PRAISE FOR _____ CATO'S
CLOCKWORK DAGGER SERIES

"Beth Cato's *The Clockwork Crown* is a satisfying follow-up to *The Clockwork Dagger,* each twist of the action pulling me deeper into the story. These are books I'll be recommending to friends, both teenagers and adults."
—Laura Anne Gilman, author of *Silver on the Road*

"Beth Cato handles this heady mix with a fine sense of language, emotion, and event, making the whole thing flow more like a force of nature than the work of a first novelist."
—*Locus*

"[*The Clockwork Dagger* takes an] intriguing approach, and a rewarding one. [It] is set in a completely fabricated universe rather than an alternate version of our own. This makes for some dazzling, uniquely detailed backdrops. It also frees Cato from having to haul around the Victorian Era's real-world baggage—and it helps level the playing field for those who aren't as familiar with steampunk's particulars."
—*Entertainment Weekly*

"*The Clockwork Dagger* was just what I needed: A steampunk adventure with an uncommon heroine, a fascinating magic system, and a young gremlin! I'm hooked and can't wait for more Octavia and Leaf!"
—*New York Times* bestselling author Kevin Hearne

The Clockwork Crown

The Clockwork Crown

A CLOCKWORK DAGGER NOVEL

BETH CATO

HARPER Voyager
An Imprint of HarperCollins Publishers

THE CLOCKWORK CROWN. Copyright © 2015 by Beth Cato. All rights reserved. Printed in the United States of America. No part of this book may be used or reproduced in any manner whatsoever without written permission except in the case of brief quotations embodied in critical articles and reviews. For information address Harper-Collins Publishers, 195 Broadway, New York, NY 10007.

HarperCollins books may be purchased for educational, business, or sales promotional use. For information please e-mail the Special Markets Department at SPsales@harpercollins.com.

FIRST EDITION

Harper Voyager is a federally registered trademark of HarperCollins Publishers.

Library of Congress Cataloging-in-Publication Data has been applied for.

ISBN 978-0-06-231398-0

15 16 17 18 19   OV/RRD   10 9 8 7 6 5 4 3 2 1

To Mrs. Quist, my fourth and fifth grade teacher at Lee Richmond Elementary, and Mr. Quist, my seventh and eighth grade newspaper teacher at Woodrow Wilson Junior High. You both told me, "Write whatever you want." I never forgot.

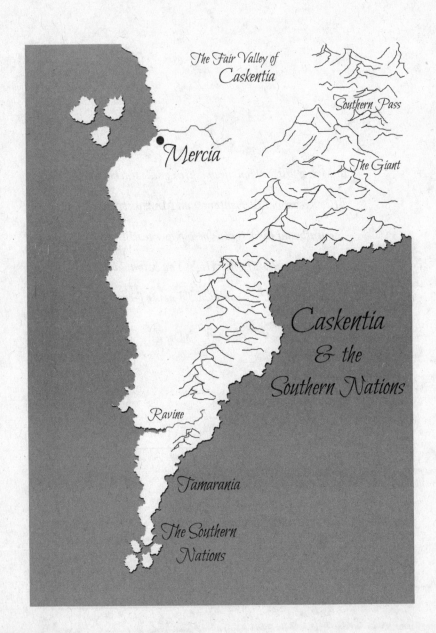

Chapter 1

As she rode through the snowy wilderness of far southern Caskentia, Octavia Leander's spirits were buoyed by three thoughts: that although she fled from assassination and capture, she was undoubtedly in one of the most beautiful places she had ever seen; that thus far they had survived a full week without any sign of pursuit by horse or buzzer; and that her companion in the hard journey was Alonzo Garret, a man who had forfeited his career as a Clockwork Dagger—and possibly his life—in order to keep her alive.

Considering the dire circumstances, he made for delightful company.

Alonzo rode ahead on a chestnut bay stallion, their gray packhorse following close behind. This far from civilization, the world was utterly quiet but for the jingling of tack, the horses' breathing and the steady rhythm of their hooves, and the radiant life songs of the horses, Alonzo, and any wildlife within close range. In particular, she took comfort in the ever-present marching-band brasses of Alonzo's life essence; she would recognize his particular notes in any crowd.

Since childhood, she had known people's and animals' health woes by their music, but only in a generic sense. She didn't hear specifics unless they had an open wound or she placed the patient in a circle to ask for the Lady's direct intervention.

The Lady's Tree moored its roots to the very spirit of the earth. Through the Tree, Octavia could heal with prowess beyond any other known medician. Lately, however, the Lady's magic had changed. Octavia had changed. Her power through the Lady had increased, and she wasn't sure if it was truly for the better.

As if he sensed her attention, Alonzo glanced back. A Waster's fur-fringed hood framed his face and contrasted with the warm nutmeg tone of his skin. A coarse black beard lined his jaw. His song was ragged in weariness, his heart steady in its anxiety. His mechanical leg—though masterfully designed—could not help but grind the joint against the flesh below his knee. She had treated him with pampria and heskool root over the past few days to ward against infection. His leg pained him again now, but even so, his smile to her was tender. Heat bloomed in her own chest, along with a sense of terrible sadness.

She had told Alonzo that she wanted to search the famed libraries of the southern nations to find out where the Lady's Tree might be found. Alonzo knew that Octavia sought a greater understanding of her own magic through the Lady, but he didn't know of all the ways that her power was changing. Or how it terrified her.

How had Octavia's blood, combined with a true branch

from the Lady's Tree, caused a massive tree to grow temporarily? That tree had acted in her defense and torn apart the men of the Waste who had tried to hold her captive. The branch that had done that was now tied to her saddlebag. It was green, as if freshly cut, and hummed with life like any person or animal.

Then there had been the moment after she had pulled Alonzo from the edge of death. She had kissed him, and with the touch of her lips she had gone beyond her knowledge of his body's song. It was as if she had become immersed in his very soul, as if she could pry apart his body's instruments and manipulate his health without any restrictions from the Lady's herbs.

That had frightened her even more than the persistent threats of both Caskentia and the Waste.

A flock of birds fluttered overhead, anxiety driving them as if they were pursued. Octavia craned around. The sky was a blanket of gray, the wind sharpened by early winter.

"What is the matter?" called Alonzo.

"Something alarmed the birds."

"To the trees, quickly."

Their horses pounded down the hill, the action reverberating through her constantly aching leg muscles. Thin snow sloshed underfoot. The forest welcomed them with a slap of branches and a shower of pine needles and ice. Roads had been scarce, signs of humanity scarcer. A good thing, in truth, though the long days of slow progress had permanently imprinted the saddle's curve into her backside.

"We should be nearing the Caskentian border. 'Tis a likely place for patrols to be wary for us." Alonzo reined up.

Octavia listened past the songs of wildlife around her. "I hear a buzzer." *That's what I get for counting my blessings. I jinxed us.*

"Yes. He is likely flying amongst the low clouds. Our tracks are bold on the snow." Alonzo pressed his horse onward, staying in the trees. She followed, brush scraping her legs. Trees crowded close.

Because of the unusual strength of Octavia's skills, the settlers of the rogue territory known as the Waste had sought to capture her and use her against Caskentia. The Caskentian royal court caught wind of this plot and, true to form, thought the tidiest solution was Octavia's death.

She had known all her life that her government was as rotten as unsalted meat left out on a summer afternoon—the sort that looks fine to eat, and makes you pray for a merciful end hours later—but she had never expected them to send Clockwork Daggers to assassinate her. But Alonzo Garret, in the guise of an airship steward, had refused to carry out his assigned task.

"It could be normal Caskentian border patrol, right? Perhaps they don't know to look for us?"

The buzzer roared overhead. Alonzo looked up with a grimace. "'Tis my hope that our feint will last longer, but I dare not be too positive. Our circuitous route has taken us a week. By now they are well aware of what transpired aboard the *Argus* and have tracked the Wasters' trail to where we did battle. If they suspect we are alive and free, our choices of destination are few."

"Well, we certainly couldn't go to the Waste, though that's where most criminals would flee. That leaves the southern nations as the obvious choice."

"An obvious choice, but not the only. There is always Mercia. 'Tis a warren. A person could lose their own shadow in those environs, and within a stone's throw of the palace."

And many stones are being thrown that way, I'm sure, knowing how people feel about Queen Evandia.

Mercia was Caskentia's capital, a sprawling city of half a million, a place of countless factories and miserable refugees. Octavia had never been there—never wished to go there, with its reputation for foul air, sickness, and utter lack of vegetation. Such denseness of humanity was the stuff of her nightmares; considering how she could hear Alonzo's song now, she dreaded to think of what it would be like to be surrounded by the starving and sick.

No trees lay ahead. Alonzo sucked in a sharp breath and reined up. "Damn."

She knew it had to be bad if he used that sort of language in front of her. She drew up alongside him. "What is—? Oh."

They had reached the end of Caskentia.

The ravine had to be some five hundred feet across, the basin of it far beyond sight. Sedimentary-rock layers rippled in various tones of red and brown. On the far side, and farther south, steam clouds billowed into the chilly afternoon.

"Factories," Alonzo said. "There are said to be many on their side of the border."

"I don't see any signs of bridges or roads."

Alonzo cast a grim glance at the sky. The sound of the buzzer had faded again. "No, and if there are, they will be well guarded. The southern nations have taken in many Caskentian refugees, but with restrictions."

"If all the unemployed and starving fled Caskentia, there'd be scarcely anyone left."

"Indeed."

They urged their horses to trot into the woods parallel to the ravine. The horses knew their anxiety; it showed in their quickened hearts and flickering ears. Octavia stroked her mare again. The white horse appeared delicate with her tapered legs and quick stride, but had revealed incredible endurance and a steady temperament over their long trek. Octavia's growing fondness for the mare was bothersome.

I must resist naming her. Maybe that will make our eventual parting that much easier—a lesson I should have learned with Leaf.

The thought of the little gremlin caused her to glance up in case she might see him for the first time in a week. Birds cawed, but there were no mews or chitters from man-made biological constructs.

The trees thinned out and showed open ground to the west. With another wary look to the clouds, they rode into the open. Clicking her tongue, Octavia encouraged her horse to gallop. Melted snow created thick mud that spattered her legs and chest; the enchantment on her robes would wick away the filth within minutes. Another stand of trees loomed a quarter mile away.

That high mechanical buzz returned to the clouds.

Octavia lifted herself higher in the stirrups, crouching low over the horse's neck. Mane lashed her face. She gritted her teeth against the burning tension in her thighs.

Alonzo looked over his shoulder. His hood had blown flat against his back, his bound hair blowing out like a miniature horse's tail. His mouth was a hard line. She almost expected the buzzer to be mounted with an automatic gun like the one that pursued them in the marsh outside of Leffen, for gunfire to follow them into the woods. They slowed as they entered the tree cover. Alonzo wheeled around. The buzzing grew louder yet.

With a grunt, he heaved himself out of the saddle. Octavia scrambled to do the same, and landed just in time to provide him with an arm for extra balance. His half leg warbled with strain. Octavia grabbed both bridles.

"My thanks," he said. His walk was stiff as he headed toward the edge of the woods.

"What are you doing?"

"I want to get a good look at the pilot." He unholstered the Gadsden .45 from his belt.

"That's a particular kind of look. This—this likely isn't a Clockwork Dagger. It's probably just a soldier."

"A soldier must perform his duty. Our whereabouts will be reported." His expression carried both regret and resolve. He walked on.

Alonzo had reminded her more than once that Caskentia would pursue them across the border. That land across the ravine was their destination for the sake of information, not as a haven.

She calmed both horses, shushing and rubbing their muzzles as if she could soothe herself as well. This pilot would be like any of the thousands she had tended at the front—a boy who simply drew a bad billet this morning.

The gunshot jolted her and the horses.

She turned as Alonzo fired again. He had crouched at the tree line.

"'Tis going down," he said.

Treetops snapped in the canopy above as the craft roared by. As awed as she was by his marksmanship, her stomach twisted with guilt. *Another life lost because of us. Lady, be with the pilot. Show him mercy at the end, please.*

"Come! Let us follow."

Grief gnawed at her as they rode through the woods. "Octavia." Alonzo seemed to read her thoughts. "With fair winds and a good engine, 'tis a mere two days from Mercia to the southern nations. If he landed and relayed a telegraph, our odds would be more dismal by the hour."

"If the pilot's hurt—" The whine of the buzzer continued, though the sound did not seem farther away. Odd.

"You know the state of your supplies better than I."

Octavia grimaced. *The deplorable state.* After her brief journey on the *Argus,* she was low on everything except wet Linsom berries to restore skin. Her supply of her most vital herb, pampria, was very low, and though she had a full bag of the dry herb she had had no chance to grind any.

"I'll try to use discretion," she said. Alonzo arched an eyebrow, clearly not believing she was capable of such a thing.

The buzzer had landed in a small clearing, engine on and roaring. Alonzo dismounted, gun drawn. Octavia followed suit, but her first priority was to untie her satchel from the saddlebag. Only with that secured across her torso, bandolier-style, did she reach for the gun in her trench-coat pocket. It was one of the Wasters' pistols, the crosshatching on the grip almost worn smooth by use. She took both reins as Alonzo edged forward.

The buzzer's motor revved at full speed, the propeller a blur of movement atop its eight-foot pole. The base resembled a somewhat flattened tricycle, all three wheels resting on the ground. The pilot had slumped over in the single seat.

"Alonzo. He's dead." From thirty feet away, she knew. His blood still wailed with its need to live, though the instruments of the full body had already been rendered mute. Octavia clenched and unclenched her fists. *I have the tree leaves, but . . . I can't. I can't. I can't heal everyone willy-nilly. Lady, please let this person deserve this fate.*

In her apron pocket, she kept four leaves from the tree that had grown from her own blood. A fifth leaf had already been used to return Alonzo from death. According to legend, all aspects of the Lady's Tree were endowed with incredible healing powers: the leaves, to bring back the recently dead; the bark, as a healing balm; the seeds, to resurrect the "fully" deceased.

Alonzo still advanced with care to check on the man. "Indeed," he said. "He lived long enough to make a proper landing, and only that."

He unstrapped the pilot and dragged him from the seat. The man wore a full brown leather suit, Caskentian standard for pilots. Octavia looked away and mouthed a prayer.

A few minutes later, Alonzo spoke again. "I found his papers. He is indeed a border monitor, though he is far beyond the normal route for his patrol. This bodes ill."

Everything about this journey bodes ill. She blinked up at the bleary sky. Clouds had plagued them in recent days. Winter's full brunt loomed far too close for comfort.

Something glinted up on high.

"Alonzo!" She yelled to be heard over the propeller. "This isn't the only buzzer!"

"Grab my bag!"

She rushed to his saddlebag. A few motions and she had his hefty pack unbuckled. She could hear the new buzzer over the sound of the landed craft.

"Octavia!" Alonzo's voice was sharp. "Hurry!"

She released both reins and dashed for the buzzer. It was a one-seater. Alonzo had wedged himself as far forward as possible into the cockpit, hunched over the small dashboard. She tossed him his bag, and then, hiking up her skirts, she climbed in behind him.

Thank the Lady my medician uniform utilizes trousers, not just bloomers.

Even so, it was an intimate fit. She drew the restraining strap across her chest. Her satchel bulged over the lip of the cockpit, her attached parasol jutting out at an awkward angle. Alonzo shoved his bag back to her and she somehow managed to wedge it beneath her right leg. Her knees hitched up near Alonzo's shoulder blades. She frowned. The seat felt warm. *Blood. Of course.* It was quiet now, cooled and apart from its body.

Alonzo's body shifted as he worked the controls. She squeaked as the buzzer bounced in place.

"Never flown these newer models," he yelled.

"That's hardly a comfort. Do you have a restraining strap?"

"No."

Being packed as tight as sardines should keep him secure enough. It had better.

"Oh Lady," she muttered as the craft lurched upward. Her stomach threatened to rise higher than the rest of her body. Vibrations shivered through her, making her teeth chatter, the motions far more immediate and violent than the engine of any train or airship. She couldn't help but clench Alonzo with both knees as they rose to treetop level and higher.

The green, gray, and white horizon tipped drunkenly. Alonzo had donned the dead pilot's hat and goggles. His hair and the helmet's leather straps whipped her in the face, so she leaned close enough to rest a cheek on his back, which also cut out some of the biting wind. She was no nesh to complain of the chill—the army encampment at the northern pass had many a soldier freeze to death on duty overnight—but sweet Lady, it was cold.

The buzzer leveled out and turned. The dome of the sky reminded her of the swirls in a polished stone. She had a glimpse of the black dot of the other buzzer and then they angled south. She only knew this because of the massive ravine. It was just as well they had a buzzer, as there was still no bridge in sight. She glanced down, awed at the ravine's depth.

We're out of Caskentia. Under different circumstances, she might have felt relieved.

She pictured the continent she knew from maps and matched it with the topography below. Caskentia, a long valley tucked against the western coast. This ravine formed the southern border. Here, the land of Tamarania tapered in a jagged peninsula with the collective southern nations at the tip. To the far north of Caskentia lay Frengia, a country known for its endless forests and bitter cold. The high peaks of the Pinnacles formed Caskentia's natural eastern border, though Caskentia had for centuries claimed ownership of the sprawling plains beyond the mountains: the Waste.

Many centuries ago, the Waste had been known as the Dallows. Then something changed—according to the Wasters, Caskentia had laid a magicked curse on the land. Whatever the reason, it became an inhospitable wasteland. Only in the past hundred years had the terrain been settled again—and half of the time since had been devoted to a near-constant war for independence from Caskentia.

War is all we know, all we've known since my grandparents' time. No wonder Caskentia thinks it's best to kill me. It's their easiest solution for any problem.

Alonzo yelled something that was lost against the wind and engine. She leaned forward. Even with the bite and clarity of the air, he exuded that particular masculine ripeness that couldn't be helped after over a week without baths.

"Watch that buzzer!" He had to yell it three more times before she discerned what he was saying.

Octavia craned around in the seat to check. "Far away! Staying on Caskentia side!" she yelled right into his ear. Alonzo nodded.

"More military, then!"

Caskentia knew they were alive. Knew where they were. The buzzer might not cross in their pursuit, but plenty more threats awaited them on the ground.

Oh Lady. I'm a medician. I want a quiet cottage with an atelier, a garden, and woods for gleaning. I don't want any of this attention. The icy wind blasted tears from her eyes and dried them upon her cheeks. The warmth of the dead man's blood was utterly gone. Her warded uniform had absorbed it.

Tall steam plumes stroked the gray sky up ahead. Alonzo aimed directly for them. Some civilization might be a good thing. Perhaps they could buy horses. There was still a good bit of wilderness to travel until they reached the city-states.

The buzzer dipped. Octavia yelped and flung an arm out to protect her satchel. Snow-crested pines crowded the ground below.

Trees. A realization struck her like a slap to the face. The blessed branch of the Lady's Tree. She had left it tied to her mare's saddle.

Octavia moaned and pressed her forehead to Alonzo's back. Of all the stupid, foolish things. A holy icon, something that had actively assisted in saving their lives, and she'd left it behind. Lost it. Over the past week, she had toyed with the thought of planting it in the ground again to harvest more leaves, but it had never happened. She was always too bone-tired after each long day in the saddle, and more than that, she was afraid of what might happen. The tree had been vicious before. It killed men. It had tried to physically grab her and force her to the safety of its branches. It was an aspect of the Lady, but nothing like the Lady, whom Octavia thought she understood and worshipped. *The grieving mother. The protector of the lost. The balm for any ill. The entity whose vines ripped the leg from a living Waster and dragged the limb across the dirt, like a dog toying with a bone.*

Now the branch was gone. The only other one she knew of was in the palace vault in Caskentia, protected behind blood-magicked wards that only the true royal bloodline could penetrate.

Then there was the actual Tree, hidden somewhere in the Waste.

She worked a hand to Alonzo's ribs and clutched him as tightly as she could, as if she were able to siphon his strength. The buzzer bobbed again.

" . . . problem!" he yelled.

"What?"

"First bullet—maybe did not miss."

It took her a few seconds to decode what he meant. The

buzzer dropped. Something shifted in its high, obnoxious whine. Oh Lady, they were going to crash.

She held on to him tighter for a whole new reason. The old fears flowed over her again. *Fire. The crash of the* Alexandria. *My parents. The village. The screams of blood, bodies, horses. Me, twelve years of age, utterly alone.*

She countered her fear with reality—the gas tank of the buzzer was small and would most likely sear their lower bodies, as it had burned her would-be assassin in a buzzer crash the week before. He had survived, though in agony.

Besides, from here it looked far more likely they'd crash straight into the woods. *Ah yes. That's much preferable to immolation.*

Alonzo's elbow angled back and he laid his hand atop hers, briefly, before taking full grip of the controls again. She breathed through her terror as she did in her Al Cala meditations. Alonzo's father had created the buzzer. Alonzo had experience in piloting. He could do this.

He guided them lower and lower. Growls and odd hiccups interrupted the steady buzz. He wound them between several massive pines, so close she could hear the life thrum of startled birds, and then they were in the open. She gasped in relief. A meadow stretched before them, factories beyond. She almost closed her eyes but couldn't.

With a final, desperate wheeze, the engine stopped completely.

This was no airship with momentum behind it. The rotor seized. They dropped in the space of a gasp.

Metal met dirt with a violent crunch. The impact jarred

through her legs and spine. Her head snapped back against the seat. Alonzo's body followed, crushing her like meat in a pressed sandwich. She listened. She knew the terror in his heart, the rush of adrenaline, how the force and pressure of gravity roiled through his body. But he was well. As well as she was, in any case.

Then she heard something more—the trickling of liquid.

"Petrol!" Alonzo shoved himself off of her.

Octavia didn't need further motivation. Her trembling hands managed to unlatch the restraints. Alonzo already had hold of his bag and leaped out. He pivoted to give her a helping hand. Her black coat snagged on debris and ripped, but that didn't slow her exit in the slightest. She stumbled into a run, gasping for breath. The saturated grassland sloshed underfoot. Her satchel slapped against her hip. Alonzo led her halfway across the meadow before he dropped to his knees on a dry rise. She fell beside him. His eyes grazed over her, worried, and she offered him a nod. His blue eyes crinkled in relief.

"Well, then!" Alonzo sat up, hands on his hips as he panted heavily. "Welcome to Tamarania and the southern nations."

EVEN THOUGH CASKENTIA HAD done its utmost to kill her, it still somewhat unnerved Octavia to be in a different country for the first time, and for it to be Tamarania of all places. Everyone spoke of the southern nations in such glowing terms: cities where people didn't starve, libraries abounded, and every child was guaranteed free schooling until age twelve. Plus, the region was known for its importation of cocoa and its numerous chocolatiers. If not for the threat of imminent death or capture, she could have played tourist.

Alonzo led the way toward the nearest factory. She felt the old familiar pressure in her chest—a life debt to Alonzo. It was the Lady's way of thanking those who directly saved the lives of her magi. It was regarded as a rare event among medicians, but the feeling had lingered on her every day of their journey. It was comforting and unsettling to know the Lady kept such a watch on her.

"Alonzo." He paused, and she rested her hand on his bristled jaw.

"Another blessing?" He looked discomfited by the attention, as he always did.

"For preserving the life of her medician, the Lady blesses you." The bothersome pressure dissipated. "Well, you do have a knack for saving my life."

New vigor carried through his stride as he continued. The blessing would enable him to heal faster and sleep more soundly, and spared her from hearing an aggravating repetition of *debt* in the back of her brain that was reminiscent of a colicky baby's cries.

"'Tis a mutual thing."

"True. I suppose you need a patron to bless me in turn," she said. Alonzo chuckled. "How far are we from the cities now?" This late in the year, the veiled sun already leaned toward the western horizon. She dreaded nightfall. Their extra blankets had been abandoned with their packhorse.

"A few days of walking, I think, though other options may be available. I believe I saw a rail line from above."

"A train! A train would be wonderful." Walking felt strange after so long in the saddle. She had some iodine for doctoring their tender feet, but not enough for extended days on foot.

"Octavia, I must urge you to act with special caution. I know on the *Argus* you intended to travel incognito. Here, 'tis essential. The southern nations do not look kindly upon magic. To them 'tis an antiquated practice, regarded with revulsion."

"The Wexlers on the ship acted like that. I've known others as well."

"This is a full culture with such an attitude, nor do they look kindly upon Caskentians." He grimaced.

"Your father. Was he . . . disowned because he moved north?" There seemed no delicate way to broach the subject of Solomon Garret. He had been a general in Caskentia, regarded as a hero when she was a girl. He was also the reason her parents were dead. He'd piloted a buzzer against a Waster airship over her village. The ensuing crash caused a conflagration that left Octavia as the sole survivor—all because she'd been a silly git and run off to the woods in search of herbs.

When she first met Alonzo, she had been appalled to learn his last name. Now she understood that he was likely the only other person who comprehended the terrible grief of that night.

"According to my mother, my father was regarded with

bewilderment by other Tamarans, as someone who stepped down from paradise to muck in with the commoners. I have never ventured to Tamarania. The few kin I have met came to visit our estate in Mercia."

Estate. A keen reminder of how Alonzo was raised among the elite in Mercia, though the inelegant manner of Solomon Garret's death had caused a significant fall in status.

"You said before that your mother maintains a household in the south."

"Yes. She lives part of the year in a flat that overlooks a blue fountain on the plaza. A cozy abode, I am sure, but we cannot go there. 'Tis the first place any Dagger would look for us."

"The gilly coins Mrs. Stout gave me. What value will they carry here?" Octavia felt the small purse as a heavy lump in her brassiere.

"Their value is not as it would be in Caskentia, but gold is gold." He frowned. "Is the Lady's branch squeezed inside your satchel?"

She flinched and looked away. "No. I—in the rush to grab everything, I left it on the saddlebag."

"Oh. I am so sorry, Octavia."

"Sorry" is such an inadequate word. I think I would have rather lost part of my leg, like Alonzo, than that blessed branch, that proof of the Lady.

They reached a stand of trees. Beyond that lay a field of tree stumps—a graveyard of mighty pines—with the log-hewn factory on the far side. It looked some five stories in height, chimneys reaching far higher. A trestle stood just beyond. A train idled there. White steam drifted upward, some men in black milling about.

"The dormitories are just over there," Alonzo murmured, and glanced at the sun. "Shift whistle should have blown a short while ago. The train's presence is auspicious. The week is at an end."

Octavia thought about what she knew of factories. "The workers will be traveling to Tamarania City for the weekend?"

"Yes. The train likely delivered fresh workers for the coming week. This crew will return to civilization. This remote locale is not a place where they would expect to run into any hitchhikers. Perhaps we can blend in."

"Let me take care of our bloodied coats."

She pulled out her parasol. Her medician wand was hidden in the handle. The copper-and-wood stick carried enchantments to dry blood and kill zymes. A few minutes later, their coats were somewhat cleaner. Alonzo rigged his saddlebag strap beneath his coat, closer to his body. Octavia almost laughed. Here they were, stinky and harried and hungry, and those were the very qualities that would likely help them to blend in with the workers.

They crept closer to the train. Alonzo had tucked his pistol out of sight, but she knew he'd have it ready if needed. A whistle blew. Workers poured from a brick dormitory. Most wore black coats, many of which had faded to shades of gray. Unlike most factory employees she had seen, these people smiled and talked amongst themselves, even if it was an exhausted-sounding murmur. Clearly, an impending return to the city had brightened their spirits.

Suddenly her acute awareness of the workers' health woes draped over her like a suffocating quilt.

Noises. Songs. Tweets, bells, off-key trumpets. Cancer, a thudding, drumming mass. The sweetness of pox. The first stirrings of a pregnancy. Dragged notes of exhaustion—plenty of that.

Cities had always overwhelmed her, but this . . . *this.* These people were still thirty steps away, more following behind, and their needs swarmed her like bees. Octavia moaned, both hands to her ears as she slid down the wall to the ground.

"Octavia?" Firm hands gripped her shoulders. "What is the matter?"

"The people. I hear them. I hear inside them." *Lady, what's happening to me?*

"Stand. I am with you, Octavia."

Yes, she had Alonzo. Her legs like gelatin, her brain addled, she managed to stand. People surrounded them. *Hums, buzzes, bleats.* Voices—familiar words. Refugees from her land. Caskentians would be more likely to recognize her as a medician. That brought a whole different kind of danger than what Alonzo had warned against.

His hand was her tether, the steady marching band of his heart clear even amidst the din.

"Separate!" a man's voice boomed. People jostled and shifted around her. *A heart skips beats like a child learning to jump rope. Stomachs moan in hunger. The baby in the womb writhes as if it knows the excitement to come.*

"Octavia." Alonzo's breath was hot on her ear. "They are separating the men and women, you must—"

"Come along, then! Board! Say your farewells, it's only a few hours' ride—"

"Separate?" The horror of that word cleaved through her mental fog. "We can't! How will I—"

The train roared. Alonzo's hand jerked from hers. She struggled to focus, to see with her eyes and hear with her physical ears. Faces around her ranged from milky pale to deep coffee in tone, men and women both. Alonzo, tall as he was, had turned toward her, the determination on his face visible above another man's shoulders. The tide of humanity carried him away.

Women's voices jabbered around her, higher in pitch. Giggles punctuated conversations. The press of women ebbed and flowed toward a black train car and groups began to split off. Octavia found herself at a short set of stairs. Passing hands had smoothed the wooden banister to burnished gold. She staggered up the steps and tripped at the top. She caught herself on a knee and forced herself up and inside.

She had been on a train once, as a child. Mother and Father took her to the beach. To her delighted eyes, the train car had been a palace on wheels, even if she realized in hindsight that the velvet seats had been bald in spots like a mangy dog and the brakes had squealed like a pen of hogs.

But in comparison to this place, the train car of her youth had indeed been a palace.

The floor had been stripped down to coarse planks. Ridges of splinters snagged her shoes. Bleak wooden benches sat in rows, many of them already occupied. No seat backs, no comforts. Women laughed and murmured as their cases slid beneath benches. They doffed their hats and smoothed their bound-up hair. Octavia sat, hatless and conspicuous. She breathed as she did in her Al Cala. It was easier to focus with fewer people close by and metal walls separating her from the rest. Her fingers clutched at her satchel as she had desperately clung to Alonzo.

The train lurched forward, steam whistle piercing, the rollicking rhythm of the wheels shuddering through the hard bench. *Where will this train stop? How will I find Alonzo?*

"Hey. Who're you?" asked a raspy voice. The woman's face was creased and dented like an apple left to rot in the sunlight. Her body rang out its exhaustion. Hollowness echoed in her abdomen. Somehow, many years ago, she had lost a babe . . . and much more.

"I'm new," Octavia managed.

"New. New, aye. Nice coat."

She looked down as if seeing it for the first time. Wasters did know how to dress warmly to survive their godforsaken plains. "Ah, thank you."

Gnarled fingers plucked at her elbow. "Wool, I think." The woman bent close to Octavia's chest and breathed in. "Yes, wool."

Prickles of unease trickled down Octavia's spine.

"Kethan's bastards. Look at that," said another woman, her body craning around to stare. "What's that cloth there?"

More eyes turned Octavia's way. Another woman leaned over and tugged back Octavia's torn coat to reveal the pristine white of her medician robes. The cloth, which was unrealistically clean despite a week in the wilderness, shimmered with its enchantment.

It made her a gleaming target.

"It's beautiful, like silk."

"That's a Percival robe!"

"No. It can't be. Here?"

"It is! I swear on King Kethan's tomb! I saw one once. My mum took me—"

"A medician. A magic user?" Expressions varied from disgust to delight to sly assessment.

Miss Percival had warned Octavia of this very risk, so many times. These Caskentian refugees would tear her apart with their need.

Octavia had a gun but only four bullets. There had to be thirty women crammed into this space, and she didn't want to kill anyone. These women had suffered—did suffer. She knew their agonies, loud as steam whistles.

The hand stroking the wool of her sleeve gripped it tight instead. Others leaned in, reaching toward her, toward her satchel.

Octavia stood. The motion of the train almost bowled her over. Her calves rocked against the bench to keep her upright.

"I'm terribly sorry, I'm just—" Octavia began.

"I need a healing. My chest . . . it hurts, I can't breathe—" *Lung cancer, bronchioles clogged like autumn leaves in a gutter.*

"My foot! It—" *was broken in childhood and set poorly. The bones grind together as if to spark a fire.*

"I need a medician! I'm sick." *The babe is quickening. The woman—the girl—is too small, too young. She starves, the babe starves. Together they breathe in the coke from the furnaces. Black nodules already stain and harden her lungs.*

Octavia's awareness—the horror of it—almost drove her to the floor. These women called to her, and it was as though their bodies, their woes, opened to her like a book. Octavia *knew*.

"I can't. I'm sorry!" Too many in need, too few herbs. Only one of her.

The women gathered around her, hunched against benches for balance, a shabby pack of wolves with snarling lips and desperate eyes. They lunged.

Octavia shoved several back. As she spun around, the stick of her parasol thwacked several more. A nose broke, and klaxons of blood began to wail. *Oh Lady. Every train car will be the same. If I jump off—I can't. I would never find Alonzo again.* She kicked someone's bag aside. An empty space gaped at the back of the room. She kicked away more suitcases as she stumbled that way. Her hand dove into the center of her satchel, to the medician blanket.

Two seconds later, she had the blanket fluffed out. The action surprised the mob. They retreated a few steps and cried out. A honeyflower-woven circle—oval, really—lay flat in the center of the blanket. Octavia threw herself into it, her fingers grazing the golden threads around her.

"Lady!" she cried out.

With an electric snap, the circle flared into existence. The heat of the Lady's scrutiny flashed against her skin, a stark reminder of the chill in the air. The women dove at her and crashed against the invisible barricade of the circle.

"By Allendia's ghost!"

"Magic!"

Howls of frustration filled the train car.

The circle of a medician blanket enabled the Lady's eye to focus on those most in need of healing. For most medicians, that borderline created a sensation akin to walking through a wall of spiderwebs. It helped contain the patient within the circle if they thrashed or convulsed. Octavia, with her unparalleled power, formed something similar to a brick wall. She could cross her circle as she reached for supplies or whatnot, but the patient could not leave until Octavia broke the enchantment.

Octavia cradled her satchel on her lap. Her arms, her body, shivered. Her parasol's staff gouged into her, but she didn't move. She stared at the women feet away, listened to their curses, their profanity.

Miss Percival always warned me and the other girls that if we went out in public in our gear, people would riot.

The thought of Miss Percival stung. Her mentor may have sold out Octavia and Mrs. Stout to the Waste, but the woman was still wise. She'd been like a second mother to Octavia for the past ten years. All those nights when the nightmares of her parents' deaths had plagued her, Miss Percival had been there, her presence a balm. Even in recent years in their medical wards at the front, Miss Percival had always avoided giving burn cases to Octavia except as a last resort.

Now, these women—her own countrywomen—would burn Octavia alive, if they could. They'd shred her apart with their bare fingers.

Frothy spittle spattered against the invisible wall and rolled down as if on glass. Several women pulled out eating knives and stabbed the barricade. Octavia flinched. Metal met nothingness with a sound like a wrench clanging on dense wood.

She had never known anyone to take shelter within a circle like this. *Another peculiarity for the list. I can float a body within a circle, and guide it beyond. My blood has grown pampria, a temporary version of the Lady's Tree, and vines. I can hear the songs of zymes, those microscopic enigmas that make people ill. And now I know the details of a person's health in greater detail than ever before.* She was suddenly so tired. So very tired, and alone.

Lady, watch over Alonzo. Help him to blend in, unlike me. Help us find each other again. Please.

"The circle only starts at the thread, not the edge of the blanket. Look here," said one of the women. Her hands trembled. At the *Look here,* Octavia gained insight into her body. The sound was dimmed by the circle, but even so, the stranger's blood burbled with too much sugar, as if she were a Frengian maple tree ready to be tapped. The nerves in her hands and feet had atrophied, unable to carry tactile sensations back to the brain.

Octavia clenched her eyes shut, as if she could force away the insight.

Knives tugged and sawed at the white edge of the

blanket. She felt the motions, but she also knew that they wouldn't impact the integrity of the circle. Blankets were damaged and frayed in the course of their use, though she had never known anyone to willingly savage one.

It's spite. Pure spite. Rage wavered through her, hot and cold.

A woman cried out in triumph. "I'll patch my coat with it! The one bit that will never get dirty." Others laughed and cheered.

Octavia's rage dwindled to pity and numbness. They wanted something of her? Fine. At least it could be of use. "The cloth absorbs blood and other matter." At her voice, the women grew silent. "Use it to clean up injuries. Use it for your monthly. Don't keep it on open flesh as a bandage, though, or it will absorb too much."

They murmured at that. "It's a trick!" cried one. "She's trying to poison us."

"No. I've heard the same about this enchantment they do. It's why the cloth glimmers."

The knives went to work again. Their anger was gone. Now they worked in eager cooperation, like rag weavers gathered to rend cloth. Octavia bowed forward in the oval into a relaxed Al Cala pose. The satchel slid from her lap and rested like a thick log against her belly.

Unbidden, the image of the Tree flared in her mind's eye. The green branches that extended beyond the clouds as if to support the sky itself. The bark, gnarled, much of it patched in rough lichen. Leaves bobbed and swayed as if to wave in greeting.

The vision of the Tree had been a tremendous comfort since it had first come to her as a teenager. Most medicians experienced it, from her understanding, though it was regarded as a private thing not often discussed. Octavia knew now that this was no mere vision. She saw the Lady as she was, day or night, whatever the weather. Nothing was distinct about the nearby mountains—though they did not have the sharpness of the Pinnacles—or the normal forest that existed like moss at the Lady's feet. By some magic, this Tree had been hidden in the Waste for centuries, yet somehow the Wasters had found it. When they held Octavia captive, they had tried to bargain for her cooperation by saying they would take her to the Tree. It had to be done by land, she knew, and the trek was hard. Beyond that, the location was a mystery.

Can you show us the way, Lady? It seems everyone is trying to kill us. Can we find refuge beneath your branches?

And if not there, where?

CHAPTER 2

Octavia woke to the rollicking grind of the train's brakes. The Lady's warmth lay as a cozy weight over her, like dirt upon roots. She wiped a trail of drool from her mouth as she pushed herself onto her haunches. The circle around her held. She had seen circles stay open for hours during complex operations that relied on doctoring as well as herbs, but certainly not with the healer bound inside. The other women, long since retreated to their benches, began to murmur and stir. They eyed Octavia as they reached for their hats and bags. Their look reminded her of the vultures that clustered on the edge of a battlefield, waiting for their turn.

Octavia did not anticipate a pleasant disembarkation.

The train screeched to a halt. She dug her elbow against her satchel, readying herself. The rest of the women stood. The door to the train car flung open with a clang. Grabbing hold of the medician blanket, Octavia lunged forward, jumping over the stairs entirely. A surprised conductor fell backward. *Incontinence*. She landed, ready to run.

Pandemonium drowned her.

Songs, bodies, thousands of them. As many as an army encampment, but all in tight proximity. A stew of humanity, with her senses more attuned than ever before.

She screamed, but even that sound was lost in the cacophony.

She ran, faces blurring around her. Dark suits, dark skins, people, people everywhere. Train whistles blasted like a whisper against the needs of bodies. *Starvation gout disease pox infection syphilis double amputation typhoid pregnancy migraine.* She ran, she shoved, she found a wall of glimmering white tile. A door. She opened it. She threw herself inside. A hallway, the lights electric. She staggered another twenty feet until she collapsed, heaving for breath, heaving from terror. The songs still burbled close by, like ocean waves hidden behind a dune.

"Lady, what is happening to me?"

She pulled the blanket from beneath her arm and pressed it to her face. The cloth absorbed her sobs as she rocked for a minute. *Enough of this. I need to find out where I am. Find Alonzo.*

Up the hall she found a map painted on the white wall: TAMARAN TERMINAL Colored lines depicted a massive facility of multiple floors and several dozen tracks. The place could easily hold tens of thousands of people—no wonder she had been overwhelmed. Even at her normal sensitivity, this place would have left her dazed and desirous of a quick retreat.

How am I to find Alonzo amidst these crowds? And how am I to cope with the noise of all these diagnoses?

The map showed several access hallways, like the one

she was in, but she could not avoid the city itself. The terminal was located at city center, at the plaza. Even as a newcomer to Tamarania, she knew of the plaza.

The southern nations were a cluster of twelve city-states. Tamarania possessed the largest area by far, though its principal city occupied only the tip at the continent's end. The other city-states overflowed islands interconnected by bridges, naval vessels, and airships. The plaza was the hub of Tamarania, and of all the southern nations. Millions of people were said to live in the immediate environs.

Millions. My brain will explode.

Octavia had heard millions of living beings before—microscopic zymes—when the Lady's magic had enhanced her hearing so she could diagnose the Wasters' water contamination. People were so much bigger and more complex, there was no comparison.

If the Lady can enhance my hearing, maybe she can decrease it. Actually—she did. In the train car, I barely heard the women's songs once I was in the circle. The magic filtered it.

Frowning, she fluffed out the medician blanket. It looked ghastly with an entire long edge hacked away. She had not properly disengaged the circle before she fled and she still felt the inherent heat of the Lady's presence. "I'm sorry," she murmured. While she'd been in training, forgetting to disengage a circle was a grave offense—the sort that earned a hundred lines and a week of doubled manure-shoveling duty. "But I do still require your attention."

She delved into her satchel to find her headband. The white cloth bore a hand-stitched emblem of the Lady's Tree on the front. It sparkled with the same enchantment as the rest of her uniform. Warding the cloth had taken many days of meditation; she hoped that the existing enchantment might make the cloth more receptive. *As if I'm one to judge the Lady's capabilities.*

Octavia sat in the circle, headband across her lap. "Lady," she whispered. At the word, heat stroked her as if she were a cat. "You have opened my eyes and ears in new ways, and now I ask something more of you. I'm too attuned to people. I must be able to walk the city. Please, rest your touch on my headband so that I may cover my ears and dim the songs around me." She lifted up the band. It grew hot in her grip. She remained that way for several long minutes, breathing through her Al Cala, and didn't let her hands drop until the cloth began to cool.

She disengaged the circle with murmured gratitude. She secured the headband to cover her ears, the embroidered side upside down and hidden at the nape of her neck. Immediately the background burble of songs vanished. She could have wept with relief as she murmured more thanks, but she didn't dare linger.

The longer I am hidden away, the harder it will be to find Alonzo.

She wended her way through more passages in an attempt to avoid the public terminal. Rounding a corner, she stopped. A body was sprawled on the floor. Even as Octavia approached, she knew this person was dead. There was no song. *Maybe the southern nations are not so different from Caskentia after all.*

She stepped closer. The body's music returned, so thready that it barely penetrated her new headband.

Octavia gasped and dropped to her knees, hands delving into her satchel. What just happened?

"Octavia." The woman's head lolled as the name gargled past her lips.

Shock froze her in place. "I—do I know you?"

The cut and shabbiness of the woman's clothes denoted Caskentian origins, her skin honey in hue. Blank eyes met Octavia's gaze. "North." Her jaw bobbed as if she struggled for more words. Frustration flashed across her haggard face.

With that, the music puffed out. She was dead. Again.

"Lady?" Octavia whispered, though she already surmised what had just happened. The Lady had spoken before through people on the brink of life and death—through a boy in Leffen, and through Alonzo when Octavia had saved him with a leaf. She had a sense that a leaf wouldn't work on this woman now—after all, she was too far gone for even the Lady to utilize as a messenger.

North. Caskentia. What had the Lady tried to say? Octavia stood, shaken.

The entrance of the terminal roared with humanity, but this time she could discern true sounds as well: overlapping voices, footsteps, the clatter of wheels, the rumbles of trains. The songs were like breeze-blown tree branches outside a window, much easier to ignore than the banshee screams they'd been before.

She studied the crowd. It was peculiar to see so many

darker skin tones, ranging from deep tan to coal. Tamarans were rare in Caskentia, which was one reason why Alonzo had stood out so much to her. *And why he was doomed as a Clockwork Dagger—too unusual, too memorable*. Now he would blend in too much for her to find him.

She followed the flow outside to the plaza and froze as elbows and bodies jostled against her.

Night draped over a metropolis set aglow. Before her was an illuminated hexagon easily a half mile in diameter. In the middle was a massive roundabout packed with more cabriolets, automated cycles, and bicycles than she had ever seen in her life. Each side of the hexagon featured a massive building that was blocks long and dozens of floors tall. Tramway tracks stacked around them. Every ten or so floors, another track made a circuit. Bridges spanned the high gaps, the trestles like fine spiderwebs. Beyond the plaza, tower upon tower stretched into the sky.

On the far side of the hexagon sat the ornate palace known as the Warriors' Arena. It was shorter than all of the surrounding buildings at a mere dozen floors, but no less magnificent. A bright stained-glass dome crowned the gray edifice. Mooring towers lined the long roof; airships bobbed from several. Long, rippling banners advertised the next Arena bout several days away.

Peculiar, how the city-states prided themselves on centuries without war even as they relished the blood sport of Warriors played out in the Arena.

Spotlights waved to and fro like gigantic dogs' tails made of rays. They beamed over airships on high, their gasbags adorned with advertisements far too distant for her to fully read from ground level.

Somehow, amidst these thousands of people, Octavia needed to find Alonzo.

As obvious as the Garret household would be to Daggers and Wasters, it also presented the only specific location for her to meet him. Now it was a matter of finding it. With her coat pulled close and satchel snug at her hip, Octavia set off across the plaza.

How can I inquire with any subtlety? She approached a doorman as he stalked a yellow-lit entry between a haberdashery and a cheese shop. The directory sign behind him listed a dozen residence floors, but no occupants by name. There were simply too many.

"Pardon me," Octavia said, smiling. "I'm to deliver a message to the Garret flat but I've lost the address."

"Shoo, girl. You look like you were dragged behind a lorry." He motioned her away with both hands.

She bit her lip to contain a retort, but she knew the man was right. Her coat had multiple rips after the train ride, and it barely managed to cover her uniform if she remained standing. If she lingered anywhere for long, she would be jailed as a vagrant.

She looked around, scanning for any clue, any idea. Another airship drifted overhead. From here she could see the ad, the familiar calligraphy and crown logo featuring two fashionable young ladies holding up slender tins.

ROYAL-TEA. A TASTY BALM FOR ANY ILL!

She snarled. A few nearby pedestrians lurched away from her, wide-eyed. That blasted Royal-Tea was everywhere. The Wasters made the concoction by brewing the dried bark of the Lady's Tree—and they were kidnapping teenage girls from Mercia to fetch the bark. A dangerous task, with the woods full of threems—beasts part equine and part dragon—to act in the Lady's defense. Ads for Royal-Tea had plastered Caskentia, and each purchase unknowingly funded the war effort of their greatest enemy.

The presence of the tea was a reminder that Wasters would be here as well, keener than ever before to kidnap her. *Because trained assassins from Caskentia are not enough to worry about.*

It also brought to mind Mrs. Stout. Octavia pressed her fingers to her lips and sent a prayer to her friend.

Mrs. Stout had been Octavia's roommate aboard the *Argus*. The vivacious and plump older woman turned out to be a childhood friend of Octavia's mentor, Miss Percival. Mrs. Stout was also the long-lost princess of Caskentia, Allendia. Her kidnapping fifty years ago had sparked the endless intermittent conflict with the Waste. The young princess had been presumed dead, and the next year, the rest of the royal family was killed in a Waster attack on Mercia. With her cousin Queen Evandia now on the throne, Mrs. Stout had adapted to life as a civilian with the hopes that it might spare Caskentia a civil war.

Miss Percival had been one of the few who knew Mrs. Stout's true identity and she'd kept the secret for decades, until now. She arranged for Octavia and Mrs. Stout to travel together by airship because she had sold them out to the Waste.

It was mostly about the money to save the academy. It had to be. But envy had to be part of it as well, and fear.

Octavia was so sick of being feared, but with these new changes, she was starting to fear herself as well.

She hurried past more lorries and cycles. A fountain glowed purple. Two boys in knickerbockers sat on the edge and splashed each other, giggling. The lit fountain—Alonzo had said his mother's flat overlooked a blue fountain. Looking around, she realized that she had passed an orange fountain already, and she didn't see any duplicated colors. Lady be praised!

After another long block of walking, she found the blue landmark and glanced at the building above. At least now she was at the right place. It was just a matter of gaining entry and going from there. Could she sneak around the back? Perhaps there was a goods entry. She walked past a doorman, looking for any placard listing residences.

"Hey! You!" The doorman lunged to grab her arm.

Octavia's hand immediately went to her torso for her capsicum flute. *Drat. Used it on the airship!* When she found nothing, her hand formed a fist and she punched at his fingers. "Let me go! Stop!"

"Stop struggling, woman. I been told to look for you. Come here." Chew tobacco reeked on his breath. *Mouth lesions.*

She stopped fighting, though her heart continued to hammer in her chest. A small twist and she could grab her parasol from its loop on her satchel. It'd make a fine cudgel.

"Who told you to look for me?"

"A Mr. Garret. Said to look for a pale young woman with brown hair and a ripped black coat. You fit the description mighty well. Hold on. He just went inside to the lobby."

She could have melted into the pavement in relief. The doorman returned to his station and scribbled a note. He tucked it inside a strange capsule and set it at the base of a clear pipe. At the press of a button, the capsule shot up the tube with a mighty whoosh and vanished through the ceiling. She stared, mouth gaping.

"What, never seen a pneumatic tube system before?" He brayed a laugh. "The message will go right to the desk. Hold here."

All the best inventions come from Tamarania. She shook her head in awe. Yet another reminder that she was in the place that invented airships, mechas, and even gremlins.

A few more minutes of restless pacing, and she heard that familiar song of marching-band brasses—distorted. Alonzo nigh broke the glass door as he flung it wide. Relief shone in his eyes. Even with noise of his song dimmed by the headband, blood screamed beneath his clothes. *Ribs. Muscle shredded. Bone chipped.*

"Al . . . Mr. Garret." She could have hugged him, but she knew it would worsen his pain.

"I was just about to head upstairs, m'lady. Now we shall go together. My thanks to you, sir." Alonzo extended a hand to the doorman, to which the man responded with a bright smile. There'd been a coin tucked in Alonzo's palm.

She followed Alonzo into an austere hallway. "You were stabbed. Several hours ago," she murmured.

"Yes. 'Tis not that bad, truly." He frowned. "You are aware of this, just as you were aware of the ailments of the factory workers?"

"Yes. My senses have strengthened in a rather obnoxious way. The city . . . has been especially taxing." She gestured to her headband. "This is all that's keeping me from crouching in a corner, aware of the screaming maladies of passersby."

Alonzo's brows drew together in thought. They stood before the black wire of the lift doors. Judging by the number of floors, they would have quite a wait. At least her senses informed her that he could manage awhile more, though in agony.

"What happened, Alonzo?" *Shallow wound. No poison, but there are always zymes to cause infections. Someone aimed for his kidneys.* "Someone was trying to kill you. Was it . . . ?" *Clockwork Daggers? Wasters?*

He stared at the ticking light on the dial that showed the lift floors. "No. None of our past acquaintances. The train car was mostly occupied by Caskentian workers of a desperate nature. One decided to liberate me of my coins and bag, and when that effort failed, my body."

"Yes. They were a rather desperate lot."

His gaze snapped to her. "Were you assaulted?"

"Don't you dare fuss over me. Must you end up injured in every single city?"

"Considering our 'smashing' arrival in Tamarania, I feel I have done quite well today."

"I'll grant you that. A straightforward stabbing is preferable to breaking most every bone in your body, not to mention potential immolation. Your piloting skills are to be applauded."

"Thank you. Ah, here we are."

The lift lowered into place. The iron gate cranked open. People exited, eyeing them and granting a wide berth. The lift man looked none too pleased to be in their company either. Octavia's tepid smile didn't seem to relieve him. Fortunately the ride only lasted five floors.

"Room 553," Alonzo said as they staggered together into a carpeted hallway. The place was staid and clean with white wainscoting and cream paint. Pneumatic tubes followed the walls and connected to each room.

"Is your mother here?" They walked past 550, 551.

"I know not. At the front desk I sent up a message that was approved by—"

The door ahead of them burst open. "He's here! He's here!" A small body lunged from the domicile. She looked to be perhaps ten or twelve in age, her kinky black hair cropped close to her skull and molded into a pastrylike swirl. Her skin shone in a bright nutmeg tone. Icy-blue eyes, just like Alonzo's, were filled with tears. Alonzo caught her with a pain-filled grunt as he was almost bowled over.

"Tatiana!" The name was an agonized wheeze.

The girl bounced in place, squeezing him. "When the

desk sent up the message, I could hardly believe it! You, here! I'm so happy!"

Octavia forced her jaw up again as she looked between them. "Ah . . . Alonzo?"

Sweet Lady. Do I really know this man at all? Is this his daughter?

CHAPTER 3

Alonzo gently pried the girl off of him. "Miss Octavia Leander, I would like to introduce my sister, Miss Tatiana Garret."

Sister. That was worlds better. "Hello there. Do take care. He's injured."

"Injured?" Tatiana looked Octavia up and down, frowning. "Who are you? Alonzo, what happened?"

"Let us discuss the matter inside, please."

The decor of the flat looked much the same as that of the hallway—generically upper class without any gaudiness. Five servants stood in line. One woman curtsied. "We've prepared his room, miss."

Tatiana bit her lip. "My brother's hurt. We need a doctor!"

"I'll get to the pneumatic, miss," said the servant.

Octavia shook her head. "That's not necessary. I'm a medician. I can take care of him."

A few of the servant girls looked aghast; the older men were more stoic in their clear disapproval.

"A medician!" The way Tatiana looked at her, Octavia might as well have announced she kicked kittens as a hobby. "Well, you're not going to touch my brother with that hocus-pocus."

Octavia bristled. "Hocus-pocus! I've healed him more than once and I'm quite qualified to do so again."

"Ladies?" queried Alonzo.

Tatiana's nose flared. Even when she was perturbed, her face was lovely—her cheeks rosy and rounded, nose pert, her lips broad. But then, a horse could be quite lovely as it kicked you in the face. "Magic. Alonzo, please tell me she hasn't *done* magic to you." At the word "magic," the servants made slashing motions across their chests to show contempt.

"Tatiana." Alonzo clutched his elbow to his side as he worked his bag's strap over his head. A servant immediately took it from him. "Do not call for a physician. We do not wish to attract extra attention. Octavia is a medician, yes, but she is also an accomplished doctor. She will tend to my wound without use of a circle. That will also spare your blessed supplies," he said directly to Octavia.

She almost growled at the compromise.

Tatiana did not look placated either. "I want her to promise that she won't use magic in my house. If she does any healing, she must do it naturally. It's just embarrassing otherwise! This is Tamarania, not Caskentia." Her tone made her opinion of Caskentia quite clear.

Alonzo nodded. "I promise on her behalf."

"I am standing right here, you know," said Octavia.

Tatiana grimaced as she nodded. "Very well. I suppose

she'll need a room, too. She *does* require her own room, doesn't she?"

Impertinent little twit. A girl her age needs a mother close by to keep her in line. A hot flush bloomed across Octavia's cheeks. "Yes. I do." She looked to the servants. "But foremost, I need boiling water, please, and clean bandages if you have them." If not, she certainly had her own.

"Yes, of course, miss," one of the girls stammered, curtsying.

Octavia looked to Tatiana. "Where can I tend to him?"

Tatiana's haughtiness faded some as she looked to her brother. "Follow me."

A countertop island in the kitchen was cleared. With the help of a chair, Alonzo managed to roll himself onto the top, groaning. Octavia set her satchel on the floor near her feet and briskly set up her workstation. Really, she despised doctoring. Not only was it slow, but it was such a gamble— wait to see if the mundane herbs worked, wait to see if infection set in.

Yet now, thanks to the Lady, my doctoring is not mere doctoring.

When she kissed Alonzo after using a leaf to revive him, she had felt an intense understanding of his body—and not in the way she wished at that particular moment. If he had had any lingering health issues, she had the sense that she could have remedied them.

Given how she was now able to hear so much more from every passing body, she wondered just what she could do. *Only one way to find out.*

She pulled out her doctoring kit. The sight of the bullet probes made her flinch; she had used one to kill the Waster Mr. Drury by stabbing him through the eye.

From what Octavia understood, Mr. Drury had been infatuated with her before they even met aboard the *Argus*. He had been the mastermind behind a poison attack that killed thousands of Caskentian soldiers; she had been the medician who, through the Lady, found the source of the toxins in the water and saved thousands more. Mr. Drury had intended to enlist her in the Waste's cause and marry her as well—all due to some perverse admiration of her wit and strength. She didn't mourn the man in the slightest, but regretted that a life had been lost at her own hands. *A loss that the Lady supported, since the Tree's leaf did not revive him.*

With a shiver, she pulled out the straight scissors and cut Alonzo's shirt. He sat upright, his hands bracing him on the edge of the table.

Tatiana made an odd keening sound, as many did when they saw a loved one's blood. "I'll come back in a while, Alonzo." She planted a kiss on his knuckle and left with a rustle of skirts.

Water began to boil on the stove—goodness, electric stoves were fast. Octavia tugged back her headband a wee bit. His agonized song flared in her hearing. *Oh, Alonzo, why must you so frequently be in pain because of me?* At least he hadn't lost his mechanical leg again.

"A servant stands just beyond the kitchen door," Alonzo murmured.

Octavia already knew by the woman's song. "To ensure

my good behavior, I'm sure." She grabbed the clean sheets the servant left on the counter, and began to shred them into strips. The cloth was silky and strong, far superior to anything she had ever used for bandages in Caskentia.

"With reason. As I warned you, attitudes are different here in the south."

"Being a medician is not an embarrassment."

"Not in Caskentia. Octavia, whenever you are complimented on your healing skills, what is the first thing you say?"

"That my power doesn't come from me. It comes from the Lady. Why—"

"That is the distinction. In the southern nations, personal accomplishment defines a person. You do not claim credit. Beyond that, magic simply is not considered fashionable."

"Fashionable. Bosh and tosh."

"I know it perturbs you, Octavia, but this is an age of science. The idea of a giant tree fostering life is considered, as you put it, bosh and tosh to many educated people."

Well, I'd like to see science explain this. Listening, she rested a hand on the smooth curve of his ribs just above the wound.

She knew the thrums of his pain, the exhaustion of his body, the coldness from the loss of blood. Immediately, she ached to reach into her satchel for her blanket and herbs. Her hand formed a fist. *I will make my own circle.* She let her eyes flutter half shut. She imagined the gold line of honeyflower around him and her herbs at ready. Pampria, for blood loss. Bartholomew's tincture, to repair his chipped ribs. Heskool root, against infection. Bellywood bark, to counteract zymes. Linsom berries, to mend skin.

Stop hurting.

Alonzo sucked in a sharp breath. "What?"

The wound was still there, same as before, but she could sense a block to keep pain signals from reaching his brain. That ability could come in useful. She began to clean the wound with water and rags.

"Octavia?" He gave her a look, the sort that told her he was well aware she was doing something impossible, again, and that he wanted to learn more.

"Shush. Let me do my job." By applying her will, the broken bits of bone pulled into place, the worst of the muscle mended. Hot prickles zinged to the top of her skull. She found herself bent over Alonzo, suddenly so tired she could scarcely move. His hands gripped her upper arms.

"I think I need to sit," she said.

"Here." He guided her to lean against his lap.

"This is rather comfortable." Her cheek rested on his thigh, gaze outward. If she closed her eyes, she'd slumber in a matter of winks, his body's thrum as her lullaby.

He managed a small laugh. His self-consciousness carried through his song. "'Tis good to know I am cozier than the cold kitchen floor."

Oh, Alonzo. He was always so frustratingly proper and polite, so *Mercian*. The man had no idea how much she yearned to wrap both arms around him and kiss him for hours on end—just to be close to him, know his full heat, the hard contours of his body. To feel just how coarse his beard was beneath her fingertips, how his muscles tensed to compensate for the slight differences between his mechanical leg and intact leg.

But he was injured still, and she was afraid of what she would know through that kiss. *What I just did without a circle should be impossible, now part of a long list of impossibilities I've committed. If I can heal through sheer focus, I could do the opposite. I could kill.*

That horrible thought sobered her. She eased herself several feet away to a stool. Alonzo studied her, arms extended as if she were going to keel over at any instant.

She waved him back. "I should eat soon. It's been an exhausting day. I have no intention of sprawling out on the kitchen floor." He arched an eyebrow, and she continued, "If my plans change, I'll be sure to let you know."

"Please do. Though I might recommend other rooms of the household, as they are likely carpeted."

"A very good point. I should create a priority list of where best to faint." She scooted the stool beside his knees and sat upon the curved steel seat.

"As if you are the fainting sort, m'lady." His blue eyes sparkled with mischief.

"What sort am I, then?" Behind her, the servant's shoes scuffed on the floor. Octavia doubted the sound was an accident.

Alonzo bowed his head toward her. "The delightfully obstinate sort." His words were a low rumble.

"Well, thank goodness for adverbs, or I might take offense at that." They froze as those shoes tapped the floor again. *A chaperone, and not just to prevent me from my hocus-pocus. Piffle.* Alonzo straightened and cleared his throat as if in reply to their watcher, and Octavia looked to his injury again.

She did the rest of the work by hand, movements brisk. With the strips of cloth, she bound his torso tighter than any corset.

"There." She slumped forward on the stool. The life-debt blessing from the Lady would speed his recovery as well. In her mind, she eased off on her control of his pain. The more pain he felt, the less tired she was. She stood upright. *Interesting. Apparently, instead of spending herbs, I spent my own energy. How's that for personal accomplishment by Tamaran standards, hmm?*

Octavia sensed the servant scurrying away.

Alonzo glanced in that direction as well, making the same observation with different senses. "How did you control my pain?" he murmured.

"I could hear the cause and squelch it. The effort did take something out of me, but I'm feeling better now, really." Worry crinkled his eyes. Before he could nag her, she continued, "Tell me about your sister. She's how old, twelve?"

"Barely ten. I did not expect her to be here, though I know my mother has often sent her south in recent years. Tamaran schools are far superior to those of Caskentia. I last saw Tatiana two years ago, when I was on leave for my leg attachment. She has . . . come into her own."

"That's one way to put it. She's managing this entire

household. That's impressive." *Ten years old. She was either a newborn or nearly born when Solomon Garret died, then.*

His smile was apologetic. "Most all of Tatiana's life, I have been away. To school, then war, then my time as a Dagger. When we are together, 'tis a special time." He frowned as he sat up, a hand to his bandages. Octavia couldn't help but admire the sight of his chest. He was an athletic man, and it showed. His skin possessed a creamy, warm undertone that simply begged to be touched.

She swallowed drily and tucked her hands beneath the ledge of the counter. "I'm just glad we're together again. I know you said this flat was the place we shouldn't go to, but I knew of nowhere else to possibly find you." Bodies approached, their songs healthy and strong.

"Yes. We cannot stay here long. My surname is enough to bring danger upon this place. For us to be physically present draws even more danger."

"What? You're going to leave already?" Tatiana stood in the doorway. Her voice warbled. "You can't go."

"Tatiana. Come here." Alonzo swung his legs to the side of the table. Tatiana leaned into his embrace, her forehead to his arm. Octavia couldn't help a twinge of envy. "What has Mother told you of my employment?"

"That you were working for the Caskentian government. Every time I write her a letter, I ask if she's heard from you. It's been months and months since you contacted her." She began to cry.

"Can you send the servant away?" he asked.

Tatiana nodded. The other woman departed with a formal curtsy.

"I have been on a special job this past while. I cannot share details, but 'tis vital that Miss Leander stay alive."

Alonzo could not see the expression on Tatiana's face, but Octavia could. The girl grimaced as if she had stepped in a fresh cow patty. "You've been hurt trying to keep her safe."

"I have, and likely will endure more travails." The siblings looked so alike, but Alonzo's accent was lilting and pure Mercian. Tatiana spoke with the casual yet rushed accent of the city-states.

"I want you to stay here with me. I can hire more guards! You've never seen the islands before, Alonzo. There are the hydroponic gardens, and the port of entry—hundreds and hundreds of airships there! You'd love it! And tonight, Cook is going to make your very, very favorite, cardamom chicken with cashews, and there will be lemon curd with shortbread for dessert. Please, Alonzo."

"We will stay tonight." He grimaced, even as Tatiana clapped her hands in glee. "But we dare not linger. Tomorrow we must seek out the best libraries of the southern nations."

"I know of many. I can write up a list."

The servant returned to the doorway. Tatiana nodded her approval at the woman's presence.

"Good." He tweaked his little sister's nose. "Do you have bolts of cloth here suitable for a grown woman's dress?"

"Yes. Gigi sews mine," said Tatiana, motioning to her dress and the servant behind her. The skirts swayed with grace. Many women had been wearing a similar cut in the plaza—no defined waist, but pleated cloth that fell straight from shoulder to knee.

"Alonzo, you're thinking of a dress for me?" asked Octavia.

"Yes. That Percival white is too fine a target."

If only he knew. "Considering everything we've been through, I'd like to keep my uniform on. Maybe a full coat would do."

"Miss, pardon me, miss." Gigi's voice trembled. "Are you asking me to sew for the magus?" A pleading note crept in at the end.

"I'm not contagious," Octavia muttered.

"Actually," said Alonzo, "I can sew it. Simply provide the supplies and good light."

"You can sew something of that complexity, that quickly?" asked Octavia.

Tatiana smiled smugly. "He's always had a good hand for sewing. He used to make dolls for me. Whatever you need, Alonzo. Just ask!" Her tone made it clear that she wanted him to need other things, too. "Now we have to get out of here so that Cook can get to work. I imagine you both want to bathe." She gave Octavia a pointed look.

"That would be lovely." Octavia smiled in the face of the insult.

While Gigi showed Alonzo the sewing supplies, another servant emerged to guide Octavia. Almost wordless, the girl pointed out a guest room and neighboring lavatory, and then dashed away.

Alone in her room, Octavia marveled at the space and luxury. She yearned to throw herself down on the honest-to-goodness bed, but knowing the filth of her body and coat, she didn't dare. Her wand sanitized things, but it couldn't match the sensation of being cleansed by water. She glanced in the mirror—she *looked* like she had spent a week in the wilderness. She stuck out her tongue at herself, just because.

Someone tapped on the door. Octavia opened it to find Tatiana. The child stared up at her, hands primly clasped at her waist.

"I want you to know that I hate you." Her tone was casual, her eyes like venom.

Octavia recoiled slightly. "I gathered that you weren't that fond of me."

"You don't understand. You can't. I learned to read and write by sending letters to my brother at the front, always afraid that he would die there. When Mother decided I needed to stay in Tamarania for tutoring, I didn't want to do it. I knew Alonzo would never come here. Father loved Caskentia, so Alonzo has to love it, too." She almost spat the words. "Now Alonzo finally comes and he's not going to stay."

"I'm sorry you're not going to—"

"No, you're not. You're going to take him away. He won't let me help after tonight."

"He's trying to protect you."

"That's what Alonzo does. It's what he's always done. But he only feels he has to protect me because he's in danger because of *you*."

Octavia gnawed on her lip and had no idea what to say.

"I saw how you were looking at him," Tatiana continued. "You think he's yours. Well, he's my brother. No matter what happens to you, if you live or die, he'll always be my brother. I love him." Her fists clenched at her narrow hips, and she turned away with a flounce of skirts. A short distance away, she stopped. "Dinner will be ready in an hour."

It was a threat, not an invitation. With that, Tatiana stalked away without looking back.

Her father dead. Alonzo absent. Her mother has practically abandoned her. So young to be filled with such hate.

Octavia closed the door again to compose herself. In truth, it was a shame Alonzo couldn't be with Tatiana longer. His gentleness, his logic, would be a great positive influence on her. Maybe that time would come later, after they survived this, after Caskentia and the Waste focused on other things. *Unfortunately, the only way they distract themselves is by seeking their mutual obliteration.*

In the meantime, she would take care when Alonzo's little sister offered any drinks, in case they contained as much poison as her words.

The nearby lavatory was as sumptuous as the bedroom. Octavia turned the bathtub tap and gasped at the immediate flow of hot water. It had only been a week and a half since her stay at the lush Hotel Nennia in Leffen, but it felt like months. Lifetimes. *A bath, hot water and all. Oh, what a sweet blessing.* Maybe afterward she could mend the edges of her medician blanket—and perhaps even grind that bag of dried pampria.

She stripped and loosened her hair as the tub filled. Steam clouded the room. She pulled the knife from her satchel's kit and set it on the ledge beside the claw-footed tub.

I certainly hope I don't need to use it, and certainly not against a ten-year-old girl.

Octavia sank into the water and sighed in bliss. Water flowed to her chest, her pale breasts buoyant, arms propped on the edges of the tub. Halfway down her left forearm, a small bandage covered the incision she used for bloodletting. The compulsion to bloodlet came directly from the Lady, usually every three or four days. Pressure would build up in her arm until she bled a few drops into the soil. Now that she thought about it, she hadn't had the need to bloodlet since they escaped from the Wasters—since her blood had temporarily caused that tree to grow.

She looked at the skin of her arm for the first time since then. An odd brown tinge framed the bandage.

Frowning, Octavia sat up. It couldn't be dirt. The enchantment on her uniform wouldn't have allowed it. She pried the bandage from the cantham wax beneath. The opaque wax showed the brown going all the way up to the fresh red of the incision; the wax prevented it from healing. She touched the colored skin. It was mottled and tough like a callus.

"How strange," she murmured, and sank into the water again.

"MAYBE THE CLOCKWORK DAGGERS succeeded, and did it so quickly that we don't even know we're dead," Octavia whispered.

"Why do you say such a thing, Miss Leander?" asked Alonzo.

"Because I am in the happy beyond."

The library occupied a rotunda that probably could have held the entire clapboard structure of Miss Percival's academy within its walls. Shelves towered a hundred feet, curved like a ship's hull, stairs and lifts leading up to exposed walkways of riveted copper. Octavia breathed in the divinity of thousands of leather-bound books.

Alonzo's grin was bold in contrast to his skin. "Holiness may be found by being in the mere presence of books, without even parting the pages."

Octavia loved it when Alonzo's poetic nature emerged—it always made her think of Father, how he muttered and cursed while he unfolded the rhythms of words as he sat by glowstone lamplight.

"It reminds me of how much Caskentia has really lost in the past half century. Not simply the men in the wars, but the books."

The greatest libraries in Caskentia had burned in the infernal attack on Mercia soon after the princess's kidnapping, and more had been lost in smaller attacks since. It was a rare delight to find a collection of old hardbound books in a single place.

"Remember our plan," Alonzo murmured as he entered the labyrinth of metal shelves. She ventured down a parallel aisle; their separation the day before made her anxious about being apart, though Alonzo had counseled that they not stay too close. Flashes of his new black coat showed through gaps in the shelves.

Alonzo had provided a veritable list of tips on searching inconspicuously for information in public. Foremost, she was not to attract attention or be especially memorable. Yellow was a color currently in fashion here, so he had styled for her a simple overcoat to cover her medician robes. He hadn't been pleased at her continued insistence on carrying her satchel—it had spoiled her previous effort to travel incognito—but he hadn't pressed the point too much. He knew it would be a losing battle. A yellow ribbon overlapped her headband and had been accented by an enormous white silk flower that could practically double as an umbrella.

Certainly, I could buy new clothes here, but these robes are one of the few things I can still claim as my own. If I had a few days to devote to meditation, maybe I could enchant a new dress that wasn't in Percival white, but that'll need to wait until assassins stop pursuing us like hungry mosquitoes.

Alonzo's other advice had been to move around often, even if she found a section of particular interest; never to ask librarians for help; and most importantly, not to save anyone with magic. The latter had been accompanied by a particularly severe look.

He stopped moving among the shelves. She stopped as well and scanned the books around her. *Such a glorious perfume, these old books.* This section focused on nationalities. She spied books on Mendalian dagger fighting, a multivolume set on the history of Warriors, biographies of the augusts, and a history of cocoa importation in the southern nations. She was glad to skim through this last as a decoy book, but was quickly disappointed to see the delights of cocoa reduced to soporific tax ratios, tonnages, and the woes of pod rot.

Alonzo circled behind her. "A few books on religion in Caskentia over there," he murmured. "Take a look and see if anything on the Lady seems new. Look for five books in red." His brow was lowered in consternation.

"What's the matter?" she whispered.

"I expected more. I must make some delicate inquiries." He walked down the aisle, a new tweed hat tucked under his arm. *Delicate inquiries. Meaning he's going to do things he told me not to do.*

She studied the shelves he had pointed her to. The section labeled RELIGION consisted of some twenty books. The red books addressed all world religions by country and regional quirk. The Lady earned a few sentences in Caskentia's section.

"The Lady's Tree is a variation on the Lord's Tree, as found elsewhere [SEE Grant, Vernon, Cashmere]. In recent centuries, numbers of faithful have declined; devotees are almost exclusively magi of the healing arts, known here as medicians. Medician schools indoctrinate their students in the faith of an avatar of God, a Tree who was once a grieving woman who wandered the Dallows. By invoking the Lady through a bound circle, miracles are achieved."

Faith has declined, indeed. I knew almost nothing of the Lady until I met Miss Percival, and my parents were both teachers and well read. If they had known of an explanation for my need to bloodlet, they would have let me know. Instead, they watched me and worried. No parent, no child, should have to endure that painful ignorance.

She checked the other nations referenced. Those listings didn't elaborate, instead forming an endless cross-referential loop. Sighing, Octavia slid the book back onto the shelf. A strange man approached. *Young, heart murmur, still suffering from the lingering effects of inebriation.* She looked up with a slight smile, even as a self-conscious flush traveled up her neck.

He wore a trim gray suit. Black kohl lined his eyes and thickened his eyebrows. "Can I help you?"

"Ah yes. I was just skimming books. On religion." *Blast it, Alonzo, I act about as incognito as a gremlin in a jewelry shop.*

The librarian's brows drew together. "You're Caskentian?" *Balderdash.* "Ah yes."

"I'm surprised, that's all. Most Caskentians can't read. They don't come in here."

She wished she could argue with him but he was quite right. She had written letters home for hundreds of soldiers, which were likely received by families that were equally illiterate.

"I'm trying to explore matters of faith. Are there more books?"

"You could check the academic studies of mythology, but no, religion isn't a relevant topic these days. If a book isn't checked out in a decade, it's sent to the basement, and after another decade without requests, it's sold." He shrugged.

"I see," she said slowly. Alonzo approached; he paused

to pull a book off the shelf, more cool and casual than she could ever hope to be. "My thanks."

It took several more minutes for Alonzo to work his way down to her. "I'm rotten at this," she muttered. "He was shocked a Caskentian could read."

"I am sorry." He turned his back to her as he skimmed a volume on regional variations within the folk art of making bread boxes. "In Caskentia, my skin sets me apart. Here, there is greater variety in coloration, but your accent will label you in an instant."

"And my literacy," she muttered. "But if I pretend to be mute, that makes me memorable as well."

"Did you find anything of interest in the books?"

"Mention of other Trees around the world, including male ones. That was new. He also said they get rid of books that aren't checked out in a long time."

"The librarian I spoke with said much the same. I had hoped that religion would retain an academic interest here."

"What do we do now?"

"Try other libraries. Await me by the gargoyle statue outside."

And so it went, library after library. If the Lady and Tree were mentioned at all, it was to rehash what Octavia had already learned from Miss Percival.

"There must be something more," Octavia muttered as they rode a tenth-level tram to yet another library. They sat side by side in an almost empty car. Afternoon sun failed to penetrate the constant clouds, though at least they were true clouds and not the persistent pollution said to smother Mercia. She rubbed her arm against her torso and sighed.

"Such books must exist. 'Tis a matter of finding them." Alonzo stared out the window.

Octavia avoided the view and kept her satchel clutched tight on her lap. Her headband helped her tolerate the number of people, but the sheer density of the city bothered her. *I'm a country girl at heart, even if it means a lack of libraries.*

"So far, it feels like hunting for a cat's whisker in a haystack. No one here is interested in magic or hokey religions, but someone must be buying the books since nothing has been remaindered in any of their storage rooms."

"An interesting observation. Perhaps 'tis time for a change of tack at our next library."

"Our last library, at least on your sister's list."

Tatiana had sobbed and wailed at Alonzo's departure that morning, pleading for him to return. Alonzo vowed he would send word somehow. After this next stop, their priority was to find a doss house in which to spend the night.

"There are other, smaller libraries on the other isles, but I fear the reception would be much the same."

A light rain pattered against the metal roof as they traversed catwalks down to the seventh floor of a skyscraper. At such a height, Octavia could see a hundred towers, maybe more, each a dark gray monolith against the mist. Still no sight of the sea, though. There was too much city in the way. A strong wind nipped straight up her skirt and made her convulse with cold.

This library occupied the full floor of a broad building. Few people utilized tables at the very front. A father sat with two young children at his feet as he read in a low rumble. A few women walked among the shelves, long skirts swaying. The rows of shelves reminded Octavia of the tidy furrows of a field.

In the fields back at the academy, the other girls will be planting tulip bulbs for spring. She rubbed the fingertips of her borrowed gloves as if she could feel moisture and grit. She had always loved planting times—she loved busywork when no one suffered.

"Walk on in," Alonzo murmured. "I will make my inquiries."

Octavia studied a display of copper novels that boasted of espionage, intrigue, and murder—published by Mrs. Stout's book company, no less. Even so, she felt her lip curl in distaste. *I fear my choices in pulp novels will be limited in the future.*

"My professor assigned me to write a paper on the obscure religions of Caskentia and how they regard magic," Alonzo was saying to a librarian. The woman clicked her tongue. "I know, I know. The man must hate me. The search has been futile. I lack the money to buy the books new . . ."

"The lot of students. I know it well." Her smile was sympathetic.

My Caskentian accent makes me sound like an illiterate toerag, but his Mercian lilt immediately makes him appear like a Caskentian student here for a proper education.

"Do you know where I might buy remaindered library books on the subject? I am desperate."

"I'm afraid I have bad news for you. When it comes to magic, august Balthazar Cody has likely bought them all. He's known for his eccentricities."

"Balthazar Cody." Alonzo tested the thick name on his tongue. "Of Tamarania, correct? Does he own . . . ?"

"The Warriors' Arena, yes. That said, there are a few books on the shelf I can show you."

An august. That would be like a councilman in Caskentia. With the population here, that's a position of great prestige. It'd certainly make an eccentricity like faith more tolerable.

Feeling awkward, Octavia pretended to study shelves as she worked her way toward Alonzo. The books here followed an inscrutable system involving decimals. She finally sidled up to him. He held a book entitled *Old Faiths* as he stroked his trimmed beard.

"I might make a Dagger of you yet," he murmured. "You are improving."

"I still feel like a blotto on a tightrope. I heard what she said. Balthazar Cody?"

"Yes. A dangerous man. My mother still speaks of him. He is a politician, through and through. It would be best to avoid direct dealings with him."

"I have those gilly coins from Mrs. Stout. Could we bribe his staff?"

Alonzo held back a chuckle. "That is certainly standard procedure in Caskentia. Here, I am more reluctant to trust. It may be wiser to explore the weak links in his household, perhaps infiltrate his staff as employees, but even that may prove difficult for a man of that ilk."

"Oh. That sounds as if it could take time." She rubbed her arms against her torso.

"Weeks. Perhaps months. Do recall that snow will soon close the passes. We will need to wait until spring to venture to the Dallows if we still intend to find the Lady."

"A task to keep us busy through the winter, then." Octavia stared at the shelves but didn't see titles.

"Not a bad thing, Miss Leander. As my father used to say, 'Idleness leads to madness.'" He paused. "I must remind you, however, that our primary goal is to stay hidden and alive. Understanding your power more, perhaps stopping the Wasters' abuse of the Tree, would be wonderful, and yet . . ."

Her throat tightened in frustration. "Finding these answers isn't a hobby for me, Mr. Garret."

"I know." His voice softened. "I have seen how your powers have changed, even in the brief time of our acquaintance. I want these answers for you as well, but most of all, you must stay alive. 'Tis enough that we have Caskentia and the Waste in our pursuit. I would rather not involve Tamarania in the donnybrook, and certainly not a man of Mr. Cody's might. I should add, he is not a mere politician. He created gremlins."

"Did he?" She looked away and frowned.

Onboard the airship, Octavia had saved and nurtured a tiny gremlin that she had dubbed Leaf. She had known it was a foolish thing at the time, forming an attachment to a wild chimera—a biological construct born of science—and it had broken her heart to set Leaf free. To her shock, Leaf had returned when she had been imprisoned by the Wasters. Using his affinity for silver, he had broken Octavia and Mrs. Stout free of their chains. Octavia was certain his appearance was no accident; she had prayed to the Lady and then Leaf arrived. He had also had an odd reaction to the branch of the Lady, acting reverential in its presence.

The thought of the lost branch irritated her. *So stupid, to lose part of the Lady like that. Now the only branch I know of in the west is in Caskentia's royal vault.*

The royal vault. Caskentia. The royals were always a subject of speculation and gossip. People still waxed nostalgic about King Kethan's Golden Age. The other library had a section on nations; perhaps this one had books on more interesting subjects than cocoa tariffs.

"I'm going to check another shelf," she murmured.

A few minutes of wandering, and she found the section. Caskentia actually had solid representation on the shelf. Bindings displayed a clear theme. *The Caskentia Problem. The Endless War. An Academic Study of the First Caskentian-Dallows War, Volume I. Technological Advancements of the Golden Age. Of Mechanical Men and Inherent Poverty: A Study of the Caskentian Proletariat.* She frowned and scanned downward. A small red volume caught her eye. *Lord Chamberlain of the Golden Age.*

The volume was one in a run of twenty, a printing of the logs of the palace lord chamberlain of both King Rathe and his son, King Kethan. Judging by the accumulation of dust puffs across the top, the topic was not of interest to Tamarans.

She squinted at the narrow type as she skimmed, rubbing at her arm. At last, a hundred pages in, she found something.

Knowing of the studious nature of our young prince, a hunter today delivered a most astonishing gift. He explored our territory of the Dallows and thereupon claims to have found the Lady's Tree of medician lore. To King Rathe he offered a branch of the Tree the size of a man's arm, by all appearances wholly alive; a leaf, that resembles most any normal foliage; and a seed the size of a shelled almond, bright green to the eye.

As to why the man brought such bounty to court, he confessed that he had been cursed since leaving the Tree's canopy. Threems nearly burned him alive, while wyrms thrashed deep furrows across the prairie. His horses, by all appearances healthy, dropped dead. When we informed the man that he had delivered a curse to the King, the hunter protested, saying the men of Caskentia's court were known to be the wisest in the land. And surely, such holy artifacts would not harm someone blessed by God to rule our Fair Valley.

Prince Kethan himself placed the pieces of the Lady's living body within the royal vault. To my surprise, he seemed troubled by the gifts rather than intrigued. "In my reading of his *History of World Trees,* Garcia said that blooded trees only produce one seed in a lifetime. If this new seed should grow in Mercia, our entire city would be overgrown!"

At this, we laughed, even as we were impressed, as always, by the erudition of the young heir and his eidetic knowledge of books. 'Tis my sincere hope that King Rathe be blessed with a long life, though the day when Prince Kethan claims the throne will surely be one of great celebration.

The volume resumed a few days later:

The words of the hunter and Prince Kethan returned to me last night as the earth rumbled. My first thought was of a mighty tree taking root and destroying the city, whereas people cried in the street that the Giant had awakened and we would all die of ash and fire. The sun soon rose and showed no ominous clouds from the mountain . . .

The Giant, being a massive dormant volcano just to the southeast of Mercia. The Waste's recent designs on Octavia had included using her to keep their infernals alive past the volcano's wards against fire magi. They had intended to undo the dormancy and destroy Mercia.

She flipped ahead but could find no other mentions of the vault or the artifacts. The slender book concluded soon after King Kethan's ascent to the throne, with Queen Varya just announcing her pregnancy. *The child who would be Princess Allendia, who grew up as a civilian named Viola Stout.*

This meant that the Tree had been sighted only some sixty or seventy years ago. *According to lore, magic keeps it hidden. Magic still must hide it to some degree. Caskentia's airships have flown over the entire Waste. A Tree taller than any building in Tamarania would have been seen otherwise. And the infernal Lanskay said the trek to the Tree was still perilous. That implies it is accessed by foot.*

As for the seed, Miss Percival had taught that it had the power to revive those who had been dead for a long while. Octavia had asked once if that meant there were people out there who were immortal as a result of the seed's power. Miss Percival had said there was no way to know, and it was not something that should be known.

"Pardon, pardon," said a woman as she pressed past. Her health rang as extraordinarily athletic—unusual for a woman—and that surprised Octavia enough to lift her head. She caught a glimpse of red hair cut in a short bob, a gorgeous contrast to ebony skin, and then the woman rounded the corner.

Octavia gnawed on her lip. *The vault was the only thing left standing after the firebombing of the palace fifty years ago. Mrs. Stout's bloodline is the key to entry. Maybe King Kethan did more research on these artifacts as he grew. He told Mrs. Stout when she was a child that they were the most powerful treasures in the vault. He knew something.*

Maybe there's still information there, along with the artifacts of the Tree. Queen Evandia can't get in because of her blood. It would all be waiting for us, locked away.

How odd that she was actually considering a trip into Mercia—and infiltrating the palace, no less—after she'd fought tooth and nail against the idea when it was proposed by Alonzo back on the *Argus*. But this was different. She wasn't going to stay there, or be in government custody. It could be a mere errand trip, that's all.

She snorted. An errand trip into the very palace of Queen Evandia. *I'm a flibbertigibbet. It'd be a suicide mission. And yet, if we made it inside the vault . . .*

She rubbed her arm again and frowned, suddenly aware of what she was doing. The area around her bloodletting incision itched. She'd have to check on the discolored skin later.

Something clunked a few aisles away. Metal whined, followed by the sound of books—hundreds of books—thudding to the floor. Metal banged and clattered again. Screams pierced the silence. Books thundered against the shelf before her. Metal smacked, hard. Octavia backstepped as the shelf in front of her tipped. Books poured down in a violent hailstorm. Screeching, she covered her head with her arms as she dropped flat.

The world turned black in a crush of books.

CHAPTER 4

Books, marvelous as they were, made for painful missiles. Hardcovers bombarded Octavia from the ten-foot-high shelf as it tipped far enough to smack into the next shelf. Leather-bound edges pounded and gouged into her back and shoulders. She yelped under the assault as books continued to slide down. Screams and yells echoed throughout the library.

"Alonzo!" Octavia called, wiggling to free herself from the pile. "Help!" She shook off enough books to free her shoulders and push herself to her knees. Electric light penetrated the emptied bookshelves and revealed dunes of books around her. Ripped pages crackled under her knees.

A body approached her from behind. With a start, Octavia realized her headband had been knocked off, as the body's song rang stronger than before. *Woman, healthy, strong. Her heart rate normal. Too normal.* Octavia had the sense to roll to one side as the woman dove at her. She whirled to face her attacker—the redheaded woman who had passed by a minute before. The stranger crouched in the crooked archway of the downed bookshelves, her skirt indecently hiked to show her knees. Her face was emotionless.

The brasses of Alonzo's song struck a frenzied melody. *Worry, concern, fear.* "She is a Dagger," he said from behind the woman. "I met her more than once in Mercia. The only other Dagger to share Tamaran heritage. Greetings to you, Esme."

The woman spun around to confront him. Books shifted and tore beneath her feet. The fallen shelves created a tilted triangle about four feet high at the peak, the space cramped and narrow. Esme carried a knife. The blade glinted with an unreal sheen, not unlike the enchantment on Octavia's Percival garb. Octavia had a hunch, however, that the knife's magic had nothing to do with cleanliness.

"Alonzo! That blade—"

"I am aware."

With Octavia on the far side, Alonzo didn't pull out the Gadsden. Instead, he hefted a knife in one hand and a sizable book in the other. As Esme lunged forward, he wielded the book as a shield as he backed toward the open hallway— guiding the fight away from Octavia.

A good thing, she realized, as she was still partly buried in books and gawking like a fool.

She extracted herself while keeping an eye on the fight. Esme was more aggressive by far, her movements sinuous as a cat's. Alonzo offered few jabs. Octavia bit back a curse. His injury still pained him and restricted his movements. *If only I'd been able to give him a proper healing!*

Octavia rummaged beneath the books and found her headband. The flower had been ripped off. No time to spare, she shoved the cloth into an outer pocket of her satchel. The domino fall of shelves had stopped, and in the distance there were cries and alarmed voices. *Broken leg. Ribs. Arm. Bruises. Concussions.* She shivered, wondering at what distance she was detecting these injuries, and afraid to know the answer.

She grabbed a book—*A History of Frengian Maple Patisseries*—and flung it. The book spun through the air and smacked the assassin in the lower back. Octavia grabbed another one—*The Inherent Violence of the Caskentian Psyche.* That one, quite appropriately, struck corner-first directly into the back of Esme's head. The woman couldn't help but glance back with a scowl, and that's all the advantage Alonzo needed. Esme screeched as he slammed her into the debris-covered floor. He twisted her wrist, snapping it with a jolt that pierced Octavia's ears and senses.

New bodies flooded the library. *Strong hearts and songs, not unlike Alonzo's. Calm in the face of chaos. These are police, soldiers. How did they respond so quickly?*

"What magic's on the blade?" Octavia asked.

"She will not answer. 'Tis a part of the training I have yet to attend." He wrenched Esme's arm more.

Esme lifted her head a tad. Across the drifts of books, she stared at Octavia. Her jaw shifted as she chomped down. With her shielding headband off, Octavia could almost taste the bitterness, reminiscent of almonds, as it gushed over Esme's molars and numbed her mouth. Her dark skin flushed, her next breath rattling.

"Cyanide!" Octavia cried. The favored poison of Mercia's elite, one she had encountered in the suicides of several officers at the front.

Alonzo wrested Esme around. Books pattered to the side. Esme's song—oh Lady, her song screeched as if rabid wolves were chasing down a marching band. Her organs shut down in a vicious cascade, each wailing and silencing as if devoured in a single gulp. Octavia wanted to hurry forward, to help. Instead, she curled into a ball, heaving as if her own body were starved for oxygen.

"Octavia!"

"I'm not hurt, it's just . . ." Hot tears poured down her face as she fumbled to pull on the headband again. She didn't care how it looked—she simply needed her ears covered, and quickly. "I can heal her." With her intimate awareness somewhat dimmed, Octavia crawled forward, wiping her face with her sleeve as she went.

She was a foot away from Esme when the new songs in the room grew close and bold.

"Do not move." The order came from the hallway beyond the claustrophobic hug of the shelves. A man in vivid blue stood there, gun drawn. Braids gilded his sleeves, neck, and along a triple row of buttons. More men in similar attire crowded behind him.

Alonzo grimaced, raising his hands above head level as he shuffled around on his knees. Octavia hesitantly raised her arms, her gaze going between the men and the Clockwork Dagger. Esme convulsed. Red froth flowed from her mouth.

"I'm a medician. Let me get her in a circle—"

Alonzo shot her a glare of warning. She felt pressure anew in her chest. *A life debt to Alonzo, again. The Lady is watching.*

The soldier scowled. "A circle? Nep. Doctor, over here! Now!" he bellowed. "You lot, come out of there. Keep your hands up."

Alonzo and Octavia crawled out on their knees, a tricky thing with hands up and splayed books beneath them. Octavia kept partially falling over her satchel and winced as pages tore beneath her weight. As she reached the end of the shelves, another soldier grabbed her by the arm—not cruelly—and pulled her up to her feet. Several other soldiers crawled to Esme. Her body's screams had dwindled to the weak mews of a starved kitten.

Cyanide that potent, that fast, placed her beyond intervention within seconds, even with a circle in place. That awareness didn't stop the knot of frustration from forming in Octavia's chest. Her fists balled at her hips.

"Check her bag," the commander said to a soldier, pointing to Octavia.

She hugged her satchel closer, the parasol banging against her arm. Alonzo gave his head a quick shake. Grinding her teeth, she relinquished her death grip. The soldier made no effort to take the satchel strap from her shoulder. Instead, he opened the main pocket and rummaged under the blanket. He held up the newly filled jar of pampria.

The commander nodded. "A medician indeed. Check the other pockets. If nothing stands out, let her keep it."

Octavia almost sagged in relief. The soldier made a quick check of the other compartments and then her coat. He took her gun without a word and backed away.

Esme's limp body lay sprawled on the carpet. One of the men, eyes averted, tugged her skirt to a proper length past the knee.

A woman in a skirted version of the blue uniform rushed up just as Octavia finished refastening her satchel. She wore a black leather medic bag against her hip.

"What's this about, then?" asked the newcomer.

"Woman took a dose of cyanide, they say." The commander gestured toward them.

The doctor crouched. Her thick black hair was pinned in a massive roll like a ball of yarn. She muttered beneath her breath as she checked Esme's pulse, opened her mouth, and glanced at her fingernails. "Cyanide, absolutely. The good stuff, from the look of it." She looked up at Octavia. "You family? Friend? Do you have any claim to her?"

"Claim?" asked Octavia. "No. She tried to kill us by tipping the shelves!"

"Perfect. I claim the body, then. My students need to see the internal results of a cyanide poisoning." The woman brushed her hands on her skirt as she stood.

"That's it? You're not going to do anything else?" The mews faded to nothing. The drumbeat, gone.

The doctor looked Octavia up and down. "What would you have me do, a song and dance and plead for help from above? Footle. There are other, living people who need aid now. This one made her choice when she bit down on a tablet."

That terrible sense of frustration threatened to over-whelm Octavia again. *I could use a leaf. We could question her, find out how she followed us here, what she has reported to Mercia.*

"Miss Leander." Alonzo's voice was soft. "No. Not on her."

Of course he knows what I'm thinking. He knows me so well.

"You're both hale, then? No injuries after this attack?" asked the commander. Alonzo and Octavia shook their heads. At that, the doctor turned on her heel and left. The soldier continued, "We're here to fetch you, and with right good timing, it seems. We're private guards for august Balthazar Cody. You're invited to his household."

"Right now?" Octavia asked.

"Now," said the soldier. He and the other men bristled with weaponry, their expressions grim.

"Well, as I was raised, invitations were best handled by a calling card and a gift of flowers, but I suppose this will do." She said this as brightly as she could, trying to ignore the worry that raced through Alonzo's song. "Lead on, please."

"I DO NOT LIKE this," murmured Alonzo.

They sat across from each other on a small passenger airship decorated in lush brown leather and gold rivets. The engine was so quiet and smooth that Octavia wouldn't have known they were moving but for the shifting cityscape beyond the window.

"It's not as if we had much of a choice."

"All the more reason to dislike it." His dark brows drew together. "We are being placed in obligation to Mr. Cody. Several patrons saw the woman push over the shelves, then all were too busy to witness our full conflict. By public appearances, his men saved us from an assassin, or at the very least compelled her to commit suicide."

"This plays into what you said before, about how Tamarans regard personal accomplishment?" she asked, and Alonzo nodded. "It must be my fault that the Dagger and Mr. Cody tracked us down within a day. My accent, my clumsiness, something. I'm so sorry, Alonzo."

"Look at it in this positive light—we can meet Balthazar Cody and directly inquire about his library." He didn't sound too positive, though. Something about this Mr. Cody obviously unsettled him.

"True. It's just as well we didn't pursue your idea of infiltrating his household. You may be able to playact as a steward, but I'd have been dreadful as house staff. I wouldn't have lasted a day before getting the chuck."

"Be gentler with yourself, Miss Leander." Alonzo paused as he glanced outside. "It might have taken two days, at least, until you tried to save some life in peril."

"More likely a matter of hours." Octavia fidgeted with her headband again and stared out the window.

Advertisements plastered the long horizontal gaps between the high-rise windows, an ad for Royal-Tea included. The calligraphy boasted ENERGY AND FORTITUDE accompanied by a large emblem of the crown as it was shown on Caskentian coins. The Wasters had a sick sense of humor to market their tea using the image of King Kethan's crown, commonly known as the clockwork crown. The crown had been presented to him by a conglomerate of metalworkers at the height of the Golden Age. As a symbol of the industrial boom, the points of the crown had been designed like the teeth of a cogwheel. Kethan increased his popularity with commoners by declaring it his favorite crown and wearing it most often, even though it was basic silver and unadorned by jewels.

King Kethan was said to have worn it as he died in the infernal attack by the Waste.

The ship's engine purred louder as the craft rose. A gauzy layer of clouds drifted below them and hid the advertisements. With a metallic clatter and a jolt, the ship docked. The engine wound down.

The cockpit door opened and the pilot gave them a nod. "If you'll come with me, sir, m'lady."

Wind whistled through the short mooring tower atop the building. Octavia was grateful for the high railing along the curved staircase. She was curious about the view of the ground below, but dared not lean to look. She all too clearly recalled the time when she had been defenestrated aboard the *Argus*.

The pilot led them to what seemed to be a long shanty in the middle of the roof. Octavia entered a downward stairwell and paused to look up. Body songs rang out from the attic—dozens upon dozens, all in an excited clamor. *Little heartbeats. Odd, disjointed bodies, yet healthy.*

"Gremlins," she whispered to Alonzo with a nudge.

Mrs. Stout said that gremlins hate being in the city, but this doesn't feel like a city, this high up. She also said people in the southern nations could talk to gremlins.

If anyone could, surely it would be their creator.

The stairwell led directly into a domicile.

The Garret flat had embodied controlled opulence. Cody's showed no such restraint. If a surface could be adorned with gold leaf, it was; if it needed cloth for texture, vivid blue velvet was the choice. The floor consisted of alabaster marble tiles large enough for an adult to stretch out supine. Mechanical detritus sat on display along the walls: metal men, armaments, artistic odds and ends from engines of all sizes. No silver, though. A wise precaution with gremlins about.

They entered a masculine den seemingly carved out of dark wood, as if they had entered a cave within a giant tree. Octavia stepped onto the carpet and stared down. The lush blue pile was as high as real grass and hid the toes of her shoes. Two bookshelves flanked a desk in mahogany with carved dragon-claw legs. A man stood behind the desk. *Prolonged bladder infection.* His unbuttoned coat revealed a curved gut girthed by a burgundy vest. His skin tone was a few shades darker than Alonzo's. Frizzy black hair, white-striped, had been cut to about three inches in length.

"You are the very image of your father," said the stranger as he rounded the desk. "Except the eyes. That blue is purely your mother." His posture, clothing, everything about him announced that he was either a horse trader, politician, or some other swindler of grand tradition.

"You are Balthazar Cody. I know of you from my mother." The men clasped hands. "'Tis good to meet you, sir." A lie, though courteously said.

Mr. Cody turned to Octavia, bowing as he took her hand. His lips hovered at her gloved knuckles about two seconds longer than was proper. "Ah, the famed Octavia Leander. My little birds tell me extraordinary tales about you, my dear."

"Perhaps your little birds shouldn't spread gossip, Mr. Cody." *Alonzo was right to describe this man as dangerous.*

Mr. Cody burst out laughing. "That would make for a dull world." He waved the pilot away.

"Your birds must work well for you to know so many things," said Alonzo. His song raced with unease. His Gadsden and knives had been confiscated, yet he was ready to uncoil in an instant.

"Oh, they only tell me so much. The rest comes from good old-fashioned spies. This is my city, you understand. It's my place to know what goes on here. Nothing brings people together like a similar taste in books, correct?"

Octavia glanced at Alonzo. His mouth was set in a grim line.

"Unfortunately," Mr. Cody continued, "you had rather poor timing in your choice of libraries. That Caskentian Clockwork Dagger, Esme Spencer, visits—visited—that library at this time each day as part of her guise as a student. When you waltzed in, she must have been as happy as a pilot atop the Warriors' mountain. A shame she had to die like that. Now we get to start from scratch with someone new."

At least the Dagger didn't follow us there. Maybe she didn't get to report our whereabouts either.

Alonzo, however, didn't look relieved. "Are you aware of why she attacked us?"

"Direct, are you? Very well. The game will be more fun if I continue to show my hand. Yes, I've intercepted recent bulletins sent down from Caskentia. You, Alonzo Garret, have been declared a collaborator of the Dallows. You, Miss Leander, have been kidnapped. By him."

Her jaw dropped. "What?"

"I am not surprised," said Alonzo. "Miss Leander, you know well how Caskentia is."

Such orders explained why the woman had not killed Octavia when it would have been easy to do so, but Octavia's death would have still been the end result. The Lady knew as much or she wouldn't have bestowed another life debt on Alonzo.

Mr. Cody sat on the corner of his desk and leaned on his higher knee. "The subject of religion has made our libraries very attractive to you. I'm going to surmise that you're most likely looking for books on medician magi. A search that frustrated you, I imagine, because I possess all the available literature on the subject. Miss Leander here has something of a reputation since that zyme contamination. Maybe you have questions on the subject, questions Caskentia can't answer. Questions Caskentia might not want answered. Yes?"

Octavia tried to keep her face impassive, even as her gut soured with dread. "You think differently from your countrymen." A shame that his genuine enthusiasm for her kind didn't make her like the man.

"Others here in the south have a narrow view of what powers are worthwhile. Power is power. It should be respected. I respect the two of you immensely, and I hope the three of us might strike a bargain."

Octavia shot Alonzo a worried look. He appeared stoic, arms crossed over his broad chest. *Daggers must stare into a mirror to practice that blank countenance.*

Mr. Cody waddled around them. "Walk with me, please." His shoes clattered on the fine floor of the hall. Octavia hugged her satchel a little tighter. A lift awaited them, the ornate doors in gold.

"We're going all the way to the shop," Mr. Cody said to the operator as the man bowed low.

The lift's motor was nearly silent as they descended. Mr. Cody clutched both sides of his unbuttoned coat. "Mr. Garret, your father had a knack for operating most all machines. I remember the first time I saw a buzzer in the skies here—quite a legacy he left with such an invention. According to your army file, you are an adept buzzer pilot yourself."

Alonzo stared at the door. Through the mesh of the lift gates, building floors zoomed by in light and dark blurs. "I can pilot," he said at last.

"What do you have in mind, Mr. Cody?" asked Octavia.

"Well, you have been in the city for only a day, so I know you haven't seen a bout, but how much do you know of my Arena?"

"'Tis a life-size version of the game of Warriors, set

before a large audience. Piloted mechas battle their way to the top of a metal pyramid."

Octavia's fists clenched. "You're not suggesting Mr. Garret pilot one of those things, are you?" *Oh Lady. People die in those matches. The audience cheers.*

"I have a new mecha. It combines my interests for the first time. The problem is, no one can pilot it. There's a bout the day after tomorrow, and my other mechas are sidelined by repairs. Here you are, like an answer to prayer."

"No one else has piloted it, Mr. Cody, or no one has survived piloting it?" asked Octavia.

"Now, now. Not all of them have died."

"Is that what you're asking of me? To treat the injured?"

"No. Doctors have handled them. My request of you is special." The lift dinged and the operator opened the portal. The dial showed them at a basement.

The high ceiling reminded Octavia of an airship repair hangar she had seen at the front. Partitions divided the floor like a giant stable. Bright electric bulbs dangled from pendulums, but the overwhelming gray of the floor and walls cast a dour mood over the massive space. The air stank of heated metal and mustiness.

"A tunnel over there leads directly to the Arena." Mr. Cody pointed.

"We're right on the plaza, then?" Octavia asked.

"Quite. I believe in being in the center of any action."

Mr. Cody led them onward. Crews worked on massive war machines twenty, thirty feet in height. The constructs were not in stark metal shades like common working vehicles; no, these were characters. One was a porcupine, its back a mass of deadly spikes. A standing cockpit occupied the space from chest to where the creature's head would be. Another was a threem from mythology. The scaled horse stood on four cloven hooves, the pilot's seat a shielded cage set into the back. The lower part of the horse's face had been removed, and several men currently shoved a long piece of pipe into the gullet.

They have it rigged to breathe fire like in the stories. Mr. Cody wants Alonzo in a machine like that.

She brought her hands together and found the small scar on her wrist, the gift given to her by the infernal Lanskay. Among Waster fire magi, it was considered impressive if an enemy soldier made it within range of touch—and therefore, they were allowed to live with a scar as something of a trophy. Counting coup, the airship bartender Vincan had called it. Octavia's mark was tiny—the imprint of Lanskay's finger and nail—and enduring it had been agony. It was nothing compared to what Alonzo had survived during the same incident. His entire arm had been burned to make her compliant. Now he could burn again.

It always comes back to fire. My parents' deaths. The village. Alonzo, tortured, only for the Lady's leaf to heal him completely as he returned from the dead.

"Alonzo, I don't like this." She spoke loud enough for Mr. Cody to hear.

"Nor do I." *Heart rate elevated. Breaths rapid. Fear.* Alonzo had survived the front. He had lost half a leg. He had no interest in the wanton waste of life.

"Miss Leander," said Mr. Cody. He paused long enough for them to walk closer together. "It's my understanding that you have something of an affinity for gremlins."

An icy sensation trickled through Octavia's veins. *How does he know that, of all things? Only Mrs. Stout and Alonzo know how I hid Leaf on the airship.* She forced herself to remain calm, as if she could mimic Alonzo's Dagger stoicism. "Why would you say such a thing?"

The headband filtered out many of the extraneous songs of workmen, but up ahead, a body rang as particularly bold. No men worked in this station. It was a body by itself, and yet . . . She frowned, trying to make sense of it. It felt like there were layers involved, and dead zones, hollow spaces like amputations.

Mr. Cody guided them around a brass partition. "As I told you already, my little birds whisper all sorts of things."

Three hearts, beating in rhythm. Atrophied muscles. A song dragging in despair. The trill of gremlins.

Not gremlins. A singular gremlin, thirty feet tall. Green skin soldered to brass extensions. Batlike wings folded close, the webbing in brilliant metal. Separate arms attached just below in full copper, the hands endowed with three fingers each, like Leaf's hands. The eyes—black, round, and filled with sorrow.

"Oh Lady," Octavia whispered. "No. No."

CHAPTER 5

This mecha was a chimera in the most extreme sense. From what Octavia understood, first-generation gremlins had been made of cats, dogs, bats, and other creatures; this monstrosity included those beasts and so much more. Short hind legs, bent like that of a crouched human, were made of copper to match the stubby arms. The body and head were largely flesh, though enhanced by metal for the sake of shielding. The long, tapered ears, as an obvious point of vulnerability, had been capped by copper spikes as if they were horns.

The gremlin chirped, the sound like a magnified version of Leaf's adorable greeting. The creature shuffled. Massive chains rattled at the movement. A twenty-foot copper oval was inlaid into the tiles; it sparked with life as Octavia crossed the line, but didn't fully activate. The chains kept the chimera well away from the boundaries of the circle.

"Good God. You have made a beastie into a mechanical," said Alonzo.

Not just one beastie. Many. *The layers. Multiple souls.*

Pieces of the whole animal bodies, reused, altered. To her mind's ear, it created a crude symphony similar to a body in ill health, but more complex. *It's like the few human transplant patients I have worked on, where the healthy body fights the new organ it views as invasive. Here, that physical fight is over, and yet...* Facts, realities tumbled through her brain.

Medicians had been part of this creation; Balthazar Cody's interest in magic now made perfect sense. It was all part of his hobby, his business. That was evident in the extravagant circle in the floor and the manner of the creature's melding. As much as Octavia loved Leaf, she wondered at the cruelty behind his creation—how could the Lady be part of this?

Octavia walked forward, hand extended as if she offered a carrot to a horse. "Hello there, little one who's not so little," she said. The long ears trembled.

"Miss Leander!" Alonzo's voice rose in alarm. She knew his elevated heartbeat, the readiness of his muscles. *His hand ready to grab a Gadsden that's not there.*

"It's okay. She's not going to hurt me." The feminine pronoun felt appropriate, though the creature was truly neuter in gender.

"My God." Mr. Cody gasped. "Look at how it's responding to her."

"And how should she be responding?" Octavia kept her gaze on the chimera.

"By now, anyone else would have been pummeled into the ground."

Throughout the hangar, all other work on mechas had

stopped. The engineers congregated behind Mr. Cody and Alonzo. Their songs formed a wall of excitement.

"Mr. Cody," said Alonzo. "Your 'little birds.' Your gremlins. They have told you about us?"

"Yes. My first chimeras use a human voice box. They act as translators for other gremlins. They do like to gossip. Word spread of a medician, a worker of the Tree, who had offered unusual kindness to gremlins. That they should all be on the lookout for her in order to offer any possible aid." Mr. Cody said this low enough for just Alonzo and Octavia to hear, not the other workers. "I have never heard of them regarding someone like that before."

"You cannot communicate with this new mechanical creature?" asked Alonzo.

"Not for lack of effort. This chimera is sullen, angry. It doesn't want to speak to me."

The black nose of the gremlin snuffled at Octavia. A few strands of hair loosened from her updo and tickled at her cheeks as the headband pushed back to her shoulders. So close, the creature reeked of metal, wild game, mustiness, and enchanted aether. *An aether magus has worked on this as well—the wings, I imagine.* She tugged off a glove and tucked it into her satchel. Shushing to comfort the chimera, Octavia rested a hand against the wrinkled green skin of the creature's face.

And promptly dropped into pulsing black nothingness.

She knew the gremlin's despair by the way the emotion manifested throughout the body—sluggishness, lethargy, a reaction she'd seen with any man kept in chains for a time.

The creature's scars were recent, the memory of pain still vivid within the body, the way a flash of light sears vision in the darkness. The muscles—she had been chained here for weeks. *The ache to move, to fly—though she can't fly far, even magicked. The weight is too much.*

Mr. Cody spoke in the background but his voice was an indecipherable roar, as if Octavia heard him while submersed underwater. The chimera's three hearts ticked faster. *The gremlin hates him. She knows Mr. Cody is the cause of all this pain.*

Through the creature's muscle memory, Octavia felt jolts of electricity that left flesh singed as each heart sparked to life again. *Once life existed, that's when the medician stepped in. Patients must always acquiesce for a healing to occur. The gremlin, confused as she was, acquiesced—anything to stop the pain. The Lady then acted with mercy.*

Octavia opened her eyes. Hot tears streamed down her face. "I am so sorry."

The chimera trilled and rubbed her face against Octavia as if to comfort her. Octavia laughed as she stumbled back a step.

"Will you look at that!" said Mr. Cody. "It's like an oversize kitten with her. Now we just need to channel the anger it has shown before and I'll win my bout. It's all about proper direction."

The heartbeats roared. *Rage. Hatred.* Those were already channeled—toward Mr. Cody. Octavia turned to face him, hating him just as much. A peculiar heat poured from her chest and into her extremities. As it flowed over her bloodletting arm, the pain of a thousand zinging needles raced to her brain. She screamed and fell to her knees. Black spots swarmed over her vision.

Body heat. Strong arms. The brass-filled song. *Alonzo.* She pressed her face deeper into his chest. His touch felt so good, so right. She breathed him in. That cinnamon scent had returned, reminding her of pampria leaves and Frengian pastries, all the finest things in life.

She blinked several times before her eyes managed to stay open. "What happened?"

"I know not." His broad hand cupped her cheek.

"Is she all right?" asked Mr. Cody. The chimera trilled low. No, not a trill. A growl.

Lady! I felt like I could have killed Mr. Cody with my glare alone, and the wrongness of wanting, craving, his death struck me in a backlash.

What is happening to me?

"I'm okay," she called, her voice hoarse.

Alonzo's brow furrowed. "I know this power of yours comes through the Lady. I worry that she forgets you are human. A copper wire can be overloaded by a current."

Octavia nodded, unsure of what to say. A dark shadow loomed over them. The chimera's massive catlike nose snuffled over Alonzo as he helped her to sit up. Mr. Cody still stood beyond the circle and the reach of the chains. Behind him, the engineers made slashing motions across their chests, their gazes on her troubled. *They know something has changed about the creature and they're blaming me, my magic. Tamarans aren't that different from Caskentians, really.*

Fear and ignorance are still there. A few more years of education hasn't changed much.

"Whatever you did, Miss Leander, I am in awe!" Mr. Cody practically crowed in delight. "The chimera looks functional. You do have a profound connection with my constructs, both little and big."

Constructs. That makes them sound so disposable, like children's toys to be battered and then thrown in the trash. Even "chimera" is a better term.

The creature's name occurred to her then: Chi.

There I go, naming things again. At least my horse was spared.

She glared at Mr. Cody. "This construct, as you put it, has been restrained far too long. It's easy to see she's in pain."

"That was a better option than killing her and wasting years of effort." Mr. Cody straightened his cravat. "Well! You have already fulfilled the first part of the deal, and before I properly proposed it."

Alonzo grimaced as Chi nuzzled his thick queue of hair. "Let us not dither further, then. What are the terms of our agreement?"

"I will grant you access to my private library for your search. In turn, Miss Leander will ensure I have a healthy, functional mecha for the bout. Mr. Garret, you will be the pilot. I'm not so foolish as to order you to win, though I do expect full participation in the battle. I'm not a gambler in that sense."

Alonzo tilted his head to one side. "This is an exhibition."

A sparkle lit Mr. Cody's eyes. "Yes. No one has brought

in a biological blend before. It's enough to make a proper show and survive."

Survive. Mr. Cody's callous abuse of magic and life made Octavia feel filthy in his very presence. *He'll use me. He'll use Alonzo. He'll use his chimera. He's already playing a game of Warriors, and the bout hasn't even begun.*

"I don't like this in the slightest." She met Mr. Cody's gaze levelly. "The very idea of the Arena sets me on edge. I've seen war. It's not a game. And you would throw Mr. Garret into the thick of that, and on a living creature that's had no say in the matter."

"Of course it's had no say. Do you ask horses if they want to join the cavalry?" Mr. Cody looked genuinely puzzled.

The man could speak with some of his gremlins, but he didn't comprehend their sentience. *Or he doesn't care.* Leaf had been bright enough to learn dozens of words within a span of hours, and he was a mere baby. Chi had all the more potential. *If she survives.*

"Octavia." Alonzo's voice lowered to a husky whisper. "I understand well the reasons for your objections. There is inherent risk here. However, Cody has acquired the southern nations' knowledge about your art. If we do not agree, I fear we will have no other recourse."

"You would give up that quickly? We've been here for all of a day!"

"Long enough to gain a feel for our odds of success. Remember, survival is our primary goal, not the Lady. Judging by how we already encountered a Dagger by sheer accident, 'tis not prudent to stay here for any length of time."

"You speak about survival and this Arena bout together. It doesn't make sense."

"People do die in these matches, but 'tis not a gladiatorial fight. 'Tis more about strategy in reaching the top. Death is not the intent."

"Ah yes, and that makes it all fine and dandy." She struggled to keep her trembling voice at a low volume. "You keep reminding me that I can't heal people here, but if you're in the Arena, if you're injured . . ."

The previous day had been hard enough, separated on train cars with no idea how to reunite, but the thought of continuing alone caused her chest to squeeze in a vise of terror. *No, not simply because of the mission to find the Lady, or because I rely on his skills to survive against Caskentia and the Waste.*

Alonzo, you can't leave me alone. Octavia couldn't say the words. They clogged in her throat, thick as logs.

He looked past her to the chimera. "I know your beastie on the airship was far brighter than one would think. This large beastie here—how much does he—she—understand?"

"A great deal, I think. Just talk to her the way I talked to Leaf. She'll show you if she comprehends. I named her Chi, by the way."

"Chi. Of course you did." He shook his head, smiling. "Very well." And like that, he vaulted up the side of Chi. His sore ribs didn't slow him, even as his song warbled at the abrupt movement. It was to Alonzo's benefit that the chimera was as surprised as everyone else. She froze in place, black eyes unblinking. Between the green wrinkled flesh and copper plating, Alonzo had abundant handholds. It took a matter of seconds for him to reach Chi's back and nestle in at the base of her wings.

Octavia sensed Chi's rising alarm and stood, arms extended. "Shush, Chi, shush. It's all right. You're strong. You can be ridden. Do you have memories of the time before you were melded? Of seeing people on horseback? It doesn't hurt horses to be sat upon. There. Relax." The heartbeats calmed, though the ears still twitched.

Though what Mr. Cody has in mind may very well hurt. Oh Lady.

"Miss Leander." Alonzo leaned over to see her. "I have broken green horses before. We will learn together." He stroked the chimera's short neck. Chi chirped—a pleasant sound.

"Have you trained a war-horse in two days?" Octavia hissed.

"No, but this is no mere war-horse. Do you understand me, beastie? Can you flare out your wings?"

With a metallic snap, the wings extended fully. They almost reached the sides of the inlaid circle. From base to wing tip, they had to be twenty feet in length. *Beautiful, and a fine target.*

"Magnificent!" cried Mr. Cody, applauding. "This will be the debut of the year!"

Frustrated, disgusted, and relieved all at once, Octavia backed away.

"Mr. Garret, we have a full training course where you can teach the chimera how to navigate the Warriors' mountain. I will show you that in a moment. Boys, go get the saddle and reins. Let's do this properly." Mr. Cody eagerly motioned Octavia closer and whispered, "Miss Leander, I know time is essential, Daggers and all. My clerk can show you upstairs to the library."

She looked at Alonzo. She wanted to linger within range of his body's song to make sure he stayed safe; at the same time, she ached to flee for fear of what might happen, what she might see, what she might be helpless to repair. *If I have to use another leaf on that man, I'll revive him just so I can throttle him.*

Then there was Chi, who had already suffered so much. Octavia knew she could tend to the chimera without a circle, though it worried her to think of how such an effort would tax her.

This deal with Balthazar Cody needed to be over and done with for all of their sakes. "Promise me that if Mr. Garret or the chimera is injured, you'll fetch me immediately."

"I can do that, absolutely. I also keep doctors on staff down here at all times."

"Very well," she said, though it was anything but. "Please show me to your library."

CHAPTER 6

Octavia had never thought it was possible to grow weary of a library, but after a full day skimming through Mr. Cody's volumes, she had reached the threshold of being so. The man possessed at least fifty books solely about the Lady and the Tree, and hundreds more on the full spectrum of magic and magi.

"Fiddlesticks," she muttered, rubbing one forearm and then the other.

The same facts about the Lady repeated time and again, circling like a flying-horse carousel. The Lady was rooted somewhere in the Dallows. She was once a grieving mother. Stories first referenced her about seven hundred years ago, but there were very few books older than that on any subject matter. Each of Cody's books on magi observed that the Tree had potent healing properties. A few stated the existence of several such Trees around the world, though the number ranged from three to seven. How that number came about at all was a puzzle, as it was universally accepted that the Trees used magic to veil themselves.

Most of the books were over a century in age and published within Mercia or the southern nations. She was surprised by statistics that made medicians sound much more common then—numbering in thousands, not a scant few hundred. Why had the number of healing magi dropped so? In the southern nations, she could see young medicians being repressed so that they never trained to fulfill their potential. In Caskentia, perhaps, many were dying of wounds, malnutrition, or other effects of the war. Five girls had died during her ten years at the academy, after all.

Octavia scribbled notes and questions as she read. Why would a Tree suddenly become visible, as the Lady had during King Kethan's youth? Why could the Wasters find it by foot now? How were they getting past the wyrms and threems that were said to defend the Tree? If these Trees produced one seed in their lifetimes, this suggested that their lives were limited to a finite number of years, but Miss Percival had always said that the Lady's Tree was immortal. Not that those teachings could be trusted anymore. Octavia had learned the hard way that the Lady defied expectations.

The data on medicians was just as redundant and useless. After seeing the same pencil notations across several books, she could only surmise they were in Mr. Cody's hand. He had circled passages that described how to build effective circles into floors or portable surfaces, the peculiar need to bloodlet, even the odds on medician skills being passed down from one generation to the next—a subject that led to very diverse conclusions.

Considering how he's made gremlins, it's vexing to think of the man searching for a hereditary trait for medicians. My own experience would discourage him, at least. My mother doctored, but I don't know of anyone else in my family with the knack. Miss Percival once said that it just seemed to happen to some girls and boys, as though we sniffed the right flower.

Reading about bloodletting made her more conscious of the continued problem she was having with her arms. The blemish around her incision had grown a deeper brown, the texture scaly. It was unlike anything she had ever seen before, and she had seen a great deal. It didn't hurt, really—it itched as though the skin stretched. Her other forearm now featured a growing patch of brown of its own.

When she had set herself in a circle and asked the Lady to intercede, nothing had happened.

The Lady's apparent denial of her request perturbed her. *I know she disapproves of what the Wasters are doing, marketing her bark as a tea. So why won't she show us a direct route to the Tree so that we may stop them? And this condition on my skin is definitely not normal, yet pampria didn't even absorb into my body, as if everything were perfectly well. Nothing makes sense.*

I need answers, and instead, the questions are piling up like autumn leaves.

Something clattered against the window. Octavia jumped in her seat and gasped, her hand instinctively reaching to where she had once kept the capsicum flute. Her fingers found only the cloth of her apron and the nubs of the buttons beneath. She pivoted in her seat.

Outside, a gremlin pressed against the glass, wings spread wide. She laughed. The chair squealed on tile as she pushed it back.

"Hello there, little one!"

The gremlin trilled. It was far larger than Leaf—perhaps the size of a bulldog—with a slight yellow cast to its skin.

"I hear you and your kin like to gossip. Have you heard about the gremlin I named Leaf? He has a bent fork on his arm." She pointed near her armpit and formed a circle with her fingers. "I hope that he's well."

With a squawk, the gremlin pushed off the glass. The small body spiraled downward. No clouds blocked the view today. She could see straight down to the plaza and the broad stained-glass dome of the arena. Airships docked at spires set at points along the roof. Tall cranes loomed, lifting pallets of goods to the dirigibles. Far across the way, the terminal building was a mutant octopus along whose tentacles trains moved. The space in between writhed with activity. Lorries and cabriolets kept to their neat paths like black ants.

The gremlin flew toward the terminal, turned to glance at her, and then arced down. He did another loop and looked back to see if she was watching, then again flew at the terminal. This time he kept going.

As if he wants me to follow. Octavia frowned.

"Miss Leander." Alonzo's song rang as the healthiest it had been since they first journeyed on the *Argus*. Several days of good food and restful sleep had worked wonders.

"Al—Mr. Garret." Despite her frustration regarding the Arena, she couldn't help but smile at the sight of him. His fitted jacket was in the bright blue of Mr. Cody's household, the flap in an unusual diagonal cut. Black jodhpurs tucked into knee-high black boots. From paintings and artwork around the library, she knew it to be the distinctive attire of Mr. Cody's Arena pilots. Alonzo looked smashing in it, as he did in most every uniform—but then, he had even managed to add artistic merits to common dungarees.

"We have a few minutes together. Mr. Cody will follow shortly," he said. Octavia fidgeted with the urge to stroke his newly shaven jaw, know the smoothness beneath her fingertips. "Have you had any luck?"

She shook her head as she motioned to her notes. "It's amazing how many different books can exist that say almost exactly the same thing. Some of the inaccuracies are downright ridiculous. One book painted medicians as divine beings that require no food, water, or sleep, because they can survive solely on people's appreciation." She rolled her eyes. "Clearly, this author never emptied bedpans in the middle of the night."

"You mean my appreciation alone cannot be your sustenance?" He pressed a hand to his heart.

A flush crept up her neck. "Your gratitude can sustain me in many ways, Mr. Garret, but it cannot replace almond chicken accompanied by a good, hard cheese."

"I suppose I must live with that."

Oh, how she loved those warm crinkles that lined his eyes when he smiled. She could imagine how they would deepen as he aged.

"Does that mean you plan to stay in my company for some time?"

"Yes." The word was soft, husky. "So long as we are not assassinated in the near future. Or until you do prefer a good, hard cheese to my appreciation and companionship."

"It would need to be an especially good cheese."

His lips quirked. "I will be wary of such worthy rivals."

Oh Lady. The intensity of his gaze rooted her in place. Giddy warmth bloomed deep in her belly as she drily swallowed. A servant whistled as he passed by the open doorway. The tension between them snapped.

Alonzo looked to the stacks of books across the table and cleared his throat. "I will be glad to join you here for a time. The beastie is as bright as we hoped. She learns words after only a few examples and understands well that her goal is the top of the pyramid. She has quickly gained the knack of how to handle foes."

Octavia's joy dimmed significantly. "The knack to kill."

"No. Killing is not the goal."

"That's right, death is a mere side effect of a pitched battle against five other twenty-ton mechas who happen to breathe fire, fly, or wield claws like scythes." She pressed a hand to her face. "I'm sorry. You know how I feel about this."

"I do. And you above all should know that I have no death wish, but this . . ." He hesitated. "I will not lie to you. 'Tis a glorious thing to sit atop that chimera as she climbs a metal mountain. It reminds me of the first time my father set me in his lap while he steered an airship. Not simply power, but perspective, looking down on the world from a fresh vantage."

Lady help her, but she wanted to kiss that man. Throttle him, and kiss him. "I don't care if it's frowned upon in Tamarania. If you or Chi is hurt, I'm going to rush down there to help."

"I pity the fools who would attempt to stop you." He motioned to the books. "These, you have read?"

"Yes. This smaller stack needs to be skimmed. There are more books on the shelf that cover religion and mythology in general."

His lips compressed. "This worries me."

"More than the Arena?"

"More that the Arena will be in vain if we have no useful information to show for our effort."

If this is a dead end, there's always the royal vault in Mercia. She was reluctant to say the words. She had a strong hunch he'd be opposed, with valid reasons. Her arms irritated her and she checked the urge to rub them.

She needed answers about the Lady, or from the Lady. Soon.

Mr. Cody's ailment announced his arrival as his footsteps still tapped down the hall. So aware of his health, she self-consciously averted her gaze as he entered. Miss Percival used to say that some people deserved to suffer. Mr. Cody, for all he'd done to gremlins, was one of those people.

"Greetings to you, Miss Leander! Pleasant reading? Any intriguing new insights?"

She pasted on a smile as she tucked her notes into her satchel. "You have an amazing collection here, Mr. Cody."

"Yes. Yes, I do." He looked between her and Alonzo.

"I'm happy to say that the buzz is growing about the match tomorrow. Someone happened to start some rumors, you see. Tickets have already sold out. Ah, and before I forget again, Mr. Garret, I heard back from your sister. She agreed."

Octavia's head jerked up. "Pardon? What have I missed?"

Alonzo leaned against the table. "I asked Mr. Cody to invite Tatiana to the bout tomorrow, to join you in his suite. 'Tis private there and easily secured."

Yes, I'm sure we'll have a pleasant conversation about how much she hates me and how repulsive the Lady is. "Something else to be excited about, then."

A woman in household livery darted into the room and bowed to Mr. Cody. "Pardon the interruption, sir, but there's a major disturbance down in the terminal."

"What kind of disturbance?" asked Mr. Cody, his brow furrowed.

"An attack occurred on the *Beautiful Varya* from Caskentia and now a woman is in labor. There's already a doctor attending. The incident has stalled all progress on the line. The backup of people is starting to impact other corridors."

"An attack by whom?" snapped Mr. Cody.

"Dallowmen, if the Caskentians onboard are to be believed, though they blame every cloudy day on that lot." The woman seemed to suddenly recall that she was in the presence of two Caskentians, and flushed as she offered an apologetic bow.

Leaf had followed Octavia from Leffen to the Waster encampment. It wasn't farfetched to think that a gremlin might follow Mrs. Stout on her train journey south. That strange gremlin at the window had definitely pointed Octavia toward the terminal.

Octavia grabbed her satchel and stood. "I need to get down there. Mrs. Stout was going to persuade her daughter to flee south, and the daughter is pregnant and due soon."

The Wasters knew the truth of Mrs. Stout's identity, thanks to Miss Percival. They would still want to grab Mrs. Stout and steal her away to the Waste—to the Dallows.

Mr. Cody looked vexed. "I don't care who this Mrs. Stout is. Miss Leander, I must protest. You already had terrible timing in encountering that Dagger at the library. To go into the terminal is to be seen by many, especially Caskentians—"

"If my friend is in danger and her daughter in labor, you can protest all you want. I'm going." The messenger stared agape as she passed. Octavia guessed people didn't normally speak to Mr. Cody as she just had. She pounded the button to summon a lift. Alonzo's marching-band brasses grew louder as he approached and stood behind her.

"What makes you certain 'tis her?" Alonzo asked in a low rumble. She whispered about the gremlin at the window. He took in this latest revelation with a nod. She could see the gears turning beyond his eyes. "'Tis good to know we have allies."

"Yes. Caskentia has its army and Daggers. Mr. Cody has his network here. Lady knows the Waste has spies ev-

erywhere as they sell that blasted tea. But here we are, allied with small flying creatures who resemble naked cats."

"You are not being entirely facetious."

"No. I know better. My friends tend to surprise me." The door dinged as the lift opened.

"If this is truly Mrs. Stout and her daughter, the labor may be a feint, a distraction," murmured Alonzo. "Or a trap."

"Do you think that will stop me?"

"'Tis best to be prepared for any possibilities."

At that, she clutched her satchel even tighter against her hip. *Unfortunately, my possibilities always seem to involve blood.*

They rushed through the lobby and into the plaza. Octavia made sure to tuck her headband more firmly into place. Even so, the sheer numbers of humanity disoriented her. She took in several breaths as she did in her Al Cala. Either she'd become spoiled by the isolation of Mr. Cody's lush flat, or her skills had become even stronger in the past day. She stared at Alonzo's bright coat as a point of focus. Foggy as her brain was, she noted that she wasn't the only one eyeing his clothes and urgent stride. People sidestepped to let them through, whispering excitedly to each other. Several lanes of steam cars stopped to grant them passage. Drivers leaned on their horns and waved at him.

"A pilot! Godspeed!"

"Cody's man! Look at him!"

"The pilot looks like that? I'll place a wager on him."

Alonzo's stride stiffened, shoulders bracing. His song

ticked higher in response—anxious, self-conscious, embarrassed.

*I didn't even think of his uniform and what would happen if
we left the building. Now we'll absolutely need to keep our time in
the southern nations brief. People will see him, know him, ask his
name.*

No turning back now. Octavia grimaced and hurried in
his wake.

The terminal bustled and echoed just as it had before,
voices, footsteps and songs stirring a maddening stew. It
took all of Octavia's concentration to shadow Alonzo. He
stopped the first employee they encountered. "The *Beautiful Varya*. Where is it?"

"Terminal A, on down. You'll see signs. You're Cody's
man? How about that—"

They rushed onward until the people compressed like
a Caskentian army division at a beer delivery. Octavia
grabbed hold of the tail of Alonzo's jacket as he barreled his
way through.

"Let us through! Pardon, pardon! My apologies!"
Alonzo almost crushed a man against a pillar as he shoved
past.

Octavia caught snippets of conversation as they rushed by.

"They said Dallowmen attacked a family!"

"Come on. It can't take that long to mop up some blood.
If it doesn't leave soon, I'll—"

"Is that a pilot? Here?"

"I got that dame's wallet! Let's—"

"—typical Caskentian violence. Such a barbarous lot of—"

Beyond the bobbing waves of hats and hair bows, the sleek silver of the train resembled an elongated bullet. This was undoubtedly a higher-class transport. At last they reached a door to a train car. Alonzo hopped up two steps only to be stopped by a steward in deep green attire.

"I'm sorry, sir, but we have a situation on board, we cannot—"

"I work for august Balthazar Cody. Which way to the woman in labor?"

The steward, though Caskentian by his accent, took in Alonzo's apparel and pointed to the right as he stepped back.

"Your uniform may have garnered us a lot of attention, but it also got us through the crowds ten times faster than otherwise," Octavia murmured as they entered a narrow passage of glossy wood and flocked wallpaper.

Alonzo grunted, clearly not pleased. "I should have given more thought to my attire. And yours."

That's right. She still wore her uniform. She hadn't spared the time to grab so much as a coat or hat.

"Speed saves lives in my job. Think on that."

"I will think more positively on it when we are far from Tamarania without assassins lurking two steps behind, all because I made a damned juvenile mistake." Anger shook his voice.

"Oh, Alonzo," she said softly. "You know, you really *are* a good Clockwork Dagger, despite how Caskentia treated you. I can prove it."

"And how is that?" His posture was so rigid it was painful.

"Esme was a full Dagger. Who won that fight?"

He conceded the point with a soft grunt.

Through the open doors, a cluster of people could be seen at the far end of the next car. "You can't keep 'er from 'er girl. Don't make me make you move, 'cause I can." The voice boomed. The man was built like a Frengian draft horse, his shoulders far wider than the doorways of the train. *Vincan!* His skin lacked almost all pigment, making him far paler than most Caskentians. He had the flattened, scarred face of a man who had naturally healed after being used as a battering ram.

"I don't respond to threats. You must let the doctor work in peace." A steward had his arms extended to block the doorway behind him.

"The man is incompetent!" An imperious tone rang out. "He may wear the title of doctor, but—"

"Mrs. Stout!" Alonzo called.

Mrs. Viola Stout, the long-lost princess of Caskentia, looked around the hulking form of Vincan and gasped in obvious relief. Her rounded face was flushed, her silver hair accented by a mustard-yellow swirl. Fresh blood smeared the bodice of her flower-patterned dress.

"Miss Leander! Thank God! Thank that Lady of yours! Hurry, hurry! To the next car up, child! The doctor in there is killing my Mathilda!"

CHAPTER 7

A man's body huddled on the floor behind them. He wore a suit jacket over faded black trousers. Blood was almost invisible on the dark fabric, a mere wet splotch, the klaxons already silenced. His soul was gone.

"How many assailants?" asked Alonzo.

"Two Wasters. Both deader'n Kethan's ashes. Them been with us the 'ole ride, bidin' their time. Didn't make to kill Mrs. Stout, just grab'er and run." Vincan was a former Caskentian soldier and the bartender aboard the *Argus*. He had been Mrs. Stout's escort back to Mercia, but evidently their partnership hadn't ended there.

"Your daughter was injured in the attack?" asked Octavia.

"No! Her labor started first. Those ruffians sought to take advantage and abscond with me. The greater issue now is this doctor! He watched Mathilda these past few hours, and all seemed fine until he cut her open—"

Octavia didn't need to hear any more. She stalked toward the steward. "I'm getting through that door."

The man's nervous eyes looked past her to Vincan and

Alonzo and he stepped aside. "You don't understand, this physician has an excellent reputation, he—"

Through the doorway, Octavia heard nothing but blood, the noise as piercing as steam whistles. The doctor knelt beside a woman. Crimson dyed his sleeves to the elbows. Mrs. Stout's daughter was utterly still. An incision split open her lower abdomen. Blood obscured the rest. Octavia dropped her satchel to the floor.

The doctor looked up, blinking as if he had just awakened. "A medician! Good God, that woman is desperate. I . . . everything here will be fine. It was a hard birth. That happens." His voice shook, as did his hands. Through the hue of blood, she heard the tremor as it echoed through his body. *This isn't a mere reaction to the Waster attack; this is a nervous-system deficiency. He can't even hold a pencil, and yet he wielded a knife.*

She listened beyond him, beyond Mathilda. "Where's the baby?" Even as she asked, her eyes found a bloodied lump on the carpet. A napkin draped over the babe. There was no song, but heat lingered. A live birth, botched.

"Sometimes these tragedies happen," said the doctor. He said the words, but by the terror in his eyes, he knew what had happened. He knew he had caused this.

Heavy footsteps shuddered through the floor. Octavia glanced over her shoulder. "I need this man out."

"You 'eard the lady," growled Vincan.

"Can't leave a patient open. I can't. It's not . . . it's not professional."

"To 'ell with this." A few long strides, and Vincan had

hold of the man by the collar. The doctor sobbed quietly as Vincan dragged him past. Octavia had her medician blanket fluffed out before the door shut behind them. She set out her jars along the mended edge.

"What happened to your blanket?" asked Alonzo. He holstered the Gadsden as he crouched down; she hadn't even known that Mr. Cody had returned the weapon. Alonzo lifted the shroud from the babe, just enough to look, and turned away with a grimace.

"The train ride to Tamarania happened. Help me move the daughter."

Alonzo took Mathilda's shoulders while Octavia grabbed the feet. Together they shuffled her to the oval. The woman was limp, her song dim. *Like Mrs. Stout was when I found her on the* Argus, *when she almost died in my stead. Such a dreadful similarity.*

Octavia's fingers pressed against the honeyflower and copper weave of the circle. Heat crackled as the magic awoke. "Pray, by the Lady let me mend thy ills." She felt no resistance, no barrier. This woman wanted to live.

Through the cloth over Octavia's ears, the music became clearer, faint as it was. *Thank you, Lady, for the discovery of that pampria bush in the swamp, and for the time to finally grind those leaves.* She scooped out a handful of the cinnamon-scented herb. The pampria drifted to Mathilda's skin and was absorbed in an instant.

Octavia had a keener awareness than ever before of the layers within a woman's body and of the damage done to a patient. She knew to add a pinch of heskool, a chunk of bellywood, and three globs of Linsom berries. Upon contact with Mathilda, each herb was absorbed without a trace. Skin drew together; the window closed. The woman's music wailed and softened. Rhythm returned.

That left one more vital task.

"Alonzo. Pass me the babe."

Octavia lifted the napkin from the light bundle on her lap and sucked in a sharp breath. *That doctor . . . ! Oh, this poor child.* She passed her hands over the stick of her parasol; blood fell away as dust. Looking up at Alonzo, she reached into her apron pocket. He nodded understanding, his lips a hard line.

The leaf of the Lady's tree was as long as her palm, its green vivid and texture pliable, as if just plucked from the twig. Octavia rolled it as if making a cigarette. The little jaw opened easily. She tucked the rolled leaf beneath the babe's stubby tongue and gently closed the toothless mouth.

As if tickled by a feather, the child shivered. Pudgy fingers convulsed and straightened, arms relaxing as they folded over his belly again. Skin melded with a tiny slurp. A red flush crept across his pale skin. Dark eyes squinted as they viewed the world for the first time.

"Oh God." Mrs. Stout's weak voice came from behind them.

"Vincan—" said Alonzo.

"You try to keep 'er out! Like tryin' to keep a bull still by the tongue, it is."

Octavia didn't look around. "Viola, they are both alive. Please step out so I can clean up. You don't need to see this."

She reached inside the babe's mouth and pulled out the leaf. Just as when she revived Alonzo, the leaf crumbled to dust in her hand.

Mrs. Stout didn't move. "I . . . I . . . Mathilda, she's alive, too? She's not moving."

"Mrs. Stout." Alonzo padded past Octavia. "Just a few minutes more. Octavia knows best." The door shut with a gentle click.

Octavia allowed herself a few long Al Cala breaths. The crisis was past. "Thank you, Lady, for extending your branches." She touched the circle. With an audible pop, the Lady's scrutiny diminished, heat fading.

Alonzo's hand rested on her shoulder and she leaned into him. He lowered beside her, his song strong and comforting. *Like my mother's humming.* A memory of sound that made her want to nestle deeper into a warm and cozy bed in defiance of the chilly morning that lurked beyond.

His lips pressed against her temple. She probably hadn't been kissed like that since she was a child. Octavia looked up at him.

"I fear we've set a terrible precedent," she said. The babe wiggled on her lap.

"Oh?"

"The last time I—we—kissed was right after I used a leaf on you. I only have three left."

His lips quirked in a smile. "I will do my utmost to defy our established pattern. Such intimacy deserves a change in scenery as well."

"Yes. We're too often surrounded by blood." The air

stank with iron. She used the concealed medician wand to clean the baby's body. "Well! Do you mind passing him to Mrs. Stout? I think there was a dining cart with napkins and tablecloths in that last car."

"I do not mind at all." He made kissing noises as he stood with the babe. She shook her head, smiling. The man must be a natural with children—quite unlike her. Octavia had rarely been around healthy babies. If she was present, the situation all too often involved crying, screaming, blood, and grief.

Not that today has changed that.

She cleaned Mrs. Stout's daughter and covered her sliced dress with a tablecloth. Another man's body lay on the floor a few feet away—blood cooled, body silent, neck broken. Ligature marks formed a purple torque around his neck.

Alonzo returned. "Mr. Cody is here."

"It's probably just as well. We'll need help to get Mrs. Stout's daughter out of here."

"He is already arranging that, and much more." Alonzo grimaced. Her bag reassembled, Octavia followed him into the other train car.

Mrs. Stout clutched the babe to her generous bosom. Napkins had been knotted into a makeshift nappy. Her eyes lit up when she saw Octavia. "Oh, child! You work miracles! My Mathilda . . . ?"

"By the Lady's mercy, she'll be sleeping for several more hours as she continues to recover."

"I have men on the way with a cart," said Mr. Cody. He

stood beside Mrs. Stout. A group of his men in blue lurked close by. "Such a terrible way for you to enter our fair cities, Mrs. Stout. I don't foresee legal issues for you. It'll be fair to say your man acted in self-defense against the Dallowmen."

Mr. Cody's cool gaze turned to Octavia. "I *am* glad you were here to help your friend's family, but in your case that action carries consequences. This doctor is a prominent local physician, one known to donate generously to electoral campaigns."

"Here I thought Caskentia had cornered the market on bribes," snapped Octavia.

"I didn't say he donated to my campaigns." Mr. Cody's smile was thin. "He is vocal, even in his recent retirement. I had him escorted from the train, but he made it quite clear he was insulted at being replaced by, as he put it, vulgar quackery."

Octavia flushed. "He cut—" She stopped. Mrs. Stout didn't need to hear the specifics. "He botched the operation. They both would have died. That doctor's impaired, both physically and by pride. Have him hold a pencil, or work laces. That will give you all the proof you need."

"You don't need to convince me. *I* know a medician's worth. I'm simply warning you about what to expect when you leave this train."

"About that . . ." began Alonzo.

"I would have discouraged you from leaving the building in your pilot's uniform as well, but as far as my goals go, this wasn't a bad thing. On my way here, people professed delight at having sighted the pilot of the mysterious new mecha."

"Our goals vary from yours," growled Alonzo.

"Yes, but we agree on certain vital points. You want to stay alive. I want you to stay alive. I'll keep you safe as I can through the bout."

Alonzo shot Octavia a grim look. *Through the bout.* After that, they were on their own again. With Mercia two days away by air, they could expect a full contingent of Daggers all too soon. And Lady knew how many were already in the city.

Not that they dared to dismiss the threat of Wasters, not with dead bodies so close by. *Plus, the Wasters know how I grew that tree with the intervention of the Lady. Caskentia may want me dead, but the Waste wants to use me, use the Lady, to kill others.*

Mr. Cody stepped aside to murmur to his men. Mrs. Stout and Vincan rejoined Mathilda in the next car. Octavia stepped a little closer to Alonzo.

"Remember what you said about us having allies?" she murmured.

"Yes?"

"All considered, you might be safest in the Arena, there with Chi."

"I could perhaps extend an invitation to you, though it may be an indecently tight squeeze in the saddle cage."

Octavia looked through an open window. The crowds still stewed, even more restless than before. Her stomach soured in dread of facing that mob again. They would notice Alonzo in his pilot's blue, but there was no denying her presence or occupation. Not now.

"It can't be as bad as our brief buzzer ride," she said, trying to keep her voice light.

"Miss Leander?" He said her name in a way that made her warm even in the bitterest of cold. "We will make it from here together. Keep faith."

She nodded, both arms clutched tight to her torso. The way things were now, it was easier to keep faith in Alonzo than in the Lady.

CHAPTER 8

Mr. Cody extended his hospitality to Mrs. Stout, Vincan, the babe, and the unconscious Mathilda. Octavia was grateful, but knew his motivation was not magnanimity. *They're just another part of his investment in that blasted Arena bout.* Mrs. Stout was everywhere at once in the flat, conferring with Mr. Cody and directing servants with all the efficiency of an army quartermaster. She may not have ruled Casken-tia, but she played despot over a stranger's household in a matter of minutes.

Mr. Cody soon retreated to attend to his duties as august. The servants dispersed. The Caskentians gath-ered around Mathilda in a guest bedroom. The woman whimpered in her bed, legs twitching as her consciousness began to return. Octavia had a good look at her for the first time. Mathilda had to only be a few years older than her—perhaps twenty-five or thirty. Her rounded cheeks re-minded Octavia of Mrs. Stout's face, but her narrow nose and broad lips must have carried down from her late father. Illustrations of young Mrs. Stout—the missing princess—always showed her as blond with curls; Mathilda certainly had flaxen-gold hair from her mother, though not curly in the slightest.

Mrs. Stout sat on the end of the bed within arm's reach of the babe. Her grandson was swaddled in a lush piece of blue flannel—a remnant from the household seamstress, if Octavia dared a guess. His face had lost some of its new-born redness and wrinkles, his expression now one of peace as he dozed on his back.

"Well!" said Mrs. Stout. "Here I've been worried sick about you both, wondering how I might possibly find you in such a metropolis. I never expected you to be our welcome party, though far stranger things have happened!"

Yes, giant trees and all.

Vincan paced between the window and door. Clearly the high floor on which the flat was located hadn't caused him to relax his guard. His body sang of abrasions to his knuckles and bruises to his torso, all minor.

"I should like to know how you came to be here, Mrs. Stout," said Alonzo.

"After we parted at that horrid Waster camp, Vincan flew me into Mercia. My goodness! By buzzer! Never in my life. You should have seen my hair afterward! We went to my daughter's home. Her husband is a sailor in Frengia for the season, but I convinced her to come south with me."

"Did you tell her?" asked Alonzo.

Mrs. Stout looked down at her lap, her nod tiny. Octavia rested a hand on her shoulder, and the older woman cast her a grateful smile. Until the incidents aboard the *Argus,* Mrs. Stout had only told three people of her true identity as the lost princess—her childhood headmistress at the academy, also known by the title of Miss Percival; Nelly Winters, who saved Mrs. Stout's life when she had just escaped from her Waster kidnappers, and who grew to become the next Miss Percival; and Mrs. Stout's late husband, the publishing magnate Donovan Stout.

The current Miss Percival had kept the secret for fifty years before selling out her old friend—and Octavia—to save the academy from bankruptcy. A financial crisis caused by the fact that Caskentia hadn't paid the academy, or most anyone else, for their work in the last war.

"Mathilda took the news well," said Mrs. Stout with a frail smile. "We packed most of her household. It should be delivered in a few days. Oh! Child, we also went by the *Argus*. Your suitcase will be forthcoming as well."

Octavia had prized that suitcase and her meager belongings, and now they seemed so frivolous. "Thank you, Mrs. Stout. I'm afraid I still need to travel light for the next while. I'll get it from you eventually."

"Vincan, it seems you have switched employers?" asked Alonzo.

Vincan grunted. "Aye. Cap'n Hue woulda kept me on, but Mrs. Stout 'ere needed someone to watch 'er back, so I said I'd come. Never seen the south."

"I'm so very grateful he did come!" Mrs. Stout clasped her hands. "Mathilda's labor pains started when we crossed the border into Tamarania. The doctor seemed like a good sort. I was so grateful to have him there, and then . . . !"

Vincan barely checked himself from spitting. "Wasters

made to grab Mrs. Stout right after the doc'r started surgery, as the train pulled into the city. Didn't seem interested in the daughter. S'all about Mrs. Stout."

"I will be grabbed by no man! And certainly not in a public venue." Mrs. Stout sniffed. "Vincan did his duty well. Then I saw how the doctor's hands trembled, and oh, I knew something was wrong! The train stopped and I dashed out to get help, and then that wretched steward wouldn't let me back in." Tears filled Mrs. Stout's eyes.

"Did the Wasters ever say anything?" asked Alonzo.

"Nah. Seemed like common swaddies to me, not like them high-ups at that camp at the ol' copper quarry."

Alonzo's face scrunched in a frown. "Sounds like they were sent to Mercia in case the mission aboard the *Argus* failed. They likely watched your daughter's household. You must continue to take care, Mrs. Stout."

"I will hire more guards! Next time, these Wasters may very well try to grab us all. I will protect mine." A cold glint existed in Mrs. Stout's eyes, one that hadn't been there before. Her recent ordeals had made her all the stronger.

"Octavia and I have already encountered a Clockwork Dagger here by accident." Alonzo looked at Octavia and away. "With this incident down below and the fuss it has created, we cannot stay in Tamarania. After we repay our debt to Mr. Cody, we must flee."

Octavia leaned over Mathilda. "I should check under the blankets again."

"Eh. I'll step out, then." Vincan practically dashed for the door. "Won't be far, missus."

"Alonzo." Octavia stopped him at the doorway. "Stay, please. Just face away." He closed the door and faced the wall. As a precaution, she still held up a sheet as she checked beneath Mathilda.

"What is this debt you spoke of?" asked Mrs. Stout.

"Mr. Cody asked for our assistance in preparing a mechanized gremlin for the Arena on the morrow, and for me to pilot his creation." Alonzo's voice echoed against the wall.

"Oh my! An Arena match! How horrible and danger-ous, and with a strange chimera at that! Child, I should hope you gave him the roughage of your tongue for agree-ing to such a thing."

Octavia was glad to have a sheet to hide behind, as that phrase brought entirely the wrong sorts of things to mind. "I'm not happy with the deal, no, but we've been paid by being given access to Mr. Cody's library. He likely has the largest collection of medician texts we'll find anywhere." She paused. "Mrs. Stout, I did find out that your father was a child when the artifacts of the Tree came to Mercia. Even then the power of the objects worried him."

"The artifacts had been there that short a time? Truly? Wherever did you find privy details like that?"

"A chamberlain's log with a small print run. It covered the period right up to your imminent birth." Octavia low-ered the sheet again and tucked it over Mathilda.

"Well, I daresay my father was well read on about every subject. He was a brilliant man, the most brilliant I've ever known. I wish that had been his greatest legacy." Mrs. Stout rubbed her daughter's knuckles and stared at the slumbering babe. "The palace library was one of the largest buildings in the entire city. I was told it was twice as big as any library in Tamarania. Of course, everything burned in the firebombing. Greater Mercia lost most all its libraries, too. In my heart, I am glad that Father never knew of that loss. It would have grieved him beyond anything."

It always comes back to fire. "Is it possible that some books on the Tree were kept in the vault?"

"Some books were in there, yes, but I haven't a clue about the subjects. I certainly wouldn't have been allowed to read anything of that sort at my tender age!"

Octavia looked toward Alonzo. "I . . . I have been wondering if we should try the vault, Alonzo. We haven't found what we need here. King Kethan knew the artifacts of the Tree were powerful and he might have kept—"

"Octavia, are you certain this is not about the loss of the branch?" Alonzo's tone was gentle.

"No. Of course it's not."

"The loss of the branch? The Lady's branch?" echoed Mrs. Stout. "Oh, goodness, how terrible!"

"Or the other parts of the Tree that reside there?" asked Alonzo.

"I already have leaves. And the seed . . . the seed scares me."

"It could bring back one of your parents."

She swallowed drily. "It could. Or your father, or anyone else we've lost. But my parents believed in the promise of the beyond. I couldn't take that from them."

If I had been given that option at age twelve, newly orphaned, my answer would have been much different, though to choose between them would have been impossible.

Alonzo turned to face her, his mouth a grim line. "I do not see this as a valid option, Miss Leander. One, the vault is located deep within the palace grounds. After the surrounding complex was razed by the fire, it was converted to gardens. 'Tis guarded, but I am ignorant of the numbers and their patterns of rotation." He held up two fingers. "I cannot simply escort you in. If my skin shows at all, my Tamaran legacy is obvious, and to cover myself completely invites suspicion." Three. "There is a reason people jest of things being as secure as the royal vault. It cannot be opened, not by door, roof, or wall. The blood magic is that strong."

Mrs. Stout looked at Octavia, her lips compressed. "You didn't tell him."

Octavia shook her head. "Of course not. You told me in confidence. It's your secret."

Mrs. Stout sighed. "Access to the vault is magicked to my father's bloodline. That's why no one can get inside."

Alonzo stared at her for a long moment before slowly nodding. "Queen Evandia is your mother's cousin. No wonder she and the current family cannot get in."

"Yes, thank God!" Mrs. Stout shuddered at the mention of Evandia. "That weepy, frail thing. She should never have ruled—she hasn't ruled, truly. The country's gone to ruin. I'm appalled to think of what she would have done with the contents of that vault. It's enough that me and mine can get inside." She looked to the babe with tears in her eyes.

"You and yours," echoed Octavia. "Where is your son?"

"My son. I haven't seen him since long before armistice, though we have exchanged letters on a regular basis. But he didn't respond now, when it was most urgent! I even went to his residence. That boy. He always had the knack to vanish when it suited him. I'm not even sure what he did in the war. He could have been a Dagger, far as I know!"

"Would he help us get to the vault?" Octavia tried to ignore Alonzo's disapproving frown. *The more I think on the vault, the more right it seems. The idea itches at my brain, almost like a life debt, even with the danger involved.*

"If he knew the truth? Most assuredly! My Devin's a good lad, and the determined sort. He gets what he wants. He's fearless! Bright!"

"'Tis a lot to ask of him, to risk the palace. We are strangers to him."

Alonzo is coming up with every possible excuse, and each makes perfect sense. And yet . . .

"I can resolve that readily enough." Mrs. Stout pulled out the notepad and pencil she always kept handy. "I had hoped to tell him in person, but, well! We have a family cipher. I'll write another letter, one that explains the matter of my history and says that he should trust and help you. He will. I know my boy!"

If we can find him. If he'll respond to us. So many ifs.

A heavy knock shuddered through the door. Alonzo rose to answer, hand near his gun.

"Eh." Vincan leaned inside. "Girl says dinner's soon and we're asked to go, if'n Mrs. Stout's daughter can be left."

"She will wake up soon," Octavia said. "So will the babe, and it'll be feeding time."

"I'm not leaving my Mathilda." Mrs. Stout tore pages from her notebook. "Here. I made two copies, one for each of you, as a precaution." She passed them along. Octavia looked down at the small page. It consisted of hieroglyphics and didn't make a dollop of sense. "Devin lives and works at a bakery called Bready or Not that's just off the palace quarter. It's where my letters have been dropped, though I have yet to catch him there myself. If you find him, do let me know? I've been so worried, and after I almost lost Mathilda and our little one today . . ." She struggled to stay composed.

"We will do our utmost to relay that to him, if nothing else," said Alonzo as he tucked the paper away.

Octavia and Alonzo walked down the hallway together. "This idea of the vault bothers me more and more," he murmured. "Any passing magi would sense your power and wonder who you were. This also puts Mrs. Stout's family at even more risk. Evandia could be made aware of their existence."

A servant passed by with fresh linens while another walked along with a cart. Octavia frowned. "We need privacy to discuss this. Here, Alonzo. Step into my room."

"Are you certain?"

She rolled her eyes. "People are going to talk. Let them. I'm already regarded as a guttersnipe because I'm a medician. If they want to gossip that I'm your ladybird, well, I don't regard that as an insult." With that, she stalked inside and gestured him to follow. She shut the door behind them and locked it for good measure.

"There. You were saying?" She faced him. The drums in his song beat a furious pace.

"Are people truly gibbering that you are my ladybird?" He said it as if he were both appalled and amused.

"Probably. I have higher priorities than gossip, and so do you. Your ultimate duty beyond that mecha-jockey gear is to be *my* Clockwork Dagger. You're guarding me even now." *Much to Tatiana's chagrin.*

She smelled the fragrant cinnamon of Alonzo's clothes, knew his familiar song. Goodness, but that uniform fit him in a delightful way.

"As *your* Clockwork Dagger, then, I must argue against this venture to the vault. 'Tis a climb into a roc's nest."

"Then what do you suggest? Really? Where do we go?"

"I do not object to going to Mercia, though I know you will detest the place most thoroughly. We may lose our pursuers for a time. Survival is our true goal, you must recall. Afterward, we could go far north to Frengia, or travel across the sea—"

"When would we be able to stop worrying, Alonzo? Ever?"

Indescribable sadness flickered across his face. "What do you truly hope to gain from finding the Lady, Octavia? And is something the matter with your arm?"

Octavia released her grip on her own arm. Both limbs ached and tingled like mad, and it almost seemed to grow worse at the talk of the vault. "It's nothing. As for the Lady . . . you said yourself that the search gives us a purpose, something beyond hiding. My powers have always been strange, but these past few weeks . . ." She shook her head. A tendril of hair lashed her cheeks. "I want answers." *I need answers. The vault has answers. I know that, somehow.*

"If we find the Lady, what then?"

She threw herself into a chair and leaned against her knees. "I don't know. I don't know what it will take to get Caskentia to forget about me, or how the Waste can get their independence and leave me alone. I still want to have a future, Alonzo. I want an atelier and a garden." She squeezed her fingers together. "I want a home."

"Like Delford."

"Delford would be a beautiful place to live, but I loved the academy, too. The tulip fields. The woods. The feel of moss between my toes. Then there's the coastline—I loved it when my parents took me there when I was young. Is it so wrong to want peace and a home?"

Alonzo crouched before her. "'Tis not wrong in the least." There was a low undercurrent to his voice that reverberated throughout her body. Even more, she knew the shift within him. *Heart rate increased. Blood flow . . . oh Lady, why do I know such things?* His callused hand curved against her cheek. "I want you to have all these things, Octavia."

"I'm scared about the Arena tomorrow. I'm scared I won't be able to save you if something happens."

His heartbeat, the essence of his life, stroked a fast rhythm through the touch of his palm. On his song, she could float away as if on a mighty river. Her awareness increased as his broad and strong lips met hers, his sandpaper bristle scraping her skin. Her hand found his neck, her fingers in his magnificently thick hair.

The bottom dropped out from her world—no, her world became his song. It rose in crescendo, blocking out the existence of the room, of the burbling city, of all the threats against them.

He pulled back. The music dimmed, the heat diminished, but her sense of him lingered. She still knew the surge in his body. *He wants me.* But this was Alonzo Garret, ever the gentleman. He stood and faced away, tugging down his jacket in the process.

He glanced at her over his shoulder. "If anything should happen to me, work your way to Leffen, to the Dryns. You know they will do their utmost to keep you safe."

Adana and Kellar Dryn knew of his identity as a Clockwork Dagger and of Octavia's unusual powers as a medician. They secretly labored for the welfare of Caskentia's people.

"I don't want a backup plan to be necessary."

"Wants and needs are separate things." His voice softened. "You need to stay alive, Miss Leander."

He left.

His scent was still like a cloud around her, his heat still on her lips. Finally, she stood to lock the door again. She worked up her left sleeve. The mottled brown rash now stretched from wrist to elbow. She touched it. The skin was still soft. The crackled lines did not bleed. She pinched her skin; it hurt, as it should. She stared at the full forearm, her resolve to find the Lady growing even stronger.

My arm looks like the branch of a tree.

CHAPTER 9

Octavia's dear little gremlin, Leaf, had had an adorable habit of springing off objects and floating to land on her shoulder or lap. When the same action was attempted by a chimera the size of a lorry, it was somewhat less cute.

The men in the hangar scrambled out of the way, yelling. Half-buckled barding trailed like banners from Chi as she glided some twenty feet. Octavia remained utterly still as the gremlin-mecha landed mere feet away. A violent gust of air rippled her skirts and hair.

At least Chi didn't aim for my lap.

"That's the longest glide so far!" crowed one of the men.

"Hello to you, too," murmured Octavia as Chi trilled and lowered her head.

"I did not get such a welcome this morning," said Alonzo. He walked toward her—no, sauntered. No person could merely walk in a pilot's attire, not with the way the jodhpurs flattered the thighs and the coat hugged the shoulders.

"I'm not sure if she's really excited because of me, or if she smells this." Octavia held up a round of hard cheese.

Chi's nostrils flared. "Leaf expressed a great fondness for cheese, so I figured Chi might appreciate the same splurge. I paid one of Cody's guards to run down to the plaza for me."

"Eh! Eh! We're not feeding the thing before the bout!" said one of the men, waving his arms as he approached.

Octavia stared him down. "Yes, and what a cockama-mie plan that is. She's gone without food since at least yesterday. Both of her stomachs are empty. If you want her to have energy, I suggest she eat much more than a round of aged vellette. She needs bread, lots of it." Octavia set down the treat.

The engineer gaped at her, face flushed. Alonzo looked impressed and amused.

"Do as she says." Mr. Cody strode up behind them. He wore a snazzy suit of midnight blue with a metallic sheen, an unneeded monocle dangling from his lapel.

The man backed away, bowing, and several other servants went running. As Chi crouched to eat, a few other engineers crept up to resume their work on the chimera's armor.

"An interesting and specific diagnosis of her hunger," Mr. Cody said, stopping beside her and Alonzo.

Lovely, I've piqued his curiosity and now he's fishing for information. Sometimes I need to keep my mouth shut, or at the very least, whisper.

"In the circle the other day, I had insights into her stomach capacity. Alonzo mentioned that she hadn't been fed." A lie, but Alonzo played along and nodded.

"I see." Mr. Cody seemed disappointed by the mundane answer.

Chi finished the cheese. Her long purple tongue lapped her lips to glean any crumbs. Trilling softly, she butted her chin against Octavia's shoulder. Chi's breath reeked of cheese with an acidic edge, and Octavia almost gagged as she took a step back.

"You're welcome, not-so-little-one," she said, laughing. It felt good to laugh, to be distracted. Tension thickened the air like cornstarch in stew, carried through every body, every flurried preparation. Maybe some of the energy seeped down from the Arena; ninety thousand people were expected to attend.

They want blood. No—they want to win bets. Blood is an exciting bonus, even among these pledged pacifists.

Alonzo rubbed Chi between the ears, right where a metal skull plate began. The chimera chirped, eyes blinking. Octavia took in the full protective barding with her eyes and senses. The extremities and wings were already largely metal, and now most any flesh was covered with some sort of shielding as well. None of it was silver, of course—most of it looked to be copper.

Servants set down bread loaves that steamed in the cool basement air. Chi bit down on a loaf with a soft crack, showing sharp teeth as long as Octavia's hand. Light footsteps tapped on the floor behind them, the song familiar.

"Alonzo!" Tatiana cried as she ran up to her brother. He met her with a tight hug, twirling her around.

"'Tis good to see you again." He grinned as he set her

down. Three men followed Tatiana, each dressed in long jackets and broad pants as befitted a spectacle in the Arena.

"I hired guards, Alonzo," Tatiana said, lowering her voice. "Mr. Cody referred me to a firm. He said they had to pass his requirements, too."

"Good. I am glad." Alonzo nodded to the men.

She looked past him, her blue eyes going wide. "Oh. Is that what all the rumors are about? Is that really a gremlin?"

"In part." Mr. Cody approached and bowed to Tatiana. "It's been a few years since I saw you last, sweet child."

"Two years at winter solstice," she said, her attention still on the chimera. "Alonzo, you're going to wear armor, right?" She didn't sound too worried, which surprised Octavia.

"Yes. I will don it in a few minutes. Tatiana, Miss Leander is here, too."

Tatiana offered a part grimace, part smile as she curtsied for Octavia. "I heard you healed someone in public yesterday. There's a great deal of talk."

"As we are already aware, Tatiana," said Alonzo. He shot Octavia a look of concern, as if she required a reminder of their need to swiftly exit the region.

A bell dinged on the far side of the hangar. "Time! Time!" called out a chorus.

Alonzo gave Tatiana another quick hug. "I am glad to see you this one last time."

"What? This is it?" Emotion choked her voice.

He pulled back and looked to Octavia. He began to bow, as was proper.

"Piffle on that," Octavia said. She stopped him by wrapping both arms around him. He was stiff for a second and then seemed to melt against her. *His heart races. He's nervous and scared.*

He pulled back enough to study her face. His blue eyes looked pained. *His song increases in tempo. He's not simply scared for himself.* "I . . ." He cleared his throat. "I will take care of Chi. Do not worry for either of us."

"That's a ridiculous thing to say and you know it."

A smile softened his lips. "Nevertheless, it must be said."

"Keep in mind that if you *are* maimed, I'll be rather cross with you." Octavia stepped back, her hands gliding down his arms.

"For that reason alone, I will take care." His fingers squeezed hers. His thumb rubbed a quick circle before he let go.

"Gear up! It's time!" said Mr. Cody. He clapped twice in quick succession. Wide doors on the far side cranked open to reveal an electric-lit passage. He turned to Octavia and Tatiana, his smile threatening to outdo the sun. "Let's head up to the suite, shall we, ladies?"

Lady, be with Alonzo and Chi. Help them survive, help them help each other. Please.

Octavia clutched her satchel to her hip as they rode a lift upward. Tatiana and Mr. Cody's men occupied most of the space.

Tatiana glowered at her as they rattled past several floors. "You have a new surcoat."

That's almost an effort at niceties. "Yes. I'm borrowing it from Mr. Cody's household."

"Green looks good on you. The black dress beneath is far different than your . . . than the other dress." The word "medician" had been dropped from the sentence like an implied expletive.

"Thank you," Octavia murmured. It wouldn't do to tell her that the full medician uniform was on beneath the thin black gown. The layers made her look especially thick around the waist and hips, but that didn't bother her vanity too terribly. Practicality overruled fashion, especially after two weeks of assassination and kidnapping attempts. She did adore the green coat, though. It was the sort of thing she would have once coveted but never in a hundred years possessed. Tamarania set all the fashion standards. "The orange of your dress suits you well, too."

"You do seem overly fond of headbands. Do they not wear hats in your part of Caskentia? Is cloth so rare?"

That insult was so poorly veiled that one of the guards even shuffled and cleared his throat. Octavia touched the headband out of reflex. She had overlapped a green ribbon on the white, but Tatiana was right. It looked pedestrian compared to Tatiana's fascinator or likely any of the other accessories worn by southern women.

"This headband has sentimental value for me," she said. *Not a lie. It keeps me from curling up in fetal position and screaming my throat raw, so I am rather fond of it.*

Tatiana managed a slight smile as her eyes went to the satchel and parasol. She didn't need to say anything. Octavia managed a toothless smile in return, almost daring the fashion assessment to continue.

"Have you two spent much time together?" asked Mr. Cody, too happy to be aware of the venom between them. They shook their heads. "Well, this should be the perfect time to remedy that! Some fine entertainment, good food. An ideal resting day."

"Mr. Cody, sir," said Octavia, fidgeting with her satchel strap. "Don't you worry about what will happen down there?"

He blinked. "Two days ago, I was desperate to have a contestant in the bout at all. The work you both accomplished with that mecha—I am still in awe. No, I'm not worried, not anymore. Mr. Garret and that chimera work in strange symbiosis. Whether they win or not, the audience is going to eat it up like churned cream, though at this point I do have complete faith that they will dominate the pyramid."

"You're not worried either?" Octavia asked Tatiana.

"People don't get hurt *that* often. I'm not worried about *his* health." Tatiana looked away, sadness flashing across her face. "Anyway, Alonzo's always been a good pilot."

Octavia nodded. "He is. Takes after your father, from what I understand. Have you ever tried piloting?"

Tatiana arched an eyebrow, the gesture so like Alonzo it was eerie.

Mr. Cody burst out laughing. "A girl pilot? Well, it could happen, I suppose. Ah, here we are." The doors parted and he walked on.

Octavia matched Tatiana's pace. "Everyone always tells Alonzo he's like his father. You have the same blood. Why not consider it?"

Tatiana pursed her lips and seemed to consider Octavia instead, then walked on past. Her entourage followed.

The suite was what one would expect of a man of Mr. Cody's status, all plush fabrics, dark wood, and riveted metal. Laughing people mingled, champagne flutes in hand, notes of indigestion and inebriation growing bolder in their bodies' songs.

A different melody stood out to Octavia. She walked past the buffet to a large golden cage in the corner. The gremlin within was the largest she had seen, easily the size of a bird dog. His wings folded close to his body, and unlike any other gremlins she'd seen, his wings and arms were separate. The seams in his flesh had healed poorly and resembled patches on a quilt, shades of green varied in each segment.

A small sign was bolted to the base: PRIME: THE FIRST GREMLIN. Near his feet were bits of silver that had been warped by his touch. She wondered if wealthy people had tossed old jewelry his way, like folks throwing dry bread crusts to ducks.

"Hello, little one," Octavia said.

"You medician." The words were a croak.

She stepped back, startled, even as she reached out with her senses to analyze the body in more detail. *A complete mishmash of parts. Cat, dog, bat, horse—a human larynx.*

"You've been healed by a medician before, recently," she murmured. She felt the scars where tumors recently resided, as if they were divots beneath her fingertips. *The body fights against itself.*

"Yessss." A pause. "You smell like tree."

Octavia looked at her arms, then around. No one stood close. The gremlin must be a permanent installation in Mr. Cody's suite, and one far less popular than the bar. "Do I?"

The gremlin leaned closer. The snout was longer than on most gremlins—more canine. "Like chimera."

Herald trumpets rang out from the Arena. Thousands upon thousands of voices flared and then faded. Octavia's gaze didn't shift from the old gremlin. "What do you mean?" she whispered.

"Miss Leander!" Mr. Cody grabbed her by the arm. "Come! Have a drink, watch!"

Even as he walked her away, she studied the gremlin. Those beady black eyes didn't blink.

The heart of the Arena stretched out in a massive rectangle, all sides surrounded by multicolored flecks of humanity. Their balcony granted an advantageous view of the metal pyramid. The man-made mountain was about a hundred feet in height. Switchbacks and platforms made some routes clear, though steep slopes and cliffs wouldn't impede some entrants, depending on their abilities.

She shivered at the sight of so many people, suddenly grateful for Mr. Cody's suite. It provided a buffer of privacy that dropped the combined songs to a low murmur.

A champagne flute was shoved into her hand. "Are you aware of how the rules differ from a standard playing board?" asked Mr. Cody. She shook her head. He leaned back on the railing, clearly relishing his role. She made sure to stay several feet away from the edge, the risk of defenestration still very much on her mind. "The Warriors' boards found in your average tavern rely on basic magic, magnets, and luck. The men place their bets and hope their chosen mecha creature makes it to the top first. Here, of course, we have intelligent pilots."

"Sometimes," cut in another well-dressed man. The others laughed.

Mr. Cody acknowledged this with a smile. He used his swelled gut to help support his glass. "The bout is thirty minutes. We use five contestants. A mecha must claim the peak for ten minutes to win, or hold it at the end. Some say you can nap for twenty-nine minutes and wake up for the good part."

"The good part. Blasts of fire, concentrated aether, geologica burrowing." She rubbed both arms against her torso. *I cannot understand these Tamarans and their standards. I save a woman and a babe's life, and as I leave the train, people hiss and slash their arms. Here, magic is all good and well if it's used for violent entertainment and monetary profit.*

Mr. Cody was oblivious to the derision in her tone. "Yes. Today has a fantastic mix. You'll see our chimera can—"

Cheers rose in crescendo. The first mecha entered the arena—a dragon, bristling with spines. Each waddled step swung a mighty tail. Wings larger than Chi's extended to their full length. The noise was deafening; clearly, this was a fan favorite. Next came a hedgehog similar to the one in Mr. Cody's own hangar, then a roc that bounded and flapped across the ground, and a golden wolf with bared teeth. Last came Chi and Alonzo. There was a collective gasp amongst the audience, then shouts of joy and outrage. Mr. Cody laughed. His comrades clapped him on the back and toasted. The man had won and the match hadn't even begun.

"Controversy is business," said Mr. Cody, raising his glass. "Let them say I broke the rules. Let them say all mechas should now be hybrids. Whatever comes . . . !" Crystal tinked as the flutes met. Octavia scooted back enough to slide her full champagne flute onto a table and grabbed a chair. She sat as far from the others as she could and leaned on the rail. Dread writhed in her stomach like a bowl of worms.

The mechas split up to take their positions at the five points of a star. Alonzo was just below, still likely a quarter mile distant. Octavia closed her eyes, breathing through her terror, breathing herself closer to the Lady.

The Tree flared in her mind, majestic against an afternoon sky freckled with gray cumulus clouds. Snow dappled the upper branches and parts of the canopy below. She swooped closer, close enough to reach for a single leaf. The Tree had many leaves of many shapes. This one resembled the leaves tucked in her apron pocket, buried beneath an overly large evening dress.

Lady, this isn't a portent, is it? That the leaf you show me could revive the dead? Outside of the vision, Octavia's arms ached. *That's not an answer.*

Octavia never used to speak to the Lady in this way. Before she left the academy, she was the perfect devotee, bowing in her prayers throughout the day, calling on the

Lady without any hesitation. Her own blasphemy bothered her. *I've changed. The way I see the Lady has changed.*

The Lady, killing Wasters. The Lady, allowing Octavia to bring back a dead little boy just long enough for him to relay a message to her. The Lady, channeling so much power to her, power Octavia didn't want.

Until now.

I need to keep Alonzo and Chi safe so we can leave this place together. I can't keep them in a circle, Lady, but I call on your focus regardless. Grant me insight to Alonzo.

With her unhurt arm, she pushed the headband to her nape. The crowd's enthusiasm vibrated through the railing like an airship engine, body songs swelling and crashing like a violent coastal storm. Beyond that, she listened.

She wanted to hear the marching-band brasses of Alonzo, the unified chaos from within Chi. The Lady had enabled her to hear microscopic zymes before—from here, Alonzo seemed that small. She closed her eyes and extended her will, imagining that she was the Lady, stretching her grace across a distance.

"Octavia—" Alonzo's voice broke into her mind, as close as if he stood next to her. Her gasp and the roar of the crowd obscured his next few words. *"That fire-breather is gaming for the first platform. Let him, beastie. We will grant him wide berth. Fire vexes Octavia like nothing else. She thinks she hides it, but I see. I likely would feel the same, had I seen what happened to my father that night. Up! Now . . ."*

Each time he said her name, she felt it like sharpened cat claws digging into her belly. She opened her eyes. Sweat dribbled from her temple. Chi had indeed bounded up the mountain. Her wings carried her beyond the swipe of the mecha-dragon's tail.

Octavia couldn't hear Alonzo now. Neither his voice nor his song.

The Lady had granted her another new insight, one that made no sense. She felt the scrutiny of eyes on her. Tatiana stood feet away, lips contorted in disgust.

"You're doing magic, aren't you? This isn't Caskentia, you know. There are things you can do there but not here."

"Does that mean you wouldn't hate me if we were in Caskentia?"

Tatiana averted her gaze as a flush stained her cheeks. "I don't know. I might hate you less, given a good reason."

"I only want to keep your brother safe. You know that, right?"

"From what Alonzo said, from what Mr. Cody said about his security here . . . it seems that when my brother's with you, he's in even more danger than he is down there." She nodded toward the battle below.

Guilt twisted in Octavia's gut. Tatiana was right. Alonzo had already had his mechanical leg ripped off, his arm severely burned, been knifed, and died, all because of her.

Down below, Alonzo had made it to the third platform, on the far side of the mountain. She could barely see Chi's wings poking upward. The dragon and the hedgehog battled at ground level. The crowd oohed and aahed in chorus. Octavia couldn't stand it. She glanced up instead. Catwalks crisscrossed the ceiling and held rows of manned spotlights, like the sort used at airfields.

Maybe if I was farther away from all of the other people, it'd be easier to focus on the Lady. Maybe I could hear Alonzo again.

"You're right," Octavia finally said. "Alonzo has been hurt because of me, but I've also kept him alive. I'll continue to do so, too."

"He wouldn't tell me much, but he said you were the most powerful medician in all of Caskentia, probably the whole continent. Is that true?"

A few weeks ago, Octavia would have utterly denied the praise. "I might be, yes," she whispered.

"You've done some good, then."

Octavia glanced over in surprise. Tatiana had said it softly, with meaning. "Yes. I certainly hope so." *Maybe some of the ice around her heart is starting to thaw.*

Tatiana shifted as if suddenly shy. "Alonzo told me I should show you around. The view here is good, but I know some other spots, too. Do you want to go on a walk with me?"

"Do you know how to get up there?" She motioned to the catwalks.

"Oh. Yes." Tatiana looked both surprised and pleased.

"I would appreciate that. Really." *If Alonzo and Chi can survive this and I can befriend Tatiana as well, I'll consider it a spectacular day.*

Tatiana motioned to her three guards. Octavia let the girl lead through the halls. They walked up several flights of stairs, metal clambering beneath their feet. The roars of the crowd trembled through the metalwork. Something dramatic was happening in the Arena.

Please, Lady, let Alonzo and Chi be well.

Tatiana opened a door. Sudden bright light blinded Octavia. The roars of airship engines quivered through the air. "The access to the dome is here on the roof," Tatiana shouted back at her. Tatiana's body radiated anxiety. *The bout is nearing the end. This is the worrisome part.*

As she had seen from Mr. Cody's flat, the roof of the arena was lined with mooring towers. Eight in all, placed at the corners and halfway points of the building. Several airships were berthed. Cranes hoisted pallets of freight. Tatiana motioned and Octavia followed, the men close behind.

"Sometimes I come up here for the view," Tatiana shouted. Wind whipped at Octavia's hair, forcing strands free from her coiled braids, but Tatiana's weave seem plastered into place. Strong hands grasped Octavia from behind, pinning her arms to her sides. She screeched. No new songs had approached. *These are her guards. We've been betrayed.*

"Let me go! Help! Help!" Octavia struggled and kicked, but she may as well have been pounding against a concrete pillar.

"No one's working up here right now. They'd miss the show," said Tatiana.

Octavia felt something deep inside her turn cold. *Alonzo's little sister? What . . . ?*

Tatiana motioned to a large shipping box about her height. FRAGILE: THIS END UP had been repeatedly stenciled across the fresh wood.

"Tatiana, no! I—"

The men lifted Octavia. Her flailing boot found the tenderness of a face. *Crunch of cartilage, wail of blood, adrenaline spike of annoyance.* She dropped inside, landing on all fours. Splintered wood scraped at the softness of her hands. A lamp and a traveler's canvas pack awaited her. With a heavy thud, an eclipse stole away sunlight. She pivoted on her hip. *The lid.* She jumped to her feet but couldn't quite stand. Even as she pressed her bowed shoulders against the wood, she felt the shudders of a hammer on nails. A board or something dense slapped directly overhead.

Holes at random intervals cast beams of light into the box, like tiny arena spotlights. "Tatiana! Let me out!" Octavia screamed, pressing her face to an air hole in the side.

"No!" The ferocity of the word ripped at the girl's throat. "You're going to get Alonzo killed! You're shaming him with all this magic! He needs to be here, with me. I'll keep him safe!"

"Tatiana, no! You don't understand!"

"Go away! Just go away! You'll be more useful elsewhere." A sob broke her voice.

The songs departed, leaving only the roars of airships. Up here, Octavia could not even hear the crowd, or perhaps the raucous noise blended with the engines. *The crowd. Alonzo. Oh, Alonzo.* She pressed both hands to her face as she collapsed on the bottom of the crate. The lamp, the cheap sort found across Caskentia, cast its sallow enchanted light across her legs.

If he's hurt, if he dies, I won't be there. I won't be able to save him. She tried to stand again, bracing her shoulders against the lid. It didn't budge. Panting, she dropped to her knees and reached for the other bag. She held up the contents to the light: a bucket, canteens of water, parcels of dry meat, Tamaran flatbread, nuts. *She doesn't intend for me to die, then. Just to dispose of me.*

"Octavia"—Alonzo's voice cut into her mind out of nowhere—*"will be sorely disappointed if you are injured. More, she will turn her vicious tongue upon me, and I would much prefer sweetness from her lips. Three minutes remain . . ."* His voice started to fade, then resurged. *"Octavia must be sick with dread, but we will hold on for her. I am sure she will bring you more cheese."*

Octavia sobbed, both arms clutched to her torso. Her parasol slapped against her hip. The roof quaked beneath her—the crowd, wild with enthusiasm. Then, nothing. She rubbed her arms together. Did Alonzo and Chi win? Did they merely survive? What happened?

Voices, distant. Octavia pressed her mouth to an air hole again. "Help! Help! I'm in a crate! Help!" She looked out and couldn't see anyone. Machinery clanged. With a lurch, the shipping crate rose. Beams of light shifted as the box turned.

"No, Lady, no. Stop this. Let them find me. Let there be a way out, please." The tiny view outside showed gray skies and towers, then the sunlight blinked out again. A new roar surrounded her, and the sense of being totally enclosed— the holding bay of an airship.

"Help! Help me!" She scooted from side to side. Through

the holes, she could see more crates. A heavy weight clanged above, the wood of the crate groaning. Something had been set on top.

"Lady?" she whispered. The buzz of an engine was her only reply.

CHAPTER 10

Thud. Thunk. The scrape of metal on wood. The whine of opening doors.

Octavia was slow to wake. Her arms ached, her shoulders were stiff, her body permanently cold. She curled her hand toward her face so she could read her pocket watch. Morning. The second morning. Two days in a crate. Now what? Something was happening. No point in yelling, not without other voices nearby. She had yelled herself hoarse before the airship left Tamarania, just in case anyone else entered the cargo hold.

On the Argus, *I was glad no one went to the hold. I was able to hide Leaf there. Now I only wish someone else would meddle about below decks.*

"Lady, is this almost over?" she asked, her voice a raw creak. "Where am I?" She stuffed her watch into her satchel and looped the strap over her head and shoulder. The black overdress and green surcoat, as her pillow and blanket, remained balled up on the floor.

Oh, Alonzo. How was he? She could only imagine his fury at his sister. Tatiana might try to play it off like Octavia had left of her own volition, but Alonzo would know differently. *He knows me. He'll try to find me. Wherever I am.*

More noises, more thudding. Something crunched on either side of the crate. The box lifted up, swinging. Octavia rolled and smacked into the far side. Sparkles circled her head like a babe's mobile. *The babe. Mathilda. They were both well when they awoke, but I should be there to check on them, to make sure.*

Another sway. She rolled again, the back of her head cracking against the wood. Total darkness claimed her.

She stirred at the sound of voices, feminine. The buzzes of their songs. *Young, healthy, one's breasts heavy with milk.* Light stabbed daggers into her stunned eyes as the lid cracked open.

"What is it! Can you see inside?" Someone squealed. Two blurry heads partially blocked out the light. *Adrenaline. Pounding hearts.* Screams. Fleeing footsteps.

Octavia knew she needed to get herself in a circle, but when she tried to rise, the vertigo spun her around like a lunatic's dance partner. She had treated many concussions at the front, but had never had one herself. *An illuminating experience.*

More voices. The light was blocked again. Deep baritones, arguing.

"Let me see." A feminine voice rang with authority. A figure leaned over the opening. "Do not let the poor girl wallow in there. Get her out, gently. 'Tis a medician."

Their grips on her forearms made her cry out, the world going all wobbly again. Strong arms cradled her. *Not Alonzo.*

Not his song. She clenched her body around her satchel, but no one tried to pull it away. A hallway blurred by and then she was in a soft and cushy chair, her sore sit bones finally achieving respite. She sighed in relief. Water flowed past her lips. Oh Lady, water!

After a few minutes of drinking with assistance, she had the strength to hold the cup on her own, her wits returning. She had done her utmost to ration her water, but it had been exhausted nevertheless. Tatiana was woefully inexperienced when it came to packing people in crates—she had no comprehension how much food and water a person required each day.

Octavia realized that she was sitting in an elegant room painted in fine cream with wainscoted lower walls. A small crowd stood in wait—serving girls, their hair capped; men in trim black suits; a woman in powder-blue velvet with white down the bodice, a hard knot of cancer throbbing within her breast. Octavia could not simply hear it in the wail of the woman's song; she could almost see it, like the harshness of light through the crate's air hole.

All of their skins were paler, too, like her own. "Where am I?" she whispered. She managed to lift the satchel strap over her head, the bag wedged to one side of her thighs.

"Mercia," answered the woman in ill health. "You have had a terrible injustice done to you." She sat in a chair, hands folded on her lap. She moved with deliberation. *Pain. Fatigue.* Her eyes were glints of blue ice, beautiful and cold at once. "Your name is Octavia Leander?"

Octavia nodded, taking in the formal Mercian accent, the eyes. "You're Alonzo's mother."

"You must be very familiar with my son to call him by his first name."

"How do you know my name, Mrs. Garret?"

"My daughter included a letter in the shipping manifest." Her lips were a thin line.

Oh, Alonzo. Please be alive and well. You and Chi both. Octavia closed her eyes briefly to compose herself. "Can we speak in private?" At Mrs. Garret's nod, the servants exited, the door closing behind them. "I'm aware of the employment you helped Alonzo acquire." She worded things delicately, knowing that many ears likely pressed against the door.

Mrs. Garret's eyebrows rose. "Are you, now?" The shrewd expression reminded Octavia greatly of Alonzo.

"His supervisors . . . they did not respect him. Alonzo in turned risked a great deal to go against orders and keep me alive."

"You're a Percival-trained medician."

"Yes. It's all terribly complicated, but needless to say, circumstances required that we go to the southern nations. We took refuge with Tatiana. She did not . . . take kindly to me, the danger I brought upon her brother."

"In Tatiana's eyes, Alonzo hung the moon and stars in the sky." Mrs. Garret sighed. The conversation was exhausting her, even as her carriage remained straight and noble. *Alonzo said before that his mother had an intimidating presence. She still does. Most people would be bed-bound and whimpering in her condition. This woman's will is made of iron.* "My daughter is spoiled. Her staff is indulgent. I suppose you think me a terrible mother."

Octavia bit her lip. She had thought that very thing in Tamarania.

"My health has been worse in recent years. I have tried to hide it from Tatiana, with her in Tamarania as much as possible, but she is a smart girl. I have been on a waiting list to see a medician here in Mercia, but with the war and so many in need and the lack of herbs . . ." She shrugged, palms upturned.

Octavia nodded as everything became clear. *Tatiana wasn't simply getting rid of me.* "She sent me here to heal you. Alonzo doesn't know about your condition, does he?" She took another long guzzle of water.

"I have not seen my son since he was fitted for his new leg. We have only spoken by letter and telegram." She sighed. "Oh, Miss Leander. I am sorry you came to be here like this. Tatiana is precocious. I have encouraged her to be an adult at too young an age, because in my heart, I was readying her to carry on when I am gone."

"Have you had any messages from Alonzo in the past two days?"

"No." Mrs. Garret had a curious spark in her eyes; she obviously wondered at this first-name relationship Octavia had with her son. "Was a threat that imminent?"

"If anything terrible had happened, I'm sure Tatiana would have sent word." Lady forgive her for the vagueness, but she didn't want to vex Mrs. Garret with news of the

Arena; the woman had quite enough to concern her. The terrible mass had already sprouted polyps in her neck and lungs. "The most potent danger right now is to you, Mrs. Garret. This cancer that started in your breast will kill you within a span of weeks if it's left untreated. If you can grant me a few hours to recover, I'll gladly tend to it for you."

Mrs. Garret pressed a hand to her chest. Instead of gratitude, her eyes flared with suspicion. "How did you . . . ?"

"I'm an unusual medician." The words didn't make her flinch anymore.

Mrs. Garret stood, her spine straight and dignified. "You are leaving much unsaid, though likely with good reason. I wish I could ask my son about you."

"I wish I could talk to him, too," Octavia said softly.

Mrs. Garret's expression mellowed. "You have suffered and need your rest. I will have dinner brought to you shortly. If you need anything else, simply ask."

"Thank you, Mrs. Garret," Octavia murmured. *The woman needs to leave or she'll collapse. She would never show weakness in front of a stranger, not even a medician.*

Octavia stared at the closed door for a few minutes, gathering her strength and her bearings. She pushed herself from the chair to stand erect for the first time in two days. Water sloshed in her belly. *I was parched like a tree after a drought.* With baby steps, she walked to the window.

Mercia. Two weeks before, Alonzo had intended to bring her to the capital to keep her safe against the Wasters, unaware that the greatest threat had come from his own Dagger peers. She had resisted coming here. Everything she had ever heard of Mercia spoke of its endless sprawl, of skies choked with constant pollution, of toxic factories, of thousands of wretched refugees.

Everything was true.

She looked upon a steel-gray sky stabbed by thousands of dark pipes that puffed out even more gray. Soot caked buildings in black. From her second-story vantage point, she watched four lanes of traffic teem with cabriolets, cycles, and lorries. On the sidewalk, women bowed beneath shawls and pushed prams hooded by oilcloth. Men wore black hats, shoulders bowed by unseen burdens. A peculiarly large number of soldiers passed by in Caskentian regimental green. No trees. No birds. No signs of life beyond pedestrians who shuffled with the vigor of automatons.

Oh Lady. Octavia clutched the curtain to stay upright. Mercia. She had been terrified to come here with Alonzo, and now she was here alone. Panicked, she touched the top of her head and then recalled that she had stuffed her headband in her satchel.

How was she to brave those streets, even with her headband? Wasters spied here—they had already followed Mrs. Stout. If Clockwork Daggers knew she was in the city . . .

Children ran along waving white flags fringed with gold—Evandia's colors. She frowned. Such banners had been popular during the recent wars, but she hadn't seen such a flag waved since armistice was signed several months ago.

A light knock echoed through the door. "Come in," she called.

One of the servant girls carried in a silver tray. She cast Octavia a shy smile as she set it on a table. "M'lady said medicians need extra meat, so Cook included an extra portion."

"Thank you kindly, and thank the cook as well. I'm hungry enough to eat the tray itself." She nodded toward the street. "Why are flags out?"

"Oh, the white flags? That's right, you couldn't have heard, sealed away like that. Armistice broke."

"We're at war with the Waste again?" Octavia stilled. Everyone knew the armistice was a mere pause in the conflict, but she wondered how Caskentia stood a chance. The army had largely disbanded since soldiers and civilians in its employ had been left unpaid.

The servant rested her hands on her hips. "It's a peculiar thing. Well, maybe not so peculiar to you, since you're a medician. That Lady's Tree from the old stories? It's been sighted, just plain popped into existence overnight. Airship brought word two days ago, and yesterday we went back to war. We certainly can't let anything like *that* be in filthy Waster hands." She shuddered.

"The Lady's Tree. Visible?"

"Yes. You worship her, don't you? As a medician?"

Octavia nodded numbly. "Yes. Yes, I do."

"Maybe once our boys have it, you can do a pilgrimage there." The girl's smile was bright. "It's supposed to cure most anything, they say. Might make your job easier! Oh, dear. I'd best get back to the kitchen."

"Yes. Thank you." The door shut behind her.

Octavia collapsed into the chair, wrapping herself in

a hug. Miss Percival's training flared in her mind. *Breathe. Exhale your troubles to the Lady.*

"What if the Lady is the source of your troubles? What then?" The whisper made her cringe, blasphemous as it was. She swallowed, mouth parched already, but she didn't move toward the pitcher.

Why had the Tree become fully visible at last? What had changed? Well, now she and Alonzo didn't have to fuss about finding it. They could simply follow the trail of blood and carnage.

She tugged off the fancy gloves she had worn to the arena. Her fingers fumbled at her cuffs, though she could already see a brown crackle pattern stretch all the way to her knuckles. *I'll need to wear gloves constantly.* Like she could hide this for much longer as it continued to spread. She peeled back the cloth. Both forearms had darkened. Her skin ached as if she were recovering from a sunburn.

The old gremlin had said she smelled like a tree, that she was a chimera. Octavia shivered and buttoned her sleeves again.

The Tree was changing. Octavia was changing, too, and quickly. She needed answers before she lost her humanity entirely.

She needed to get inside the royal vault.

CHAPTER 11

The next morning, Mercia's arteries were crawling with wagons and cabriolets. Open army lorries contained soldiers crated like chickens to market. Masses of people walked the sidewalks and high catwalks overhead. A fetid perfume of sweat, coal coke, burning exhaust, and manure weighed down the air. Quiet didn't exist. Steam horns blared, tramway cars chimed, and beneath it all lay the constant buzz of thousands of engines, like a dull toothache, ever present and impossible to ignore.

Then there were the songs.

Always, Octavia had heard the soft notes of infection, the staccato of old war wounds, the emptiness of lost limbs. She knew from an early age to despise cities and the way they overwhelmed her senses. Now the vivid, intrusive strains stacked atop each other like a hundred battling symphonies, so many of the instruments off-key and off rhythm.

Many people across the realms were ill, but for some reason the misery rang more profoundly in Mercia, as if the city itself amplified illness. It very well could, judging by the foulness created by so many factories.

She stood in the gateway to Mrs. Garret's building and breathed through her Al Cala meditation. She pictured the Tree, its branches battered by some distant storm. *That's how I feel.* The headband helped, but it was cheesecloth straining a flooded river.

Lady, I must do this. Help me. Please. I don't understand why I feel such a compulsion to get inside the vault, but I know the task must be done before Alonzo arrives in Mercia.

Last night's buzzer message to Mrs. Garret had been easy enough to interpret:

Parcel sent in error. Sending man to retrieve. ~Tatiana

Mrs. Garret had been delighted that her son was on the way to Mercia, and delighted by life overall. Octavia's healing of her had been a slow, deliberate procedure, akin to plucking dispersed dandelion seeds from a grassy field. But the task was done, and Mrs. Garret would live.

Octavia should have been relieved that Alonzo was rushing her way. If he smuggled himself aboard an airship—hopefully in more comfortable confines than Octavia experienced—the journey was two or three days. He could be in Mercia as soon as tomorrow.

It will be safer for him if I infiltrate the palace myself, with the aid of Mrs. Stout's son. Please, Lady, since you are guiding me that way, let there be something of use in the vault. Books, scrolls, tablets—something about your nature, something that will help me understand. I can meet Alonzo afterward and we can journey to the Tree.

Her legs propelled her into the flow of pedestrians. Diagnoses bombarded her. She bit her cheek to force back a scream and walked on, bullish. Mrs. Garret had provided her with directions to the palace quarter about a half mile away. Beyond that, Octavia had told Mrs. Garret nothing of her destination or intentions. The less Mrs. Garret knew, the safer she would be.

After all, her house received a medician in a crate from Tamarania. The servants' gossip has already spread over town. Spending the night was all I dared, and even that was foolish.

Her arms hugged her torso as if she were freezing. She wore the green coat from Mr. Cody again. Mrs. Garret's servant girls had murmured in delight over it. Octavia found it odd to be considered fashionable for the first time in her life, and under such horrid circumstances.

Another pox case walked by, the telltale sweet odor clear to her trained nose. *Caskentia has been exterminating full villages to prevent pox from getting into Mercia. Fools. It's here. It has been here all along.*

Block after block, she walked, foul factory smoke billowing from somewhere upwind. Many other walkers wore face masks of black or faded gray cloth. Tamarania's buildings had towered high and yet there had still been a sense of roominess; in Mercia, skyscrapers crowded like vultures to feed on carrion. The windows were fewer or boarded up, streets narrower. A tram rumbled overhead, the trestle rattling as if it'd fall apart.

The spires of the palace emerged from between buildings. The elegant caps of the towers reminded her of spun sugar, though overcooked to an ugly black. Signs designated the palace quarter ahead. Gates and guards marked the boundary. She spied a plant at last—dead vines clung to the wall.

The buildings here were somewhat statelier—columns and porticos and wrought-iron fences. Pedestrians wore more colorful and elegant clothes, a relief to Octavia; her swank coat helped her to blend in. She walked along the periphery street, eyes desperate for any bakeries. Signs, many bleached gray by time, covered the sides of buildings. Royal-Tea advertised again and again—oh, how the Wasters must laugh, knowing Queen Evandia likely looked out her window to see their ads each day.

She walked a full half mile and saw nothing. Turning around, she asked a newspaper vendor for assistance and paid him a copper for the help. The shop still proved difficult to see, tucked away on a third floor and only accessible by a rusted metal staircase on the outside of a building. Gaps in the steps were almost as large as her foot. By the time she reached the third floor, she felt an odd strain in her lungs. *It's the air here. No wonder I'm hearing so many breathing problems.*

A handwritten sign in the doorway read CLOSSED. A common Frengian misspelling of the word.

Octavia stood on the landing for a minute. It was quieter with the street far below, the bodies farther away. She jiggled the cold doorknob. It fell off in her hand and the door swung open.

"Hello?" she called, stepping inside. No happy smell of fresh bread welcomed her, though a yeasty scent lingered nevertheless.

The room was shallow, some five feet from door to counter. White shelves were almost empty of bread and pastries. Cheap glowstone lights had been mounted in the ceiling and walls. A crooked light socket gaped as if missing an eye.

"Hello!" she called again.

"We're shut!" The voice was feminine and high.

Octavia closed the door behind her and set the knob on a sill. More of the fog in her brain dissipated. "I'm here looking for someone."

"They're not here!"

She followed the voice. Behind the counter and a doorway almost naked of paint, the kitchen floor was a dismantled mess of metal parts. Two legs kicked beneath a hollowed-out stove. "I said we're shut." The words echoed.

A young woman, no older than fourteen. Drums, flutes, a cello—the melody familiar.

"I need to find Devin Stout. His mother sent messages through this shop."

"There's no one here by that name." *Heartbeat accelerated.*

"You know the name. If he's not here, tell me where to find him. The rest of his family is in danger and so is he."

"That's living, isn't it? Ow! Damn it!" She slurred her words. Slender hands grabbed the lower lip of the stove and shoved the rest of her body out. "Sorry. Hit my head." The girl sat up with her legs crossed. She wore robes in the Frengian style, a rope securing the folded cloth at the waist. The bell-shaped sleeves looked stained and frayed. White-blond hair reminded Octavia of Mrs. Stout's daughter, Mathilda, but this girl's skin was a deeper tan that spoke of a definite northern heritage. A cleft divided her upper lip, but by the girl's song, it didn't extend to cleave the palate. Large red acne spotted her cheeks.

At a glance, Octavia surmised the girl was an orphan. She knew that look in her eyes. Octavia had seen it in the mirror herself at that age, and in far too many other children to count. The loss of one's family was akin to an amputation. It left emptiness, uneasiness. This girl, at least, ate and had a roof overhead. She was luckier than many. Octavia shuddered to think of what would have happened in her own life if Miss Percival hadn't found her.

"What's your name?" asked Octavia.

"Rivka." The girl appraised Octavia in turn. "If you know how to write, you can leave a message on the counter, or give me a few minutes and I'll write it."

Octavia took a deep breath, actually surprised that the girl was literate. "I can't. I need to speak to him myself."

A man's song strained by constant agony. Burns. Skin pulled taut. "Tell me, then."

The gravelly voice caused her to spin around to face a man who was over six feet in height, his black suit slack as if dangling from a rack. A black mask covered the lower half of his face, and above that the skin was mottled and tight.

An infernal magus laid hands on each cheek and wiggled his fingers, as if molding clay. Rare, for a Waster to count coup in such a severe way. What sort of soldier was this man, to earn that peculiar honor? The infernal scar on Octavia's wrist was a gnat's kiss compared to this.

"I can relay the message to him," said the man.

"No. I need to speak to him myself."

The man stared at her, intending to intimidate. She wasn't cowed. She glared back, listening beneath the pain. The melody was familiar. She would have known Mrs. Garret after being near Tatiana and Alonzo; there was no way this man would fool her after she had spent so much time with Mrs. Stout, Mathilda, and the babe—and in the clarity of a circle, no less. Rivka's song revealed her clear connection as well.

"You're Devin Stout."

The songs shifted around her. The man's in anger. The girl's in anxiety, fear.

"You realize I'll have to kill you," he said lightly.

Whatever she had expected of Mrs. Stout's son, it wasn't this. "That would make your mother quite cross."

"That doesn't take very much. Give her a copper novel and a gin and tonic, and she'll be better soon enough."

"She left you notes last week."

"Ah yes. That she was moving to the southern nations and hauling my sister along. That I should do the same. Never explained why." The tautness of his skin strained the words.

"I have a message to give you directly from her. It's in my—" As she shifted to reach into her satchel, he moved as well, fast and sinuous as a snake. Behind her, the girl whimpered.

"I don't trust easily. Pull it out slowly." He motioned

with a copper-toned Vera .45. Octavia pulled out the cipher and extended it to him between two fingers. He plucked it away and nodded.

"This is from Mother, all right. Girl, put that stove back together. You're supposed to be running a bakery, not dismantling more damned contraptions."

"I needed to open it up. There was a clog, and then I found—"

"Clean it up," he snapped. He held the note to the dim light and squinted, and then he began to laugh. Deep, wheezing laughs. *His lungs, seared, scarred.*

"So, it all comes out now." He lowered the note. "You're Octavia Leander, a medician. That explains the satchel. Packed with goodies, I'm sure." Octavia hugged it a little tighter. "I'm supposed to help you break into the palace."

"Yes."

"Because I'm King Kethan's grandson."

"Yes."

"This is supposed to be a surprise."

She hesitated. "Yes?"

Mr. Stout shook his head. "Oh, my mother. She's so bright with her ciphers and mysteries, her desperate need for intrigue, that she misses the most obvious details. All my life, people stopping me in the street. 'Oh, you look like the old king. Best not let Evandia see you.' In the army all the crusty old swaddies say, 'You look far too young to be another of Kethan's bastards.' My nose, my cheekbones, my hair. By all accounts, I was something of a throwback.

I wonder if the infernal who did this"—he motioned to his face—"thought the same. Maybe he did me a favor."

Metal chimed and dinged as the girl resumed her work.

"Are you going to help me?" asked Octavia. *The vault. The vault. I must get inside the vault.* The urgency itched in her mind, along the lengths of her arms.

"Ah, you're that sort of woman. Full of sass. War did that to a lot of you, unfortunately. Rivka's like that sometimes, aren't you, girl?"

Rivka recoiled. Bits of metal dropped from her hand. She snatched up a washer as it spun like a Mendalian dervish.

Octavia felt a wave of nausea and disgust as she looked between Mr. Stout and the girl. *Dogs are usually treated better. Even dogs that are about to be eaten. No daughter should be treated this way.*

His daughter . . . Mrs. Stout doesn't know she already has a grandchild. Devin Stout has kept this child a secret since he was scarcely more than a child himself.

He fanned himself with the note. "The surprise here is the vault." She could tell he grinned beneath the mask. "I like the idea of taking the most valuable treasures of the realm from Evandia. I like it immensely."

"Hold on. Take? I want inside for very specific—"

"Then lay your claim. You've obviously helped my mother. I can give you first dibs."

Lady, what am I getting myself into? "Books and anything related to the Lady. Mrs. Stout said there are . . . pieces of the Tree in there." *He doesn't need to know that King Kethan believed they were the most powerful things in the vault.*

"Pieces of the Tree. What are those worth, with everyone marching off to see the full thing? Well, that's your choice. I'll get whatever else I want, then. Maybe it'll finally be enough to leave this damned kingdom."

"Where do you want to go? The southern nations?"

He shook his head. His pale blond hair, cut crude and short as if by handfuls and a razor, bobbed at the movement. "Ah, the southern nations. Everyone talks up the city-states like they are so grand. No. I want to cross the sea, and without indenturing myself. I want to leave this wretched place and never look back."

"Your mother would worry for you."

"My mother. My dear mother. The true heir to the throne." He snorted. "All her stories of growing up as an orphan with the prudish Percivals and how the grit of the field never washed from beneath her nails, and here she was, the missing princess. I figured she was one of King Kethan's bastards, really. It seems more appropriate that she's legitimate. Suits her."

He looked to a crooked calendar on the wall, squinting, and flipped through several months to find the current page. "What day of the week is it? Ah. Well. Tonight's the night, then. I know the boys on duty." He walked to the counter and tipped a burlap bag of flour onto a slab of wood.

"You want to do this tonight?" Octavia's heart pounded at the thought, but at the same time she was relieved. Get in, get out. Succeed, fail. Let it all be done before Alonzo arrived.

"What my dear mother doesn't know—among many,

many things—is that I am intimately familiar with the palace. I had to guard the old doss house when I was first conscripted. I know every crack and cubbyhole. I can get us in."

"What, were you a Clockwork Dagger at the palace?" Octavia asked. She rubbed her foot against her calf.

"Ha! The first rule among Clockwork Daggers is you never say you're a Clockwork Dagger. You say nothing, make people wonder."

"People will assume the answer is yes."

He smoothed the flour with a swipe of his hand. "People are idiots. A man can't be defined by what he was, but by what he is. I'm the humble owner of a bakery and engage in various other entrepreneurial pursuits, when the mood suits me. Now look here." With his fingertip, he drew a square in the brown powder. "The vault is on the far side of the grounds. Guards always mutter that the old side is haunted, cursed. Not like the newer side of the palace is any better. It all burned in the attack." He shrugged, box coat loose on his shoulders.

"Cursed? Like how the Wasters claim their land is cursed?"

"The whole bloody continent is cursed. You look around Mercia? People say there are no trees here because of the factories, but you take a gander at a daguerreotype from forty years ago, the skies are clear and there are still some plants to be found. The Waste is better for growing things these days. At least battles turn over the soil, and blood and flesh make good fertilizer—girl, don't dent any-thing!"

"Sorry, sorry," Rivka said. She picked up the part she had dropped.

Mr. Stout gestured over his shoulder. "She might grow up to be a decent mechanic, so long as some buck doesn't get her in the pudding club these next few years. Harder to assemble an engine with a babe strapped to your teat. Now see, this is where the gate is."

He rambled on, sketching out the map in flour, discussing the locations of guards and going off on a dozen other tangents.

Octavia listened and pressed her arms against her body. She scratched her boot against her calf, shifting from foot to foot, but it did nothing to ease the irritation buried beneath cloth and leather.

Irritation just like the skin of her arms.

The bark was spreading.

CHAPTER 12

Octavia stared out the small window at the front of the bakery and couldn't see a single star through the quilt of smog. Buildings pressed in, neighbors with no comprehension of personal space. Faint glowstone lights lined the street below. Electric wires crisscrossed in thick tangles though few windows revealed bright glows. Everything felt darker, gloomier, especially after the modern brightness of Tamarania.

"Caskentia is known for two straightforward approaches to life," said Devin Stout. He sharpened a knife against a whetstone. "If negotiation is possible, use bribery. If negotiations aren't an option, murder is. Unfortunately, murder is the messier of the two, and we have to wear Evandia's white livery to get in."

I won't think of that possibility. We can get in and out without any deaths. "A shame I can't just wear my uniform as it is," said Octavia. Instead, she had layered a palace housekeeper's plain frock over her Percival gear. Considering the chill of the night, she was grateful for the extra warmth.

"It's daft that you insist on wearing that Percival swag

at all. You look like a stuffed sausage, though really, a lot of the servant girls at the palace do, so you'll actually blend in." The man was like a cruder version of his mother—his mouth constant, his tact thin.

Mr. Stout and Rivka had left the bakery for part of the afternoon and returned with livery for each of them to wear. "I like to pop into the palace every so often, see if there's anything new," he had said. As if the royal palace were a community garden that might offer new flowers in bloom.

The fact that the palace was so porous, so susceptible to bribery, wasn't a surprise. Octavia wasn't a moppet in a nappy; she knew how Caskentia operated. The shock came in Mr. Stout's attitude. He didn't know fear. His heart rate didn't spike. To him, this request to break into the vault didn't seem like a big fuss.

Rivka felt differently. Mr. Stout had insisted she come along. Octavia had argued against placing the child in danger, but he stated that they were a package deal. Rivka hadn't argued one way or another, but the terror was there, melded too readily with her song. *She's accustomed to constant fear in his presence.*

There had been no chance to talk to the girl alone. Mr. Stout kept her in his shadow. Octavia wondered where her mother was, why he had kept the girl's existence hidden from Mrs. Stout. Was it shame over Rivka's harelip? Her obvious Frengian heritage? Octavia couldn't see Mrs. Stout being bothered by those things.

"Let's go, then." Mr. Stout swaggered out. His coat dangled past his buttocks, the trousers showing the chicken-like scrawniness of his legs. Rivka wore a smaller version of Octavia's attire and carried a basket burdened with more white laundry. Her eyes were round and solemn against her darker skin, her chin often tucked as if she could hide her upper lip.

Octavia had folded some of the laundry and half stuffed it into the top of her satchel, as if the entire bag carried more of the same.

Auto and foot traffic had dwindled as the hour neared curfew. Octavia was thankful for fewer bodies about, though the idea of wandering after hours worried her. Criminals would still be about—the police worst of all.

"Kethan's bastards! Move yer wagon!" roared a lorry driver, laying on the horn. Some young bucks strolled along, hats at jaunty angles, while young women scurried in tight packs like prey animals. The air stank of a peculiar mix of rotting fish and ammonia. They crossed to walk along the outside of the palace walls. Gray bricks extended some ten feet high, the top crested with spikes.

Mr. Stout motioned to a gate as they walked on by. Iron bars reinforced battered wooden planks. Paint layered the wood in myriad colors. It reeked of urine. "Everyone calls this the protest gate, or the bloody gate. Evandia's tower overlooks it, you see. It's a good place to come for a piss, if you're willing to risk a potshot from the guards up top."

"Everyone hates Evandia," Octavia murmured. The brick wall was battered and patched, made ancient by abuse.

"I don't hate her, not like some do, though she's done a

right job of botching the kingdom, hasn't she? I know many a man who's starved these past few months, all because the army disbanded without providing so much as a copper."

"How long did you serve?" she asked.

"Too damn long," he snapped, then shook his head. "See, I was a boy at an academy here in Mercia when my notice came. Fourteen years old. This was back when the Wasters started their firebombing runs—those fast airships, infernals up top."

Back when Solomon Garret invented the buzzer. Back when one of those same attacking airships went down atop my village. The fire. The screams and klaxons of blood. Octavia forced away the scar of memory and focused on Devin Stout.

"I had a week to go home and kiss my mother, sell my horse, and off I went to be a good soldier." He lifted his face mask enough to spit into the dead weeds along the pitted stone wall. "Good soldier. I was too good. And this is what happened last year." He pointed to his melted face. The shadows cast deep lines into the visible skin. "I don't blame Evandia for all of that. Her generals? Her Daggers? The Wasters? Yes. Evandia, she has all the mind of a child, anyway."

"Mrs. Stout has said much the same," Octavia murmured.

"From their childhood acquaintance? I do wish I could talk to dear old Mum. Get the *real* stories. She used to say she lived in Mercia as a child. An understatement, that." He looked toward the palace and shook his head.

Octavia found her opportunity. "What about you?

Were you raised here in Mercia?" she asked Rivka.

The young woman eyed a passing steam car. "Yes, up in the towers."

"Rivka here scarcely walked on street level until she came down to the bakery," Mr. Stout cut in. "Always up on those catwalks and tramways on high." He gestured toward the built-up sprawl to the east.

"How did you come to be down here?" Octavia asked.

Rivka looked at Octavia and Mr. Stout and back at the sidewalk. *Something terrible happened.* It carried in the girl's anxiety, in the sorrow that suddenly slowed her heart and created physical constriction in her chest.

"Here." Mr. Stout motioned them to stop. A metal door led inside the grounds; the surface was dented like the ocean in a storm, with some gunshot holes for good measure. A small window, more of a slit really, showed the movement of a shadow on the other side. Mr. Stout flashed a gilly coin. Octavia had provided him with three for this mission. A few coins from Mrs. Stout remained tucked away in Octavia's brassiere.

"Devin," growled the shadow on the far side.

"Thom."

"See you're out walking the rabbit. Who's the new bird? Bit too pretty for you, eh?"

Octavia bristled and opened her mouth to tell the man what was what. A soft elbow jabbed her side. Rivka met her eye with a quick shake of her head.

"Yeah. We're needing to walk in the gardens. Rabbit needs to eat greens." He flicked the coin through the gap.

"Shiny. Walk is fine, Devin, but don't make any messes now."

"Never."

"Well, if you do make a mess, wait a few minutes, at least. My watch's nearly up." The gate cracked open.

Like that, they were inside the palace. Stone buildings flanked the walkway. They were mere feet from the street, but already it felt quieter. Mr. Stout led the way around outbuildings weathered in gray and black.

Octavia's gloved fingers brushed the crackled stones. "I thought the infernal attack destroyed the entire palace."

"It did, except the vault."

"These buildings look five hundred years old."

"That's Mercia for you. Factory exhaust, most likely. Think on what it does to the lungs. Actually, you probably do. Now hush. Be a good servant girl."

She bit her lip to contain her annoyance.

Ten, fifteen minutes passed. Other servants shuffled past. Octavia tensed at each passerby but no one paid them any heed. Mr. Stout slipped a coin to another passing guard, the man acknowledging them with a tip of his hat as he walked on. It was fascinating and disturbing, the access this man still had. *But if he was a Dagger, maybe they think he still is one. Maybe he is.*

That thought chilled her. What if this was a trap? He could have spoken to anyone when he was out this afternoon. She cast a glance at Rivka. The girl was no tenser than before. If she knew something was going to happen, surely she'd give Octavia some warning.

Oh, Alonzo. You were so right to warn me against this. I have no idea what I've become enmeshed in.

Octavia smelled the moisture of the palace garden as they rounded a bend. She smiled, relieved to be in the presence of greenery, and then she stopped cold. "What is this, Lady?" she whispered.

The garden was alive, but not. Common trees she knew from the country looked like twisted, stunted things, like people constricted with lockjaw. Pine needles and leaves dangled, green yet limp. Lower plants fared no better. Flowers had no energy to bloom—petals slumped partially open as if asleep. She stooped to touch the soil. It was appropriately moist. Was this caused by a lack of sun? Factory toxins?

"It's been like this as long as I've been coming here," Mr. Stout hissed. "Now come."

She scurried to catch up with him. Foot stones flaked and crackled underfoot, as if heavy machinery had driven along this way, which was quite impossible due to the narrowness of the path. Intermittent glowstone lamps cast spooky light and showed that bushes were trimmed, leaves were raked, and other basic care was attended to. The garden's condition wasn't for lack of love and effort. *I'd certainly want to dig into this needy plot of land.* That longing for the academy's gardens, for her own cottage, swept over her again and she forced it away.

"Something feels very wrong here," Rivka whispered.

"There's a reason people say it's haunted." Mr. Stout shrugged.

Octavia's skin prickled with sudden heat. She quickly backstepped, tugging on Rivka as she did. "Magus," she hissed. *At least it won't be a Caskentian infernal. The city's wards are a blessing in that regard.*

Mr. Stout immediately stepped behind a tree. She caught a glimpse of the Vera concealed against his wrist.

Octavia breathed in, willing her senses to extend. The smell struck her then, that particular ozone scent. "An aether magus." She had to get out of range before the newcomer sensed her own magic. She turned down a side path, hugging her satchel a little closer. Rivka's footsteps followed right behind. Through the bushes, she saw a tall shape.

"Who's there? Pally?" a woman's voice called.

She already sensed me. Blast it! Octavia walked faster, trying to lose the magus. Up ahead was a gray building, but a different sort of gray than the rest. Its stones contained the iridescent shimmer of heavy enchantment, same as her medician robes.

The hue and cry of blood caused her to stop in her tracks. Rivka bumped into her. The laundry basket dropped with a thud. Octavia turned. Blood wailed, its agony pouring, protesting as it spilled onto the ground.

"No, no, no," Octavia whispered, breaking into a run.

Mr. Stout was wiping his knife clean on the aether magus's skirt. The woman was folded over on the side of the path, throat slit. The blood was black in the absence of light. Octavia lifted her satchel strap over her head.

"No," he said. "She was going for that." He motioned to an alarm bell about ten feet away.

"I can heal her and the Lady will keep her unconscious—"

"You bring her back, I'll kill her again. We don't have time to waste."

Oh Lady, what have I done by coming here? Behind her, Rivka made an odd crooning sound in her throat.

"You don't know how long I've wanted to do this." Mr. Stout spun the knife in his grip. "Now I can. Now I won't be coming back here again. You two get along to the vault. I get to resume my old guard duties." He grinned. *Heart slightly accelerated, not panicked at all. He's . . . enjoying this.* "Don't dawdle now."

She should hurt him. Stop him. Her fists clenched with the yearning for her capsicum flute. Oh Lady, they hadn't even gotten inside the vault yet—as far as she knew, it could all be books or the items of the Tree, nothing with the kind of value he anticipated. *The war broke his mind. He's the gambler, betting it all because a lucky pink-nosed cat crossed his path.*

Mr. Stout's grin widened. "Let's be honest now. You told me how I can get into the vault. Do I really need you along?" He didn't aim the gun but she knew the tension in his muscles.

"Your mother wouldn't appreciate that."

"My mother. My mother has never really appreciated anything I've accomplished, so this would be nothing new. Now go, you two. Get in the vault, find me something good. I'll be having more fun out here."

She stared him down a moment more and then turned away, brisk steps taking her back toward the vault. Tears blinded her. "Lady," she whispered. "I'm sorry. I'm sorry. Another innocent like the soldier in the buzzer. Be with her. Ease her passing." Rage burned in her lungs.

Rivka panted beside her. "How are we going to get inside if he's back there?"

Octavia almost stumbled. "You don't know?"

"Know what?"

"He's your father." As soon as the words emerged, she regretted them. *He intended her to find out now, like this. Why?*

"No." It was almost a yell. "He can't be. I knew my father. I . . . thought I knew him. He . . . he died at the northern pass. The zyme poisoning."

Oh Lady. He was one of mine, one I failed. "How did you end up in the bakery?"

"After armistice, a man lived up on our building roof. I—I didn't know him as Mr. Stout then." Emotion thickened her voice, quickened her song. "The building burned. My mama . . ."

Fire. Octavia blinked back tears as she walked. "I'm sorry. I lost my parents in a fire, too. Waster airship conflagration atop my village."

"Oh."

"He took you in after . . . ?"

"Yes. He just gave me the shop and said live here, work here. Mama used to bake bread out of our flat. Frengian sweets, Caskentian loaves, Mendalian flatbreads, she did it all, taught me. That's—that's where I've been since."

Octavia slowed down as they approached the vault. It shined, even with only scant glowstone lights scattered throughout the garden. Smooth marble pillars lined the portico, the tops and bottoms carved into snarled roots. The roof was steeply peaked, like a building up high in the Pinnacles where winter snow fell by the foot. Something chattered in the eaves. She wanted to think it was a sentinel gremlin looking after her.

"The vault. I never thought I would see it myself," Octavia murmured. *Please, let there be something in there. Don't let this be futile like Mr. Cody's library. An innocent woman just died for this.*

Within arm's reach of the iron door, the ward sparked against her skin. Menace resided in the enchantment, like a silent, poised guard dog breathing on her face. If she reached forward, she'd likely lose her hand, or worse.

Blood magic. Not evil, but powerful. The protection exists for a reason.

Devin Stout. He's a coward. He's been here before, maybe he's seen what contact with the enchantment does. That's why he sent us.

"What do I do?" asked Rivka, her voice small. She stopped beside Octavia.

"Hold out your hand. An enchantment like this will challenge you. You'll probably feel a flare of heat, maybe even some pain. Don't scream. Don't run. Grit your teeth and bear through. You're strong and you are of royal blood. It'll know you."

"I'm of royal blood." Rivka sounded dazed. Loops of pale hair draped from the sides of her servant's cap. She extended a hand and gasped. Octavia looked between the girl and the building. *Please, Lady, let this be the right thing. Let good come of us being here.*

Heat flashed from the building—a sign of the enchantment's great potency—followed by a small pop. The door opened as if someone had turned a knob. Rivka looked at Octavia, eyes wide. The menace in the air disintegrated.

"It . . . it talked to me. It welcomed me. I—I really am royal." She shook her head. "It asked who was with me. I told it you were a friend. It said it'd know if we were here for ill intent."

Octavia had little experience with enchantments like this. Maybe the magi who laid the ward were bluffing. In any case, the vault was letting her in, so she wasn't about to quibble. Rivka set down the laundry basket and pulled a glowstone torch from within the layers. They entered side by side.

The blackness was as viscous as oil. No glowstones. Certainly no electricity. Rivka panned the weak yellow light around the open space. The floor crunched underfoot—the tiles had deteriorated even more than the pathways of the garden. Shelves had collapsed inward, random spikes of wood still nailed in place. Octavia touched a piece of wood. It was soft, fibrous like heskool root. It practically dissolved at the pressure of her fingers.

"What happened here?" she whispered. Had to whisper, in the stillness and sanctity of such a place. Her boots found something soft—piles of dust. Considering the placement beneath the shelves, she imagined it to be the remnants of books. Despair clogged her throat.

"Miss Leander." Rivka's voice was high. "I think something moved back there."

Octavia's eyes followed the beam of light. A new body's song met her ears—weak, distorted, like nothing she had ever heard before. A body in death wailed and blared, and this body did just that, tiredly. It was a symphony forced to play the same dirge for years on end. A stench grew stronger, closer. Rivka whimpered and stepped back. Octavia grabbed her hand and a firm hold of the torch.

"Who's there?" she called. She clenched the torch, ready to wield it as a cudgel. *What's there?*

"Who here is of my blood?" The voice creaked like settling floorboards.

Cold chills trickled down Octavia's spine as her tongue struggled to form syllables. " . . . I asked first."

The laughter was as brittle as the stones underfoot. A figure stepped into the faint light, a man as tall as Octavia. Pallid skin stretched over a naked body that was scarcely more than bones and sinew.

"I am King Kethan of the Fair Valley of Caskentia," he said. "And who may you be, m'lady?"

CHAPTER 13

King Kethan. She took in his wretched condition and everything about this place, and she couldn't doubt him. Somewhere in the back of her mind she heard the echo of Mother's voice: *If you should ever meet the King and Queen . . .*

Heeding the memory, she bowed her head and curtsied low.

"Your Majesty," she murmured.

"M . . . Ma . . . Majesty." Rivka's voice emerged as squeaks as she followed Octavia's example.

"Rise."

She did, biting her lip as she focused the light to the side of him so as not to blind him or highlight his nudity. He reminded her of mummified soldiers she had seen in the Pinnacles—boys who had gone missing years or months before in a previous bout of war. At that elevation, everything dried out. Skin sucked in close to the bone. Teeth were bared by curled-back lips. The King's body had grown emaciated in such a way. The visible spaces between his ribs were deep enough to swallow fingers, and his lips parted slightly in a permanent grimace.

"I beg your pardon for my shameful state of undress, m'ladies," he said as gently as he could. His voice resembled metal wheels on gravel, his accent lilting and Mercian. "By your reaction, you did not expect me. I gather that you were not sent here by Evandia."

"No. No, we weren't." Octavia's brain felt numb.

He looked at Rivka. "You, sweet child, look like you are my kin. What is your name?"

"My . . . my name is Rivka. I ju-just found out I'm your great-granddaughter."

"Are you now? Has so much time passed? 'Tis impossible to tell in this place."

Octavia took a steadying breath. "Your Majesty, my name is Octavia Leander. I'm a medician. I am also good friends with your daughter, Allendia, who now goes by the name of Viola Stout."

A strange choking sound escaped his shriveled lips. "Allendia . . . lives?" Light as a blanket, he crumbled to the ground. The strangeness of his song grew more erratic.

Stupid, stupid. Of course he didn't know she was alive. Octavia dropped to her knees. His song baffled her. She didn't know how to understand it—to understand him. She tugged off her glove and pressed her hand to his arm.

Her awareness of the world shrank to a blip of light against midnight. His heart, a frail, poisoned thing. Everything inside him was toxic, discolored, foul, worse than any concoction stewed by the Wasters. And yet he existed, a soul encased in flesh. His stomach had shriveled like an apple left for weeks in the sun, but it wasn't empty. An odd growth rested there, a cancer of a different sort, and most definitely not of his body.

Octavia slammed back into her own consciousness, dizzy.

"Miss Leander? Miss Leander?" Rivka's voice was frantic at her ear, her slender hands clutching her shoulder.

"I'm here. I'm well." Disoriented as she was, she managed to tug the glove on again.

"Tell me of my daughter, please." King Kethan's skeletal hand grabbed her arm, his wrinkle-lined eyes moist with emotion. She resisted the urge to jerk away, afraid of renewed direct contact with him.

"She's about sixty now." *Older than her own father. King Kethan is emaciated and looks ancient at a glance, but he's not.* Rattled, she forced herself to continue. "She has a bold spirit. She can talk off anyone's ears. She loves novels and ciphers, and has written dozens of books herself. She married a book publisher and has two children—"

"Of course she did, my clever girl. She would know to marry the source of her greatest joy." He released his hold and leaned back, smiling. The rictus made her shiver.

"Your Majesty, I . . . how did this happen? You . . . everyone thinks you died in the infernal attack on the palace over fifty years ago."

"I did."

Wretched as his condition was, there were no burns. He was unblemished by fire, the same way Alonzo was after being healed by the Lady's leaf.

Octavia pressed her fingers to her lips as she looked

around the vault full of rot and dust. "Oh Lady. The leaf. They used a leaf on you." *Is this what the leaf does to a person? It prevents them from ever dying?* The horror caused her to clutch a fist to her stomach. *Alonzo, ending up like this? And that babe? What will happen to the babe?*

Faint sounds carried from outside—scuffling, yelling. Rivka walked toward the door.

King Kethan frowned. "You know about the Lady's leaf?"

"Viola—Allendia—told me. Your Majesty, is anything else in here? Has it all . . . ?"

"Rotted? Yes."

Octavia took a few breaths to compose herself. *Even if we reach the Tree, I won't know what is happening to me, or what may work as a cure. Here I hoped that the illogical pull to the vault had some meaning, but now I need some new vision or clue. And Alonzo and the babe—I won't know what can be done for them either. If anything.*

"I had hoped for books about the Lady and the Tree, information. Things are happening. The Tree has just become fully visible—"

"It has? Oh God. At last. I must leave this place. I must go there." King Kethan stood.

"He's killed more guards," called Rivka, leaning inside. Octavia nodded to herself as everything clicked together like teeth in a cogwheel. *I am here for a reason.* "Your Majesty, this can't be a coincidence. Come with me. We'll go to the Tree together. Rivka! Pull out some clothes from that basket."

At the doorway, King Kethan paused and then stepped beyond the threshold. Octavia followed. The door closed itself. The ward flared into place as if they had never entered.

"Here, Your . . . Your Majesty," said Rivka. She held clothing out to the King. He was paying no heed, staring up at the mottled gray skies over Mercia, tears streaming down his cheeks. His grief, his awe, was a palpable physical sensation within his body.

"I have not been outside since I awoke," he whispered. "'Tis beautiful."

After fifty years in a tomb, even Mercia's murky skies and dismal gardens are paradise. "Your Majesty, we need to hurry. Let me help you." Octavia tossed the torch back to Rivka. She draped a white robe over his shoulders. It fit him like he was a toddler playing dress-up in adult clothes. She managed to haul up the hem and tie the waist so that he wasn't likely to trip.

He looked slightly less ghastly in the scant light outdoors. His face was gaunt and clean-shaven, skin gray, his stringy and colorless hair draped to the shoulders. The stench of him wasn't as strong as it had been inside, yet was still very much there. She pulled the hood over his head and grabbed hold of his sleeve to shake him from his wonderment.

"This way, Your Majesty." He walked faster, distracted as he was. *Odd. His bare feet are consistently tender but his skin isn't tearing or reacting at all.* "I can't keep calling you by your title in public. 'Kethan' may also stand out too much." It was not a popular name.

"You may call me Mr. Everett, Miss Leander."

Everett. She vaguely recalled that as the old royal surname. She gnawed on her lip. With his shoddy appearance and stench, he didn't look like a proper gentleman. Perhaps if they played at being family . . . "Would it be acceptable for me to call you my grandfather?"

He considered that for a moment and nodded. "That may be most prudent. Less formality will enable us to blend in more in public."

Klaxons of blood wailed on the path ahead. Three bodies, still warm. The aether magus had turned cold, her blood viscous and mute. Devin Stout was uninjured. He stood with his gun in one hand and a clean knife in the other, heavily panting. The burn scars in his lungs strained his breath.

"What's this?" Mr. Stout growled. He pointed the knife at King Kethan.

"This is what we found inside the vault. Everything else is gone."

"Gone?" he snapped. "You're lying." He looked between her and Rivka. He knocked the basket from her hands. The worn reeds snapped on impact with the ground. Clothes and the torch tumbled to the path. He stomped through the tangle of laundry as if to find something hidden. He glanced at the dead bodies, his lips in a grimace not unlike Kethan's. There was no regret on his face, just raw anger and frustration.

"Was it necessary to kill them?" Octavia hissed.

"Yes. What, you would have had me gag them and tie

them to a tree? That takes time and rope, and I had neither."

"Murder is sometimes the laziest course of action," King Kethan murmured.

"We need to get out of here," Octavia said, walking on.

Mr. Stout caught up with her in a few long strides. "How can everything in the vault be gone? Evandia's not kin of Kethan. How did she even get inside?"

"As a young man, prior to my marriage, I did not behave with discretion," King Kethan's voice creaked. "As a result, there were numerous offspring. I acknowledged many and contributed to their upbringing as was appropriate."

Fifty years locked away without companionship, of course he's willing to say whatever comes to mind.

And Mrs. Stout would be appalled to know that the tavern footle was fully true.

Mr. Stout stared at the man walking alongside him.

"Yes, this is King Kethan," Octavia murmured. *Lady, help us. I do not trust Mrs. Stout's son.*

"But . . . the fire . . ." The cogs seemed to turn in Mr. Stout's mind as they briskly headed down the path. "How can he be the King?"

"He is. Without question." A few servants passed by. They shot King Kethan some puzzled looks but no one stopped them. "I didn't exactly have time to interrogate him for the full details," she whispered.

Mr. Stout scowled. Other people were far too close to discuss the matter now.

"All different. All changed," King Kethan mumbled.

Octavia's heart raced with each passerby, wondering

who might sound the alarm, or if any more magi lurked nearby. At last they reached the gate. A new guard stood there.

"Bart," said Mr. Stout, shaking the man's hand and passing along a gilly coin.

Far, far across the grounds, a bell began to ring. The guard looked past them, frowning. "Good God, not another middle-of-the-night drill. Was told you'd be back this way. Good timing, I suppose." He opened the gate. "You hear about the Arena match down in the southern nations? Rich bloke made a bloody mechanical gremlin. Won the whole bout."

Octavia almost let out a whoop. Alonzo and Chi had won! Lady be praised! She could have danced there on the cracked sidewalk just beyond the gate.

"That so? We'll need to catch up over Warriors later."

"Bah. Guess you expect me to buy now." The guard tucked the coin into a pocket and swung the gate shut. "Now you all best get straight home. It's past curfew, though Ronnie's on street patrol here this week."

"Good to know. He owes me a beer, too," said Devin Stout. The guard chuckled.

Eerie quiet lay over the street like a shroud. "Mercia," breathed the King, the word rapturous.

Octavia's legs felt like elasticized rubber as she climbed the rickety stairs. All the day's stress seemed to quiver through her at once. *We made it out.* King Kethan craned his neck during the whole climb as he took in the skyline and heavens, as if checking to make sure the celestial bodies were still there. They entered the bakery and Rivka jammed the door behind them.

"Well then." Mr. Stout walked a tight circle in front of the counter. He slammed his hat down and smoothed back his pale hair, the most visible trait he shared with his grandfather. "You're King Kethan. Alive. How?"

King Kethan stood in the center of the room. With his billowing robe, he looked like a saint out of an illustration in a religious tract. "When I was a boy, pieces of the Lady's Tree were brought to the palace. A hunter in the Dallows had found the massive Tree and climbed into its heart. He grabbed what he could, and as he was set upon by threems, he fled. He escaped with a branch, a leaf, and a seed, so he said. My father investigated and found the truth—the hunter had had a bag full of leaves, which he gave to his family so that they might live forever. They chewed the leaves and died in a most excruciating manner. The rest he personally delivered to the palace."

Octavia perked up. "I knew the first part of that from a chamberlain's log, but not the latter."

"Our chamberlain wrote of the incident? He always was a fool." King Kethan shook his head, clearly disgusted.

"This bloke sounds like the first Waster to attack Mercia," said Mr. Stout.

"Perhaps. Relations with settlers in the Dallows were starting to disintegrate at that time as they demanded irrigation rights, though I believe he was motivated by grief more than by politics." Kethan stared into space. "You asked how I am still alive. I am not. I died in the fire attack by the Dallowmen. I do not remember the exact moment, only that I was in the throne room and everything turned red."

"The Lady's mercy," whispered Octavia.

"Do not speak to me of mercy." Infinite sadness moistened his eyes. "I awoke to agony, to the feeling of my burned body born anew. I remember . . . I remember the sensation of my clockwork crown's metal being pushed from my scalp, my face. It had melted in rivulets. The cooled pieces of metal struck the floor like dropped nails." He shivered.

"Evandia was there in the vault with a few other counselors, the ones who had been in the country during the attack. Evandia was the age of Rivka here. She told me that my Varya had been dead for weeks, as had I, that the palace had been obliterated. Evandia did not want to rule. She wanted me alive. Her council had sought out one of my bastard children in order to break into the vault. They forced the Tree's seed down my throat and waited a day. When nothing happened, they forced the leaf between my teeth and made me chew it. They did not know of what the leaves had done to the hunter's family so many years before." Kethan pressed a fist to his stomach. "Even now I can feel the seed like a weight."

"The seed didn't react fast enough, so they used the leaf as well," Octavia murmured, her mind racing. "Did the seed need time to germinate?"

King Kethan shook his head. "I awoke, fighting against them. Fighting against the seed. A deep sense of peace is all I remember from my time beyond the infinite river. I hope my Varya would have been with me there, and I—I expected Allendia to be there as well. I did not wish to return to life."

"Of course not," murmured Octavia.

The leaf is poison if it's chewed. The Wasters learned that same lesson. And the seed . . . The Lady's Tree oversees millions of people, animals, flora, across hundreds, thousands of miles. The seed holds that full potential within its shell. If that kind of concentrated power is melded with the toxins of a misused leaf . . .

Mr. Stout frowned. "If I understand this correctly, you carry a seed in your gut that brings back the dead? Even the dead and burned?"

"Yes," said the King.

In two long strides, Mr. Stout had the King by the hair and pinned him against the counter. Octavia and Rivka cried out, Octavia reaching for her capsicum flute yet again to find it gone. *Lady!* She grappled with her satchel to shift it behind her. The parasol's handle smacked against her hip.

"Here's how I see it," said Mr. Stout. "You're dead. No one will miss you. But I can use a seed. I can sell it. I can leave this damned place, buy a dirigible, go over the sea where no one looks at me and thinks, 'Look at the poor soldier some infernal counted coup on.'"

"Devin, no!" snapped Octavia. "He's your grandfather!"

"My grandson?" whispered the King, really looking at Devin Stout for the first time. He had been too distracted by the outside world. "Through . . . Allendia?"

"Yes. Allendia. Viola Stout. The famed missing princess." Mr. Stout said it singsong. "The war you started over her has gone on for fifty bloody years. You burned and died. Seems fitting, really, that I'm burned, too." He pulled back the knife long enough to rip away the face mask. His lips were a deep pink smear of flesh. "See the legacy of your war? I heard my own blokes stand over me and leave me to die. 'Face like that, not worth living.' By the time I crawled to the road, no doctor, no medician could mend this damage or stop the pain." With his facial muscles so tight, his words slurred as they rushed together. Spittle trailed from the corner of his mouth.

"I came back to Mercia, burned like this. I found the bird I knocked up years ago. I see the babe we had, almost grown up, near as ugly as me." He wheezed a laugh. "To think, I could have been born a royal. Should have been." *Racing heart. Adrenaline. The ugliness of rage.* "The people in the city want a revolution, they want Evandia off the throne. I tell you, it won't be me sitting there. Caskentia can rot to nothing, far as I care."

The knife entered King Kethan's gut with a brittle, juicy sound. His blood didn't scream—it wailed like banshees trapped down a mine shaft. The King moaned, his head falling slack.

"No!" screamed Rivka. "No!" She threw herself at Mr. Stout and flailed his back with her fists. He dismissed her with a single mule kick. She pounded against the floor, addled but unhurt.

In one slick motion, Octavia had the parasol free of its loop and switched her hold. She brought the polished wood and copper wand down on the back of Devin Stout's head. She knew precisely where to strike. She knew the pressure behind her arms—strong by farm labor—and the density of his skull.

She knew where best to crack through to the soft gray matter beneath, just as if cracking an egg.

CHAPTER 14

"Oh, Lady," Octavia whispered as she recoiled from Devin Stout. His body, his blood, pleaded for healing. The chemical stink of brain tainted the air. She set the parasol on the counter and backed away until she found the wall. Peeling paint crackled against her back.

Rivka shakily stood. She was tall and lean, her body still hesitant to bud into a woman's curves. Her lips distorted in a sneer as she walked up to her father.

"You killed Mama! You killed her! You were my father all along and you never said . . . !" Rivka kicked Mr. Stout in the ribs, the gut. Octavia lurched forward to grab her around the shoulders and pull her back.

"No," she said gently. Rivka sheltered her face in Octavia's shoulder and dissolved in sobs. Octavia held her and stared at the two bodies on the floor. *This poor girl. No wonder she knew terror every moment in his presence.*

King Kethan did not die. His distorted song scarcely altered. It had flared when the knife sliced in, but as she listened, the tune dimmed as his abdomen came together again. The blood that had oozed out—thick as oil, the coloration as deep as copper—dissolved as if she had passed a wand over him. He sucked in a long, rattling breath.

Devin Stout continued to die. He needed to die.

If I were a better medician, a more compassionate person, I would use a leaf on him. He's Mrs. Stout's son. She loves him. Yet Octavia stared at him and didn't move.

His blood's cry dwindled to a whimper.

"He was my grandson." King Kethan's voice rattled like bared tree branches in a windstorm. Rivka stiffened in Octavia's arms.

"Yes."

"The war did that to him. My wars."

"Only in part, perhaps. His mind . . . maybe something was always wrong there, in some deep place no medician could ever touch."

"Octavia Leander, you need not feel any guilt. I absolve you of it."

Her smile quivered. "It's not that easy."

"No," he said. "It never is."

Rivka trembled. "He's not dead? The King?"

"No. This isn't the first time you've faced death again since you returned, is it, Grandfather?"

He stood with a whisper of bones. "No. I tried to end myself in many ways, as did Evandia's men, when they realized what had been done. No mortal blade can slice the seed from my flesh. No maggots can gnaw it out. This is why I stayed in the vault. In truth, we knew not what to do, not with the Tree still hidden."

Mr. Stout's body was silent.

Rivka pried herself away from Octavia's hug. She walked a wide berth around Mr. Stout, as much as possible in the tight space, to the King. King Kethan's face showed shock as the girl embraced him. He smiled as he wrapped his baggy-sleeved arms around her.

"You. You remind me of my Allendia," he said.

"I'm glad he didn't kill you, too," Rivka said, words muffled against the robe. His song radiated a strange sort of harmony for the first time.

I killed Mr. Drury. Now I killed Devin Stout. And so many have died because of me—the magus and guards in the palace, the buzzer pilot, people on the street in Leffen, even birds. Lady, forgive me. In time, help me to forgive myself.

Her feet scuffed on the floor. It crackled. She frowned and stooped down. The tile floor, already heavily worn, was fragmenting into crumbs. Paint chips lined the floor, too. She brought her gaze to the walls. When she had been standing around earlier, she had noticed fissures and bubbling in the paint. Now it curled and littered the floor as if someone had been picking at it.

"Oh Lady," she breathed. The sickly-sweet stink of Kethan lingered in the air. "The rot in the vault, the garden, maybe the whole city of Mercia. It's from you, isn't it?"

He patted Rivka's shoulder and she stepped away. "When I was first confined in the vault, I thought that if there was any good in my continued life, it was that I at last would have time to read all the books." Terrible grief draped over him again. "Then the books began to disintegrate between my fingers, turn to dust on the shelves. Everything in there, even the swords, the muskets, everything crumbled. I had thought the wards of the vault contained my . . . miasma."

"The Lady's Tree blesses all life. The seed inside you is wallowing in the leaf's poison. You—you've become a kind of antithesis to the Tree."

Grief, shame, shivered through him. "I am a curse to our valley, as the Dallows is cursed."

"Wait. The curse on the Dallows—it's real?"

"Yes. Over six hundred years ago—closer to seven hundred now—Caskentia warred with the Dallows. Magi were not as rare then. Hundreds marshaled their powers together to lay waste to the plains. Their dark enchantment spread as a pestilence among the people, the crops, the soil, but people healed once they returned to Caskentia. The Waste remained abandoned until my father's time, when our growing population compelled people to cross the mountains again. The poison was not as potent and so they settled."

"That time frame. Seven hundred years ago—that's when the Lady was said to have lost her family and become the Tree."

"In my reading, I encountered the same. *And lo, the Lady lost her final babe while it still suckled upon her breast, and she looked to God and cried for mercy, and for no more mothers to suffer. And so the bark began to grow on her skin and the leaves in her hair and she smiled, for she knew her shade would cool children at play.'*"

Octavia stared, hot nausea roiling in her gut. *I've made*

no such cry, yet I am still turning. "I recall that tale from Miss Percival. I . . . I have always heard about your knowledge of books. Is it true that you memorize most books upon first reading?"

"Yes. I set the life goal to read most every book in Caskentia's great libraries." His smile was ghastly and yet fond. "In my studies, I found that Trees are said to exist around the world, most always hidden. They produce a single seed, always at the end of their life."

Octavia mulled everything over and tried to avoid rubbing her arms and legs. *I am becoming a tree, but why? Did something happen when I bled onto that branch? I haven't had to bloodlet since, and that is when my skin started to change. If my body is changing on its own, what's the real purpose of the seed?*

She looked at the dead man on the floor and turned away. "Let's talk in the kitchen, please." As she passed the counter, she grabbed her parasol. By its nature, the wand had already shed the bits of hair and skull, but she still felt peculiar with that familiar grip in her hand.

Rivka walked to a cabinet and grabbed a stack of sweet Frengian flatbreads. She passed two to Octavia. "Mama always said when life makes you cry, eat some bread, because it always tastes better with a little salt."

"Your mother, she was Frengian?" asked the King. There was no judgment in his words.

"Yes. She came down to work the factories, and after she had me, she baked bread at home. Can you . . . are you able to eat?"

King Kethan stared at the sweet bread, longing in his

eyes. Golden turbinado sugar crusted the bubbled top of the yeast bread.

Octavia listened to his song. "He can, actually. The seed is in his stomach but there's room for food as well. I think he'll actually gain muscle and energy if he eats."

The seed. I can even feel the texture of it in his stomach. The hull is intact, even as it marinates in poison. If there were a way to remove it, it might still grow a new Tree.

And King Kethan would truly die.

Rivka smiled as she handed him the rest of the bread.

They ate and did not speak for a few minutes. Bits of turbinado sugar melted on Octavia's tongue like tiny snowflakes, the bread's texture soft, chewy, and thin. King Kethan closed his eyes and forced himself to eat slowly, though occasional murmurs of bliss escaped him. *Even a day old, the bread tastes like heaven to me, but for Kethan . . .*

"Either medicians have changed greatly in a few generations, or you are most gifted." King Kethan brushed raw sugar from his fingertips. His cheeks had actually gained more color. *His body has fed on itself for fifty years, with the seed keeping him alive regardless. He could eat nonstop for days and become more passably normal. But we don't have days. I don't.* Her skin ached.

"The Lady has been too generous to me, especially these past few weeks. I had planned to journey to the Tree, even before finding you in the vault."

He pondered that. "Our paths have merged in a peculiar way."

"How far is it to the Tree?" asked Rivka.

"I don't know, but if the army's heading that way, it shouldn't be too hard to find out." Octavia looked down at her robes. "Winter is beginning. We'll need to pack well." She mentally ticked through the supplies they'd need. The gilly coins could buy them horses, perhaps—a cabriolet would never make it over the pass in winter.

"Our rooms are in back," said Rivka. "I don't have many clothes, but there's all of . . . of Mr. Stout's things. I can wear his clothes. So can the King."

"Rivka, you can't come with us. This is a dangerous journey," said Octavia. She heard a very soft pop and looked up. The paint in the ceiling erupted in a long fissure. She grimaced. "We're on the third floor of a ten-story building that was rotting even before I arrived. We can't linger in the city, not with this aura around you, Grandfather."

I can't wait here for Alonzo. The realization physically pained her. What she wouldn't give for his solid presence right now.

"Where am I supposed to go, then?" Tears softened Rivka's eyes.

"The southern nations. Your grandmother is there, as well as your aunt and a new baby. Mrs. Stout would be delighted to have you there."

"I . . . She saw me here at the bakery, but we didn't know . . . She might not . . ."

King Kethan crossed to Rivka and tapped her chin to force her head up. "Show no shame. 'Tis not deserved." She granted him a little nod and a shy smile.

"Mrs. Stout won't care. She's as fierce as a threem. She'll

take care of you—no one will dare give you grief with her around. I can buy your passage south."

"He . . . he carried money on him, too. I bet there's more hidden in his room," said Rivka.

Pain sparked through the marrow of Octavia's arms. She froze, breathing through the pain as in her Al Cala. *The change is deeper than my skin.* She rubbed at her arms as the agony faded, even as she felt the itchiness along her calves.

"We need to go," said Octavia, surprised at her own voice. She actually sounded calm.

"'TIS THE SAME, yet so different," murmured King Kethan. He stood at the iron railing along a tower roof overlooking his old domain.

Octavia felt the weight of the night on her like God's fist. *The palace, the King, the death of Devin Stout.* All she knew now was that they had to keep on moving until daylight, when they could escape the city. Escape . . . to the Waste. Such an incomprehensible thought.

Rivka had given them directions to catwalks on high that were not restricted by curfews. The tramways would be shut for a few hours yet, but from here Octavia could see the track and the hop-skip of the trestles through and around buildings, all cast in the eerie light of glowstones. Windows gleamed like cat eyes in the blackness.

Trash littered the rooftop. Bottles, mostly, as broken as the men who drank from them. No one was sleeping on the roof tonight, but she couldn't afford to let down her guard. She shivered at the memory of the train ride to Tamarania—

the feral glints in the women's eyes, the way they hacked apart her medician blanket. Thank the Lady that the circle shielded her.

The medician blanket.

Octavia fluffed out the damaged blanket. "Grandfather? Come and sit in the circle, please."

His stride was stronger than before; the food had done obvious good. He carried one of Mr. Stout's knives at his waist and had told her he'd spent many hours practicing the movements of the Five Stars while in the vault. In his youth, he had been known for his athleticism and horsemanship. Such skills could only help them now.

"Medicians attempted to treat me many years ago, to no avail."

"I'm not going to treat you. I have something else in mind."

King Kethan sat in the circle, legs crossed. They had raided Devin Stout's meager wardrobe. Thank the Lady, the two men were of a similar build. The King's scraggly long hair was tied back at his neck; that alone made him look more civilized. Octavia again wore the green coat over her uniform.

Her fingers grazed the circle. "Pray, Lady, heed my call." The heat descended on her, cozy against the cold of the night. She breathed as in her Al Cala. The Tree flared in her mind. There was no moon. The Lady was black on blackness, the wind was as weary as Octavia. No airships, no visible changes.

The King's song grew stronger in the confines of the

circle, as it should. His chaotic, clacking melody sounded as if a classroom of toddlers had been handed musical instruments and told to play. She wondered what other court medicians had thought, hearing this, and how long Evandia's council had let them live afterward. His illegitimate offspring had never opened the vault again either. Gossip had never spread. Evandia had surely silenced anyone beyond her trusted circle. *Lovely thought, that.*

"Lady, days ago you guarded me within this circle. You know well the King's condition. You have likely fought to balance it for fifty years." In answer, the full canopy of the Tree seemed to bow. Branches cracked like gunshots. Octavia froze. *What just happened?* Swallowing, she continued to whisper, "We cannot leave Mercia until curfew lifts. We require respite like that offered by your branches. Let this circle contain his aura of decay, and let us remain here in safety."

The Tree did not move again. Octavia pressed a fist to her chest and then opened her eyes. The King was studying her with curiosity, rather like Alonzo. *Don't think on him. You know you can't linger in the city in wait for him, even if this works.*

She walked to the edge of the roof and grabbed a splintered board a bit larger than her hand. She set it just beyond the circle and then crossed the boundary. Warmth flashed on her skin.

"We'll know if this works by watching this wood," she said.

"Then we had best set my pack and yours outside of the bounds."

She bit back a curse. He was right. She helped him to ease off his pack, which they had fully stuffed with more clothes, food, canteens, and most anything else of potential use. She slipped off her overloaded satchel as well; it'd do her no good if her jars cracked and food spoiled.

The oval was large enough for an adult to lie down, legs and arms slack, so there was adequate space for the two of them to sit and face each other. The King's rank odor was unpleasant, but she'd live. The wards at the front hadn't exactly smelled like honeysuckle.

"My guess is that you come from the North Country." King Kethan folded his hands together.

"Yes. Far north, though since I was twelve I lived at Miss Percival's academy."

"Ah, the academy. I visited there several times as a boy. 'Tis a beautiful place, especially with the tulips in bloom. Do they still grow there?"

Homesickness stuck in her craw. She nodded so that she wouldn't speak and sob. Even with the coldness of the other girls, even with Miss Percival's aloofness in recent months, she missed that place fiercely. Her fingers twitched as if she could feel the tulip bulbs, the grit of the field.

"Yes," she finally managed. "It's planting time now. Selling the full plants in spring still brings in much of the academy's income." *Maybe, with the money from selling me and Mrs. Stout, the girls are eating better. They will need the energy for these long days in the field.*

"A curious thing. Miss Percival came to Mercia mere days before my Allendia vanished."

"What?"

King Kethan stared beyond the blanket, as if into the past. "She asked about the Lady, if there was anything at the palace that connected with the Tree. She said something about dreams pulling her there. I told her no, of course. My senior Daggers were most concerned that rumors of the vault's contents had spread. 'Tis something I thought on, in my time in the vault, as I pondered anything of relation to the Lady. I have wondered why Miss Percival came and what she wanted."

Octavia's mind raced. "Mrs. Stout—your daughter—told me Miss Percival and one of her students found her injured outside of Mercia. They saved her life and took her to the academy. They were going to bring her back to Mercia when . . . when the infernals attacked."

He bowed his head. "Then I thank God she stayed there with the Percivals. The dreams of the headmistress must have brought her to Mercia for that very purpose."

"Maybe. I've had several strange coincidences like that now, such as meeting you. Until a few weeks ago, I thought I had a perfect understanding of the Lady." She pressed her arms closer together. "Now her nature is changing. She's visible to everyone. You carry her seed inside. You can't die. So many things." *The Lady, reviving that dead woman in Tamarania long enough for her to speak. The way her vines ripped apart the Wasters. The way she is changing me.*

"Garcia's *History of World Trees* said that seeds only formed near the end of a Tree's lifetime. The Lady made this seed over seventy years ago, at least. If her life was intended to end, my miasma may have strained her all the more. Perhaps the magic that veiled her has now failed."

"That . . . feels so wrong to me, to think of the Lady dying. Blasphemous, really. It goes against everything I know. It doesn't seem *right*."

"The Lady is grandiose and magical, but she is a Tree, and trees by their nature are finite." He tilted his head toward her. "So are you, Miss Leander. The sun will not rise for several hours yet. You must rest."

"But I—"

"Octavia Leander." He said the words, not with regal formality, but like a father. "I do not sleep. I will be on watch and will wake you if anyone comes to the roof."

Blinking her bleary eyes, she touched the piece of wood beyond the circle. It was still solid. She folded herself forward, her body inches from his tumultuous song. Her eyes closed.

"*MISS LEANDER. AWAKEN. A* strange creature lurks beyond the sanctity of your circle."

She sat upright. *I was asleep?* She could have sworn that she had just closed her eyes. Kethan pointed over her shoulder, and she turned.

Sunrise blushed the eastern sky as pink as a healing scar. Like a miniature gargoyle, a silhouette sat on the railing. Batlike wings flared out. The dismal light reflected on a silver object, like a bracelet, at the base of its wing.

"Leaf," she whispered.

At his name, the gremlin chittered and glided at her,

landing inches beyond the mended edge of the blanket. "Leaf! Oh, Leaf! It really is you!" She touched the circle. "Thank you, Lady, for extending your branches," she stammered without a pause to breathe.

As soon as the barrier dropped, Leaf was on her. He dashed in a crazy circle from shoulder to back to shoulder to breast, chattering all the while. His stubby fingers clutched at her clothes as his wings grazed her ears. His body was the size of a young kitten's, his weight as heavy as a handful of eggs.

"Oh, Leaf! Where have you been all this time? I heard you've been gossiping about me." She shook a finger at him. His long, tapered ears wobbled. "I can't say I mind terribly since it led us to a good friend in Tamarania, Chi. I imagine you've heard of Chi already, too, since people are even speaking of her in Mercia." Octavia cooed and scratched at Leaf's chin.

King Kethan politely coughed into his hand. "If I may inquire, what exactly is this creature?"

"Oh! Of course. This is a chimera, a construct out of Tamarania, a mix of magic and science. They were originally created in laboratories but they nest now and create their own young. Leaf here is a mere baby, but he's bright and he's already saved my life once." *The Lady may not have bestowed the weight of a life debt, but I will never forget.*

"A biological creation? How fascinating. May I?" He extended a hand, palm up.

Leaf stared at King Kethan. One long ear was higher than the other. He mewed and leaned from Octavia's arms, his little black nose sniffing. With a small hop, he landed on the King. Leaf didn't seem quite sure how to react to a man neither living nor dead. He crept up the King's shoulder, sniffing all the while, mewed again, and glided back to Octavia's arm. He rubbed at the glove over her knuckles as he perched on her wrist.

"Sorry," she said.

"Do not apologize for his survival skills. I know well what I am." The King looked away, that grief in his eyes. "I wonder if even horses will fear me?"

I hope not. "The sun's up now. We had best get a start. Leaf, are you here to make the journey with us?"

An affirmative chirp. The gremlin's song was much stronger now—disturbing, how different it was after just two weeks.

"Leaf, if you're spreading more gossip, can you somehow connect with Alonzo and let him know where we're going? Perhaps send him a gremlin to guide him our way?" She paused to swallow down her worry for him, her need to see him. "I wish I could leave him a note but I'm not Mrs. Stout, who grew up with royal spy codes, or Adana Dryn, with her mastery of Waster ciphers. Such things make no sense to me."

"I would help, if I knew what codes he might comprehend."

"I appreciate that, Grandfather."

A smile carved canyons in his desiccated face. "This man, he means a great deal to you."

"Alonzo Garret." Octavia said his name like a prayer.

"A veteran of the recent war. He was an apprentice as a Clockwork Dagger, sent to kill me before I fell into the hands of the Waste. He defied his orders, and the past few weeks . . ." She spread her hands. "Clockwork Daggers now have orders to kill us both."

"To kill a medician of your skill." The King shook his head. "The rot in Mercia is not fully mine."

"No. It's not." She bobbed her arm up and down, causing Leaf to extend his wings for balance. "Can you help Alonzo, little one?"

Leaf placed his tongue between his sharp little fangs and blew a perfect raspberry.

"Well then," she said, laughing. *When did I last laugh and smile this much?* "I'm not sure if I taught him that. I do hope you remember how to hide in my satchel, Leaf?"

At that, he sprang to land in her open bag. His stubby tail waggled in the air like the tip of a thumb.

"Bright creatures," said King Kethan. He stood, joints creaking. His hair draped across his shoulders again; the leather tie fell to the ground in pieces. *That effort was in vain.* "You must tell me more about them."

"I just spent some time with their creator in Tamarania. I'll tell you what I can." She stood and straightened her coat and skirts. At the tug on her coat's hem, the seam gave way. She leaned to look. The threads had loosened. She checked the seams at her shoulders and the pockets. The threads were weak, and the weave of the thick cloth itself had softened. Light powdery residue covered her fingers.

"The cloth is decaying," she said. "Yours will do the

same." *Winter will be harsh enough, but how are we to survive if our clothing rots from our bodies?*

"I am sorry."

She checked her medician robes and the blanket as well. The enchantment afforded them extra durability, but she wondered how long they would truly hold up. The magic was woven for endurance and cleanliness, not to confront years of elemental decay within a span of hours. She packed the blanket away. Leaf writhed in an effort to create a new niche in an already fully loaded satchel.

"You can't help it, Grandfather," she said. She gave Leaf's head a quick rub and pulled the flap shut.

The piece of wood by her feet had splintered into chunks.

Her hand went to her face, as if to find new lines. *I wonder what his presence is doing to my body?* Her arms and legs ached, the feeling now almost familiar. *I wonder if I will end up looking like an old tree?*

She said it in her mind as if it were a joke, but she didn't laugh.

Chapter 15

Octavia had thought the train into Tamarania had been a rickety old thing, but the tramway line through Mercia made everything else look gleaming and bright. The cars rattled like a cabriolet rolling on bare rims. Windows had been knocked out and replaced by iron bars or nailed-on boards or nothing at all. Wind howled through the gaps, whirling hair and skirts and drowning out the sound of woeful songs from bodies all around. Wooden bench seats had been worn smooth by derrieres.

It was a wonder the whole thing hadn't been scrapped in the last war, with metal so precious, but its necessity was soon clear. Mercia was massive. She knew, logically, that half a million people lived there, the bulk of Caskentia's population, but she had no comprehension of how far it sprawled, how many towers scraped the bruised sky, how many factories squatted across wide blocks.

The entire city wears black and gray, as if it's in mourning.

King Kethan was quiet as he stared out the window, his aged face stoic. She recalled the stories her parents had told, that during their parents' day, the city of Mercia had abounded in gardens. The Golden Rose City, they once called it, after a creamy orange rose cultivated as a symbol of the Golden Age of King Rathe and King Kethan.

Octavia's village had grown such roses. They burned with everything else.

The tram braked with a squeal like an injured horse. Leaf lurched in her satchel, and Octavia disguised the movement by bouncing the bag on her lap. No one had noticed, though. Workers shuffled out, hats pulled low. She and Kethan exited last. The King's legs had left an imprint on the wood, like a burn.

How will we do this? He'll rot any saddle, rust any cabriolet. It will take long days to cross the pass, even if the weather is decent, and I dare not think how far the journey across the Waste will be. A nauseous ball of fear rested in her belly. It seemed that each positive development was countered by three negatives.

The far eastern fringe of Mercia was lined with massive boxes belching black smoke. Beyond that towered the Pinnacles, the snowcaps heavier than when Octavia last saw them. Bodies wailed of burns, black lungs, choked bronchioles; children's bodies were stunted by lack of food and knew abuses no one should know. She forced back a sob and walked faster. She pressed Rivka's straw hat more firmly against her head, as if she could grind the headband beneath it into her skull and make it work better.

I want to save them all. Once, I thought I could. Alonzo would be relieved to learn that I'm more prudent, but it only makes me sad. Like I've given up.

Black military lorries rolled by, more and more as the

blocks passed. Soldiers in Caskentian green strolled the streets. Many of the uniforms showed wear—indelicate mends, faded color, poor fit—obviously retrieved from some trunk or wardrobe, or another body. She was surprised to see so few horses. When a cart finally did approach, the gelding in the shafts reared and lunged away from them. The whites of the horse's eyes showed, terror screaming in its song and lungs. Octavia and Kethan shared a grim look.

What now? What will we do?

"Fort Wilcox is just ahead," she murmured to Kethan. "When I served at the front, I stayed at the northern pass, but I knew many men who were processed through here. This will be the ideal place to find out where the Tree can be found."

Please, Lady, let the southern pass be the best route. If we must go north as well . . . I don't know.

"Infantry cannot have journeyed there yet. We need sailors. Let us walk toward the mooring towers and find the closest pubs. 'Tis the perfect time for the night's pilots to settle in for a pint."

Black masts lined a far edge of the brick-walled fort. Not far away they found a tavern. CID'S WRENCH, read the sign, and showed a carving of a bearded man with thick goggles. Men's voices boomed through the windows as piano keys bounced to some ragtime tune. Pillars flanked the door, each plastered with sheets bearing images of airships and lists of names. ARE OUR BOYS, read the barely legible scrawl above.

"No." King Kethan stopped Octavia's approach to the

door. Mr. Stout's black hat cast a heavy shadow across his face. "You do not belong in there and—do not argue—you know well that they will not talk with you as a peer."

She grunted and looked at him askance. "You know little of recent history, Your—ah, Grandfather."

"I know pilots," he said, and with surprising swiftness he pressed through the heavy door. At least his smell didn't stand out with the factories nearby, and any airship crew would reek of aether.

"Balderdash," she muttered, looking around. She couldn't linger out front. Little traffic flowed down the street, pedestrian or otherwise. She walked to the next storefront, a shuttered tobacco shop, and tucked herself in a niche on the portico.

She pressed a hand to her satchel. "How are you doing in there?"

It writhed in response.

With almost no one else around, it was easy to focus on Leaf and his body. Exhaustion strained his wings from long days of flight. *Where did you go, little one? I should place you in a circle later, provide some pampria.*

"—hard to believe, the Wasters taking a direct stab like that," said a man, his voice carrying down the street.

"You daft? 'Tis not hard to believe at all. They killed the whole royal family in my grandpap's day."

"True enough. At least they never made it past the garden. Thank God for Clockwork Daggers last night, or Evandia . . ." The voices faded away.

Interesting.

A few minutes more and the King emerged. He looked both ways in search of her. Octavia crept from her hiding place. As they reunited, she noted that his body sounded the same as before, with a small alteration.

"Beer?" she asked, an eyebrow arched.

"You could not expect me to blend in if I ordered an aerated water, did you, Granddaughter?" He motioned with his head and they resumed their walk east. "'Tis customary for young pilots to buy a pint for an old man. I daresay that was the finest drink I have had in all my life." He covered his mouth as he emitted a small burp. "Your pardon."

"You're excused." *Oh, Mother. What would you think of this scenario?* "Two soldiers walked by, discussing a Waster assassination attempt in the palace garden last night."

"Yes. Talk abounded. 'Tis a necessary and sound strategy for Evandia's court. Propaganda has its purposes, especially on this eve of war."

"Was there any other footle?"

"One of the pilots claimed to have seen the Tree. His peers ribbed him on the subject, but by his manner, I judge he told the truth. 'Tis due east of us, only a few days' ride on the plains. Caskentia is astonished. The Tree is along a major flight route south of the Arlingtons, where our dirigibles often dropped bombs to discourage settlement. Wind shears always pushed airships away from that particular point. Now they theorize that the wind was part of the enchantment."

"A solid week of riding, then, more with snow." Her calves and arms throbbed. *If I have that much time before I'm ready for planting.*

"The pass was never improved? No rail? No. Of course not, not with the wars."

"I've never even heard of a rail being considered there."

"We had many grand plans." His voice was so soft she almost missed his words against the rattle of wheels.

Octavia's grand plans seemed just as fruitless. No horses were to be found; not that any would have let the King ride, anyway. The livery stables were shuttered, the proprietors gone, or in one case, drunk.

"Every horse, every damned one, requisitioned without a coin to me. Needed for the war, they say. Needed to feed their damned soldiers, I say."

The King read Octavia's mood and stayed silent as they walked beyond the fort, beyond Mercia. The snowcapped Pinnacles lay directly ahead. *What would Alonzo do in this situation? He could pilot a buzzer, though three-seaters are very uncommon. He probably wouldn't have qualms about stealing a horse if necessary, though I haven't even seen many horses today to steal, if one would even tolerate the King. Lady, what do we do?*

Octavia's legs throbbed, and not merely from all the walking. Every little itch across her body reminded her that the bark was thickening, spreading.

Leaf squawked and rustled about. She glanced around. Paved roads were far behind them. Ahead, the dirt road contained ruts deep enough to hide small children. Farmhouses were few, traffic minimal, all of it going east.

"I'll let you out," she said. "But you must hide from other people."

Leaf burst out of her satchel like a green fireball, chittering all the while. She tried to smile. Leaf's wings stretched as he soared higher and she felt a pang of worry—was he leaving so quickly?

"There were more woods in my day. More farms." King Kethan studied the green countryside. "Such land stretched all the way to the marshes at Leffen and down to the Giant." He faced south to where the volcano dominated the skyline, its deep crags permanently white.

Octavia reached into her open satchel and pulled out bread rolls. She passed one to the King, and kept the other with tiny bite marks in the crust. Kethan's teeth crunched into the stale roll.

We must press on. If nothing else, I can help the King cross the pass. If he can make it to the Tree, where all of this began, there must be something that can be done for him, for Caskentia.

A military lorry rattled past. Her next taste of the roll was all dust. *The Wasters mentioned they had a settlement near the Tree. That will be Caskentia's focus of attack. Judging by the bustle, the airship bombardment will happen within days, with ground forces following.*

How many will die in the battle? How many more because they try to chew the Tree's leaves? Oh Lady, I'm glad you're visible for our sake, but your presence is going to create a massacre on all sides.

"I spy the gremlin again." King Kethan pointed southward, where a small blip moved in a way unlike any bird.

"Good, I'm glad he—" She stopped as if choked.

Something approached them from a fallow field in that same direction. She saw a blur of movement and heard a familiar high-pitched voice, like that of a teenage girl.

"*Ridemeridemeridemeridemerideme.*"

"The branch," Octavia whispered. "It can't be."

"What is it?" asked King Kethan, a hand to the knife at his waist.

It galloped over the slight rise in the field: Octavia's glorious horse, brought for her by the Wasters, the faithful mount through her trek to the southern nations. The mare was no longer white but green and brown, formed of ropes and gnarls of bark. The horse was underneath, dead beneath living barding. Chlorophyll pumped through a body that still wore flesh. Constricting vines bound a broken foreleg and made it function. The mane and tail were tattered masses of hair blended with vines and leaves.

"God have mercy," King Kethan whispered. "Is this some kind of chimera from Tamarania as well?"

"No." Octavia could barely speak through her horror.

The horse bounded over a fence and stopped before them. Blank white pupils stared her through, hooves dancing on the hard dirt. The saddle was still there, stirrups and all, as if the growth had been very careful to preserve it. The branch was no longer visible on the saddlebag—it was just another piece of wood, a part of the greater whole.

"*Ridemeridemeridemerideme.*" The horse's lips did not move to speak, but rigor mortis bared the teeth as if it posed for a dramatic statue for some town center.

"What happened?" The King looked to her for an answer.

Leaf chattered and landed on Octavia's shoulder. She was too numb to even greet him. "I . . . this was my horse, the one I was riding to Tamarania. At the ravine, I had to leave her behind. In my hurry, I left a true branch of the Lady's Tree tied to the saddlebag. The horse . . . is dead. No normal horse could gallop that far, that fast. This . . . this is a different sort of chimera." *One like me*.

She pressed a fist to her chest in acknowledgment of her beautiful mare. The branch must have goaded the horse onward, leading to starvation or sheer exhaustion, and had taken over the body at some point. It was impossible to tell now. *Lady, let that horse have known mercy*. It was not a prayer or request, but an order.

"We have our horse," the King said quietly.

She nodded. "We do."

They rode.

THE MARE, GRAFTED WITH the Tree's branch, galloped with the snap and rustle of wood as if in a windstorm. Twigs prodded the muscles to movement. Octavia bowed over the saddle horn, greenery lashing at her face. The King sat behind her with one arm around her waist. Her satchel thwacked her lap in constant motion.

King Kethan sobbed those first few minutes of the ride. She turned her head to question him, but before she could ask, he said, "To ride a horse again, even this horse, after so long . . ."

She patted the hard strings and knobs of his knuckles to show she heard and understood.

Each long stride covered tremendous stretches of ground. The hills, which would have been a day or two's walk away, surrounded them within hours. The horse did not slow. Did not need food. Did not need rest. It needed only to gallop east. Farmers with wagons stopped to gawk. Soldiers roared and blared horns as they zipped past. More than a few took shots at them. Octavia submerged her hands in the tangle of greenery to grip the reins. The pressure of her thighs and heels still found some of the softness of the former horse as she directed it to zig and zag. Their mount immediately resumed its steady course.

The horse knows where it's going more than I ever would.

Sometime in the early hours of the night, they entered the mountains. The cold caused her to hunker lower, the heat of her own breath in brief clouds against her face. King Kethan's body didn't carry warmth, yet his presence was a solid comfort. Every so often, Leaf ducked into view, chittering as he made a grand loop. All around them were rocks, snow, and desolation. This was a place paved and stripped by decades of war. They passed valleys where fortifications stood as frosted ruins, and more where feeble campfires illuminated the night in brief flashes. Men stared, agape.

Mr. Drury once told me that Caskentia always blames the Waste. He was right. These soldiers probably think this horse is some monstrosity from the Dallows. They would be right, too, in a way.

The factory exhaust of Mercia was left behind. Stars sparkled with fierce clarity made even fiercer by the intensifying cold.

At last, heeding the call of her bladder and sore muscles, Octavia forced the mare to a stop. Her attempt to dismount resulted in her falling almost face first onto the ground. Her numb hands punched through wrist-deep snow. The sensation made her gasp with shock, but at the same time she was relieved to feel anything at all. She had known too many boys who lost extremities due to exposure at the northern pass. *This change in my body must be helping me to tolerate the temperature, like a tree surviving the winter.*

Still, the very human part of her was nauseous with cold. Her teeth chattered with violence. Suddenly her coat sleeves fell forward over her arms. The gorgeous green coat had split in half. Where the King had leaned against her, the fabric had dissolved to powder. She rubbed her fingers together. The gloves had disintegrated in patches.

"Octavia?" King Kethan landed beside her with grace. His nose and hands had blackened with cold, but the skin beneath already burbled with regeneration.

She stood, tottering as she shook free of the mangled coat. The horse pawed at the earth, clearly anxious to move on. A slow tendril of vine crawled around a fetlock and hoof and into the snow. The vine pulsed, like a person's neck as they craned to drink water. She shivered, this time not from the cold.

"Privacy," she said, and stumbled for the shelter of a nearby rock. She still had enough wits to know she should be leery of mountain lions and pitfalls, though her ability to react to such threats would have been laughable.

After a few minutes, she shifted her skirts back into place. The friction against her gloves was enough to tear the fabric. She shook the useless remnants from her fingers. In the glow of starlight against snow, she saw her hands for the first time in hours. Exhausted, overwhelmed, she screamed.

Octavia's fingers were gloved in bark. The joints still moved, though stiffly. Was that from cold, or was it a permanent thing? *Will I have trouble twisting open my jars? Holding a pen? What will Alonzo think?* Horror, pity, fear—she couldn't blame him for any of those reactions, not when she felt the same. A sob quaked through her chest.

"Octavia." King Kethan was there in a matter of seconds, his knife unsheathed. He saw her hands, extended in front of her, and stopped. His expression was harder to read. A few steps more and he sheathed the blade and took her hands in his. She fought against the pull into his song. He faced the palm up, lightly touching the backs of her knuckles, taking in the texture.

"Do you have feeling?"

"It's not . . . it's not from the cold, it . . ."

"I see what it is," he said gently. "Had this begun before you ventured to the vault?"

"Yes." The word formed a harsh cloud.

"I wondered, when a medician of all people was the one to open the vault, when such a horse arrived in answer to prayer." He stepped back, pressing a fist to his chest as he bowed his head. "My Lady."

"Wait. No. You're the King. I don't deserve respect like that, I—"

"Do you not realize what you are? Octavia Leander, of the North Country, you are the true vessel, the one who is meant to carry the Lady's seed. You are the Tree's true heir."

Her chest shuddered. A dozen denials flared in her mind, all of them pointless. "What more do you know? What haven't you told me?"

"Let us ride."

It was a relief to hide her hands in the horse's leafy mane again. *If I can't see it, it's not happening. It's not real.* Without any guidance from Octavia, the horse wheeled about to resume its eastward gallop.

"I have spent decades pondering the enigmatic nature of the Tree and my condition." King Kethan's voice rattled against her ear. "The fact that seeds can bring back the dead is well chronicled. 'Tis my belief, though, that this is not meant to be a permanent resurrection."

"Everything is finite," she said, echoing his earlier words.

"The ultimate purpose of the seed is to create a new Tree. The Lady's powers are fading. She cannot hide from humanity any longer. She has likely dragged on these past fifty years, past endurance, with these wars and my essence weighing on her all the more."

"But why am I changing when I don't have the seed yet?"

"Your blood has always connected with the Lady, has it not?"

Bloodletting. Every medician felt the pain, that sensation that their arm would burst lest drops of their blood met the ground. A few seedlings would immediately sprout from the watered earth. Octavia had been stunned when her blood recently caused the Lady's own blessed pampria to sprout, and then there was everything that happened in the Waster camp—her blood and the branch creating a full tree, and the combination of blood and Royal-Tea forming an army of vines in her defense.

"You're saying this is something innate inside me, a part of being a medician?" She tried to calm herself with deep breaths. "As if I'm the perfect fertile ground, water, and climate for the seed to grow?"

"The connection is there. This must be another facet."

"What happens if there is no seed available? What happens if the seed *is* available?"

"I know not."

Will my bare feet touch the ground in these coming days and I'll suddenly sink in roots, as the horse did? Will I be able to move afterward?

She had been quiet for several miles when King Kethan's hand squeezed her waist. "I am sorry. I know my commiserations are inadequate, and yet . . ."

"You probably understand what I'm enduring more than anyone." She clenched his hand for a moment as she thought on his delight when he tasted the flatbread and the beer.

If I become the Tree, will I taste water and dirt through my roots? Plants know saltiness in the soil, but what of sweetness? Never again to know the true flavor of chocolate or maple or to have turbinado sugar melt upon my tongue. Because I won't have a tongue.

The selfishness of the thought bothered her. The inability to eat seemed so minor compared to the holy powers of the Lady's Tree, but it was so very *human*.

The landscape passed by in blurs of white and gray and cold. Deep snow had fallen, and recently, but the horse did not hesitate. Octavia's feet carved trenches in the snow as the mare plowed through. She dozed at long intervals to awaken with a start, Kethan holding her securely in the saddle. The sun glinted in the distance. They made few stops. King Kethan's clothes drifted around him in soft tatters, his body blackened beneath. His pack was gone, the straps giving way at some point. Half the clothing, food, and water, lost. More than half, really, because as they rode her satchel had been the easiest place from which to grab food. Octavia cursed for not thinking of the danger to his pack before, but it would have rotted away even if she had tied it to the saddlebag. The saddle itself was gone. Sometime during the ride, the leather rotted through and had been replaced by a seat of wood, moss, and vine stirrups. The transition had been so subtle she had not even noticed until they dismounted. The enchantments on her medician gear, satchel included, still held for now, though she was glad she had packed extra clothing as a precaution.

Thank the Lady, she thought out of habit, then felt a turn of disgust. Miss Percival's betrayal stung, but this turn by the Lady hurt far worse.

Will Alonzo even know what happened to me? Or will it seem to him that I left his mother's house, left a body behind in a bakery, and vanished?

By evening they glimpsed flatness beyond the Pinnacles. Clouds crept in to steal the starlight. The mare's hooves clattered into the hills. Ice crusted the gray stone fortifications of Caskentia's final encampment. There were buildings and tents, the most bodies they had encountered since leaving Mercia. *My skills are even stronger if I can detect their songs at such a distance.*

With a start she jerked her hands from the reins long enough to touch the top of her head. The headband was gone, blown off somewhere in the pass.

DAYLIGHT FOUND THEM IN the Waste.

The yellow plains stretched out to the dull gray of the horizon. Snow hid in shadows and dips. Compared to the Pinnacles, it was warmer here in the place of her childhood nightmares, but still cold enough to kill. *The Waste.* A place described as a living hell. Dry, due to the rain shadow of the Pinnacles; cursed by Caskentia, so the Wasters claimed, to make the dry soil all the more infertile. Oh, how everyone used to make a mockery of that curse—"the only curse is their lack of farming skill!"

To think it had been real all along, and Mercia's blight all the worse.

Their horse abandoned the road and leaped over gullies—no, not gullies, abandoned trenches. A downed airship lay in a black scar. Ribs of framework jutted into the sky. Not far away lay another airship. The conflagration had been so intense that the metal had collapsed inward.

Hydrogen. An older model, likely an older crash. Exhausted as she was, she didn't even flash back to the conflagration that seared her childhood.

Strange holes punched into the dirt, as if oversize gophers had been at work. The pits ranged from five feet to twenty feet in diameter, each round.

"Wyrms," King Kethan said by her ear.

Another native peril of the Waste—creatures that burrowed through the earth and swallowed entire ranches—entire troop divisions—whole. She had known other children in her old village who had been threatened at bedtime, "Go right to sleep or the wyrms will get you." Octavia had always thought that threat was excessively cruel.

Southern Caskentia had been the sort of wilderness that inspired the soul. The Dallows was the sort where you wondered how you would die, with the sad awareness that no one would find your bones.

And yet people settled here, determined to make new lives for themselves. A sinuous line of smoke curled into the evening sky. Octavia reined up. A settlement at last.

"I still don't see the Tree or any new mountains in the distance. We're out of food and almost out of water." She dismounted, holding on to the gnarled wooden lines of the horse to keep her upright.

"Any homes closer to the Pinnacles were likely obliterated by Caskentia."

Octavia nodded. "We have to take the risk of asking for hospitality. Maybe, if we're lucky, they won't shoot us." She granted him a quick glance as he hopped down. His current clothes draped in mere tatters. His long hair hid his face as he turned away. "I've worked in the wards, Grandfather. I've seen it all."

"That does not mean I wish to be seen in such a way by my granddaughter."

This kindness—this willingness to love—is why people loved this man in turn. It's why Mrs. Stout still guards her memories of him with such tender ferocity.

Octavia pulled out spare clothes for him that she had brought for this reason; she still had a gown for herself, just in case. She dug deeper in her satchel and found an old pair of black gloves from Rivka. The sight of her skin in broad daylight forced her to swallow down hot bile. She jerked the covering over her hands, aching to call out to the Lady. Instead, she seethed.

Octavia looked to the dome of the sky; it seemed strangely larger here. Leaf was nowhere in sight, nor anything else in flight. Trees had been scarce, and what they had passed had been bent and twisted, like men who had spent twenty years hauling coal by a yoke.

"Horse," she said, holding the thickened muzzle between her hands. The muscle beneath had not started to rot—perhaps due to movement, cold, or the strange nature of its magic. "I avoided a name for you, thinking that I might spare you. Shows what a bunch of superstitious tosh that was. I'm sorry." Grief weighed on her chest. "You need to wait for us, out of sight, and come when I call."

"Ridemeridemerideme?" The query returned for the first time in days.

"We will ride again, but the Lady knows all about the

dangers of starvation and dehydration. You won't have ful-filled your duty if I arrive dead." *Or so I think.*

The horse seemed to consider this, and walked away.

Octavia and King Kethan staggered through limp grass over a small rise. She studied him. He looked ill, but not dead. Their time in the warmer weather of the Waste had allowed his skin to recover from frostbite.

A ranch sprawled out before them. Brown fields consisted of tidy furrows, corrals beyond. She was puzzled by how the smoke directly rose from a hill, and it was only as they drew close that she realized it was a sod house. The nearby barn was likewise carved into the Waste itself. Yellow-gray grass furred the roofs. To a far side was a dirt road, one of the few they had seen that day.

Tall poles with bells were spaced out along the fringe of the field. With no other trees about, they truly stood out.

King Kethan followed her gaze. "Wyrm alarms. Earth-quakes will set off the bells."

"What good would that really do?"

"Would you rather die fighting with a gun in hand, or while you sleep in your cot?"

Octavia was quiet for a moment. "There's no right answer. I'd prefer not to die at all."

King Kethan inclined his head with a smile.

Dogs struck up a howling chorus and bounded out to meet them. The three scraggly mutts stopped cold about fifteen feet away and stared in utter silence.

A man stepped into the doorway of the sod house. He held a rifle with the grace of a person who knew how to use one.

"Greetings!" called Octavia. "We're travelers in search of hospitality." *Please don't shoot us.*

"Good God, did you make it over the pass dressed like that?"

Octavia was taken aback—it was a woman's voice. "We had more, but we lost some to soldiers, and our horse—"

"Needn't say any more." The woman in man's garb whistled sharply. The silent dogs scampered back toward the sod barn. She frowned at the mutts, clearly puzzled by their behavior. "Soldiers take what they will." She looked Octavia up and down, her already dark skin flushing more. "They didn't—"

"No," said Octavia. "I'm not hurt."

"Small mercies. I grant you the hospitality of my house. My name is Bruna."

Octavia stepped across the threshold first. She recalled that Wasters more readily accepted first-name familiarity. "I'm Octavia. This is my grandfather."

"Mr. Everett," said King Kethan, his voice raspy.

"The road has been hard for you both. Please, come to our table, we just began our evening repast."

It was not difficult to find the table. The dugout consisted of one room. The table was in the center, formed of old planks. A woman and two children sat there. Octavia did not need to see below the woman's skirts to know one leg was fully gone to midthigh, the stump poorly cut. The worst of the infections were past, but they had left a lingering strain on her song and in her young face. The two children looked almost like twins, though their songs differed slightly. Their eyes were wide at the shock of seeing guests.

"Pardon me if I don't stand, I've been ill," said the woman at the table. "I'm Farrell. Please share our meager feast and accept our salt, for we are glad for a wayfarer's presence."

That sounds like an old poem, the sort Father would have known.

"We wayfarers are glad to share in this feast, though we bring little more than our company," answered King Kethan. Octavia looked at him with surprise. Farrell and Bruna smiled, each with a fist to their chest. After a nudge, the two little ones followed suit.

Here I thought they would shoot us on sight as obvious Caskentians, but then, so many Wasters came from Caskentia. Octavia sat on large rock that placed the table at about her chest height. The fare was indeed meager, but her mouth watered at the sight of roasted rabbit with root vegetables and a small stack of flatbread. Bruna split their portions onto two battered tin plates.

Octavia's fingers shook as she attempted to grip a two-tined fork. Her thumb didn't want to flex. She took small, precise bites and savored each taste as if it might be her last. *It may well be.* At the very least, her stiffened skin prevented her from shoveling in food.

"You are a medician?" asked Farrell.

Octavia froze. The query sounded innocent enough, but by this point, she knew better. "I am." *No point in denying it, with my satchel and full robes.* "We're on a pilgrimage to the Tree. Have you seen others?"

The two women shared a grimace. "A dangerous time for that," said Bruna. "We've already been told to retreat further into the interior."

"Stupid wars," growled Farrell. She tore meat from the bone.

"We lost our husband last year," Bruna murmured. She stretched down the table to take Farrell's hand. "Now we have each other."

"And me!" piped up a little girl.

"Yes, we have the four of us."

"And a home we broke our backs to dig out of this goddamned caliche." The Waste was known for its rocklike layers of sediment.

"Am I to understand," said King Kethan, "you constructed this homestead just this year? Since armistice?"

The two women nodded, their faces hard. *Everything about them is hard. They can't be older than me—I'd guess them a few years younger. Most women here die by thirty. Most men . . . well.*

The soft putter of an engine drifted overhead. Everyone at the table froze. "God, is it starting already?" asked Farrell.

"It's just another airship flying to the Tree," whispered Bruna.

"Just another airship. How many times are they going to simply fly over?"

Kethan walked to the door. He kept his body to one side. *Habit of a soldier, with the wall to shelter him in case of gunfire.* "Caskentian flags. 'Tis coming in lower, within firing range." He didn't need to say it; they heard and felt the increasing roar.

"Kids, to the cellar," snapped Farrell.

"Can I take my meat?" said the little girl.

"Yes, take it all. Come on." Bruna took the boy by the hand and guided them to a corner of the room. She lifted a hatch in the floor.

Octavia joined King Kethan. "Do you think they're looking for us?" she whispered.

"We were seen all through the pass, and there can be but few homesteads here."

Dread sank into her stomach. *Please, Lady, no battles here. I'm so sick of people dying because of me.*

"I will talk with them." King Kethan walked outside.

"What stripe of fool is he?" snapped Farrell. She stood, reaching for a crutch made of bent metal. "A man can't show himself to a Caskentian airship here, not unless he wants suicide."

He's doing it because he can get shot and revive. "Sometimes he's more bold than clever."

"We're looking for an unusual beast and rider." The words crackled through a megaphone. "Have you seen anything?"

She wondered where the horse was hiding; surely it couldn't be far away.

King Kethan held his arms up as he shook his head in an exaggerated movement. "No, we have not!" he yelled back, his voice carrying surprisingly well over the low roar.

The airship was similar to the *Argus* that she and

Alonzo had ridden on. The hull was recessed into the underbelly of a great silver gasbag. Where the side windows had flanked the dining room of the passenger airship, this army craft boasted gunnery from most every window. Few guns aimed dead-on, but if the craft drew parallel to its target, the firepower was immense—even as it exposed the full balloon of the craft. A military rig such as this would have extra aether wards in place to toughen the skin against bullets and other missiles.

Something flew from the portside window and spiraled close to the barn. Octavia pulled the door to, throwing herself on the ground. Behind her, the other women did the same. They waited. No sound, no explosion, no hiss of gas. Octavia crawled to the door and cracked it open. King Kethan was walking across the grass to investigate. The airship hovered in place, silent but for the engine and rotors.

The King glanced back toward the house. "'Tis a piece of silver, an old serving dish," he yelled.

"A silver dish?" Octavia echoed to the women, confused. Their murmurs reflected the same confusion. *If Leaf were here, he probably would have gone for it, but why would an airship look for Leaf?*

Bells rang along the periphery of the homestead. She thought she had imagined the sound, confused it with noise from the hovering airship, but seconds later, a bell on the dugout wall joined in.

"Oh God, the low airship must have attracted it. Kids! Out!" screamed Farrell.

"Attracted what—? Oh Lady," said Octavia, remembering what Kethan had said before. *A wyrm.*

King Kethan ran back toward the house. Beneath the airship, dirt sprayed upward like a fountain. The craft reared as the wyrm emerged. The head—the visible body—was the size of train cars in sequence. Its skin was the color of dirt with a slight pink hue, like a common earthworm, and it had no discernible eyes. The wyrm lashed upward. The ship lurched away with the crackle of gunfire.

The wyrm roared. It was a strange, hollow sound. The head was a solid mass. The song—it had no song. Octavia had no time to puzzle over that now. Dirt shivered from the ceiling as the earth rumbled. The children screamed. The airship turned, exposing the far side of the craft. Bullets whistled and thudded into the dirt walls.

Cold, hard rage flared in Octavia. *They didn't miss the wyrm. They're shooting at the house because they can.*

Sprawled on the floor, she crawled to the children. They crouched to one side of the cellar hole. The little boy sobbed, a thumb wedged in his mouth. The little girl's bushy black hair was powdered in brown.

"We'll be buried alive!" cried Bruna.

Farrell crawled to them. "Don't talk like that!"

"Do wyrms always attack airships?" asked Octavia.

"Loud noises pull them in, the vibrations. The wyrm will grab the ship if it's in range," said Farrell. Mud smeared her face. "Your grandfather . . . ?"

"I don't know." She crawled back to the door. King Kethan might not be able to die, but she still worried for him. The gunfire directed at the house had stopped, though shots still rang at a distance.

New shafts of light pierced the dirt front wall where it had been penetrated by bullets. The ground shook, hard. The wooden supports in the ceiling groaned. Dirt fell somewhere behind Octavia. The children screamed again. The wyrm roared. Each time it shifted, it was like a small earthquake. She looked outside.

The airship stayed just out of range as if toying with the beast, gunfire smattering into the exposed head. No blood screamed. Whirls of dirt created a brown fog across the yard; she couldn't see King Kethan. Through the cloud, she heard a distinctive crackle and a blue flash. Octavia averted her eyes as the boomer exploded. The airship hovered closer, whirls of dirt choking her.

"Don't," she whispered to the airship, to her own countrymen, even as she already knew what they were doing. She slammed the door shut and threw herself down again. The boomer smacked into the roof of the house. Another cascade of dirt fell.

"What is that?" cried Bruna.

"A boomer," yelled Octavia. "Used at the front to terrify horses, deafen soldiers—"

"They're luring the wyrm onto us!" said Farrell.

The airship thundered close overhead, waiting. The sod house shuddered as the boomer exploded. The women and children continued to wait. *Why isn't the wyrm attacking?* In response, another boomer sparkled as it flew past the window. The stench of aether-infernal magic blew indoors, the stink reminiscent of hot cooking oil. More dirt shifted from above.

The airship pulled away. A gunshot, two. They sounded distant, not like an automatic from the airship. Octavia pulled herself to the door, her satchel dragging beside her. More gunshots. She cracked open the door to see a large object on the rise just beyond the furrowed field—a mass of green and copper, metal wings flared out.

Her breath caught. *Chi.*

Chapter 16

The airship hadn't missed the strange sight either. It circled around as more shots were fired from below. *The airship was scouting for Chi, not us. That's why they threw down silver as a lure.*

The puncture in the airship's gasbag appeared as a small black hole. Octavia couldn't believe her eyes—an airship shouldn't be that easy to shoot down, but then, Alonzo was a marksman and a trained Dagger. *He knows its vulnerabilities as few would.* In the space of several breaths, the hole widened to a rippling gap with a silver flap of skin. The ship angled hard as the nose smacked into the edge of the field with a violent eruption of dirt.

Without her headband, she clearly heard the songs of the men inside: the snaps of cracking bones, the dull thumps of concussions, and cacophony of blood and bodies, followed by the klaxons of flesh afire.

She couldn't smell it, that charring of skin and muscle, the reason she hadn't been able to eat meat until well into her teenage years, but she knew it. She knew the particular screams of a body on fire, how it lit up the brain with brilliant dazzles of pain.

Mother. Father. The neighbors, the village, the horses. Red on black, flames scraping the night sky. Mud of the field sucking down my feet, rooting me in place.

A terrible scream rang in her ears. The raw pain from her own throat told Octavia that the sound came from her.

King Kethan stood in the yard, filthy, his face carved in wrinkles of concern, and then she was past him. Deep concussive blasts knocked her off her feet. She tumbled over, sharp grass gouging her like needles. She bounded up again at a run. Her legs throbbed, the skin stretched taut with new growth, but she refused to slow.

Stop the screams. Stop the suffering.

Heat lashed against her. The gasbags flared and just as quickly expelled their contents, the flames dwindling yet still high. Something terrible shook the ground. Some small, sensible part of her brain remembered the wyrm and that she should be concerned about it, but all she knew and breathed and tasted was fire and ash.

"Octavia! Octavia!" Strong hands gripped her shoulders and spun her around.

The triumphant brasses of a marching band. Hunger, dehydration, exhaustion—exhilaration.

"Alonzo?" she whispered.

His nutmeg skin was dark with accumulated sweat and grime. Crescents of filth underlined his eyes. Goggles sat atop his forehead. Her gloved hand hovered over his cheek, afraid to touch him, as if he wasn't real.

"You're here? Really here?"

Another violent shudder and flash of heat. Alonzo

shoved her down, wrapping himself around her. He stank, but his touch, his presence, was pure Alonzo, and oh Lady, did she need him at that exact moment.

The screams within the airship went mute.

"I am sorry, Octavia, I am sorry. I had to shoot it down. I saw you in the doorway, the wyrm, the boomers, what the ship was trying to do. I had to shoot it down."

She closed her eyes and pressed her face to his shoulder. The oiled duster was smooth against her skin. "I know." She knew, even as she tabulated more deaths to weigh on her soul. *A ship of that make, with a full gunnery crew, held as many as forty. None escaped. None.*

The fire roared.

A child cried, the sound high-pitched and anxious. She looked back toward the dugout. It was gone, collapsed in the concussive blasts. King Kethan stooped over as he unearthed the little girl. He held her up as she screamed again.

"Oh no." Octavia pried herself free of Alonzo. "There are two women and another babe in there." She tore across the grass, her senses already straining to find them in the rubble. Just as when she scrutinized Mrs. Garret, she detected a glow with her mind's eye.

"Help. Medician." Farrell's words were weak, but boomed in her ears as a summons.

"We're coming!" she screamed.

King Kethan frantically dug with a small trough. "They should be about there," he said, pointing.

"I know." She knew exactly where they lay. She heard the screams of broken ribs, the heavy bleed of a scalp wound, the choke of blood in the lungs. Alonzo was at her side. "There." She pointed a few feet from where Kethan had gestured. Alonzo dug in with both hands.

Octavia took a few steps forward. "Oh, Bruna," she whispered. Her gloves delved into the dirt and dry grass. Behind her, Farrell coughed and hacked as Alonzo unearthed her. The heaves made the woman scream in pain. *Three ribs. Internal bleed. Needs pampria.* But Octavia didn't stop digging. Kethan joined her, then Alonzo.

They found the still form of Bruna. The back of her skull was a mash of blood and hair. Sheltered in the arch of her body, the little boy bawled with quiet convulsions, unharmed but for his terror. Alonzo whisked him away. Farrell cried out.

Octavia didn't hesitate. She dug out one of the Lady's leaves, the third. Bruna's broken jaw hung askew as Octavia turned her over.

"No!" King Kethan yelled, his bony fingers prying at her arm. "You cannot—" Panic galloped through his song.

"The leaves are only poison if they're chewed." She met his terrified gaze. *In all we've endured these past few days, this is the first thing that has scared him, the idea of someone being poisoned the way he was.*

"You are certain?" he asked, trembling.

"Yes. I know how to use them." Seeing the certainty in her eyes, he backed off, sagging as if deflated.

She crouched beside Bruna and pressed the leaf beneath her tongue. Gently, she shut Bruna's jaw. Over her, King Kethan's breaths rattled. Bruna shivered as if tickled in her sleep. The jaw shifted into place with a loud click. The purple rings beneath her eyes sank into healthy skin the color of fresh-baked bread crust.

"Alonzo, keep the other woman back," Octavia said, not needing to turn around. Farrell, even in her agony, was trying to reach Bruna.

Bruna's brown eyes opened, blinking. Before she could try to speak, Octavia pried open her jaw and removed the leaf. It dissolved in her hand.

"God does have mercy," whispered King Kethan, a slight sob in his gravelly voice.

Bruna frowned as her eyes focused on Octavia. "You . . . you need to hurry. The Tree is waiting."

Octavia bowed her head. The Lady had sent her a message again, just as she had done with the dead woman in Tamarania and times prior. That border between life and death seemed to be the only time that the Lady could directly speak to a person. "I know."

"You can't keep me from her! Bruna! Bruna!"

Bruna's face distorted in horror as she regained full control of her body. "Farrell? The little ones?"

"They're all out. Farrell's badly hurt, but I can tend to her. Don't—don't tell her you died." It seemed like a silly thing to say, but Octavia felt the need.

"No, no. Not now, anyway. Later."

Octavia nodded, then scooted back to make room for Bruna to scramble up. Dirt showered from her clothing as she rushed to the rest of her family. Sobs and wails brought tears to Octavia's eyes.

"Octavia." Alonzo offered a hand to help her up, but as she stood, she found his focus wasn't on her. He looked at King Kethan and pressed a fist to his chest. "You have the look of the Stout family, yet you cannot be Devin Stout."

"I am not. You may call me Grandfather, for now." King Kethan saluted him in turn. "And you are the Alonzo Garret of whom I have heard so much. 'Tis an honor to meet you."

Alonzo looked at Octavia, clearly curious. "I know that my fool sister sent you to Mercia. I am consumed with both awe and dread to know what befell you in the city."

"That story will need to wait until we're done here." She ran her wand over both hands as she trod across the dirt ruins to where Farrell and Bruna sobbed together. Out of the corner of her eye, she saw a green blur and heard the songs of three happy bodies—those of Leaf with the two children. The gremlin hopped and chattered and sent them into titters.

Of course Leaf is back. He must have led Alonzo and Chi in our direction. He was working to bring us together all along. I deserved that raspberry.

"Bruna, I need to heal Farrell, now."

Bruna pulled back from her gentle embrace. Alonzo and King Kethan helped to move Farrell to the medician blanket. The circle flared to life the instant the men stepped back. The Lady was here, watching, waiting. Prodding them on like a child herding cats.

Lady, you are the grieving mother, the one who understands laments. Know that I'm thankful you're here to heal and comfort, but I'm still bitter. I'm tired. I'm tired of all these deaths that follow in my wake, this suffering.

The heat, the sense of the Lady's presence, did not waver or react.

Octavia read the needs of her patient. A hefty scoop of pampria; Bartholomew's tincture, to bind bones; heskool and bellywood bark, as a precaution. The circle dissipated the instant Octavia knew the healing was done.

"Thank you, Lady, for extending your branches," murmured Octavia, from habit more than anything.

"Yes. Thank you, Lady," said Farrell. She looked straight at Octavia as she spoke. Odd chills crept up Octavia's spine. King Kethan passed the metal crutch to Farrell as she scooted back. Bruna knelt beside her.

"I think we lost everything but each other," said Bruna.

"Then we didn't do too badly," said Farrell.

"How far to the next settlement?" asked Alonzo.

"East, maybe half a day's ride," said Farrell. "During the war, we retreated to the far fringe of the Dallows. Most of us had the sense to stay there, even after this last armistice. We should have listened, but we wanted land of our own. I should have listened." She looked away, her face twisting with rage. Bruna reached for her again.

Now that the crisis was past, Octavia was suddenly aware of the dwindling light and the chill against her sweat-soaked skin. Beyond the songs of nearby bodies, the world seemed strangely quiet. Even the flames had died down to a distant crackle. *We all need to get out of here. If exposure doesn't kill us, the missing airship and the plume of smoke will bring Caskentian military at full throttle and gallop.*

"The wyrm vanished in the midst of everything. What

about Chi, Alonzo?" she asked. "I only saw her at a distance. You rode her all the way from Tamarania?"

"Indeed." He glowered, arms crossing his chest. As he moved, she could see that beneath the oilskin he still wore his jockey attire from the arena. "At the conclusion of the bout, Tatiana tried to excuse your absence, but I knew you would not leave, not with us in peril. It did not take her long to confess the truth. As for the beastie, Chi would not permit me to leave the hangar bay without her. Her intention was clear."

"Goodness. You came even further than my horse. She had the reinforcement of the Lady's branch, and she still didn't truly survive."

"Your horse? The white mare?" asked Alonzo, brows drawn together.

A sudden, terrible thought flashed through Octavia's mind. "Did Chi eat or rest at all?" She set off for the rise where she'd seen Chi.

"No, not truly. I dismounted a few times each day, but Chi did not wish to pause for long. She seemed compelled by a greater force."

The Lady.

Octavia forced her stiff legs to walk faster. "Chi's body is alive like any animal's. Her needs are biological, even if her extremities move as machines. She can't . . ."

They stopped at the rise.

The massive chimera had collapsed into a meditative Al Cala pose, folded forward like a small child. The wings had tucked in close to her back. Her armored head bowed, face planted to kiss the grass. Thick mud caked what was visible of her legs. Of her chaotic, powerful song, nothing remained. Chi's momentum had kept her going all those miles, but like a horse run too hard and not rubbed down afterward, the chimera stopped, and stopped completely.

A small wail escaped Alonzo's throat, a sound Octavia had never heard him make before. He rushed down to Chi and rested his hands against the slick membrane of a wing. "Can anything be done?"

He has to ask, but he knows. Octavia stood back, fists balled at her hips. "It's not your fault, Alonzo. You wouldn't have been able to stop her from coming here. She probably died immediately after you dismounted. Her hearts, her body, everything shut down. There's no trauma. No bullets from the airship struck her. Her . . . her souls are too far gone for a leaf to work."

As if responding to his name, Leaf fluttered to land between Octavia and Chi. He was utterly silent.

Alonzo embraced the massive chimera. "She took care of me, in truth. In the Arena, we were a team. She understood me, as you said she would. This long ride, she chirped, and she listened. I had total faith that she knew the path to you by magic or instinct far beyond my comprehension."

"You told me once that you only had battlefield faith," she said softly.

"What have we endured these past few weeks if not a constant battle?"

They remained still for several minutes. Alonzo leaned

over Chi with his arms wide, his face turned away. Octavia placed a hand on one of Chi's tapered ears. The horned accessory was gone, revealing a thick ear tip flecked with white whiskers. Alonzo murmured something she couldn't quite make out. Smoke and emotion stung her eyes. She looked away, blinking. The wind shifted more and the foulness of heated aether made them both cough.

Alonzo stood upright and looked toward the source of the smoke. "I do wonder," he said, voice hoarse, "at the presence of a Caskentian airship this deep in the Waste. I saw many of our soldiers these past few days, and Chi and I did not even follow the pass. What of armistice?" He kept one hand on Chi's shoulder.

Octavia stroked the large ear. "War's been declared again. The Lady's Tree is now exposed somewhere to the east of us. Caskentia saw it by air, and of course, nothing like that can ever be left in Waster hands."

"The Tree, visible," he murmured. "Why such a change?"

Why such a change indeed. Octavia looked at her gloved hands as despair welled within her chest. *Because, Alonzo, I'm changing into a Tree. The King thinks I'm supposed to be the Lady's replacement.*

She needed to tell him. Alonzo had always been forthright with her, even when it imperiled his job as a Clockwork Dagger. But telling him meant saying the words aloud, meant they were true. The stories always said that the Lady pleaded with God to save everyone and that she welcomed the change and everything it meant. *I want to help everyone.*

I do. But not like this. Not to lose my own humanity. Not to lose Alonzo and whatever may come in our future.

"We must burn Chi, lest she fall into the hands of Caskentia or the Waste." His voice was thick.

"Yes."

"Octavia. About the airship. I am sorry . . ."

Hearing her name caused her skin to prickle in an odd way. "It's the same as that buzzer pilot before. I know, Alonzo. I hate it, but I know. They would have killed us by gunfire or lured the wyrm into attacking us. You did what you needed to do."

His brow furrowed. He looked as if he didn't believe her.

"I thought you wanted me to be more accepting about this kind of thing?" she asked. "Isn't it more reasonable? Better than trying to save everyone?"

"Yes. But 'tis not *you*."

"What am I anymore?" Hysteria edged her voice. She almost screamed out the truth, but took in a deep breath instead. "I'm sorry, Alonzo. I've seen so much death this past week, more than usual. Worse than usual." A pause. "I had to kill again. Mrs. Stout's son."

His blue eyes widened as he stepped toward her. "Octavia, for you to do such a thing, there had to be a good reason, just as when you defended yourself against Mr. Drury."

She leaned into his shoulder and he wrapped his arm around her. Oh Lady, he stank of a week of compounded masculine musk and hundreds of miles of dirt, but he was Alonzo and he felt so good. As always, he knew better than to shush or offer ridiculous consolations. He was simply there, solid as an old oak, respecting her in weakness just as he respected her in strength. His fingers found the exposed nape of her neck and brushed away the whirls of hair that had escaped her tightly coiled braid. The touch of his callused thumb caused her to shiver, and not simply for the joy of physical touch.

I could be pulled inside his body again, so easily.

"Octavia." When he said her name, she felt it like a flicker of heat, like when he was in the Arena and he spoke to her. *My eavesdropping began each time as he said my name. He evoked me, just as how I call out to the Lady and direct her attention within a circle.*

The realization stole her breath. *I really am becoming the Tree. A new Lady.*

Her legs buckled.

Alonzo made a small sound of surprise as he caught her full weight. She knew the scream of his exhausted muscles as he lowered her to the grass in the shadow of Chi's body. Alonzo stood again and reached for something on the chimera's saddle.

With a soft chirp, Leaf bounded to within inches of Octavia's face. Something akin to concern created wrinkles in his forehead.

She leaned closer to Leaf. "You talk to the Lady," she whispered low enough that Alonzo couldn't hear. "I know you talk to her. Tell her I don't want this."

Leaf squawked in dismay, flapping his wings.

Alonzo crouched over her. "There is water in my canteen, and food—"

"No. Not now. We need to go."

"Are you able to walk? I can . . . I can take care of Chi, if granted a few minutes."

Octavia gritted her teeth and made herself stand. Alonzo waited within arm's reach in case she fell again. *Just as I looked out for him when he lost his mechanical leg.* Leaf landed on her shoulder with a whisper of wings. Octavia faced Chi and placed her fist to her chest.

"Chi, your creation was a cruel thing, but your souls were noble and cohesive. Thank you for caring for Alonzo. I'm sorry you were sacrificed in such a way. You deserved better. You deserved a whole shop's worth of cheese."

Emotion clogged her throat. She turned and walked away, leaving Alonzo to say his farewells in private.

She could hear King Kethan's approach. He had been shot three times when the airship had strafed them but the wounds already had sealed. Beyond the worsening wear on his clothes, he was as well as he could be.

"I began to worry for you," he said, matching her stride as she walked back toward the ruined sod structures. Pink and orange light gleamed over the Pinnacles.

"Alonzo rode a hybrid of gremlin and mechanical war machine here from Tamarania. The first of its kind. She—Chi—was forced to go and go and go, as my horse was."

"To suffer the same fate, though with no branch?" he asked quietly.

"Yes," she whispered. At that, Leaf trilled. He was

being unusually quiet. *He's mourning in his own way, like when so many of his kind were slain on the* Argus. "Alonzo is going to take care of her."

"As a warrior should tend to his fallen steed."

"Grandfather, this change in me. I . . ." *Oh Lady, I can't even hint at it.*

"You do not wish him to know."

Octavia looked at King Kethan with relief. "Yes."

"He is not an idiot. He already worries for you."

"And I worry for him, with my every breath. We're going to the Lady. I'm going to talk to her. This . . . it doesn't have to be this way." *It doesn't have to be me. Please, Lady. I have given so much of myself to you, to Caskentia. Allow me this selfishness.*

"Octavia, have you given thought as to what this world would be without the Tree?" He motioned with his head. "Look around. Nearly a millennium has passed and the Dallows is still known as the Waste in spite of the Lady's efforts to heal this land. Look at Caskentia. Mercia." His voice broke. "I know the good that Percivals rendered in my day. You have tended our boys at the front, you and your sister and brother medicians. What will this world be if there is no Lady to answer your prayers?"

No Lady. No medicians. No healing magic. Only doctoring, as crude and slow as it is.

Her chest felt so tight she could scarcely breathe. Sensing her distress, Leaf made a sound akin to a purr and paced from shoulder to shoulder in a way that usually made her giggle. Not even Leaf's antics could brighten her spirits now. "You can't—you can't place that burden on me, Your Majesty. I'm sorry. I know how that sounds. You just spent decades locked in a tomb, all because of the Lady's leaf and seed."

"Evandia believed she was doing the right thing when she revived me. She was scared, desperate. I will not deny that I have known frustration and anger during my captivity. If not for the books in my mind, I would have succumbed to madness."

"The books you memorized?"

"From the age of fourteen, when I began to keep count, I read fourteen thousand three hundred and fifty-one books." His voice softened. "I remember much of them. When the books in the vault crumbled to dust, I read from the library here." He tapped his temple. "I read the years away."

"The Lady has stood for some seven hundred years," she whispered. "I don't have your memory. I don't . . . I don't want that fate. I want to save people, that's true, but I never wanted to lose myself in the process. I want . . . I want to be *me*. I want to live, as a person. I want to grow old." *I'm only twenty-two.* Her words sounded so petty and whiny, even in her mind.

The Lady was so powerful, so full of potential to help thousands of people and beasts in need. And yet . . .

Octavia wanted to breathe in an icy morning wind, taste the brittle nuttiness of hard cheese, wiggle her toes against a carpet of moss, feel a horse's sloppy lips against her palm. She wanted to smile at her patients to let them know all would be well. For the vicious claws of young, purring kittens to prick her lap. To hear the feisty, satisfying snap of snow peas in her grasp as the pods parted from the vine.

King Kethan sighed. "You are no fool, to wish for such things. You do not crave suicide or full self-sacrifice, not with a full future before you."

This is why he was prized as one of the wisest men to have ever lived in Caskentia. I always knew we lost a great deal at the start of the wars, but I never knew how much.

"What should I do?" she whispered.

"The Lady is known for compassion. At the Tree, surely there is a way to speak to her directly. I do not see a confrontation with her as wrong."

"You just aren't sure if it will do much good either."

He held his hands palms up. "I am in search of my own answers, my own peace."

Tears stung her eyes. *Peace. An end to this war. A home. A garden. An atelier. Alonzo's smiling face. Animals, people who need me. A place to belong.*

She couldn't linger on such thoughts. "Let's hope we get the answers we want. For now, we need to figure out how to get the three of us to the Lady, and how to get this family to safety."

Charred patches marked where debris had fallen in the crash. The airship's wreckage continued to smolder, a few flashes of orange bright in the new darkness. Like a strange shadow, one of the wyrm's tunnels gaped before them. Octavia kicked through the turned dirt to stand on the edge. The tunnel dropped straight into the abyss. Leaf sprang from her shoulder and glided in a circle before landing again at her feet.

"What do you know about wyrms?" Octavia spoke loudly to be heard by both the King and Bruna. The other woman was still some thirty feet distant.

"They have always been a hazard of the Dallows," said King Kethan.

Bruna stopped on the far side of the ten-foot pit. "They're attracted by noise, but sometimes they act as if randomly. They are especially bad in this area. Some people settle again and again only to have their homestead destroyed, as if they are being run off. We chose this acreage because there weren't any holes."

"But what *are* they? Has anyone killed one?"

Bruna shrugged. Dried blood showed as black, broad streaks across her shirt and trousers. "You always hear claims, mostly from men in their cups. I've never seen proof of one dead. Shooting them doesn't seem to do much. They move fast enough that dynamite can't get them in time."

"You noticed something, Granddaughter?" asked Kethan.

Alonzo approached, a new weariness in his stride. She waited for him to join them.

"I noticed the wyrm wasn't alive. It didn't have a heart, or a song, or its own distinctive soul. It was like a plant."

Like a plant. Wyrms known to plague the area. Run people off.

"Are there any fragments of the wyrm on the ground, something caught by a bullet? I need a light." Octavia fumbled inside her satchel for a glowstone.

"Here," said Alonzo, pulling a stone from his pocket. He extended the weak light and began to pan across the ground. A minute later and Octavia did the same. They walked side by side, their steps slow. Leaf hopped in front of them at the edge of illumination.

After several minutes, King Kethan knelt down. "I believe this is its flesh."

He pointed to something that resembled a brown scrap of leather about the size of her palm. At first glance, Octavia might have dismissed it as part of a uniform or tack from the airship, but this wasn't burned.

"It would be easier to identify this if it spoke like the branch," she muttered under her breath. But then, the leaves hadn't had a voice either. However, there was one thing to which even the processed Royal-Tea had responded. She turned away from the men as she pulled her faithful scissors from her pocket.

"Octavia, what are you—"

Before Alonzo could stop her, she levered the blade enough to penetrate the fabric of her glove and the skin beneath, then stooped to press her blood to the thing on the ground.

Leaves and vines lashed outward with the brilliant chaos of a sneeze and just as quickly withdrew into the scrap of bark. Bruna screamed.

"Well. That was unexpected," said King Kethan. Leaf mewed agreement.

"Wait until you see what she can do with a keg of tea," said Alonzo.

"Shush, you." Octavia was surprised to find herself smiling. "Well, that settles it, then."

"Settles what?" asked Bruna. "What was that?"

"Wyrms aren't animals or monsters at all. They are the roots of the Lady's Tree," said Octavia. "If they're attacking a settlement, take it under advisement that the settlement is too close to her, and move elsewhere."

"Too close?" Bruna's eyes were wide and white in the dark. "We can't see the Tree from here even now! Taney has a settlement near the Tree. How come it's still there?"

That name made Octavia grimace. Grand potentate Reginald Taney ruled over the Dallows, and his plot to kidnap her and Mrs. Stout had started this whole mess.

"A tree's roots stretch far, far beyond the canopy," murmured Alonzo. "Maybe their camp is on caliche, or 'tis so close to the Tree that exploratory roots would destabilize the massive trunk."

"I'm sure someone has tried to follow these tunnels before," Octavia said to Bruna.

"Well, yes, but tunnels collapse or folks never return."

King Kethan nodded with a thoughtful hum. "Wyrms do not usually come out this far, but this one had a purpose, I think. It created a direct path to the Tree."

Octavia started walking. Leaf landed on her shoulder again and tucked his wings close to her shoulder. "Yes. Which leaves one more matter. Let's get the others."

Farrell shakily stood at their approach. The two little ones huddled under a blanket at her feet. A meager burlap bag of salvaged belongings sat to one side.

"Lady," Octavia whispered. The presence, the essence of the Lady, lurked close to her consciousness. If she closed her eyes, she knew she would see the Tree, feel the same breeze she was feeling on her skin right now. "The horse. I need it, but I need it to save this family. Please. So many have died today. Let them be saved."

A strange certainty rested in her gut. She knew the horse approached.

Octavia faced Bruna and Farrell. "There's a strange horse coming. It's . . . okay if you find it terrifying. It scares me, too, but it won't hurt any of you. It's part of the Lady's Tree."

The two women looked at each other uncertainly, their hands clutched. "Magic, then. The good sort?" asked Farrell.

"Yes," said Octavia. *I hope that's not a lie.* Hoofbeats approached. Alonzo sucked in a breath.

The remains of the mare, twined in wood and growth, looked like a macabre equine sculpture in the dim light of Alonzo's glowstone. Octavia cradled the horse's muzzle between her palms.

"These two women and children will ride you," she whispered, her voice carrying in the tension of the night. "Make the saddle fit them. Keep them safe. If they need to stop briefly along the way, let them. Deliver them to the nearest Dallows ranch. Once that's done, go to the Lady's Tree and let my beautiful horse's body know peace there. Let white-star jasmine grow on her grave." Octavia paused. Leaf was a soft and solid weight on her shoulder, his mew a hot breath by her ear. "I should have named her Jasmine."

"Theyridetheyridetheyridetheyride," whispered that excited voice.

"Yes." She found the reins where they tangled in the growth of the mane. As she stood there, the horse's back distorted, stretching with the groan of branches and snap of brittle bones. Octavia swallowed down her revulsion and sadness. "Farrell, Bruna?"

They approached with trepidation. Alonzo and Kethan helped Farrell up first. A stirrup of vine extended to encompass her foot, a gentle vine draped over her lap. The same occurred with the two children and Bruna. Their terror, the rapid beating of their hearts, echoed through Octavia. She pressed the crutch to the horse's flank, and vines immediately twined to hold it upright like a banner.

With all four settled into the saddle, the horse wheeled away, transitioning from canter to gallop in a matter of strides. They vanished into the dark plains.

"I feel," Alonzo said, "as if we have much catching up to do on our walk."

Octavia nodded as she looked to the men lit by the frail yellow light. "First things first, then. Let's do this properly. Alonzo Garret, you were right to see the resemblance to Mrs. Stout in Grandfather here. I'd like to introduce you to King Kethan of the Fair Valley of Caskentia. King Kethan, Alonzo Garret."

Chapter 17

Octavia had never been afraid of the dark—only of the way that blackness made fire seem all the brighter. However, she had never before been in blackness so absolute, so oppressive. Their glowstones glinted like mere fireflies against the midnight ink of an entire ocean. Even more, she couldn't escape the keen awareness of the weight and press of the cold earth above—a weight that could crush them in an instant. The wyrm's tunnel didn't smell like a pleasant, freshly turned field either. No, its dank flavor coated her tongue and irritated her lungs as if it could crush her inside and out.

The Lady continued to pull them along like marionettes, but that didn't make anything certain. Octavia could still die. There had been too many close calls. Back in the Waster camp, she had already defied the Lady's will once; the blood-watered tree had tried to force her to take shelter in its branches, and Octavia had refused, knowing she must save Alonzo instead.

At the end of this, I'll defy the Lady again.

That certainty left bitterness in her gullet that was far

worse than dirt. First Miss Percival's betrayal, and now this turn from the Lady. The itchiness of bark growth had now spread to her hips and prickled along her shoulders and chest.

In the dim halo of light, Alonzo studied the walls, the floor, the ceiling. The wyrm—the root—had created an almost perfectly circular tunnel. Dry dirt clumps and debris crunched underfoot. The path zigged and zagged. It had been about a ten-foot drop into the pit, followed by a slow downward slope, though it didn't take long for the route to level off. Leaf had not entered the tunnel at all. He hovered at the edge of the pit, his chirps echoing for a time. She could only assume he'd flown on to meet them at the far side.

The walk had given them abundant time to summarize what had befallen King Kethan and what they each had endured in the past week. That done, they had fallen into a silence miles long. They had likely walked ten miles already, or maybe it was a hundred. There was something about the timelessness of such darkness that could drive a person mad.

King Kethan's boots made rubbery smacks as they disintegrated beneath his feet. His breaths were a tense rattle. His anxiety had increased as they walked, and she wondered if that was more because of the dark confines—so like the royal vault—than because of their actual destination.

Alonzo tripped on a fragment of root and caught himself on a knee. He waved her back before she could come to help. Octavia knew he was unharmed. She studied him with her more mundane senses.

His black coat, battered as it was, had an elegant flare with each powerful stride. The oilskin gleamed in the dim light. His thick long hair, bound at his neck, still managed to look magnificent even after his trek; she envied someone with hair that could maintain such body.

Silly, to think on such things after all they'd gone through, all they still must do. But at least Alonzo was here. His presence soothed her, gave her the same feeling as sitting on the porch of the academy after a day of treating patients and seed sowing, a hot mug of honeyed apple cider in hand, a full moon on the horizon. He was *comfortable,* even if all of her life expectations had collapsed into rubble as soon as they met.

Miss Percival had counseled her to shun the presence of men, as nothing useful or proper could possibly happen in their company. Octavia snorted softly. She still excelled at being useful and proper, even if she was in love.

That's what this was. She was in love with a half-Caskentian, half-Tamaran former apprentice Clockwork Dagger, a temporary airship steward, a man with a maniac of a sister and a regal mother, and a peculiar knack for sewing.

He tripped again. King Kethan helped him up this time. "My thanks," said Alonzo, somewhat abashed. "I plead exhaustion."

"As do we all," said King Kethan. "'Tis noteworthy when even the deathless grow weary."

Alonzo was tired, true, but that wasn't what was causing his steps to drag. It was more like he was being tripped.

She bent to touch the object his foot had found. It was a loop of root. At her touch, it lashed like the tail of a surprised cat and withdrew into the ground with a soft rumble. No need to confirm the identity with a drop of blood.

Sudden fear made her all the more cold. "She plays favorites," Octavia whispered. "This is a warning."

The Lady is finite, as Kethan said. She's also limited in her power. Most medicians would spend an hour trying to accomplish what I do in minutes. She obviously hated the Wasters—her vines shredded the men apart in their camp—and when I tried to revive Mr. Drury with a leaf, she refused to let it work. She . . . reinforces life, but death is harder. She cannot simply kill someone from afar. If so, surely Mr. Drury would have dropped dead long before I even met him.

With her parents dead and Miss Percival estranged, Alonzo was her family. He represented the grand potential of the future. The Lady had let her leaf work on him before because Octavia needed him to survive. She had even needed him hours ago at the sod house.

What if he has fulfilled his usefulness? Oh . . . oh God. Like my mare, my Jasmine. Like Chi. A courier, a lorry, that's to be discarded at its destination.

The tunnel was suddenly all the more menacing.

The ground wouldn't collapse beneath him, not with her just steps behind him. Tripping could injure him, cause him to require a healing. If they were a few feet apart, a cave-in could easily separate them, with her on the Tree's side. The Lady couldn't manipulate things physically before—she could only speak through those on the cusp of life and death—but now they were nearing the actual Tree.

A few quick strides and Octavia hooked her arm around Alonzo's as if they were about to stroll through town together. He looked at her in surprise, then smiled.

I'm going to keep you safe. She pressed her arm closer. "We couldn't see the Tree from the homestead, so how far away could it still be?" The words echoed.

"The Dallows is famous for its visibility, though it was a hazy evening. It must have been at least fifty miles distant, likely more. We could not see the mountains either."

Hearing the possible number of miles ahead worsened the burning in her feet. She should probably apply iodine to her soles soon. "And I thought our walk through the swamp was bad," she said, trying to lighten her voice.

"My legs fully function this time."

"Always an advantage," she said. "Though I would have help to carry you now."

"I would be glad to be of assistance." She couldn't see Kethan's face, but the smile was in his voice. King Kethan paused to pull off Devin Stout's old boots. The soles had finally eroded through.

Something echoed. Something none of them had done or said. Octavia stopped. "Listen." She scarcely breathed for what felt like five minutes. The sound came again.

Alonzo stiffened. "Hide your light," he whispered.

"The root could be returning," Octavia said, but she didn't believe it. By the men's expressions, they didn't either.

King Kethan motioned to a ridge on the left side of the tunnel and then gestured behind him. Alonzo opened his mouth and Kethan cut him off with a wave of his hand. "I know well that you are offended by the need to hide behind your liege, yet I can catch bullets in your stead and live."

Alonzo nodded grudgingly. Octavia ducked behind him, one hand on his back, and tucked her glowstone into a pocket of her satchel. A second later, Alonzo's light vanished as well. The world turned absolute black. Octavia couldn't help a small squeak of fear as she scooted closer to Alonzo. His fingers found her arm and they gripped hands. Her gloves, cut and abused as they were, allowed more of his song to reach her. She willed her breaths to be slow and steady and tried to focus on the rough texture of his skin, the heat of his body.

It's so dark, I wouldn't even know if I closed my eyes. I could fall asleep while standing, like the boys on guard duty who'd come into the ward with an embarrassed flush on their cheeks and a busted nose.

"I spied a distant light." King Kethan's whisper was barely audible.

Alonzo's body shifted as he pulled out his gun. Octavia adjusted the satchel strap so she could slip her parasol free. The weight was heavy and reassuring, even as she grimaced at the thought of the last time she had used it as a weapon.

Voices echoed. Words jumbled together. A light blinked, pure and white—most definitely more powerful than glowstone. Alonzo's body was coiled like that of a cat stalking a bird.

"—goes on all eternity. We'll get back, and the bairns will have bairns."

"It only feels like eternity because you can't shut yer yap."

"'Better to speak, to speak out loud,'" sang a voice, husky and pretty, "'than in darkness go mad.'" The verse earned a smattering of applause. *There must be five, six men.* "I could sing more, but only in trade for more water rations to soothe my throat."

Octavia knew that voice. She bit her lip to swallow a gasp, her fingers immediately going to the small burn on her wrist where the man had counted coup.

"Lanskay, the infernal," she whispered, as low as she could.

"Wasters," Alonzo whispered to Kethan.

Of course it was Wasters. They possessed a settlement at the base of the Tree. It only made sense that they would investigate, especially with Caskentia's attack looming. A tunnel meant vulnerability. Anyone who read copper novels knew that—the heroes always infiltrated the castle through the sewer to take the enemy unaware.

Octavia, Alonzo, and Kethan might have an advantage of surprise, but she knew the Wasters were excellent marksmen. They didn't survive the wilderness otherwise. Her fingers tightened over the cloth of the parasol.

A white light suddenly emerged around a bend. Octavia cringed and looked away, retinas burning.

Alonzo shot first.

The Wasters cried out, feet scrambling on dirt. She could just detect the songs of their bodies. She glanced back. A large, round lantern, the sort used for nighttime airship landings, lay on the ground some fifty feet away. Its beam was aimed toward the far wall, granting gentle illumination. She could barely make out the gray movements of the men. A bullet pinged their way, then another, but not close.

"Let me," Octavia whispered, nudging Alonzo. *Miss Percival always used to say that some people got what they deserved. This is one of those times.*

He hesitated a second and passed the gun to her. She raised it and followed Lanskay's song, the sheer heat of him. He kept moving, likely whispering strategy with his men.

She fired. Lanskay cried out, his song rising in crescendo with fresh blood. "Fiddlesticks," she muttered. "I was a better shot as a child. Yet again, it's not a fatal blow to him, but at least he won't be able to shoot with that hand."

"Lanskay?" Alonzo asked.

"Yes." She could well imagine Alonzo's thoughts: that she had asked for the gun, willingly fired it, then regretted that the shot hadn't killed. "I remember what his men did to you before," she said in a small voice. *They burned you. I smelled the flesh of your arm, cooked as if on a campfire.* Her stomach twisted at the memory.

He could have whispered so many things. Reaffirmed that the Lady understood self-defense, that Octavia shouldn't do anything that made her feel guilty, that he would take care of her. Instead, his hand found her shoulder then fumbled to her cheek. His thumb brushed away a tear she hadn't realized was there.

"We're Dallowmen!" called Lanskay. He inhaled with a hiss—one of the other men was binding his hand, quieting his blood. "Hold your fire!"

Stalemate. Retreat was not an option, not this deep into the tunnel. "Even if we make it past them," Alonzo whispered, "they likely placed more guards at the entrance."

"We may even enter at their settlement," added the King.

Octavia ground her teeth together. "I've already been held captive by the Waste. I'm not keen on repeating the experience." They had wanted to use her to obliterate Mercia before. What would they do with her now?

The Wasters retreated beyond the beam of their fallen light. *They already know we must be enemy Caskentians since we didn't immediately hail them. We should have had the King speak up immediately.*

We still can.

"Grandfather," whispered Octavia. "You're unknown to them. Many settlers out here are from Caskentia. Your accent won't seem that strange."

"Hmm. Yes," said Alonzo. "Say you have been our captive, our guide into the Waste. You will be treated kindly by them."

"I have little concern for kindness right now," King Kethan said slowly. "I must journey to the Tree with Octavia, and before they know of my miasma."

"Our immediate concern is just escaping this tunnel alive," said Alonzo.

"Whatever being alive means in my case. Yes." King Kethan shifted in the darkness. "Help me! Help!" he cried, voice raspy.

Octavia felt the Wasters' songs shift in alarm, adrenaline spiking anew.

"Who goes there?" called Lanskay.

Alonzo scuffed his feet on the ground and King Kethan played along, with some grunts for good measure.

"They're coming closer," she whispered. "Lanskay will sense my magic soon."

"They made me guide . . . them!" cried King Kethan.

If Octavia had been able to hear her own song, she knew it would have radiated terror. *I escaped them once with the Lady's help. I will again. She wants me to get to the Tree. She'll do whatever she can so that I can continue.*

But Alonzo . . .

She fumbled to find his hand and twined her fingers through his. He stepped back, the heat of his body a blessing against the deep, cold darkness.

"Alonzo." She pressed her lips close to his ear. "I love you."

I love you, I love you, I love you.

"And I love you, my dear Miss Leander." He brought her knuckles to his lips. Her stomach twisted in a cozy knot. He loved her. It didn't come as a surprise, but hearing the words, feeling him so close to her, made the statement all the more agonizing and poignant. "Please do not do anything hasty or foolish."

"Me?" she whispered with a small gasp. "That goes for you, too. Don't lose a leg again."

"I will do my utmost to stay intact."

No time remained for sweet words. The full heat of Lanskay's power prickled her skin. Through the blackness, she heard the infernal's sharp hiss of breath. "The medician?" he asked.

That says a great deal about his power, for him to discern my identity in the darkness, at this distance. The scar he had left on her seemed to tingle through the layer of bark. "Didn't you know me by my aim?" she called. "I never seem to get a proper shot at you."

"Is the Tamaran with you as well?"

"I would hate to disappoint you," said Alonzo.

"We told you the way to the Tree was a difficult journey, but I suppose the Tree has made it easier for you, yes?" Lanskay chuckled. An odd tension rang in his voice. "I shouldn't be surprised to find you here, truly. You two could be of the Dallows, as tenacious as you are."

Alonzo gave Octavia's hand a final squeeze then let go. "We seek passage to the Tree."

"It isn't so simple as that. The name is Garret, if I recall? You cannot buy a ticket from me as if I am gatekeeper at an airship. We are at war again."

"We never stopped," said Octavia, sadness in her voice.

"Who is the Dallowman with you? Since Mr. Drury's medician is there, I trust this man's in good care?"

Mr. Drury's medician? A growl escaped her throat.

"I am unhurt," called King Kethan. "They have treated me well, other than forcing me through this darkness. My name is Mr. Everett."

The Wasters conferred in low murmurs. The people of the Dallows had peculiar notions of honor, and she hoped that her ploy with the King hadn't backfired. At this range, it would be very easy for Lanskay to cast fire in their direction, and if they had no care for the safety of Mr. Everett . . .

"We will escort you to our camp, where we will confer with Taney," said Lanskay. *The grand potentate is there. Of course.* "We ask, upon your honor, for your weapons. In turn, we will commit no abuses to you."

"Until we arrive in your camp," muttered Octavia.

He continued. "Miss Leander is to be treated as a highest daughter." The way he said her name made her skin prickle.

"Godspeed to us all." King Kethan's voice was a soft growl. "Granddaughter, we will find a way to continue together. Mr. Alonzo Garret, you are a Dagger in the truest sense and a credit to Caskentia. Majolico."

"Majolico," Alonzo whispered in turn.

That's the same word he used with Mrs. Stout to prove he was a Dagger, or at least one in training. It seems to bear more meaning than a mere code word.

There was no chance to inquire now. Wasters surrounded them. One of the men hauled the lantern closer. Alonzo handed over his Gadsden, two knives, and his pack. Lanskay offered him a curt nod of respect—the Wasters did not search for more weapons. The infernal's face split in a grin as he faced Octavia. He pressed a fist to his chest and bowed, his pale blond ponytail draped over his shoulder.

"Last I heard, you had vanished into the wilderness of the southern Pinnacles. Even I wouldn't wander in such a place at the edge of winter. It is good to see you survived." Sincerity warmed his voice.

"I won't lie and say I'm glad to see you. I suppose you

want to take my satchel again." She rubbed the strap be-tween her fingers. Frustration clogged her throat.

"Actually, no. Let's be honest. Holding your bag hos-tage did little to control you before. I doubt it would do so this time." He motioned to another man. "Run ahead. This old man Everett is barefoot and it's a long walk through this tunnel."

"I am not feeble," said King Kethan.

"I mean no disrespect." Lanskay bowed to him. "Even with my heat, I know this place is bitterly cold. It doesn't take long for a man to lose fingers and toes. Allow us to help. We've worn through shoes on our patrols, many times."

One of the men used a torn blanket and rope to wrap Kethan's feet. They resumed their walk. With a glare of challenge to the nearest men, Octavia worked to stand beside Alonzo. No one tried to touch her; in fact, they looked afraid.

It's not just that they are supposed to regard me as a high daughter. They've heard stories about what happened before. They know I grew another tree, that most of the guards were killed, that only their potentate and Lanskay survived. Lanskay even looks at me in a different way.

By now, she should have been accustomed to being feared, but that sad knot still twisted in her chest.

Lanskay walked with King Kethan. Octavia was a little worried that Kethan might misspeak, as ignorant as he was of recent history between Caskentia and the Waste, but soon enough his easy manner had Lanskay nodding and chuckling.

More sounds echoed up the tunnel. It took several more miles of walking to discover the source of the noise—a makeshift cabriolet mounted on chain-wrapped wheels.

Lady, keep Alonzo safe. Don't let anything happen to him, please. Losing him will not make me cooperative.

Lanskay bent close to the driver, a man in a full leather cap and goggles, and they conferred for a moment. Lanskay looked to his compatriots. "No attack has taken place yet, but more of our men have arrived." That earned a few grunts of approval from the Wasters. He gave Octavia an odd look. "I'll be escorting you back to camp."

The driver sat in a separate compartment, leaving the four of them to squeeze into the cab. Rust bled along the metal seams in the door; she hoped the trip was not too long, or the King would rot the cabriolet out from beneath them. The windows were boarded up like a Caskentian tram, which only added to the feeling of claustrophobia. Several glowstone lights had been mounted in the ceiling. Their legs tangled together in the narrow floor space just as their songs collided in Octavia's mind, as disparate as they were: Alonzo, his brass marching band exhausted but as resilient as ever; King Kethan, his chaotic rhythm consistent; Lanskay, his music heated like his skin and his touch, a rhythm suited for an inappropriate, intimate dance. The wound to his hand pained him, but he remained stoic and didn't request a healing.

The vehicle made a tight turn, tilting her into the window, then rolled onward. The engine noise was soothing, though the roughness of the tunnel floor translated into constant, vicious jolts and bumps. Alonzo and Lanskay cursed in synchrony as their heads smacked into the metal ceiling. They continued in silence for a long time.

"It won't take long now," Lanskay yelled to be heard.

Octavia could have laughed at how relieved that made her feel—relieved to soon be in a Waster camp. Anything would be better than this tunnel.

"What is the word on Caskentia's movements?" asked Alonzo.

Lanskay raised a pale brow. "It would seem more appropriate to question you on that issue, but then, the Queen's agents sought to kill the medician, so I suppose you're not friends of the green soldiers now." He shrugged. "We have shot down four airships thus far, but expect a full force by air within the next two days, before winter sets in."

"'Tis a gamble to fly over the pass any season of the year," murmured Alonzo.

"Ah, but they cannot abide the thought of an icon like the Tree in our possession. They'll throw everything they can at us, even if it's dung. The army will have special sustenance, though. A few weeks ago, Mr. Drury signed a sizable contract with the Caskentian army. We're to supply them with Royal-Tea. Isn't that amusing?"

"I find nothing amusing about using the Lady's bark in that way. She's not a business venture or a joke." *If he had the audacity to use me, my bark, in that way . . . oh Lady. No. I won't think of myself like that.*

"I still wonder about what you did before, summoning that tree, using Royal-Tea to create vines. It was most remarkable." Awe softened Lanskay's voice as he saluted her with his wrapped fist.

She had no response.

"The driver had other news as well," he continued. "Word that a friend of yours is in camp. I will speak with Taney to arrange a meeting."

Panicked, she looked at Alonzo. His face was unreadable. "A friend? You can't have captured Mrs. Stout." *Please, no. Let Mrs. Stout be safe with her daughter in Tamarania, let her be there to show Rivka all the love she deserves.*

King Kethan's song shifted, anxious.

"Ah, Mrs. Stout. No. This is not Mrs. Stout, though we hope to see her again."

Who else could it be?

"Mr. Lanskay," said Alonzo, ice in his voice. "I do believe you said you would not commit any abuses during our transit. Baiting Miss Leander could be considered such."

"Yes. Yes, I suppose so. I'm sorry, Miss Leander. I meant no offense." To her surprise, his apology sounded genuine, even emotional. Lanskay looked at Alonzo. "You're forthright and honorable, unusual for a Caskentian. You earned your burns before, even if she likely healed them once you made your escape."

They still don't know Alonzo is—was—a Clockwork Dagger. Nor did they see that Mr. Drury shot him in the head and killed him.

"Answer me this, though," continued Lanskay. "I know my friend Mr. Drury must be dead. Which one of you committed the deed?"

Octavia and Alonzo looked at each other. Alonzo opened his lips, but she spoke first. "I did, in my own defense." She met Lanskay's gaze and waited in dread for his reaction. Alonzo's song ticked faster as he readied himself to react.

No anger drummed in Lanskay's already rapid heartbeat. "I'm not surprised. He respected you a great deal, Miss Leander. If he was going to die, he would have preferred it to be at your hand."

She was wordless with revulsion. Octavia stared to one side as if she could see out the window. Lanskay's tone was strangely reverential. He hadn't treated her like this before; with a twisted sort of respect, yes, but not this . . . worship.

Even though the vines I created almost killed him, it's as if the whole incident has caused him to favor the Lady.

The cabriolet's wheels struggled as they began a slow, steady incline with switchbacks that sent her sliding between the door and Alonzo.

Suddenly light seeped around the outline of the door. Light. She touched a sunbeam, amazed at the sight after so long underground. *We walked the full night through.*

The terrain evened beneath their wheels. Just as Octavia was certain she could have closed her eyes and slept, the songs of bodies flared beyond the walls of the car. Hundreds, thousands. A town's worth. Out of habit, she reached to check her headband, belatedly remembering that it was lost somewhere in the pass. Whimpering, she covered her ears with her hands, but that did nothing. The cacophony blared, louder than it had ever been before, even in Tamarania and Mercia. Men. Soldiers, their bodies bearing the evidence of battles between Caskentia and the Dallows. *Amputations, deafness, burns, syphilis, headaches, a thousand other ailments, dozens together in some bodies.*

"Is she sick?" asked Lanskay, leaning toward her. The magic of him boiled on her skin, his song like a trumpet played inches from her ear.

"The Tree. I must be so close that . . ." Her voice trailed off into a whimper.

"Miss Leander." Alonzo leaned closer. His music soothed her, as always, even as it threatened to drown her.

"I need to get indoors. Away from people. In my circle." Each utterance of her name was a jab.

"This, we can do." Lanskay opened the door.

Noise poured in like a tidal wave, her name floating throughout like flotsam. "Miss Leander. "The medician." "The one who made the tree . . ." "Her, the one who . . ." "She's a trained Percival?" Octavia's vision dwindled to fuzzy colors.

It's not simply their bodies. It's their attention. Is this what it's like when the Lady is deluged with prayers? She suddenly understood what it truly meant to use holy names in vain.

"No. Let me. Separate us after, if you must, but permit me this." Alonzo's voice sounded as if it echoed down a tunnel. *A tunnel . . . I thought we escaped it.*

Alonzo's presence wrapped around her. His song, his very heartbeat, pressed against her ear. She wanted to argue at the indignity of being carried like a babe but could not. It was all she could do to stay conscious beneath the barrage.

"I have you," Alonzo murmured.

"This way!" Lanskay called across a great distance, his tone almost panicked.

There was more brightness than in the tunnel, but she still had a sense of being beneath deep cloud cover and shade. Bodies blurred around her, as did walls made of logs weathered to a cozy brown. The noise dimmed but lingered close, her name, her identity, flicked across a hundred tongues. Something soft against her back—was she in Mrs. Garret's house again, in Mercia? Just pulled from that crate? No—that place was painted in crisp white, not made of logs.

"I am taking your satchel off your shoulder," Alonzo said, bending her enough to lift the strap over her head.

"What else can I do?" Lanskay's words were a rush. "Water? Food? Anything?"

"I do not know. Miss Leander, I am going to set you in the circle."

She hadn't even touched the blanket when the heat of the Lady's awareness flared across her skin. Alonzo jerked back with a cry—not of pain, but of surprise. Octavia caught herself on her hands. The boundaries of the circle crackled and drowned out the noise from beyond. The flood withdrew. She suddenly became aware of her loud, desperate breaths, as if she really had almost drowned. Sweat soaked her robes through, even as the cloth absorbed it.

"I'm going to get help." Lanskay's radiant heat faded.

"Octavia." Her head jerked up at her name. Alonzo crouched at the edge of her maimed blanket. The concern on his face made her want to cry. "What is happening?"

Something I can stop. That I must stop. "I have to get to the Tree as soon as possible. You . . . you can't come. You'll be safer here."

"Safer? That makes no sense."

"Whatever happens, Alonzo, know that I love you, and I love Caskentia, too."

"Mr. Garret." A Waster stood in the doorway, his song new and so very young. "Please come with me. The women will need privacy." *Women?*

Alonzo stared at her, agony in his blue eyes. Octavia reached across the barrier. His hand clenched hers as if they were about to be pulled into a tornado. *I'd kiss him, but if my head goes beyond the circle, I'll go senseless again.*

He let go, reluctantly, but his gaze stayed on her as he backed up to the door.

"When all this is done, I will find you a cottage with an atelier and garden, just as you hoped for in Delford. I promise." With that, he left.

Oh, Alonzo.

Octavia closed her eyes as she folded into a meditative Al Cala position, just as she had done a decade ago beneath Miss Percival's desk. Those days when the nightmares of fire were too much, the isolation of the other girls a burn of a whole different kind. Such comfort there, simply being in the presence of Miss Percival as she scribbled away on her desk above.

Even at age twelve, she had heard the soft notes of Miss Percival's song. It always reminded her of being in the quiet of the woods—flutes like birdsong, the rhythmic rattle of branches, the light whistle of a breeze. However, in recent months it had been racked by anxiety; the birds had sounded as if their hatchlings had fallen from the nest, and the trees rattled as if broken by storms.

Tears squeezed from her eyes. Tired as she was, it took her a moment to realize the song was not solely in her memory.

Octavia raised her head. "Miss Percival."

CHAPTER 18

Until the recent financial duress of the academy, Miss Percival had always been one of those women who aged with particular grace, her hair silver and straight, her face endowed with gentle creases. Now the only gentleness resided in her tear-filled eyes. Hard lines traced her mouth, while heavy bags lay like pillows beneath her eyes. She knelt a few feet outside of the medician blanket. Octavia knew by Miss Percival's song that she was physically unhurt, though exhausted and strained. Not like those traits were anything new.

"Miss Leander."

"You sold me!" Rage flushed Octavia's face. "You sold both me and Mrs. Stout to the Waste. The Waste!"

Miss Percival flinched as if she'd been slapped. "I had no choice."

"Yes, because you had to save the academy." Octavia rocked back on her folded legs, trying to contain the urge to scream senselessly. "I understand that. I wouldn't want the other girls to be homeless or without herbs. But how you did it . . . and to Mrs. Stout . . ."

"I was told you both escaped?"

"Does that disappoint you?"

"No. No. I'm glad. Viola . . . She was always resilient."

"Resilience only goes so far when you're handed over to men who want to use you to undermine and destroy both Mercia and Caskentia, and likely kill you if you don't cooperate. Not to mention what Caskentia would do if they knew certain privy details."

"So you know who she is." Her voice was a whisper.

"Yes. I know. I know far too much."

"The Wasters were going to kidnap you regardless of whether or not I helped. By cooperating, I gained enough to make the academy solvent, buy herbs, and establish savings."

"I'm sure you negotiated for a good sale. Maybe you even clipped a coupon from an advert."

"Oh, Miss Leander. You have no idea how hard it was to say farewell to you, knowing what I did."

Octavia's throat felt so tight she could scarcely breathe. "Hard for you? What about these past few months, ever since the zyme poisoning? Since then, when you've looked at me at all, it's been with coldness, your tongue sharp about whatever I did. Even the other girls were surprised and wondering, and they didn't even like me before . . . before I heard the zymes."

"You want me to say I was jealous?" That now-familiar hardness returned to Miss Percival's voice. "Very well. I was jealous. But that's not why I sold you, that was all—"

"To save the academy? That justifies things nicely.

Never mind that the Wasters wanted me to keep their infernals alive past the wards on the Giant, all so they could awaken the volcano and obliterate Mercia. Yes, all good and well to save and clothe ten girls by killing half a million people."

Miss Percival's caramel skin blanched. "Awaken the Giant to destroy Mercia?"

"What, you thought they would simply resume the war again, kill people the slow and inefficient way? You're here. They probably intended for you to go to the Giant in my stead."

Miss Percival stared at her knotted hands in her lap as her mouth opened and closed several times without uttering a sound. She wore full Percival medician gear, her robe and apron sparkling. No headband, though—Miss Percival had always preferred to wear a full cap to cover the bun atop her head. As her satchel was missing, Octavia imagined that the Wasters had it in their possession. Miss Percival wouldn't have relinquished it willingly.

"They returned to the academy a week and a half ago." Words finally emerged in a murmur. "I feared that they had come to take back their money, but they said no. I had upheld my part of the bargain with honor. However, they said they still needed a medician, with you gone. I . . . I left the academy in Sasha's care." Sasha, being twenty and most senior now that Octavia was gone.

They took you because you were next best. Octavia didn't need to say the cruel words out loud. Miss Percival knew.

"We arrived in Mercia and discovered the Caskentian military was assembling. The Tree was visible. This changed whatever plan they intended." She swallowed. "We couldn't take the passes, so it took us a week to get here."

"You arrived this morning."

"Yes."

"Have you seen the Tree?"

Tears filled Miss Percival's eyes. "Yes. It's . . . how did you not? Are you blind?"

The latter was said with the concern of a medician for a patient. Octavia didn't want Miss Percival's sympathy. It made it harder to stay angry. Right now, though, there were matters more important than wounded feelings. "Have you ever heard of a medician's abilities getting stronger in a short amount of time?"

Miss Percival looked strangely composed. "Stronger, how?"

"Body songs getting louder. More specific, more intimate. The medician doing more . . . things a medician shouldn't be able to do."

"Yes."

Octavia's gaze jerked up. "You have?"

"Has your skin changed as well?"

"Yes," she whispered. "How—"

Miss Percival was quiet for a minute. "When I was a girl, my headmistress went through something similar. If a body was in a circle, the sound was overwhelming for her. Her circles themselves became more solid and binding. Mind you, she was never as strong as you, but it was still a notable difference. At the same time, a strange, rippled growth appeared on her arms, like the bark of a tree."

Octavia leaned forward. The electric essence of the circle sparked against the tip of her nose. "What happened? Wasn't she headmistress for some thirty years?"

"Yes. This was early on. I was only ten. She had strange dreams and visions of the Tree that pointed her toward Mercia. They persisted for several weeks along with the other symptoms, so eventually she listened. I traveled with her."

The age of ten. Mercia. The visit King Kethan spoke of. Octavia bit her lip and nodded for Miss Percival to continue.

"We had an audience with King Kethan. To be in the presence of that man . . ." Awe softened her voice. "My headmistress told him of her dreams, that we had been guided to the palace for some purpose, some need at the palace. He politely told us he had no idea what that might be. We stayed a few more days but couldn't get another audience. Finally, we gave up. We didn't know we left the city at the same time as the Waster kidnappers."

"You found the princess."

"Yes. Dying. I was so young. Such a child, but I fought to save her. We didn't realize who she was for several days. Viola . . . Allendia . . . she was so terrified. She knew there were traitors in the palace. We had no safe way to get word to the King, and Viola was fragile, so we waited."

"What about the visions? The growth of bark?"

Miss Percival hugged her arms tight against her torso. "The symptoms slowly grew over the next few months. We planned to return to Mercia with Viola. With her, we could surely find out what the Lady wanted. I . . . I actually knew more than my mentor by that time. Mrs. Stout had told me a secret about the palace, about the Lady."

"The vault," Octavia whispered.

Miss Percival's eyes widened. "You . . . how do you know?

"I told you, I know many things. Go on."

"Yes. The royal vault. I was certain we were being pulled to the pieces of the Lady there. Then, one day Miss Percival's skin began to heal, her circles returned to the way they had once been. A few days after that, we heard news from Mercia about the firebombing."

"When you made this deal to sell us to the Waste, you told them the secret about Mrs. Stout's identity, but nothing about the vault. Why?"

"All these years, rumors said that the royal vault was impossible to open. Whether that was true or not, it seemed to me that the items inside must have been destroyed. That's why the symptoms went away. There was no point in telling the Waste about something that no longer existed."

In truth, the seed had been used on King Kethan. Maybe the Lady was at a loss about what to do, how to get it back, until now. Until her power began to fail completely.

King Kethan's words came back to her—a world without the Lady's healing power, of full reliance on the science of doctoring. Octavia shivered. "I need to get to the Tree, but . . . you know how I've always heard songs, even without a circle?" At that, Miss Percival nodded, her expression thoughtful. "Now I hear everything as a scream. I know everything. I know the location of every chancre. I had added an enchantment to my headband—"

"Wise, since it was already steeped in medician magic," Miss Percival murmured. *As if approving of my performance in a lesson in class.*

"But it's now lost and the people out there . . . I hear them, I *know* them." Octavia gulped. "The circle is keeping me sheltered and sane."

"There are likely two thousand people out there, more arriving as they prepare to make a stand. The Tree must be calling you, as my Miss Percival was once called to Mercia."

As I was called to Mercia's vault, too. "Yes."

The two women regarded each other. Octavia wondered what Miss Percival thought would happen at the Tree—if it was obvious to her what the skin of bark really meant. If so, she didn't show any sign.

"May I look inside your satchel?" Miss Percival asked.

Octavia frowned. "Yes?"

The satchel was still on the bed, the top left gaping after Alonzo had rushed to pull out the medician blanket. Miss Percival rummaged a bit, but it was mostly empty with the blanket out and most of their survival supplies depleted. "Here we are." She unfolded the surgical kit. "Your scissors are missing?"

"They're in my pocket."

"Hand them here, please, Miss Leander."

Scowling yet curious, Octavia pushed her scissors across the woven circle. Miss Percival sat. Pulling up the hem of her dress, she began to cut.

"What? Miss Percival, you—"

"Someone obviously cut your medician blanket—I recognize your stitch work in the mending. Yet it never occurred to you that you had more magicked fabric of your own, did it? Your mind gets stuck like that sometimes." It was said gently, words punctuated by the snips of scissors.

Octavia was of half a mind to refuse the fabric when it was pushed her way along with the scissors. She could cut her own dress, after all. Frustration tightened her throat as she thought of all the petty words she could toss Miss Percival's way. *"This doesn't mean I forgive you." "I suppose there's no point in letting this go to waste."* Or to say nothing at all, just glare.

None of those would make her feel better or mend the rift between them.

"Thank you," she said softly.

"I know it's nothing. It doesn't make me feel any less guilty."

For that, Octavia had no words. She took the fabric, put it on her lap, and opened her mind to the Lady as she had in Tamarania. It was no surprise that the Lady was very much *there*. A minute later, she tied the cloth to cover her ears, the knot at her nape. Taking a steadying breath, she tapped the edge of the circle.

"Thank you, Lady, for extending your branches." The heat crackled and faded away.

"You make it look easy, the way you ask it of her, the way she responds," whispered Miss Percival. Yearning twisted her voice.

"Is this easy?" Octavia snapped. She yanked down the high collar of her uniform to show the itchy skin beneath. Miss Percival gasped, both hands to her mouth. The reaction sent a wave of fear and nausea through Octavia and made her all the more glad she hadn't pried off a glove to see the change with her own eyes.

"I'm sorry. Oh, Octavia, I'm so sorry."

"Don't be so informal, Miss Percival. All these years, and we're truly strangers."

A soft knock shuddered through the door. "Miss Percival?" asked Lanskay as the door slowly opened. The bullet wound to his hand still pained him, though it had been cleaned and wrapped anew. "Were you able to help her?" His worried gaze scanned Octavia as if for an injury.

"Lanskay, please don't tell me that you've become infatuated with me as Mr. Drury was." The songs of six other men lurked in the hallway beyond, Taney and Alonzo included. *Curious that they keep Alonzo out of sight. I wonder what game they play.* Octavia folded her blanket and tucked it away. The scissors went back in her pocket.

The infernal fully stepped inside the room. He looked relieved and somewhat bashful. "No! My wife wouldn't take well to that. My concern is out of respect for you."

"Yes. Which is why you said I had a *friend* waiting for me here. You were there when Taney told me that Miss Percival sold me. You know how she betrayed me and how that hurt."

Miss Percival faced away, her shoulders braced.

Lanskay looked around as if he had walked into the wrong room. "I . . . er."

"As direct as ever, medician." Grand potentate Reginald Taney entered, one arm extended to push back Lanskay. "Lanskay's respect for you is real, as is mine." With that, he faced her with a fist to his chest as he bowed. "You should be honored by the thought and attention Lanskay has given to the wonders you wrought when we last met. He's on his way to becoming a scholar on the Lady and the Tree."

Taney had the persuasive cadence of a master orator, a kind of magic in his presence that earned attention and respect. Thick black muttonchops framed his jaw, the growth strange against his extreme youth. Taney couldn't be past his midteens. He'd been born into war, the same as Octavia. He wore a suit jacket over a bleached-white shirt and tan dungarees, garb similar to his fellow Wasters. A broadsword strapped to his back looked incongruous. She recalled seeing it during their last meeting, and guessed it held some symbolic meaning related to his being a potentate.

Three soldiers followed him in, Alonzo between them. His song rang of sound health. He looked at her, relief palpable in his face, and then to Miss Percival in her gear. His eyes narrowed. *He knows who she is.*

Octavia closed her bag and looped the strap over her head again. She bit back a groan at the severe ache in her shoulder. No time for pampria now. "The feeling isn't mutual. I'm sure Lanskay told you why we've returned for a brief visit."

"A visit, yes. To think, I bargained with you using a trip here as the reward, and you managed it on your own. It does seem that your Lady helped, becoming visible with such interesting timing."

"The Tree certainly isn't helping your cause. Maybe you should rethink harvesting her like a field of wheat."

"Wheat can be temperamental. The Lady's Tree is being temperamental, too. Like a typical woman." He snorted. *As if he knows anything about women, at his age.* "Medician, I want to know how you make trees appear."

"What?" asked Octavia.

Taney's gaze on her was even. "We know you have a strong relationship with the Lady. You made a tree appear before. Now the full Tree has become visible here. I want you to make it disappear again."

She couldn't help it. She burst out laughing. "You think I can control the Tree and make her appear and disappear like the ghostlings in children's puppet theater? Really?"

Taney scowled. The other men looked at one another, clearly unsettled. *Most people have more sense than to laugh at Taney, I'm sure.* Octavia sobered. She needed to act with more sense as well if she was going to finagle her way to the Tree and keep Alonzo safe.

"The timing on this cannot be an accident," said Taney.

She could play along with this. "No, it's not. It's visible now so that I can find it. I'm supposed to go directly to the Lady."

"Why?"

Why indeed. She knew if she looked at Alonzo at that moment, she would burst into tears. *We would have my cot-*

tage and garden. We would. Octavia swallowed down her grief for the future that might have been.

"I don't know. Dreams guided me here, and they told me to bring along the man we traveled with, Mr. Everett." Disturbing, how practice made it so much easier to lie.

Lanskay shook his head. "You'll find that a challenge. Men don't enter the woods beneath the canopy. Well, they do. They just don't leave."

"The threems." Miss Percival spoke up for the first time. "They guard the Tree, as it's said in the tales? Passage is only granted to the innocent."

Octavia nodded. "Which is why the Wasters—pardon me, Dallowmen—have been kidnapping teenage girls from Mercia to harvest the Lady's bark to make Royal-Tea."

Miss Percival faced Octavia, mouth gaping in horror. "Her bark? Used for that advertised *tea*?"

"Unfortunately, Mercian girls are not that innocent. Many have vanished into the woods." Taney's bare lips curled in disgust. "Our daughters are more pure, but we'd rather spare them the dangers of the trek here."

Octavia sighed. Taney, yet again, had no comprehension that morality, innocence, and virginity were not all one and the same, nor an exclusive trait of young girls. "All I know is that I am supposed to bring Mr. Everett. If the Tree wants him, I'm sure the way will be clear."

She could sense Alonzo trying to catch her eye. He wanted to be included in the mission, as part of this dream. She wanted him to come—to be her rock, her source of humor, her distraction—but more than that, she wanted him to live. *Wyrms haven't attacked this settlement. He'll be safer here.*

"What else will come of this?" asked Taney. He stroked at his muttonchops.

"If the Tree becomes invisible again, you just might avoid obliteration. That could be seen as a perk."

"Caskentia has mapped the Tree's location and that of our camp, medician," said Taney. "It was never seen from the air before, but they could still land and launch an invasion, even if it hides."

The Tree hid for centuries. A new Tree would likely be able to hide fully as well, and for a long time. Not that they need to know that.

Lanskay inclined his head. "A ground war is far preferable to airships with payloads of flaming oil, complemented by a Caskentian infernal on high." *The voice of experience. How many such drops has he done on Caskentia?* She stared at him with open disgust.

"Miss Percival." Taney faced her. "Since our other plans for you must wait, I will have you work in our wards. I trust that Miss Leander here has recovered from the episode she experienced upon arrival?"

"Yes. Will my satchel be returned to me?" The hardness in Miss Percival's posture reminded Octavia of herself. *Well, I had to learn it somewhere.*

"To heal my men, yes." Taney turned to Alonzo. "There is still the question of what to do with you."

"Don't you dare torture him again." Octavia's voice shook.

Alonzo remained utterly cool in the face of this threat; his song showed his inner distress.

"Lanskay tells me this Mr. Garret acted with full honor in the wyrm's tunnel. He has also kept you alive through recent events."

Alonzo opened his lips, but Miss Percival's voice rose first. "Knowing Miss Leander, she can manage quite well in keeping herself alive without full reliance on any man."

Octavia felt an odd twinge of joy. That sounded like the old Miss Percival, the one who taught her that childbirth alone was proof that women were not the weaker of the species.

"Our survival was an effort of teamwork," said Octavia. "I don't want any harm to come to Mr. Garret."

Miss Percival pressed her lips together, one eyebrow arched. There was a question in her eyes—*who is this man whom you so obviously care about?*

"Then keep that in mind while you go to see your Tree. If the Tree can still be seen by air at sunset, each half hour of the night and morning, he will burn. Twenty units of prairie justice." Taney clasped his hands at his back and smiled at Octavia. Behind him, Lanskay looked outright appalled for a split second and then shifted to a mask of stoicism.

Octavia wavered on her feet. *Twenty units of prairie justice.* She had treated men who had endured such torture. Each toe, each finger, burned from the tip down until it was cauterized at the base. Medicians could do nothing to restore the lost extremities. Even worse, the manner of destruction made it impossible to attach mechanical replacements unless the remaining hand or foot was amputated as well.

Mr. Drury must have thought so little of Alonzo that he never told his superiors about how the man had only one leg. Not that fifteen units was a vast improvement.

Miss Percival shot Octavia a clear look of concern. *She always did her utmost to assign the burn cases to other girls, even in more recent months.*

"Is that realistic?" asked Octavia, her voice hoarse. "How far is it to the Tree? There's the forest at the roots . . ."

"We are in the forest now. It's about three miles to the trunk. We'll supply our best horses and equipment." At Taney's nod, a man in the doorway left.

King Kethan and horses. How will this work? "It's winter. Daylight is short. We need to get going. Can I speak to Mr. Garret briefly?"

Taney frowned and looked between them. "Yes, but with Lanskay present. Miss Percival, walk with me. I have some urgent cases to bring to your attention."

"Of course," Miss Percival murmured. "Miss Leander . . . I hope I see you later, but if I don't . . ."

"I'm sure you'll see me, one way or another." *Maybe in your Al Cala.*

Miss Percival's expression was troubled as she left. The other men followed, leaving Octavia with Alonzo and Lanskay.

"Well," said Alonzo.

"We survived the tunnel," said Octavia, her voice forcefully upbeat.

"We did. We cannot say we lazed about today."

"Goodness no. You know me. I can't abide laziness. Always busy-busy."

"For God's sake, get on with it," said Lanskay. He walked to the doorway and stared into the hall, his long pale ponytail dangling down his back.

Now that they had a modicum of privacy, she stared down at her boots. The leather at the toe appeared whitened and worn, the preservation enchantment obviously tested by Kethan's presence. The skin of her feet itched.

Alonzo cleared his throat. Octavia glanced at him, a lump in her throat and her eyes burning. He studied her as if for the last time, icy-blue eyes appraising her and reminding her of that brief moment they shared back in Tamarania.

"Alonzo, if I don't make it back—"

"Do not dare speak in such a way."

"I will, and you'll listen." She took a breath to force away a sob. "Thank you for everything. I wouldn't have wished these past few weeks on anyone, but if I had to go through this, I'm glad I was with you."

"Octavia." Her heart and senses lurched at the sound of her name. Alonzo leaned forward. As their lips touched, her awareness of the outer world dimmed. She felt her consciousness begin to drop into the ocean of his body, and she fought back. Teeth grinding, will resolute, she mentally clawed her way to full awareness of the physical sensation of his kiss: the softness and strength of his lips, the coarseness of his mustache and beard, the tenderness of his fingers at her neck as he drew her in. Beneath it all, she knew the rapidness of his heart, the flow of his blood, the way the yearning of his soul translated into his rapid breaths.

Lanskay cleared his throat.

She and Alonzo stared at each other as they pulled away. She clutched at him, desperately, her gloved fingers so small next to his.

"If I lose any toes or fingers, worry not. I will return to Kellar Dryn when this is done." He tried to make it sound as if this was no big deal, like he could dash down to the market to buy more bread if they ran out.

"I like your body parts. I'd prefer you to keep them as flesh. Not that I have anything against your mechanical leg."

"'Tis my preference to retain flesh as well."

"In the interest of your digits, I need to go."

"Take care of yourself foremost. Please give my best to Mr. Everett, and my regrets that we met in such poor circumstances."

"I will."

With that, she walked away. Blinded by tears, she had taken several steps into the hallway before she realized she had no idea where she was going. Lanskay's magic crackled against her skin as he joined her. Behind her, she sensed several other guards with Alonzo as they headed the other way.

"How do you stand it?" she asked him. She held up her arm to motion to where he had scarred her. "To burn people. To torture them."

"It's my duty as a man of the Dallows. We need the curse on our land undone, to live in autonomy. This skill with fire, it is something I do. A job." His voice lowered. "I do not relish the idea of torturing him later. You're both favored by the Lady's Tree. I hope you succeed."

"A job. Burning people alive. I watched you kill one of

your own men, the one who made a lewd comment to me."

In the corner of her eye, she caught the motion of him pressing a fist to his chest. *He salutes the very man he killed.* "Yes. Sometimes it's necessary, but all for the sake of the greater cause. Our freedom. A return to a normal life."

"A normal life, a life without war. What does that even mean for any of us?"

"We must all dream of something that comes after peace, yes? After a true armistice? For me, it would mean a return to my homestead, and to teach children's choir." Lanskay stared into the distance, a smile stretching the severe lines of his cheekbones.

"Maybe you'll see that day," she murmured.

"I have one favor to ask of you."

Her eyes narrowed. "What?"

"When you return, if you see the Lady, you will tell me what she's like?" He cleared his throat as if embarrassed. "I've seen the Tree itself for years now. I came to take it for granted, in truth. But when I saw what you created before . . . if anyone can see the actual Lady, it will be you."

Octavia stared at him. *Lanskay makes it sound like he's a new convert.* In the past, the revelation that any nonmedician had an interest in the Lady would have delighted her. Now, with her own faith broken, she knew emptiness.

Another sort of emptiness rang in her senses as well. With a pang, she realized she was out of range to hear Alonzo's song.

CHAPTER 19

As she stepped outside, Octavia understood why the world seemed so dark when she left the tunnel-rigged cabriolet. The settlement lay in the deep shadow of the Lady's Tree.

The trunk may have been a few miles away, but it was also miles wide. Past the canopies of normal trees, the Lady's trunk was a rippled wall of green and brown and the impenetrable black of nooks and crannies that never saw the sun. Her lowest branches were well above the normal woods. Specks of birds hovered like ground pepper. Octavia craned her neck. All she could see was green. All she could smell was green—that lush freshness that made her think of verdant early-spring mornings when the tulips and weeds shoved their way through the wet soil.

The Tree. She saw the Tree.

Despite her anger, despite her wavering faith, Octavia dropped to her knees and into a folded Al Cala pose. The sobs she had held in check now gushed out, racking her chest, contracting her entire body.

This was the Lady she had seen so many times when she closed her eyes. This was the breeze that had somehow stirred in her bedroom and dried her tears for so many years.

"Miss Leander?" Lanskay cleared his throat.

"I know. I know." Octavia pushed herself upright. To think, two weeks ago she had been awed to simply hold a green branch the size of her arm. *Lady, you are beautiful.* In answer, that familiar breeze touched her cheek, gentle as her mother's sleeve once was.

Voices and songs buzzed around her. The new headband did its duty as she followed Lanskay along a well-tamped dirt street flanked by wooden boardwalks. The settlement was a full-fledged town several blocks in length, the weathered buildings all logs and shingles. Somewhere beyond, though, was an even greater aggregation of bodies. Without even seeing it, she knew the army encamped there to defend their stake in the Tree.

No mooring towers in sight; they would have been useless while the Tree was veiled. Taney will have his ships pestering Caskentia and trying to slow its army down, but I see his urgency in hiding this camp again. If Caskentia manages to get airships with infernals overhead, this place will be like a black cat in a snowbank. It'll be a massacre . . . but one with positive aspects as well.

Caskentia could win the war at last—and Mercia no longer contains its cursed king. We may have a chance to blossom again.

But there would still need to be a Tree to continue healing the land.

Like pinpricks, she felt the attention of Wasters, the repetitions of her name. Men bustled all around—rangy soldiers with hardened eyes like feral dogs, boys hauling packs, wagon after wagon of supplies and machinery.

A high, frenzied neigh cut above the noise of battle preparations. She followed Lanskay across the street.

King Kethan stood at a corral. He wore new clothes like that of any Waster, plus boots and a frayed-rim bowler hat. He'd even been provided with a new tie for his long hair. The horses in the corral reacted as if to a mountain lion—they crowded at the far side, the lead mare braying a challenge.

"Grandfather," Octavia said, catching Lanskay looking at her askance.

Kethan faced her with a strained smile. "I fear our manner of transport will be problematic."

"Not if I can help it. Lanskay, where are our horses?"

"Over there. A man's bringing them around."

She assessed them with her eyes and senses together and nodded approval. Wasters knew their horses. The legs were sound, feed adequate, hooves trimmed and shod. As they neared the King, the horses' nostrils flared.

Alonzo's not going to lose so much as his little toe. Not if I can help it.

"Stop there," Octavia said. She approached, a hand extended for the reins. The Waster looked at Lanskay for approval and then backed away. "Shh, shh. Listen to me." She leaned close between the horses. They immediately calmed, ears perked.

She had healed most all kinds of animals before. At the academy, some days were more about livestock than people. The difficulty was that animals, like people, had to acquiesce to a healing—at some level, they had to understand.

It didn't always happen. Octavia didn't need a healing now, but she did need understanding. If she encircled both horses with honeyflower, it would strengthen her insight, but she had neither the herbs nor the time.

But they were in the shadow of the Lady, and Octavia possessed power of her own.

"Lanskay, what are these horses' names?"

"Names?"

"Yes. Names."

He conferred with the grooms. "Doxy and Chocolate."

Names possess power. She knew that, as she flinched at the men's whispers. "Lady, here in your shadow, with this change in my blood, hear me," Octavia murmured. Heat prickled against her skin as if she had initiated the forming of a circle. The men felt something, too. Boots scuffed as they backed away.

"Doxy." The bay with a white snip on her muzzle perked up her ears. "We will travel with a man who smells like death. He is a good man. Let him ride you." The horse's black eyes stared into Octavia.

"Chocolate." Despite everything, the name made Octavia smile. "You will be mine. The man's smell will bother you, as it should, but don't let him scare you away." Chocolate whickered and rubbed his face against her arm, as if pleading for a lump of sugar.

"Thank you," Octavia murmured. Like that, the heat faded. She realized, then, how quiet it was. She turned. All the activity in the street had stopped. No one stood within twenty feet of her—no one but King Kethan, Doxy, Chocolate, and the small herd of horses that now lined the corral to stare. Several of the Wasters held their shotguns slack in their grips.

"Um. What?" she asked, glancing around to see if she'd missed something.

King Kethan approached, his steps slow, a hand held out toward the horses. "You glowed."

Like Adana Dryn. Like the Saint's Road. She looked at her arms and saw the same white cloth as always. "Am I still glowing?"

"No. It ceased."

"That might have actually come in handy in the tunnel." She laughed, the sound edging on hysterical. The pitch of her voice seemed to alarm the horses more than Kethan's presence.

Lanskay edged forward, his motions tentative as if he might drop to his knees before her. "The saddlebags are packed with enough food and water for the day."

"Understood." *We won't try to escape.*

"I hope to see you by nightfall." He grimaced and stepped back.

She and Kethan mounted up. The horses were nervous, sidestepping with twitching ears. Octavia pressed Chocolate to a trot as they headed out to the street. She couldn't help but note King Kethan's smile and the strange calmness in his song. He was riding a true horse, and his joy seeped to his very soul.

I love to ride horses, too. The rhythm, the breeze in my face, that sense of flight over the ground. So many things I've taken for granted, as part of being human.

The traffic was still at a stop as men stared after them. She flinched at the distant mentions of her name, her identity, the words striking her like flicked beans.

Someone will ask Alonzo what I did, how I did it. If I make it back, he'll demand answers, too.

Actually, he'll demand even more answers if I don't return. And I'll likely hear every query.

A thin belt of green meadow separated the settlement from the thick woods. The road dead-ended there, dwindling to a mere footpath. Octavia took the lead. Shrubs and vines towered above her. The smell was intense, as if she could chew the greenery in the air. Birds sang and rattled in the branches above.

Chocolate's ears flicked, his coat shivering as if he was harassed by flies. Then Octavia felt it—the prickling warmth like that of a circle. "Grandfather, I think we crossed the line into the Lady's domain, quite literally."

"I agree." Kethan's voice was a low rumble.

The sounds of animals intensified. The trees crowded ahead like cats at feeding time, branches and leaves in a tight, verdant weave. She couldn't see the Tree now but she felt its looming presence, the shade covering them like a strange sort of nightfall. It occurred to her that she should be very cold—it had to be near freezing—but she felt fine.

An odd pile of bones and long green branches was stacked along one side of the path. The branches buzzed slightly with the life essence of the Lady. Octavia stared, taking in the large shape, then noticed green movement amidst the bones. She assumed it was a snake and prepared for Chocolate to lurch away, then noticed the leaves, the shape. *My horse. Jasmine.*

As she rode by, white buds opened to her as if in an offering. She pressed a hand to her chest and bowed her head. "Peace to you, sweet mare," she whispered.

"'God take you, warrior steed, to fields of clover, not bone,'" intoned King Kethan.

Tears burned her eyes. Caskentia still used that prayer when they burned and buried horses that fell in battle. It was one of the few times she had ever seen soldiers cry.

They crossed a churning stream and rode up an embankment. The path thinned, the light at their backs vanishing completely. The King's heart raced, his song more chaotic. *He's nervous.* So was she. This was no normal forest. Foxes, raccoons, and vague shadows crawled through the undergrowth. Five deer flashed through the trees. A moose stared at them, his antlers broad and heavy as if he carried the world upon his skull. It was as though every animal on the continent was congregating here, whether they belonged in the Waste or not; maybe somewhere, saltwater seals played in a pond where small whales breached. At this point, nothing would surprise her.

Heat seared Octavia's skin as if they approached an infernal. They did. She reined up.

The threem strolled into the path some twenty feet ahead. In the deep shade, the gray body was cast in black, its scaled skin sleek. The equine form stopped to regard them; it stood about fourteen or fifteen hands in height, comparable to a common riding horse. Eyes glowed red. The muzzle curved outward like the snout of a sea horse, the nostrils large and tinged in crimson. It had no mane. Instead, a double black ridge of scales trailed from forelock to croup, where a leonine tail lashed. It moved with the grace of a snake, exuded the mood of a nightmare.

Beneath Octavia, Chocolate convulsed in sheer terror, song lurching. Octavia immediately dismounted. A glance back showed King Kethan doing the same. Octavia grabbed the reins at the bit as she made soothing sounds.

"Grandfather, did you learn anything about threems in your extensive reading?"

"That they are not supposed to exist." He sounded more intrigued than frightened. "'Tis beautiful."

"It is, but so is a fire, and that's what it will breathe at us if we don't elicit some level of approval."

"I must venture forward first. I am no innocent, not by any definition."

"Neither am I. I've killed. I've been party to too many deaths these past few weeks."

The threem's song was unlike anything she had ever heard. It consisted of frenzied drums, like a herd of horses in a gallop across cobblestones. She had no idea how to parse those musical lines.

"Lady!" called Octavia. "Neither of us is innocent. We know that. We can't change the past. Please let us by, threem."

The threem's finely tapered ears flickered. *It under-stands, just like a gremlin.* She had a hunch that cheese or silver wouldn't win a threem's heart—no, it was too digni-fied, too noble. Her mother's advice repeated in her mind again, what Octavia should do if she ever met royalty.

Octavia curtsied, her satchel jostling against her hip. She heard Kethan move behind her.

Sinuous as a ripple of silk, the threem stepped on across the path and vanished into the piled vines. Octavia released a breath she hadn't known she was holding. "My mother always said manners were of vital importance," she said, grunting as she remounted. She shifted the satchel to a more comfortable position.

"Mothers are wise in that way."

Chocolate was still skittish as they crossed where the threem had trod. "My mother would also go apoplectic if she knew I was calling you 'Grandfather' and not genuflect-ing most every time you breathed."

King Kethan laughed. "When I cross the infinite river, I will tell her that I granted you full permission and that it was a joy to know you as part of my family."

Emotion caught in her throat. "That . . . that means a great deal to me. I . . . I like the idea of you and my par-ents being together. I think you'd get along like gremlins and silver. Our families . . . I'm glad you got to meet your great-granddaughter Rivka, but I so wish you could have seen Viola—Allendia."

"I wrote her a short letter in the village. 'Tis addressed to Balthazar Cody, to be forwarded to my daughter. A courier left with it not ten minutes before we reunited. I know you will speak to Allendia, if you can, but I wanted this chance to send her my words and tell her of my pride."

"Was it in code?"

"Must you ask?"

"She'll treasure it beyond anything in this world. I don't know how it will go when—if—I talk to her in person again, I . . ."

"Grieve for Devin Stout's choices, but do not feel guilt for his death. I may spread rot, but he was rotten."

"I know that. Logically," she said softly. Her sudden need for Alonzo's presence, his strength, almost doubled her over. Exhaustion soaked her to the marrow. When did she sleep last? Or eat? There had to be food in the saddlebags, but they needed to press on, regardless of how her mouth now watered at the thought.

I like how crusty bread crunches between my teeth, how maple syrup is silken across my tongue. A silly thing, to wish for a paper-wrapped bar of chocolate here and now, but even camp beans and stale crackers would grant a certain kind of joy. It would mean eating. Tasting. Chewing. Doing things a Tree cannot do.

Something chirped above and a green being floated down from the trees. Leaf, gliding down like his namesake.

"Oh, Leaf!" *This is better than any chocolate bar.* Being a trained war-horse, her mount barely reacted as Leaf landed on the low nub of the saddle horn.

He chittered a greeting and leaped up to Octavia's shoulder. He pattered a rapid circle around her head and then sat on her left shoulder.

"Greetings to you, gremlin," called King Kethan. Leaf chirped in his direction.

"Come to say good-bye?" she whispered.

He made a crude noise that normally indicated a need to treat with bellywood bark.

Songs drifted out of sight. *Young, healthy, female. Slow to approach.* Octavia held up a hand to stop King Kethan. "Hello?" she called.

The girls emerged like a pack of wolves, slinking, wary. They wore black oilskin coats like so many Wasters, but many of these were singed by fire. *Salvage from when a Waster didn't show proper respect to a threem.* Their visible skirts were tattered and torn, their feet bare yet unhurt. "Hello," Octavia repeated.

"I know you." One of the girls stepped to the forefront, smiling. Her yellow hair was tied back in a braid, but Octavia recognized her from when it had been wild and free. The girl couldn't have been any older than fifteen.

"Yes! You were the one in the Waster camp two weeks ago! I was so afraid for you." Octavia shifted to dismount but the girl held up a hand. Leaf groused and settled himself on her shoulder again.

"We'll walk you along this next rocky stretch but I don't want to delay you. *She's* waiting."

Octavia counted nine girls as she rode on. The youngest looked to be about twelve, the oldest maybe sixteen. "The Wasters assumed you'd all been eaten by threems."

"The bastards!" snapped the youngest.

The yellow-haired girl nodded. "The threems don't bother you if you give them space and respect. The second anyone raises a gun, they're toast. Literally."

"You're all from Mercia?" Octavia asked. They nodded. "Considering all the tea they make, there must be more girls."

That earned scowls and expressions of dismay. "There are hundreds," said a girl with dusky Frengian skin. "Most of them are so scared they do their job and get the bark. The Wasters tried to get lots of sisters, so while one is out working the other is kept hostage."

Oh no. These girls must reside in the settlement. More lives to be lost in an attack.

"Is there no outcry in Mercia?" asked King Kethan, rage clear in his voice.

"Some," said Octavia with a grimace, and nodded to the yellow-haired girl. "I saw a newspaper article about you, with a picture of your father." The path rose, strewn with boulders, and Chocolate slowed to place each hoof with care.

"Of course you did. Daddy has money." She didn't look happy that she was missed; instead she seemed disgusted.

"The Tree is visible to the air now," Octavia said. "Caskentia is preparing to attack. If they bomb—"

"They won't," said a girl.

"You're going to become a new Tree," said the other.

"He has the seed. She's so happy he's finally here," said another.

Eerie, how they all speak in a sequence. "How do you know...?"

"We're her daughters now," said the yellow-haired girl. "When we sleep here, we dream wonderful dreams."

A girl with curly black hair held up her arms. "My hands are finally healed. I used to work a sewing machine twelve hours a day."

"My step-pa don't beat me no more."

"I'm not ever leaving here!" At that, they all smiled and nodded.

I don't doubt that some of their situations have improved, but certainly there are people back in Mercia who love and miss them. But their minds . . . their smiles . . . they seem almost vacant.

The soft patter of a waterfall grew louder as they followed a switchback. The air—it was so clean, so pure, it almost made her giddy. At the curve, Octavia reined up. "Oh Lady," she whispered. That was not blasphemy.

The sight before her was the most beautiful she had ever seen. The waterfall began high up on the Tree, pouring from a shadowed crevice, and fell for at least a quarter mile. Shafts of light angled downward. Multiple rainbows wavered in the mist. The Tree's surface consisted of mottled, vertical strips covered with lichen patches that would have been meadows if stretched horizontally. Long-necked pink birds glided past the water like cherry blossoms adrift. Far below lay more trees. Gnarled roots led down to a small lake that looked to be flecked with birds of every possible color and size. At water level, the roots had eroded to resemble tumbled river stones.

She couldn't speak. Words could never have done it justice. Leaf's little body rumbled in an honest-to-goodness feline purr.

It took effort to prod her horse onward and drag her own gaze away, but even then, she looked over her shoulder until the vista was obscured by rocks and brush. The path grew steeper. The girls followed, picking their way among the boulders, their feet sure as goat hooves. The way was littered with dry red bark fragrant like a fine spice mix—a dash of cardamom, cinnamon, and nutmeg, reminiscent of all the glories of a Fengrian bakery. Octavia thought of Rivka with a quick prayer. Up another rise, and she could see the Tree itself ahead. The path led directly to a cleft in the trunk.

The Lady is there.

Tingles warmed her skin. Redwoods lined the grassy path, their shaggy tops extended far beyond sight. She had only seen such trees along the northern coast. She smiled until she rode alongside.

They were rotting, and not a dry rot—their trunks oozed a viscous gray substance like motor oil, the smell of greenery replaced by a foulness like rotting fish. The needles were still green but somewhat limp, as if suffering from a sudden drought.

"It's affecting the entire forest, like a disease. Even some of the animals are getting sores like this," said one of the girls.

"This is the sickness of the Waste, even after all these years," Octavia murmured. "The Lady is still here, yet this is happening."

"Not for long," said the girls in unison.

They passed the final normal tree, its stink heavy in the air. Only the darkness of the cleft lay ahead. She and the King dismounted.

King Kethan stood before his horse and stroked her long muzzle. "I am glad to have ridden one last time," he murmured. "Thank you." Doxy snorted at his hand, no longer afraid. He smiled.

Octavia looked around, at a sudden loss. "I don't want to set the horses free. I want to think that I'll need one to ride back."

"We cannot go beyond this point," said the yellow-haired girl. "We'll stay here until nightfall. If you don't return, we'll take good care of them, and so will you, after." Her bright smile sent a vicious chill through Octavia as she handed over the reins.

"Miss Octavia Leander. Granddaughter." King Kethan opened both arms in an unmistakable gesture. She didn't hesitate with her hug. His arms were thin cords, gentle in their strength. Leaf hopped to his shoulder and did a quick circuit around both of their heads. "'Tis my sincere hope you shall ride away, and ride on with Mr. Garret. You possess my eternal gratitude for your kindness to me, but even more, to the land I love greatly and have burdened so."

"Peace and mercy to you, Grandfather." She pulled back, the dust of his deteriorating clothes falling away from her enchanted robes. With a small chirp, Leaf leaped from

Kethan and glided to Octavia's shoulder. He sat upright, his wings tucked close.

Side by side, Octavia and Kethan walked into the darkness.

THE ENTRANCE TO THE Tree evoked the blackness of a dank basement at the end of a long, wet winter, when the root vegetables are starting to soften and the mold grows fuzzy and bold. A cold breeze stroked Octavia, like the breath of a frozen god. Even if she had pulled out her glowstone, it would have done little good against the spirit of this place.

Octavia's feet knew to walk on. She could hear Kethan beside her, his new Waster boots clomping heavily. His song showed anxiety and calmness together. She waved a hand in front of her, worried about walking into something. Her steps slowed at the thought of walking into nothing at all, even if it seemed unlikely at this stage. *Make it this far, fall into a crevasse. That does seem like my sort of luck.* Leaf chittered by her ear.

Soft light lay ahead, like the first blush of dawn behind thick clouds.

Rough cloth brushed her face. She recoiled with a gasp, swiping it away. The object tore off in her hand and she recognized the smell then—tree moss. It fragmented in her grasp. Against the light, she could see more swaths of moss ahead. They fell in mighty tufts, like heavy curtains in a fancy hotel. She tried to dodge the moss, as did Kethan, but it seemed to dangle every few feet. Looking up, she couldn't see a ceiling. Moss stretched up as if it attached to an invisible sky.

They emerged in a domed chamber. Polished wood formed the walls, the brown and red whirls begging to be touched. Swaths of moss dangled down but most of it stopped well above their heads. The floor was the same wood as the walls, though covered in a sheen of dust and disintegrated moss. Theirs were the only footprints.

"Foremost of all, the answer is no." The woman's voice emerged from nowhere, everywhere. She sounded young, her accent foreign.

"No?" echoed Octavia, spinning around to find the source.

"You are the most appropriate vessel for the seed. You have been since you were born. I knew the instant your mother and father came together. I knew you in the womb. I knew your first breath. I knew that someday, you would come here. I would make sure of it."

How, Lady? Why me?

"I will answer the best that I can. Yes, I heard your questions. I can hear you when you think of me, just as you now hear people close by when they speak of you."

A spirit Octavia's height formed in the center of the chamber. The white mist was tinted in color as if the being stood in fog. Beautiful caramel skin and luxurious thick, coiled hair showed her Tamaran heritage. She wore an antiquated version of medician gear, the robes accented in Dallows sky blue, the body beneath curvaceous and strong. As she stepped forward, the contents in her pockets chimed in various notes, the sounds of glass jars and coins and various other treasures.

Beyond that, the Lady had no song. No life.

"My human body, of course, is long gone. I am projecting my form as I best remember it. It took me centuries to make this sanctuary, a place to house the echo of my humanity, the only place where I can still speak aloud." She faced King Kethan. "No, no. I'm not ignoring you. Never. Not even when you were locked in the vault. I couldn't afford to ignore you, or the seams of life would have utterly unraveled."

"I am sorry." The words escaped his throat with a sob. King Kethan collapsed to his knees.

"Oh, Kethan." The Lady said his name with the intimacy of a wife, a mother, a sister. "This was never any sort of judgment against you. No karma, no divine retribution. This was all Evandia's very human desperation to have you live again as king, and her impatience as you fought against the seed. I have seen many people die when they chewed the Tree's leaves, but not even I knew what would happen to someone who ingested both the seed and leaf."

"I have only yearned for mercy. For my Varya and Allendia," he whispered.

"I know." The Lady walked up to him, jingling with each step. She glided like a dancer, no footprints in her wake. She laid a hand atop his head and he leaned against her hip as he sobbed. Though she appeared vaporous, the Lady was solid to him.

"There was no way to save him from afar?" asked Octavia.

"You are going to learn that there are great limits to what we can do. We encourage life. We're zymes in the soil, chewing through decay. We're gremlins, and know each piece of their living flesh." The Lady grimaced. "We're aware of everything, but it's impossible to focus on more than a few things at a time."

"Hence the use of a circle," said Octavia.

"Yes. Circles grant us a space to focus. To act outside of a circle, to act outside of our direct influence, is draining. To scratch your cheek to save your life, to make that boy in Leffen speak with you, taxed months of my life away."

Scratch my cheek? Octavia struggled to understand, then remembered the odd sensation of a branch scraping her face when she stood on the street in Leffen—it seemed like so long ago. The invisible branch at her cheek had caused her to turn just in time to dodge an assassination attempt.

Minutes later, Octavia thought she had saved a small boy struck down in her stead. The boy had come back to life long enough to utter the enigmatic phrase *"Listen to the branch, look to the leaves."*

"You prognosticated," said Octavia. "You knew I would encounter the Tree's branch and the leaves."

"No, I didn't," the Lady corrected gently. "Nothing is as straightforward as that. I see dozens of paths. I saw many where you may have met with either the branch or leaves, or none at all. As Kethan astutely noted, the Tree is finite. I don't see beyond my continent. I have lived. I will die."

"What of God and—"

"God? What of God?" The Lady burst out laughing.

The hysterical pitch of her voice caused Kethan to jerk away and Leaf to edge back on Octavia's shoulder. "Don't go into this expecting divine insights from above. The prayers you hear—and the curses—are the ones that go to you. That means very few outside of the battlefield wards, these days. As for what comes beyond life, Kethan would know more than me." She shrugged, her black hair swaying. "In all my years, he's the only one who fully crossed beyond and returned to stay."

"I . . . I remember almost nothing of my time between life and this half-life."

"I know." The Lady sounded supremely disappointed. "But the fact that you returned at all is vital. Your body's song went somewhere and it came back—reluctantly—but it came back."

The floor groaned beneath Octavia. Leaf squawked and took flight. Branches emerged from the smooth floor and, in the space of seconds, formed a high-backed chair.

"Sit." The Lady pointed at Octavia. "Your legs are hurting."

"I—I'd like to stand, I don't know how much longer I—"

"Trees stand. They don't have the luxury of sitting."

Octavia sat. The chair was smooth, the green wood stripped of any twigs or leaves. It perfectly fit the curves of her hips and buttocks. She was reminded of how Alonzo's body fit against hers—his lips, his height, his hands on her waist. Grief clogged her throat. *I'll never know more than that.*

"If you see dozens of paths into the future—"

"Octavia." The Lady said her name, and Octavia felt

like she'd smacked her head into a metal beam. Suddenly she was glad she sat. "You were born to be the next Tree. I didn't shift your cells. I didn't make you a medician. The magic was there, brought together by your parents. When you were able to float a patient beyond a circle—when you listened to the rhythms of zymes—I was amazed along with you."

Octavia froze. That sense of isolation she had known her whole life had always been balanced by the surety that the Lady knew, she understood.

"Of course I knew and understood." The Lady flicked a wrist as to dismiss the thought. "I understood you were here to take my place. In that, maybe there was divine intervention. I have already gone fifty years longer than I should, and with Kethan's burden and the factories and the war . . . I think I only have a few days left. The roots are rotting out."

"Lady, I don't want—"

"Do you think I care what you want?" The spirit of the Lady rounded on Octavia as her words quaked through the walls, the floor, shivered moss from above. Leaf squawked from up high—she could spy him as he clung to moss near the ceiling. "I'm not God, to satisfy all your wants and wishes. I can heal. That's all I can do, and I can't even heal everyone. The shortage of blessed herbs—that's not simply because of the war. It's my own weakness. There were days, in the Tree's youth, when medicians planted full fields of pampria. Row upon glorious row. Now there's no magic left in the soil to spur the growth. I can't even deny all healings to those who I wish to die—those Dallowmen, harvesting the very signs of my death, my peeling bark, and making tea from it." Octavia felt flecks of spittle from her vehemence. "It takes more effort to kill than to let live."

"She wants to live and love." That came from King Kethan. He still knelt on the floor, his gaze level.

"Yes! Everyone wants the same, and what can I do? Almost nothing, even as I'm aware of everything from the bud of a single larkspur to an old man's final breath. Even more, I know them at the very end and they know me, even if they never heard of the Lady and the Tree."

Like the boy who died in Leffen, who spoke of her; Alonzo's message when he returned by the grace of the Tree's leaf; the woman at the sod house.

"This is cruel," said King Kethan.

"LIFE IS CRUEL." The Tree convulsed. There was a long pause. Octavia felt a cool breeze again, like the long breaths of Al Cala meditation. "Octavia knows the value of the lives she saves because she knows her own loss. She knows that her whole village burned in the span of minutes, and who was left to mourn? Her, the Garrets, and the families of the thirteen Dallowmen of the *Alexandrio*. No one else in Caskentia cared. They each knew their own grief. She's a good medician because she cares. She *remembers*."

The Lady turned to her again. "I know you want to continue as a medician, but you can't. Without a Tree, there are no more herbs, there is no more healing magic. I am not even sure if you would still be able to hear bodies' songs here. Perhaps if you went across the sea, to the land of another Tree, but not here. But even if you could hear them, soon enough there wouldn't be any blessed herbs. You might be able to hear and do nothing."

Octavia wanted to coil into a tight ball of agony. "If you haven't always been here, what kept the land going before? Was there another Tree?"

"Of course. Otherwise medicians would have not existed. But he was weak, as both a medician and as a Tree. His legacy was the jealousy of Caskentia, the curse on the Dallows."

"And you," Octavia said.

The Lady laughed like a gale at sea then stopped, her expression one of surprise at the sounds she herself was making. *Does not know how to laugh anymore.* Octavia took care to edit her own thoughts to keep them her own.

"Yes, I suppose I am his legacy. I know what the tales say of me. 'The mourning mother.' 'The one who begged God that she might treat the suffering.'" Venom dripped from the words. "When I talk about the cruelty of life, I know it. Yes, I mourned. Yes, I mothered. But becoming the Tree is not a proclamation of morality, no more than surviving a threem is proof of virginity. The Tree creates magic, and the magic creates herbs and medicians, and the best of medicians becomes the next Tree, and so the cycle continues."

"Who were you, Lady? Before?" asked Octavia.

The spirit's mouth opened, her expression one of puzzlement. "I . . . I've been called Lady for so long. I don't remember my old name." She shook her head. "But I . . . I had three children. Their names, I know. Cameron, Aidan, and Cassandra.

"When they call me the mourning mother, it's because my grief shook through the land. It haunted the dreams of medicians. It caused pampria to weep red. I was forced to leave my children as orphans. It's because I had to know their laments to the Tree—because I raised them with faith—and could do nothing to help when Cassandra died in child labor at thirteen, when a wagon crushed Aidan's spine at eighteen and left him paralyzed until he brought a knife to his gut three months later, when Cameron strangled five consecutive wives and cursed them for his impotence."

Octavia's lungs felt heavy, her body cold. *No sympathy toward me. No choice.*

King Kethan bowed his head, a fist pressed to his chest. The Lady faced him with a tender smile. "Yes. You know what it's like, to a degree. To lose a child and be powerless against it. To be bound in one place when your mind is everywhere else." The Lady rested a hand on the top of his head again. "So many thousands of books are bound to your soul and memory. Their ultimate loss is the only reason I grieve to do this."

There was a split second when Kethan frowned in puzzlement, and then a spine of wood erupted from the floor at a ninety-degree angle. It impaled Kethan with a horrible crunch of atrophied organs and flesh. Other branches spontaneously crackled forth and grabbed hold of his shoulders to clutch him upright. His song wailed, the screech of a toddler blowing into bagpipes. Even knowing this was the Lady, Octavia couldn't help but lunge forward, her hands reaching to open her satchel.

The chair bound her. Green branches snared her ankles, girthed her lap, and forced both arms back to their rests.

"Kethan!" His name sobbed out of her. Octavia needed to be there, to lay her hand on his brow, to ease his passing as she had eased that of so many soldiers at the front. She craned against the restraints and screamed. "Peace to you, Kethan! Go to Varya! Allendia loves you. She's never forgotten you."

Octavia knew Kethan heard her by the shift in his song as it softened—that through the frenzy of his pain, there came the peace of a steady flute. His agony didn't ease. His wound didn't heal. This time, he was truly dying.

The Lady stood between them, her expression impassive as she watched Kethan. Her hands rested atop her rounded hips.

"Let me go to him!" Octavia yelled.

"*I* have him." The Lady said it with tenderness.

The spear of the Tree moved. It retracted and traced a circle like an oversize scalpel. Kethan moaned, his frail form falling slack in the branches' grip. His lungs, his body, deflated.

Leaf squawked and dove downward. One of the branches lashed him aside. He impacted on the far wall with a fleshy smack.

"Leaf!" Octavia screamed. Her wrists and shoulders burned as she tried to thrust herself forward in little jolts. In response, the branches squeezed. She couldn't so much as wiggle. Octavia knew by Leaf's song that he was merely bruised and dazed, but that didn't stop her rage.

"Chimeras." The Lady shook her head, her lips curled. "Men meddling with things they shouldn't. But I can't stop all life. It just happens sometimes, even in a circle."

Kethan's song dimmed.

Leaf crawled to her. He dragged his wing, the one that wore the silver fork. "Come on, Leaf, come on," she whispered. *Alonzo could have been swatted in the same way. Still could. Death is harder, but she can still kill.*

The branch withdrew from Kethan. Its forked end balanced a nugget the size of a hulled almond. The Lady plucked it up and held it to the light. "So many years since it was stolen. So many years it has been in the wrong vessel. But now . . . now. Peace to you, Kethan," said the Lady.

Hot tears streamed down Octavia's cheeks. "Good-bye, Grandfather," she whispered. As if he'd been waiting for the words, his soul departed their world.

"Soon enough, peace for me as well. Once you're rooted, Octavia, my time is done."

The Lady walked to Octavia, smiling, the seed cradled in the plush nest of her palm.

Chapter 20

Octavia fought against the branches of her chair. The green tendrils tightened their hold. "Lady! Please, no!"

"Octavia, you want to save everyone. You've told me so many times."

"Not like this. I never thought . . . not like this."

"I know it's hard. I don't think it means as much without that sacrifice. I fought the seed, too, just as Kethan did." The Lady nodded to where the King knelt. As Octavia watched, his body sifted into mere dust. *Just as the Tree's leaves disintegrate after being used. That's all we are in the end. Dust.* "However, in our case, we're alive when it goes in. It hurts. Every sort of birth hurts. I was told that if you give in, the process is done in a matter of seconds."

The Lady stood directly before Octavia. The seed in her palm looked benign, like a green almond out of the hull, its surface rippled with long vertical lines. Her touch had evaporated the leaf's toxins and Kethan's remaining viscera as if she had used a medician wand. A vine slithered around Octavia's ribs, then another. A twig twined around her neck; another circled the top of her head like a diadem. She couldn't move.

"You're the finest medician magus I've ever seen." Tears glistened in the Lady's eyes. "Thank you." The dankness of the earth lingered around her like a perfume.

A branch, a vine, something wrapped around Octavia's chin and pulled her mouth wide open. The Lady's fingers touched her lip, the texture cold like roots on a winter morning. Octavia shivered. The seed was pressed onto her tongue. Octavia immediately tried to shove it out. The Lady tsked and rested her hands on Octavia's throat. The muscles contracted.

Octavia swallowed the seed.

I don't want this, I don't want this, I don't want this. She wanted to chant the words endlessly, as the branch used to speak, but sudden dizziness overwhelmed her. Even restrained as she was, the world swam for a moment.

Her legs and back impacted on the floor, the satchel smacking heavily beside her. The chair was gone. She rolled to stare up. The lichen draped and swayed. She felt the seed in her gut. It wanted to grow. The potential was so *there,* like the taste of rain before a storm. She just had to acquiesce—ha! This wasn't acquiescing, as a patient did in a circle. The seed needed her to give up.

Octavia. Pain stabbed through her head again. *I imagine you'll fight awhile more, so I must preserve my energy until you root. Bless you, Octavia Leander, and blessings to our land.*

The Lady was gone. Gone in her human form, in any case.

Leaf faintly chirped.

"Leaf?" Octavia whispered. She rolled to her side to find him. He crawled closer, his song battered but still strong. *Concussion, bruising to the membrane of his wing, bloodied nose.*

"We have to get back to the settlement. We need to get to Alonzo. I wanted . . . I should have given him a proper good-bye before. Now's the chance. I can get you to Miss Percival, little one. She'll set you right. I . . . I don't think I'm up to healing anyone right now."

Nausea didn't adequately describe how she felt. Her gut seemed strangely full, as if she'd starved all day in the bustle of the wards and then eaten a full loaf of bread at the end of her shift. That sense that she didn't feel sick yet, but she would suffer very soon.

Here I thought Miss Percival's betrayal was the worst that could happen. That was like stubbing a toe; this is an amputation. Of the foot, leg, everything.

Octavia crouched. Her head still swam a little, but she no longer felt like she was on a crazed buzzer ride. Her fingers clumsy, she opened the main pocket of her satchel. "Here, Leaf." She scooped him up. The tips of his ears trembled. "I know. We were both betrayed. You worked hard for her. We both did." She tucked him inside the satchel. Leaf emitted a soft chirp.

Walking took extreme focus. Left foot, right. Left foot, right. Rest. Walk. The dark passage didn't seem quite so impenetrable with the gray of the outside world directly ahead. She stepped outdoors, drenched with sweat.

Screams lit up the path ahead. The girls, idling beneath

the rotting redwoods, stared at Octavia in utter horror.

"Glad to see you, too," she mumbled.

"How are you here?" cried the yellow-haired girl.

"I walked." Chocolate and Doxy stared at her, ears perked. "I might need help mounting."

"You shouldn't be here!" shouted the shortest girl.

"Did the Lady tell you that?" asked Octavia.

"She doesn't say much anymore," said another girl. "But we know she's dying. We know you're the new Tree, but you're still walking around!"

"Terribly sorry to disappoint." Octavia leaned on Chocolate. She pressed a hand to her face. The skin felt sweat-soaked and rough, even through her gloves. The gloves—how pointless now. She discarded them. Mottled green and brown bark covered the backs of her hands, her palms discolored but still flexible. She touched her face again and felt the fissures. A low moan escaped her throat.

Octavia gripped the saddle horn. She managed to get one foot into the stirrup, but weakened as she was, she couldn't lift the rest of her body. Chocolate danced sideways and almost sent her face first into the dirt. She scrambled up, panicked. *No. I don't want to touch the dirt.* "Help?" she whispered to the girls.

They were gone. Fled down the path.

"Well then. What now?" In the deep shade, it was impossible to tell the time of day. Leaf pried himself partially out of the satchel. A loud chirp erupted from his little body, then another.

"Leaf, what is it?"

Flapping wings and murmured songs filled the air over-head. The sky turned green with gremlins. Huge grem-lins and small, full chimeras and natural-born ones. Their bodies told the strain of days of flying, hours of hunger. *All to come here, to help me.* They hovered to grab her robes, her arms, the backs of her legs. Octavia was lifted upward, and her screech of alarm turned into a wild laugh.

"What, am I made of silver instead of wood?" she asked.

A scarred gremlin the size of a four-year-old child cradled Leaf in her arms, her broad wings fanning Octavia with each mighty stroke. Like Prime back in Tamarania, her wings and arms were separate.

Octavia rose higher and higher. Some of the little gremlins even gripped her satchel so that she didn't feel its weight. She twisted to check on her bag and found that someone had even shut the top flap for her.

They hovered as high as the lower branches of the Lady's Tree and flew forward. She could see the winding footpath she had followed with Kethan. Doxy and Choco-late galloped with dust in their wakes. Cold wind blasted Octavia's face and reminded her of the open windows on the *Argus*. *Though I won't be pushed out a window this time.* In fact, she had no worries of falling at all. Treetops passed just feet below. Birds cried greeting. Smoke rose from the settlement ahead.

"Dis." It took Octavia a moment to realize the large gremlin was speaking. Through the fog of bodies and songs, she made herself focus. This gremlin had vocal organs like

Prime and a bowed pelvis that indicated that she had borne offspring. "Dis dank you."

The cold air blasted tears from Octavia's eyes. "And thank you." The gremlin grunted and turned away, Leaf cradled to her chest. Thick seams lined the protruding ripples of her vertebrae.

They all came from afar. Leaf's work—maybe Chi's as well. If we had still been at the homestead, or farther away, I imagine they would have guided or carried us all.

The gremlins cried out en masse. From the distance came an answer—another flock, green specks against a cloud. Gratitude welled up in her chest—no, not gratitude. Love. The pressure filled her chest as if with a life debt, but she knew this was something more.

"I bless you. I bless you all. Every gremlin," she whispered to the wind, willing power into the words as if she were an aether magus. The gremlins shivered, though their hold on her never weakened. She heard their weariness, their aches, as it all faded. A cry came from afar—an acknowledgment.

She closed her eyes as if falling into her Al Cala meditation, but this time she didn't see the Tree. Now she *knew* the map of Caskentia and the Waste and how the current of her thanks flowed over the plains, eddied around and over the Pinnacles like a tidal wave, dipped into the saltiness of Nennia Bay, coursed through the smoke-thickened skies of Mercia. Her gratitude swirled among the towers of the southern nations to those alcoves above the clouds, and north to Frengia, where gremlins numbered few, but still mewed their thanks in a small chorus.

They said her name, whatever it was in their speech. She knew by the way the sound made her head throb.

"To me, you're all living creatures. Yes, you were created out of cruelty, but that makes you no less valid," she whispered.

A lightning bolt of pain shot through her abdomen. She screamed. The world wobbled again, dismayed cries of gremlins all around.

The seed is sprouting. By using the potential of its power, I gave in a little without it even being a conscious decision. Oh . . . balderdash. She didn't even know how to call on a higher power now, without the Lady to rely on.

Octavia breathed through the pain as she had asked women to breathe through labor, and soon it faded back to a dull ache. "We're almost to the village. Set me down in the woods. I know how men treat gremlins, and this lot's ready to fight. There. The path."

She alighted on the trail with surprising grace—grace that vanished the instant they let go. Her rubbery legs dropped her straight to the grassy earth.

Whereupon her blood tried to burst out of her skin.

It was like the urge to bloodlet, but it welled up wherever her body touched the ground, even through cloth. Screaming, she shoved herself upright and grabbed hold of a sapling. The pressure in her skin abated. Her boots, at least, granted her an adequate buffer. The gremlins fluttered around her like oversize green butterflies.

I need a walking stick. Octavia looked around and breathed in the glorious fragrance of jasmine. She was steps away from where her mare had joined the forest. There had been long sticks there among the horse's bones—likely created to reinforce the structure as the flesh failed. Carefully, she staggered to where the jasmine mounded as if it had flourished for years. From the blooms, she pulled forth a curved green stick that resembled a spine. It quivered in her hand but didn't speak.

Her power is fading quickly. When she manifested and acted physically, it sped her end all the more. Octavia couldn't help but look back toward the looming Tree. Evening light cast it in pale yellow.

Evening light. Alonzo. *I can still see the Tree.*

"Oh no. Oh no. I have to get back. Gremlins, you need to go away, far away. Don't try to steal any silver from here. I—if I—there might be a battle here. You don't need to be caught in it. Please, go!"

At the word, the flock took off. She felt a backlash of dread, wondering if the order to the gremlins carried a consequence, but she didn't feel another direct pulse of pain.

The gremlins had listened because the request came from her, not because of the will of the Lady.

Two gremlins remained: the large one and Leaf.

"Leaf, you need to go, too," she murmured as she started to walk. The large gremlin picked up Leaf and waddled alongside Octavia. "I love you, little one. I don't know what will happen here. It's enough that Alonzo is here and at risk. Go southwest. Go to Mrs. Stout in Tamarania. She'd love to see you. There's a lovely cheese shop there. Oh, Leaf . . ." He chirped and held his arms out to her like a babe. Leaning on her stick, she scooped him up from the other gremlin. He cuddled against her shoulder and mewed, his long ears rubbing and bending against her jaw. The pain in his song broke her heart. "I want to heal you, but I'm afraid to. I'm afraid of what would happen if I drew on . . . that power right now. I'm glad you have a friend to help."

The older gremlin returned Octavia's grin with a fang-tipped smile.

Octavia could see men and horses on the full street ahead. She stood at the edge of the woods. "You might be able to fly in a few hours, but take it easy." A pause. "This is where we need to say farewell."

His little catlike mouth pressed against her neck in what was clearly a kiss. Her throat burned with checked tears as she passed Leaf down to the mother gremlin. The big gremlin chirped and took to the air. Blinking, Octavia walked on. She didn't look up as she heard his mews, his battered song, as they faded away.

As she entered the village, men slowed in the midst of loading wagons. Machinists froze as they leaned into the engine compartment of a steam car. Horses stopped, ears perked, not responding to the goads of heels and spurs.

"Be nicer to that horse," she snapped.

"Yes, m'lady. Of course, m'lady," the Waster stammered, shame coloring his song and speeding his heart.

The throb in her gut worsened. *I imagine the Caskentian soldiers poisoned by the Waste felt like this as their symptoms began.*

If only my ailment could be treated by a scoop of bellywood bark.

She sensed the approach of Lanskay and an aether magus before they emerged from a building. Lanskay froze, shock evident on his face, before he continued forward. He waved the other magus away.

"I'd appreciate it if you could tell me where Alonzo is," she said.

"Good God. What happened to you in there?" he whispered.

"You're a married man. You should know better than to say something like that to a woman."

"Have you seen yourself?"

"I didn't stop to look for a mirror in the woods. And no, I don't want to see myself." *If I look that bad, how will Alonzo react?* As much as she wanted to see him, she was suddenly terrified. What if he looked on her with horror? Like some monster? *I am a monster. A chimera made of old magic.*

"I'll take you to him. Come. Do you want me to take your satchel? To help?"

She laughed, weakly. He cast her an odd look. "Medicians never surrender their satchels. Mr. Drury never could comprehend that." She leaned heavily on her stick as pain warbled through her ribs. "You know what? I don't suppose it really matters anymore. Here."

They continued down the boardwalk. Lanskay carried her satchel against his chest with the reverence of a page bearing a king's crown.

"The settlement is emptier than it was before," she said.

"Our front lines at the pass fell. Caskentia is on the way.

We expect a bombardment within hours." He sighed. "We were prepared for winter, not this. Too many of our airships are to the far east."

She heard nearby concentrations of songs and suddenly *knew* where everyone had gone. "Wise use of the wyrm tunnels. Hide there for a few days and then launch a surprise attack, hmm?" *There would be a lot more tunnels now, with the roots rotting and retracting.*

Lanskay's expression was somewhere between awe and terror. "How do you know where they are? If Taney heard you . . ."

"He has better things to do right now I'm—" Pain erupted through her gut, a fiery porcupine with all quills extended. She wanted to call on the Lady, on God, on anything, but it took all her concentration to breathe and remain conscious. Heat pulsed through her stomach and across her skin. Gasping, she leaned all her weight on the branch and gritted her teeth. *I used the seed's power without even trying. It just felt . . . natural.*

"Miss Leander . . . ?" His words echoed strangely against a high buzz in her ears. He hovered close but seemed scared to assist.

Sweat coursed down her temple and jaw. Her vision, narrowed to a tunnel, began to return to normal. "You were fine with burning me, but you won't actually touch me when I need the help."

He hesitated. "You're not the same now."

She was reminded of why she despised the man, even as she allowed him to carry her satchel. "You're the same.

You're a coward. You burned people alive as you stood up on an airship deck. You burned me right after I saved your life, and it wasn't to honor me as a worthy enemy soldier. It was to save your own pride after you choked to death on your own plug of tobacco. You don't understand honor." She thought of King Kethan with a wave of grief.

Lanskay didn't anger; instead, his song altered in a way she could only translate as shame. "As you say."

She released a long breath. *Since I was young, I hated how people feared me. I never expected that fear to cow one of the highest commanders of the Waste, and an infernal at that.*

The Lady might fascinate him, but he's still Taney's man through and through. He burned me. He'll burn Alonzo.

Lanskay opened a door for her. Men saluted as they passed. By the anxiety in their songs, she knew it wasn't because of Lanskay.

Alonzo stood by a blacked-out window as she entered. The marching-band brasses nearly made her weep in relief. Her breath, her heart, froze as he turned to face her.

No hesitation. No terror. He crossed the room with his long strides and met her with an embrace. The stick fell to the floor. She buried her face against his shoulder, both arms hooked around his back. Octavia sobbed softly as she breathed in the dust and sweat of half a continent. He felt so good, so right.

Agony spliced through her stomach like repeated stabbings, the blows fast, the blade deep. She tried to scream but managed a whimper.

Alonzo held her as her legs gave out. "Right here," he

said over her shoulder. One of the other guards shoved a chair beneath her. Alonzo lowered her as if setting down a porcelain rose. His hand touched her cheek and she flinched. Not from pain, but that he touched her skin as it was now.

The two other guards exited. Lanskay shut the door behind them and remained, his presence a furnace in the corner of the room.

"What happened?" Alonzo asked.

She studied him as if she could paint him later—if she had the skill. Strands of his kinky, thick hair had worked free and framed his brown-skinned face. His broad, strong lips pressed in a tight line of concern. His icy-blue eyes sparkled with tears, not mischief. Tight scruff lined his jaw and lips.

"I think I prefer you clean-shaven," she said.

"I could endeavor to get a razor, if I am permitted."

Octavia smiled. "I wanted to see you again. I needed to."

"What happened out there? Is he . . . ?"

"Grandfather crossed the river."

Alonzo bowed his head. "Godspeed to him."

Someone knocked at the door and it opened a crack. "Lanskay, sir," came a soldier's voice. "Taney sends word that it's sunset and he sees the Tree."

"Wait a few minutes. I will relay a reply." Lanskay closed the door again.

Octavia's gut pulsed. She pressed both hands to her stomach. "Give me a few minutes and then you won't be able to see the Tree. I just need the chance to say farewell."

"Octavia, I must know what is the matter, what you have tried to hide from me."

How can I put it into words? She looked down at her hands. "The Lady . . . is not what I ever expected. The seed? It's here."

He placed his hand over hers on her belly, in what seemed like a sad mimicry of the tenderness of a man learning he was to be a father. "What is going to happen?"

Another knock on the door. "It's Miss Percival," Octavia said. "May as well let her in." She felt the potency of Alonzo's frustration at the delay. Pain lashed against her. She reached for him, bracing herself on his biceps.

"Oh, sweet Lady." Miss Percival breathed the words.

At least those words don't attract my attention yet. I wonder how long it will take to accept that name? Miss Percival once said that it took her weeks, months, to adapt to being called that title. Yet Mother said it took her all of a day to adjust to my father's surname.

Octavia Garret. I could have adapted to that.

"It's really happening," Miss Percival whispered. She stood over Octavia; her magic tingled around her like a swirl of gauze. "I've been healing in their wards here, and my circles won't even awaken now. I—"

"The Lady's nearly dead." Octavia tilted her head against Alonzo. His hands stroked a line down her back.

"Dead?! But the Tree looks fine!" Lanskay stepped toward the blacked-out window and turned away with a guttural sound of frustration.

"You can't see a rotten core."

"You are to be the new Tree." Alonzo's voice was soft.

Octavia couldn't say the word. She nodded into him.

"My God," whispered Lanskay.

"I wondered after you grew that tree two weeks ago. I wondered what it truly meant." Alonzo held her as she gasped and cringed against him. "Lanskay, is there a bed here?"

Her breath rattled. "I can't stay. The Tree . . . if I accept the seed, it's supposed to be fast. I can . . . I can hide the settlement, then Lanskay won't have to . . ."

"Damn Taney." Lanskay stalked back and forth. "Prairie justice, to a man who's already proven himself as honorable, and as we all face fire. You're both . . . you're both chosen by the Lady." His song warbled off-key at his internal agony. Octavia lifted her head in surprise. "No. I will not do it. I will not burn him, Octavia Leander. Not his fingers or toes. Not a speck of his flesh." The pain of his insubordination eased some as he voiced the words. He knew he was doing the right thing—what the Lady would want.

Me. But not just me. The majesty of the Lady's Tree, whatever that means to him.

"Thank you," she said softly.

"There's a cot down the hall." Lanskay jerked his head. "Come."

Alonzo carried her. The cot was a sheet stuffed with straw tick, the whole thing reeking of mustiness and unwashed man. Not that she was particular at this point.

"Tell Taney I'm watching the prisoners," Lanskay said to the lingering soldier.

"That's it, sir?"

"That's it. Taney has plenty else to concern him. Go!"

Miss Percival set down Octavia's satchel and the green stick. Octavia managed a light laugh. "After all I've been through, strange how comforting it is to see that old satchel. You'll need to take it back to the academy so the other girls can—"

"Stop, damn it!" snapped Alonzo. He knelt by the cot and clasped both her hands. "You will not distribute your belongings, certainly not your satchel, as if you are at death's door."

"My goodness. You're swearing. I do believe I've vexed you. Well, I'm not at death's door. Quite the opposite."

Alonzo closed his eyes, his forehead and brows creased. "Of course. You cannot die."

"I could try a circle again—" began Miss Percival.

"No!" Octavia screamed with another bolt of pain. "Using any magic—no. Can't risk it, not now."

"Then can you please explain?" she asked. It was the quiet voice of a teacher waiting for a student to prove herself.

"His secret is meaningless now, and most would not believe anyway." Alonzo squeezed her hand. Octavia nodded. He looked up at Miss Percival. "The man we traveled here with was no Waster. He was King Kethan of Caskentia. The royal vault housed artifacts of the Lady, including a leaf and a seed. When King Kethan died in the Dallows' infernal attack fifty years ago, Evandia's court attempted to revive him."

"Imagine the compounded potential of the Lady, all bound in a single seed," Octavia whispered. "King Kethan . . . carried that might, but it blended with the toxins of the crushed Tree leaf. He . . . he caused the sickness and rot that's the hallmark of Mercia. He's why bricks crumble, why no plants grow. And he . . . he couldn't die. He was locked in the vault since. Until I . . . I got him out. Brought him here."

"That sick old man was King Kethan?" Lanskay's voice was soft with awe. With a wave of his hand, he illuminated the two lamps in the room.

"The Lady forced me to swallow the seed." Octavia met Miss Percival's gaze. She paused, breathing through another torrent of agony that lanced through her hips and chest. "The Lady isn't at all like we were taught. She was bitter. Angry."

"All the stories said she was human . . ." began Miss Percival.

"She came into her full power, but her soul is still human, and everything that means."

Alonzo kissed Octavia's knuckles. She stared at her hands, almost numb in disgust at the thickness of the bark on her skin.

"Octavia—"

"Alonzo, I love it when you say my name, but . . ." *Breathe through it.* "Names have power. It hurts to hear it."

That seemed to pain him in turn. "I am sorry."

Octavia panted heavily. "I have to do this. I don't have any choice now. If there's no Tree, there's no magic, only doctoring. The herb shortage . . . it wasn't just the war. The Tree, it heals the whole continent. Lanskay, the stories are right. The Waste was truly cursed by Caskentia, but the Lady's been fighting to heal the land for seven hundred years. Then Mercia . . . the King . . . argh!" Alonzo gripped both of her hands as Octavia's spine arced.

"Fifty years." Miss Percival shook her head. "Everything goes back to then."

Sweat sopped Octavia's brow. "Once I've rooted, people will be healed, and the land will be healed, and—"

"Do not talk like this!" Alonzo yelled. His breath rattled and he rocked forward, placing his forehead on their entwined hands. "I am sorry, Oct—I am sorry."

"Oh, Alonzo Garret. Do you have any idea how much I love you?"

Tears flooded his blue eyes. "Likely as much as I love you, Oct—'tis infuriating to not be able to say your name."

"Then say it."

"I will not hurt you."

"That's what started this whole thing, isn't it? I'm very grateful for your reluctance to see me hurt or dead, Alonzo."

Miss Percival began to sob quietly.

"I need to get out into the woods. I'm not sure how quickly a true Tree grows, and if . . . if it's anything like that branch . . . Alonzo, if you can't help me, then Lanskay . . ." Octavia sat up. She pressed a hand to her abdomen. It had gone hard like a belly in early pregnancy.

"I will stay with you as long as you will have me," said Alonzo, standing.

"Then I'd have you forever, but I won't ask that of you. You need to lead a full life." *You need to love again. I can't say it now, but I understand it.* Octavia took a deep breath as she stood and leaned on the wall.

"Stop it!" Miss Percival's voice was shrill. "You can't do this, Miss Leander. You can't."

"I don't have a choice. I'm the Tree's heir."

"You may be the best medician, but I'm bound to the Lady as well." Miss Percival fumbled with her button at her cuff, then with a snarl, jerked up the cloth. The button pinged onto the floor.

Miss Percival's forearm was mottled with brown bark.

Chapter 21

Miss Percival stared at her own arm. "My skin began to change a few days after you left the academy. The other girls complained of the same symptoms—the itchiness, the brown coloration. The more powerful the medician, the more pronounced the symptoms. But I've seen this happen before."

Octavia struggled to focus through the wavering pain. "When you were a child. You said your mentor was called to Mercia."

"Yes. She was called, but she wasn't the only one. Then the bark grew up both my arms and along both calves. I was the most powerful girl in training, more powerful than even my Miss Percival. She dreamed that the Lady needed me at the palace, but when we journeyed there, the King denied that there was anything of the Tree in Mercia."

"You found Mrs. Stout as you returned north. But what . . . what happened with the bark on your skin?"

"It continued to slowly grow for months, until we had word of the infernal attack on Mercia. After that, we all healed." She took a deep breath. "I knew my skin had looked like bark, but I had no idea why. I never would have thought that I was intended to be the next Tree. But now I can be."

Alonzo looked between them. "What is it you are saying, Miss Percival?"

Miss Percival bowed her head. Wisps of silver hair draped from beneath her white cap. "Tell me, student of mine. What was my favorite saying?"

"I'm supposed to choose just one?" The sentence ended with a hiss of agony.

"Very well. What was my favorite when the soldiers decided to sip whiskey and race horses, or smoke while on front-line patrol?"

"'Sometimes they deserve a little pain.'"

"Yes." Miss Percival looked down at her hands, blinking rapidly. "I sold you to the Wasters. I knew you might be caught in cross fire with our own boys, or live a terribly short life like most women in the Dallows, but I told myself that it was all for the welfare of the school."

Miss Percival's gaze met Octavia's. "This—this is the right thing for the academy, for you. I will take your burden."

She does love me still. Lava seemed to burble in Octavia's stomach. She screamed, the world flashing in black. Arms strong as steel snared her before she struck the floor.

"I have you," Alonzo whispered, his voice husky at her ears. *Always.*

He lowered her to sit on the floor. Miss Percival crouched to one side. By the door, Lanskay watched, his slender arms crossed over his chest. The limited light that was cast on the sharp angles of his face gave him the exaggerated visage of a puppet.

All medicians are heirs of the Tree. It makes sense. We all bloodlet. We all carry that magic, that potential for something more. "I . . . appreciate the sentiment, Miss Percival, but unfortunately, the seed is inside me now. Evandia's minions tried to cut the seed . . . out of King Kethan and they never could. The seed wouldn't budge. He couldn't die."

Alonzo's fingers gently stroked her face. "Yet King Kethan is dead and the seed is now with you. How did this occur?"

She stared at him. "Oh. Oh! The Lady's branch gutted him."

They stared at the walking stick on the floor, its hum of life so quiet she had almost forgotten it was there. A new tidal wave of pain rocked through her. Her vision dappled in black.

With a few strides, Lanskay had hold of the stick and unsheathed a knife at his waist. Octavia's brain fogged over in pain. *He's going to try to steal the seed like Devin Stout did, but he knows how to succeed.* She tried to speak and only a soft creak emerged.

"I'm a fast whittler. I'll make it into a short spearhead for you." Lanskay snapped off a portion of the stick as he granted her a tight grimace of a smile.

The pain abated. She deflated, sensing the trust and conviction in his words. "Thank . . . thank you, Lanskay. I judged . . . I judged you harshly before. Because of when you burned me."

"No, you didn't." His tone was brusque as he began to carve. Octavia flinched at the branch's high scream. He carried on, unable to hear it. "I burned you for that exact reason. I have taken great pride in my job as an infernal. I'm good at what I do." He shrugged. "I just wish—I wish I had the chance to be good at other things as well."

Miss Percival motioned to Octavia's satchel. "You said before it was best not to use a circle. Therefore, this must be done with no blessed herbs, no calling on the Lady for direct aid. May I use your tools?"

Octavia nodded. A bell pealed in the distance. They all paused.

"Damn it all," Lanskay said softly. "Caskentian airships are in sight." The bells stopped. In the lingering quiet, Octavia heard the distant roar of airship engines.

Everyone else has evacuated. We're sitting ducks.

"I'm sorry," said Octavia. "You should all—"

"If you suggest that we should abandon you, I will be compelled to scowl at you," said Alonzo.

"Could run for the woods," said Lanskay.

Octavia remembered the horrible sensation of her blood welling against her skin as if roots were about to burst out. "No. Bloodletting already causes . . . if I bleed directly on the ground now, if my skin touches it . . ." She paused, breath ragged, and lowered her voice. "But we're not completely without the Lady's aid as the attack begins. Alonzo, I still have two leaves."

"We number four," he murmured.

Miss Percival passed the wand of Octavia's parasol over

a swath of floor, and again over the surgical implements laid out to one side.

"Miss Percival . . . I . . . you . . ."

"Student of mine." Her tone was brisk. "I need to do this. I may be second best these days, but I'd like to think I'll still be adequate for the job. What I did to you was wrong, even if it was for the academy. This . . . this is right for all of you."

"The academy . . ." Octavia began.

"I've listed you as primary heir for five years now, since you proved yourself as a ward matron in our first stint at the front. Mind you, the solicitors will likely give you grief without full proof of my death, but with that lot it's always something. Can't expect them to include a clause regarding clients turning into giant trees." Miss Percival granted Alonzo the sort of matronly glare that could make generals squirm. "I'm assuming you'll be there to help things along."

"Most assuredly," said Alonzo.

"Good. Let's stop dithering," said Miss Percival, clapping her hands as if to gather the girls-in-training. The roar of engines grew louder.

I wonder if the Lady saw this as one of the possibilities for the future. If she did, I doubt she cared. I doubt she cared about anything that would happen after she forced the seed on me.

Alonzo set Octavia down. He leaned over her, almost completely blocking the light. His magnificent ponytail draped over his shoulder, just as it had when they first met. She still yearned to bury her fingers in the kinky strands, though now she had neither the strength nor the energy to do so. It was all she could do to clench her fists at her hips and breathe through the pain. Lanskay crouched beside Alonzo with the walking stick portion in his hands. Its fine point resembled an oversize green pencil.

"The seed . . . will keep me alive up until . . . the leaves . . ."

"I know." Alonzo rested a palm against her cheek. She could scarcely feel a tear as it coursed down the crevices of her face and met his fingertips. "Live, Octavia."

The pain at hearing her name was a gnat's sting compared to everything else.

"Men. We must begin," Miss Percival snapped. "You must step back, Mr. Garret."

Alonzo's grip withdrew. His fingers dipped into Octavia's apron pocket and emerged with the two remaining leaves. His eyes searched hers one final time, and then he retreated.

Miss Percival began her doctoring in brisk moves. She untied Octavia's medician apron and tossed it aside. "It will expedite things if I cut through your dress."

"I . . . I trust your judgment."

Miss Percival's hard expression softened. "Thank you for that."

Octavia felt the tug of her robes as they were sliced through. "Dare not . . . use the chloroform breather. Not sure how that . . . would affect the seed."

"I agree, though it means you'll feel everything."

"I already do," she whispered, writhing at another spike of pain.

Guns fired. Hoofbeats pounded down the street, men

yelling. The roar increased overhead. *It must be Caskentia's whole fleet. The ground forces will only linger a few days behind. They . . . they never made it this far into the Dallows before, not with a concentrated drive like this. They never had a target so close, so vital.*

"We'll have fire drop on top of us," she heard Lanskay say.

"You need not stay." *Alonzo.*

"I feel as if I should be here. I can shield with fire, for a time."

For a time. The words echoed through the ripples of agony, as if they traveled down a long tunnel. *Not that blasted tunnel again.*

"Mr. Garret. Mr. Infernal. I'm afraid I need your help to hold her down. She's convulsing." *I am?*

Octavia knew their songs as they came to either side of her. Alonzo's marching band rang with sound health, even as it struck a frantic pace that could outrace a threem. Lanskay's presence sparked against her skin as if he would burn her again. That scene flashed in her mind—Lanskay utterly still with death, Alonzo's screams from torture still echoing, Lanskay's gratitude in the form of a searing mark on her wrist. She lurched away from him, from the pain of memory.

"Octavia! Stay still." Miss Percival's voice stopped her, as it had stopped her cold so many times. *Did I forget to put the bandage roller away? Did I leave a jar open, or forget to apply a wand, or—*

A line of heat traced down her gut. She knew that kind of heat: blood. She saw a flutter of bodies in memory. Soldiers, green uniforms burned and sliced away, their stomachs bared for treatment. Skins in hues from milky to caramel, wiry hairs tracing downward from their navels. Others exposed far more than mere skin. Pinks and reds, a narrow spectrum hidden within their abdominal cavity. Pain. She understood their pain, the agonies in their songs. It bothered her. This kind of pain was wrong; it needed to mellow, to calm, to find its pianos and soft strings again.

Odd. I'm not supposed to feel their pain, just hear it.

A little voice whispered from a different memory. *If you give in to the pain, it will be over in seconds. Just let the seed grow.*

A strong masculine hand squeezed hers. His life beat was the stuff of parades and floats and waving banners, the sort of celebration—armistice!—that could make even a soul in mourning smile again.

"Octavia. You hear me when I say your name, so I say it now. Fight, Octavia Leander. Fight."

Alonzo Garret. Garret. The son of Solomon Garret.

A roar grew louder above. She tasted heat. The grip on her hand tightened. The other hand on her arm prickled with magic. *Infernal. Waster. Don't trust him. He would have killed your parents. He's killed many. Burned them.*

But he didn't burn Alonzo again. He could have.

"You are doing well, Miss Leander," said Miss Percival. That voice, those words—Octavia wanted to preen with pride. She'd do most anything to hear that praise again. Then, in a mutter, "This much blood, if not for that seed . . . even when I doctor, I use a circle to listen. Give me the stick."

"Lanskay, here," said Alonzo. "If you cannot keep up the shield, before it falls, place this beneath your tongue. Do not chew."

A leaf? But there are only two. Alonzo, you can't . . . Octavia tried to speak, to see.

"A Tree's leaf! Poison!"

"Not if you do as I say. Miss Percival, the seed—"

Something tore inside Octavia, pulled away with a juicy lurch.

"I'm extracting it right now, young man."

Something splattered on the roof above. *Oil.* Liquid sloshed down the nearby wall, pattered on the window glass. Yelling. The tingle of Miss Percival's power, so faint, then—so different. A roar consumed the world.

Octavia struggled to make her tongue move, her body shift, to somehow tell Alonzo to save himself, though she knew he would never be that selfish. He'd give the leaf to Miss Percival or to her, and Octavia couldn't stop him.

Don't die, Alonzo. I don't want to wake up and find your bones at my feet. Please, no. Not that. Anything but that.

She felt a huge shudder above her head. Even with her eyelids closed, she saw brilliant yellows and reds. Heat breathed down on her.

The burning began in her legs and then she knew nothing else. Pain crushed every sense in her body.

Blackness.

CHAPTER 22

My feet rooted to the mud of the field. Night sky. The air-ship a massive flaming meteor. The village. Home. Mother. Father. Red, bursting and bright.

Then morning. Birds sing. Light pours through the half door to the kitchen.

Mother hums as she chops carrots on the thick wooden cutting board. Father sits at the table. He has leaned so far over his book that his round glasses have nearly slipped off the tip of his nose. They both turn to look at me as if I've slammed the door. They look strangely older, grayer, like grandparents rather than parents.

"Octavia Louise Leander." Mother plants her fists on both hips. "You are not supposed to be here. Turn around this instant."

Father closes his book; he does not even replace his bookmark, which says a great deal about his urgency. He adjusts his glasses. "This verse Kethan recorded from memory is an absolute joy. I'll read it to you later, Octavia. Much later. For now, you'd best listen to your mother." His warm smile crinkles long lines in his face.

I backstep, chagrined. "But—"

Mother shakes her head. "Go, my sweet girl. Go plant tulips.
Ride horses. Tend to your patients. Besides, Alonzo is wait-
ing for you."

Alonzo is kissing me. Alonzo is alive.

Awareness returned to Octavia.

She knew the texture of his lips, the scrape of his skin.
Their mouths are open. They'd never kissed like *that* before.
Not that she was averse to the idea. She moved her lips but
they didn't quite work, for some reason. Her eyes weren't
working either. Everything was black, the impenetrable
black of that terrible tunnel. His song was as strong as when
they first met, no longer plagued by intimate details beyond
the absence of his lower leg.

Something was wedged beneath her tongue.

She smelled fire—burned wood.

Octavia opened her eyes.

Alonzo's lips were locked over hers. She wiggled her
tongue. His tongue jabbed hers in return, and not in a particularly romantic way—more like *don't move*. Not a difficult
request, as her extremities tingled as if they'd fallen asleep.
Alonzo's arms were underneath her and hoisted her up. She
glimpsed an overcast sky through thick billows of smoke.
For some reason, she had no urge to cough. She breathed
through her nose, the air fresh and pure. Debris crunched
beneath Alonzo's feet as he walked. Something bumped
against her legs. Alonzo stopped.

"You're safe here," said Miss Percival. "Don't fear the fire."

How many times over the years had Miss Percival said similar words to her? Those late nights when Octavia couldn't sleep, when she had taken shelter beneath Miss Percival's desk and sketched herbs within her cavelike refuge.

Alonzo's lips withdrew. The leaf protruded from his lips like a ridiculous tongue. That's what had been in her mouth—they had shared the leaf. He shifted her to grab the leaf, and as he did, it evaporated to nothingness. Fire illuminated the side of his face with a golden halo and showed his brilliant white grin.

"Octavia. How do you feel?" he asked.

"Peculiar. It's been a rather dreadful day, hasn't it?" Her mouth felt strange and sticky, her tongue somewhat thick.

His laugh boomed out and he held her closer. Her hands clutched at his fully exposed back.

"Alonzo? Do you realize you're half naked?" His flesh was clean, his song perfect. Strangely perfect, all things considered. His mechanical leg proved the quality of Kellar Dryn's workmanship again and was intact.

"Yes. I fear the protective powers of the leaf do not extend beyond flesh."

Logic began to function in her brain. The Lady, the pain, the attack . . .

"What happened? Set me down please. Miss Percival? Where are you?"

"Easy, easy." Alonzo set her down. Her soles met springy grass. Grass? "One question at a time. As for Miss Percival, she is behind you." He said this gently, as if bracing her for bad news.

"I'm here, Miss Leander. I don't think I'll be able to talk for much longer."

Octavia turned and faced a tree. Miss Percival's body was still visible within the trunk—the swell of her hips, the nubs of her breasts. The trunk extended past her body, twenty, thirty feet, with branches beginning just above her head. From her extended arms sprouted leaves in a dozen colors and shapes, from five-pointed maple to the red of pampria. The leaves above looked green like the ones Octavia had carried with her these past few weeks. Shreds of shimmering white cloth adorned the grass at her roots.

"She's beautiful, isn't she? More beautiful than I even imagined," said Lanskay. He sat a few feet away, naked as a babe on bath day, staring up in awe.

"Lanskay! You're well?" Octavia had to ask it, even if the strength in his song already told her this. She was surprised at how relieved she was to see him.

"That leaf kept me alive, as promised. I owe you my life again, but I vow to you, this time I will not burn you."

"You had best not," growled Alonzo.

Tears filled Octavia's eyes. Miss Percival was beautiful, but then, she always had been. "Miss Percival, I . . . your song is so different now, I can't read it. Are you hurting? Did it . . . ?"

"I swallowed the seed and didn't fight. The change was instantaneous. I never hurt, not as you did."

Octavia drily swallowed. "I . . . I'm glad."

"It's amazing, Miss Leander, all the life here, but oh,

there's so much suffering. The Lady did her best, but she was tired. I see so many things to do!"

"That sounds like you, Miss Percival, always with your lists. Staying up late to grind herbs, do your paperwork, and a thousand other things."

"I feel more alive than I have since I was a girl. The war—it took so much out of me, out of all of us, and then the debt . . . I can never apologize enough for what I put you through."

"I think you've more than made up for that." Octavia felt Alonzo's hand on her shoulder. She leaned so her cheek pressed against his knuckles.

The smell of smoke lessened. She looked beyond the new Tree. The immediate buildings of the Waster settlement had been obliterated. Fire lit up the night all around them, and as she watched, the closest flames were squelched. She stared for a second, trying to make sense of it in the dim light.

A forest—a jungle—grew around her as the moments ticked by. Vines crested like waves, silhouetted against an inferno, and then crashed down. Debris crackled, fire hissed, and then only smoke rose from the site. All around, it was the same. Trees, flowers, bushes. Through the stink of burned wood came the perfume of life and fresh greenery. Saplings sprouted steps away. Pampria—the cinnamon odor so clean and sharp—tumbled from the ground in an instant embankment of red leaves.

She couldn't see the other Lady, but she sensed the Tree's looming presence. The new forest would soon meld with the old, if it hadn't already. Good. The other Lady would be hidden. She could die in peace, without having her bark violated, and the creatures in her realm wouldn't suffer.

Through the haze and high canopy of branches, stars glittered. A strange serenity blanketed the place. There were no gunshots, no cries, none of the expected cacophony that came with a battle. No roars of airships above.

"Where's the Caskentian fleet?" Octavia asked.

"They retreated as soon as I set roots and made us vanish," said Miss Percival. "All they could see were blank plains. They will be back, but it'll do no good. Not for generations. People will only find me if I wish them to." Her voice grew fainter, word by word. "Mr. Infernal?"

Lanskay stood. "Lady?" His tone was reverent, his voice quavering, his eyes downcast.

"Tell your countrymen what you've seen. Tell them that not even Caskentia will be able to call this place the Waste within a few generations. Work with Caskentia, please. Work together. Caskentia has industry but you'll have the harvest."

"It's all we've wanted, Lady." Lanskay bowed his head. "Thank you."

"The initial bombardment killed many in the tunnels, and as my roots spread, the rest of the earth here will be unstable. Take the survivors away from here as quickly as you can. If you get too close again, the wyrms will warn you. Go."

Lanskay saluted her with a fist to his chest and, naked as he was, repeated the gesture to Octavia and Alonzo. He stumbled away. Alonzo cleared his throat.

Octavia looked at him with an eyebrow arched. "You do realize I've seen and treated thousands of naked men? Not very glorious labor, at that. Bedpans and surgery."

"My own backside was exposed to the fire. There is a reason I must face you."

Noted, with delight. At the thought, she glanced at her own clothing. Her enchanted robes, magicked though they were, had not been proof against fire. Her sleeves were burned to the elbow, her skirts and boots quite scorched. Her hands—the growth of bark was gone.

As the minutes had passed, Miss Percival had been further absorbed into the Tree. *This is why the previous Lady projected the memory of her body. Her true self had simply become rings in the center of a trunk a mile thick.*

"I'll miss you, Miss Percival."

"And I'll miss you. Truly I will. But you're all grown up. If not for our duties in the war, you would have left ages ago to form your own practice. There was—I never told you about Delford, the place that was your destination when you left—"

"I know the truth. I know that Delford's need was a lie. It's okay. I wanted a home. I'm going to have one."

The academy. A place I always loved, even if the other girls made my life difficult. The barns, the corrals, the fields—my tulips. The whole North Country, so verdant and green, the air fresh, the industry of the south far away. Home. I'm going home.

Octavia wrapped her arms around the Tree. Her hands couldn't touch at the back.

"Oh, Octavia." The voice was a whisper through the branches.

Octavia stiffened. "The Tree's leaf—Alonzo and I shared it. What does that mean? Our lives . . . ?"

"There are so many paths. So many." The whisper shook the branches. "Live. Live. Every moment you—"

The human voice stopped completely. Octavia waited a minute more, the trunk growing in her grasp, before she stepped back. Miss Percival had plenty of other matters to attend to. A shut office door used to be the old warning system that she wasn't to be bothered. This . . . this was something more.

Octavia walked a slow circuit around the Tree, trailing her fingers on the thick ridges of bark. She glanced up. "What's that?" She pointed to something about seven feet up in the lowest full branches.

"I am not sure." Alonzo stood just behind her. "Miss Percival? Might we have your assistance?"

The branch shook on its own and the object dropped straight into Alonzo's arms: Octavia's satchel. Singed to a deep brown, the strap severed at long last, but otherwise intact. She glanced inside. The jars looked sound, packed securely as always.

Octavia pressed her fist to her mouth but she couldn't contain the giggles. "All the things this poor bag has endured, and here we are."

"Here we are indeed. You even permit me to hold your satchel now."

"Yes. I won't even threaten you with capsicum."

"Such generosity, Miss Leander."

It was so good to hear her name without any accompanying pain. "I have my moments. I doubt it's any accident that I still have my bag. Here. We need to follow Lanskay." From her bag, she pulled out Rivka's gown, the one she'd brought along in case her robes disintegrated. At the look on Alonzo's face, she burst out in laughter again.

"It will help your dignity. Somewhat. We'll need to get you proper clothes before we leave the Lady's shadow and find true winter." She would not think of the sources of those clothes. Not yet.

"Somewhat. Yes."

She bit her lip as he pulled the shift overhead. It was as basic as a gown could be, not even adorned by lace. Tall as he was, the skirt ended just above the knee. As Alonzo moved, bits of his old clothes floated to the ground. His boots creaked ominously. He stood straight and affected his regal demeanor.

"Well then," he said.

"Well then." She cleared her throat. "Lanskay went this way." She started walking.

"The tunnels."

"Yes. There will be injured people. We must help them get away from here." *Which makes our current levity all the more vital. Somber work awaits.*

"I'd still prefer that you lead the way, Miss Leander."

She glanced back at him. "You could borrow my medician blanket, for an extra layer of dignity, but I will need it back soon."

"My lack of functional trousers is a small inconvenience compared to everything else. I should hope that my current attire will not distract you too much." A pause. "I am not sure if anything could distract you from your duties, truly."

She laughed, full of absolute joy for being alive, at the life ahead. "You're right. Not when people are in need. But later . . ."

Octavia didn't need to look at his face to know Alonzo had arched his eyebrow as he gave her one of his looks. "Later, Miss Leander?"

"I could use more distraction later." She walked faster, as if she could make later come a little sooner.

CHAPTER 23

Octavia breathed in the dankness of the purple dawn. The North Country had emerged from winter with humidity so thick she could taste it like fine wine. She loved it. She loved how the tip of her nose turned red and numb, how her breath created dragon puffs, how the mud squished beneath the overly large boots she used for barn labor. From the corral, a horse whickered a greeting. The songs of small bodies drifted in her wake. The cats knew it neared milking time.

"You'll get your oats soon enough," she called to the horse. The cats meowed in protest. "Yes, I know you are starving, you poor things." The glowstone lamp swayed in her grip.

The entire yard was fragrant with the scent of jasmine. The vines grew in thick tumbles beside the house and along the entry gates, the white flowers mere specks in the thin light. The blooms had opened only the day before. *Miss Percival knows they are one of my favorites.*

Yellow outlined the doors of the academy's second barn, so recently converted into a mechanist's shop. Octavia smiled to herself and slipped through the gaping doors. Alonzo's legs jutted from beneath an old tank he was attempting to alter into a plow. The guts of it were bared and gleaming in recycled copper and steel.

"How long have you been up?" Octavia asked as she fixed the lamp onto a hook.

"An hour. Sleep evaded me, like a sparrow with a cat."

"I hope you're not too tired later."

Alonzo emerged to grant her the full weight of his stare, one eyebrow raised. "I assure you, I am quite prepared for the challenge of the day."

"Marrying me is a challenge, is it?"

"Surviving you has been a challenge from the very start."

Octavia laughed as she grabbed a bucket. "Well, I won't argue with that."

He scrambled to his feet. As always, Alonzo Garret adapted to his uniform. These past few months, he had taken to wearing the dungarees and calico of a farmer, even if his commanding stride recalled the way he moved in the trim pilot's uniform of Tamarania. Octavia had caught most of the girls making moony eyes at him, and she couldn't blame them, really. Mrs. Stout would undoubtedly do the same when she arrived later in the morning. Octavia fully expected the woman to drag her off for a mortifying one-sided conversation about marital duties. The hints had already come in letter form. Now the winks and nudges would occur in person. Appalling as it would be, Octavia could scarcely wait to see her old friend and her old friend's granddaughter. Rivka had already written of her plans to commandeer the academy kitchen.

There would be somber moments as well, though. Mrs. Stout had mentioned, with unusual subtlety on her part, that she had received a surprising letter and they would discuss it more in person. It would be difficult for Octavia to tell her about King Kethan and Devin Stout, but Mrs. Stout was resilient. Not unlike Caskentia.

Spring was supposed to be the season of life and change, but for Caskentia, much had come in winter.

Mercia had erupted in blooms. Saplings and bushes had burst from the wide cracks in asphalt and cobbles. Vines crept up sooty tenement walls. Rooftops resembled meadows of verdant wildflowers. The walls of the palace, people said, wore garlands of golden roses. The skies were still an ugly gray, the factories still full of work, but by all accounts, the mood of the place had changed. Men fastened blossoms to their lapels. For the first time in generations, children presented bouquets to their mothers and grandmothers.

Part of that joy had also been due to the abdication of Queen Evandia.

That event had come suddenly. Rumors abounded of heart attacks and strokes, and the truth simply was not known. Her son had claimed the throne. Nothing was known about him; he had been raised within the confines of the palace, and probably about as wise to the ways of the outside world as a house cat exposed to its first thunderstorm, but it still signified a change.

The death of the grand potentate of the Dallows had altered politics as well. With Taney gone, crushed in a tunnel, a brief squabble for power had ensued, which resulted in an infernal being in charge of the Dallows for the first time. News had been almost nonexistent for weeks, with winter efficiently isolating the nations on either side of the Pinnacles, but already word spread of a religious resurgence. It had happened in Caskentia as well. The Tree may have vanished again, but it had been seen. People considered the Lady with new interest—as an entity no longer confined to the rare art of medicians.

The southern nations were undoubtedly rolling their eyes at the quaint ways of their northern neighbors. Mrs. Stout would be sure to inform them of the gossip.

"The other girls still slumber?" asked Alonzo.

"Other than those on the night shift, yes. The two men in the ward were sleeping well. They should be fully healed and awake within hours."

A dog barked. Octavia and Alonzo turned simultaneously, Alonzo reaching for the Gadsden he kept holstered at all times. *Old habits die hard, even with a regime change and new priorities for Clockwork Daggers.*

"It's too early for the milk pickup, though the Dryns weren't sure when they'd arrive . . ." Octavia grabbed a shovel and followed Alonzo into the yard. Annoyed cats— multiplying by the minute—trailed behind.

Octavia and Alonzo watched the wagon slowly roll up the drive. The draft horse in the shafts looked as if he had survived more than one bout at the front, but his song rang as aged but healthy. An older woman and young boy sat together. In his efforts to keep warm, the boy had curled himself up on her lap like an oversize puppy. The dog barked greeting and the horse barely flicked an ear. Octavia whistled the dog back.

"How can I help you?" she asked, though she already knew. She sensed the boy's magic. He bolted upright to stare down at her. *The first time he's sensed another magus, I'm sure.*

"I'm looking for Miss Percival." The woman's voice was weary with age and lack of sleep. She stared at the jasmine by the gate for a moment, obviously confused to see it abloom so early in the season.

"I'm Octavia Leander." *For a few more hours yet.* "I'm headmistress of Miss Percival's academy, though I will keep my true name."

"My grandson here." The woman draped an arm around him as he continued to stare at Octavia with wide dark eyes. "His arm, it kept hurting him. Awful pressure, he said. He cut himself on purpose, and flowers sprouted from the ground. That's a medician thing, it is?"

"Yes." *Another one. The third since we arrived. Miss Percival is busy, as always.* "The academy here is for girls—"

"We live east of Vorana. He was scared out of his wits. I wasn't about to drive down to Mercia to find them boys' schools. Took all night to come here."

Octavia and Alonzo looked at each other. Alonzo took hold of the reins. "'Tis a long ride and surely you are weary. Permit me to tend to your horse."

Octavia stepped toward the main house. "Come, I'll

walk you in. The other girls will be starting breakfast and we can talk more after your bellies are full."

"I haven't come to seek charity. I have my own farm—"

"It's not charity, but hospitality. If you want to work afterward, I understand, but some rest will do you both good."

At that, the woman nodded. Stiff-legged, they disembarked. Octavia walked them to the house and apprised Sasha of the situation. Octavia returned to the livestock barn as Alonzo finished rubbing down the old draft horse. The cats glared.

"They are settling in?" he asked.

"Yes. It didn't take any coaxing once they smelled the fresh bread."

"What is your estimate of the boy's age?" He guided the horse to a stall and set a board in place to secure him.

"Eight or nine, I'd say." Octavia paused and stared toward the house. The jasmine scent had followed her as if she wore perfume. "Miss Percival always said that keeping boys about was begging for trouble."

Alonzo snorted. "And what do you say to that, soon-to-be Mrs. Garret?"

"I say she was absolutely right." She blew a strand of hair from her face. "Fiddlesticks. We may as well draw up plans for a boys' dormitory."

"There is adequate room if we build on the eastern side."

"You sound as if you've already planned this out."

"In my past occupations, I found it wise to think several steps in advance. 'Tis easy to imagine that more young medicians will arrive as the new Tree does its work."

"Goodness. Let's build a cattery and a full gremlins' nest while we're at it."

"If that is m'lady's wish," said Alonzo. He bowed as if he played steward again. A pleasant, giddy warmth rose in her chest. *Lady, I do love this man.*

In answer, a tingle of power made the hairs on her arm rise. The Lady was always listening.

Octavia looked about. "Drat. I don't know where I left my shovel. There's simply too much to do today. I don't know how Miss Percival managed."

"I do. She had you."

"And I have *you.*" She leaned to give him a full kiss on the mouth. *Another advantage of being an early riser—none of the girls are about to giggle at us.*

"A cattery and a full gremlins' nest." He shook his head, his ponytail swaying from side to side. "A building devoted to gremlins. As if they are not already spoiled rotten."

"I don't know. Leaf, what do you think?"

An affirmative chirp rang from up high in the rafters, followed by the chorus of a dozen more gremlins.

"I think you've been outvoted," Octavia said. Alonzo adjusted his hat and muttered. She gave him another kiss and his fake scowl softened. "Come now. You may have moved to the country but you didn't think I'd let you get bored, did you, Alonzo?"

"You, allow boredom into my life? Never. Nor would I have it any other way."

$\mathcal{A}$CKNOWLEDGMENTS

This was my first sequel novel and my first book written under contract. It was all kinds of terrifying. I'm grateful to so many people for their supportive woots, advice, and animated cat gifs. I can't name everyone, but I do want to give some shout-outs.

To the awesome writers who critiqued the manuscript and made it a much better book in the process: J. Kathleen Cheney, Rebecca Roland, Rachel Thompson, and Rhonda Parrish.

My thanks to everyone at Codex Writers for giving me space to rant, rave, and celebrate. I'd feed you all cookies if I could. Sara Dobie Bauer deserves special kudos for enduring my babbling in person.

Crystal Light with caffeine boosted my mana when I needed it most. Hooray for grape and strawberry-flavored power-ups!

My gratitude to my superagent, Rebecca Strauss, and the team at DeFiore and Co. I always know you have my back.

Everyone at Harper Voyager has been so supportive. I

BETH CATO

can't thank you enough. Deep appreciation to my editor, Kelly O'Connor, and my publicist, Caroline Perny. You're better than maple fudge. That's saying something.

I have the most awesome and pleasantly eccentric family ever. My love to my mom, dad, and brother Scott. Porom the cat has been my loyal footstool through all my drafts. Thanks to my husband, Jason, for putting up with me, even if I turn into a frothing madwoman during revisions. As always, love and hugs to Nicholas.

Finally, I want to acknowledge my cat, Palom, who was the inspiration for Leaf. Cancer stole away the loud, nosy, extroverted cat I love so much. He deserves some immortality.

About the Author

BETH CATO hails from Hanford, California, but currently writes and bakes cookies in a lair outside of Phoenix, Arizona. She shares the household with a hockey-loving husband, a numbers-obsessed son, and a cat the size of a canned ham.

Follow her on Twitter @bethcato.